Typewriter
Beach

Typewriter Beach

A Novel

Meg Waite Clayton

HARPER

An Imprint of HarperCollins*Publishers*

TYPEWRITER BEACH. Copyright © 2025 by Meg Waite Clayton LLC. All rights reserved. Printed in the United States of America. No part of this book may be used or reproduced in any manner whatsoever without written permission except in the case of brief quotations embodied in critical articles and reviews. For information, address HarperCollins Publishers, 195 Broadway, New York, NY 10007.

HarperCollins books may be purchased for educational, business, or sales promotional use. For information, please email the Special Markets Department at SPsales@harpercollins.com.

FIRST EDITION

Library of Congress Cataloging-in-Publication Data
Names: Clayton, Meg Waite, author.
Title: Typewriter Beach: a novel / Meg Waite Clayton.
Description: First edition. | New York, NY: Harper, 2025.
Identifiers: LCCN 2024038906 | ISBN 9780063422148 (hardcover) | ISBN 9780063422087 (trade paperback) | ISBN 9780063422094 (ebook)
Subjects: LCGFT: Novels.
Classification: LCC PS3603.L45 T97 2025 | DDC 813/.6—dc23/eng/20240823
LC record available at https://lccn.loc.gov/2024038906

25 26 27 28 29 LBC 5 4 3 2 1

Hollywood is a place where they'll pay you a thousand dollars for a kiss, and fifty cents for your soul. I know, because I turned down the first offer often enough and held out for the fifty cents.

—Marilyn Monroe, from *My Story*

To hurt innocent people whom I knew many years ago in order to save myself is, to me, inhuman and indecent and dishonorable. I cannot and will not cut my conscience to fit this year's fashions.

—Screenwriter Lillian Hellman, in a May 19, 1952 letter to the Un-American Activities Committee of the U.S. House of Representatives

PART I

February 1957

Her hair—that was the first thing they changed, even before they changed her name, before her first screen test, and months before Hedda Hopper wrote that bit in her gossip column about her being "sixteen and innocent, and yet somehow elegant." They dyed her Hitchcock blond, Grace Kelly-in-*Rear Window* blond—a cool shade that was the "elegant" part of sixteen, and not really her. She wasn't sixteen, either, and no real girl could be as innocent as they meant her to be both on screen and off. But with Grace Kelly newly married to the Prince of Monaco, all of Hollywood was scrambling for "the new Grace."

By February of 1957, Isabella Giori herself was in the running. She was ten months into a standard seven-year studio contract under which every role she read for was the same girl, no matter how different the men she might play opposite. Rock Hudson. Cary Grant. Tab Hunter. The male leads were surly-but-soft-hearted boxers or cool-headed-expensively-suited executives or rough-and-tumble-but-quirky-brilliant journalists, while Iz was forever that same sixteen and innocent and elegant without a stitch of complexity or brains. Her first movie wouldn't even be released until May, and she wasn't the female lead in it, she was just the little sister. But now she was walking into the Universal Studios lobby, where Alfred Hitchcock himself was there to greet her.

Hitchcock was just a smidge taller than her five-foot-six, his long face exaggerated by his two-hundred-plus-pound baldness, by his perfectly tailored suit, by the way he lifted his chin just so and looked at her slightly slantwise as he silently took her measure. But his eyes were bright, intelligent, mischievous.

"Miss Giori," he said.

She was there to audition for his new movie based on the French novel *From Among the Dead*, with Jimmy Stewart playing the lead—a part she was keen to get. Hitchcock's women were never simple-minded ingénues. They were smart daredevils taking down uncle-murderers or undercover agents infiltrating the Nazis or, for this new film, a cunning trickster who was two women at the same time, not exactly evil but not exactly not. It was a role that would open the way for Iz to play far more complex characters than the studio had in mind for her, if only she could get it. Rumor had it that Hitchcock sent two dozen American Beauty roses to Vera Miles's dressing room every morning, that he was in love with her even though she was married to *Tarzan* star Gordon Scott, and that after using three different actresses in his latest films—Doris Day, Shirley MacLaine, and Miles—it was Miles he would choose to be his new Grace. But surely he wouldn't be auditioning Iz if he'd already made his choice.

Hitchcock called the elevator, saying in that deliberate way of his, "I don't trust stairs. They are always up to something."

And when she genuinely laughed—a sucker for a good pun, or even a bad one—he stood observing her, his fingertips together in front of his many chins, not smiling but exuding an uneasy excitement.

He responded in the same deadpan voice, "Excellent."

He took her to wardrobe, where they were joined by a petite older woman with boyish dark hair and round, tinted glasses. "She's just the same size, isn't she, Miss Head?" he said, and he personally directed the choosing of a dozen combinations of clothing, shoes, and jewelry, which Miss Head hung around the fitting room so the director could see them all at once. Evening gowns. Cocktail and daywear dresses. Skirts and tops and sweaters and trousers.

"And gloves," Hitchcock said.

Miss Head took Iz's hands in hers, then pulled out a dozen pair of gloves all in the same clean white: lacy two-button shorties and four-button day gloves, three-quarter-length and elbow-length and opera gloves, and an unsettlingly familiar pair of crocheted driving gloves.

"The pink, please, Miss Head," Hitchcock said.

Just minutes later, Iz was looking at herself in a three-way mirror, feeling a creep of dread at the reflection there. Even her hair now looked like Grace Kelly's when she wore this same pink pleated skirt and driving gloves in *To Catch a Thief*. But what did it matter? She wanted Hitchcock to want her for this part, and she wanted her studio to agree to lend her to him.

"Your posture is excellent," Hitchcock said as he led her to a set, where he pulled out a red velvet dining chair at a table for one for her. He unfolded her napkin and set it in her lap. "Legs crossed at the ankles, please," he said.

He lit the candles himself as a young man served her a plate of filet mignon and a salad dressed with rich red tomatoes.

"I'm to eat, Mr. Hitchcock?" she asked.

Hitchcock, now standing across the little table from her, signaled the cameraman to begin filming.

"The steak, please," he said to Iz.

And he had her filmed cutting into a bloody steak with her white-gloved hands while he told wildly inappropriate jokes.

Did he mean to put her at ease with the jokes, or to make her uncomfortable? He took pleasure in making a woman laugh, that was clear from his not-trusting-the-stairs pun. And she did laugh despite herself. But she had never before felt so self-conscious about how she chewed.

After she had eaten a single bite of the steak, Hitchcock said, "Thank you, Miss Giori. That will be enough."

She wanted to protest—surely he would give her a chance to actually audition!—but already he was sliding her chair back to allow her more easily to stand and escorting her to the dressing room.

"The green now," he said to Miss Head.

Iz blinked back the relief of getting a second chance as she was stripped of the pink outfit and the gloves, now marred with a single red dot. Was that where she had failed Hitchcock's expectations, with the tiny splatter of steak juice?

As she was quickly dolled up in the gown, her hair and makeup again adjusted to Hitchcock's satisfaction, she resolved to do whatever he next asked her to do ever so much more perfectly.

She walked smoothly in dyed-to-match heels, maintaining her pleasing posture, as he led her again to the set. She lifted her weight gracefully this time, more ladylike, as he slid her chair forward. She crossed her legs at the ankles without having to be asked. Unfolded her own napkin from the fresh place setting and laid it in her lap. Smiled as engagingly as she could manage as a fresh steak was served. And after Hitchcock nodded to the cameraman, she cut into the meat carefully as again the camera rolled.

A dozen outfits, every one of them served with a fresh steak even though she ate only a single bite of each.

That was it. After she swallowed a final bite in the final outfit and laughed at a last inappropriate joke, he slid her chair back and she was dismissed.

"You don't want to see me act, Mr. Hitchcock?" Trying to quell a rising desperation.

He placed his fingertips together again, not at his chins this time but lower, disapproving. She felt more than saw the others turn toward his silence: the cameraman, the crew member hesitating to clear the last steak, Miss Head standing in the doorway with the makeup and hair girls behind her.

Iz didn't move except to unfasten the four-button day gloves she'd been so careful not to stain, pull them from her hands, and carefully fold them.

"'Well, if there's one thing I know, it's how to wear the proper clothes,'" she said—a line from *Rear Window* delivered with a good approximation of Grace Kelly's breathily sophisticated petulance.

She offered Hitchcock the gloves.

He raised those pressed-together fingers to his lips and eyed her slightly slantwise again. It seemed a very long moment before he laughed—a slow, deep laugh that seemed to rise up from someone he'd once been but had long ago forgotten.

"The best actors are those who can do absolutely nothing extremely well, Miss Giori," he said, finally taking the gloves. "You will have learned otherwise, and if I choose to borrow you for my film I will have to undo the damage wrought by other directors, as I always do."

TWO WEEKS LATER, ISABELLA STOOD in Benny Thau's office, listening to the studio head read bits of an article about a blacklisted director to Eddie Mannix, whose presence did not ease her nerves.

Mr. Thau looked up at her finally, and said to Mannix, "So what I hear about her is true?"

"That our Miss Giori here eats a good steak?" Mannix said.

"A good steak *or twelve*," Mr. Thau said, and the two men laughed, and Iz did too. She was humiliated, but she was expected to laugh with them even when it was her they were laughing at.

Thau tapped his newspaper and began another self-indulgent studio head soliloquy, this time not about the blacklisted director in the newspaper article, but about how very few of the studio's own people he could protect before the new round of House Un-American Activities Committee hearings began in just twenty-nine days. In the decade since the Hollywood Ten were imprisoned for refusing to tell Congress what political party they favored, as the country cheered on Wisconsin senator Joseph McCarthy and his dire warnings of a society "riddled with communists and homosexuals," the studios had arranged to protect their top directors and writers and actors through "executive sessions." They sent them to secret locations to testify for hours or even days, to "clear" their names with HUAC by naming others they suspected of communist sympathies while avoiding the shame of being seen ratting out friends. Iz had signed the loyalty oath everyone working in the movies now had to sign, but still she, like all of Hollywood, feared she'd be next to have to testify. As little as a whispered suggestion that you might once have stumbled into a meeting or picked up a progressive magazine or simply chosen the wrong friend could end your career.

Isabella waited patiently for Mr. Thau to finish. She was just weeks away from Oscar night, which was to be her unveiling. She wasn't a nominee, but the studio was dressing her up all gorgeous in a gown made especially for her and a borrowed string of million-dollar pearls that had once belonged to Marie-Antoinette, and they were sitting her right between their best actor nominees so that everyone would wonder who this unknown beauty with Kirk Douglas and Anthony Quinn was. "We like to reward good work," Mr. Thau had told her, but she supposed it would also provide a bit of early publicity for *A Little Summer Romance*, starring Hugh Bolin and Janet Leigh, with perhaps "introducing Isabella Giori" added to the opening credits.

Mr. Thau tossed his newspaper aside, finally. "All right, Isabella," he said, "unless you want to end up back in Podunk, Pennsylvania, let's get you on up to Carmel tonight."

"Tonight?"

"Mannix here will drive you himself."

Mr. Thau slid a folded piece of paper across the desk to her: *The Jade Tree Motel, Room 101, Tuesday, March 12, 8 p.m.*—tomorrow night.

"Hitchcock did admire your 'fire,' Isabella," he said, "but I'm not sure his project is right for your first lead."

Thau wanted to maintain control of her image, he meant, rather than ceding it to Hitchcock. And the decision about what parts Iz played belonged to him, as did any payment for her work.

"And he's concerned you look too young," he said.

Even at twenty-two, she still looked sixteen.

A SIXTEEN-YEAR-OLD GIRL IMPROBABLY PEERING in through his cottage's half-open Dutch door, wearing a cotton robe thrown over ratty pajamas—that was what Leo Chazan must have seen the morning Iz first met him in Carmel two weeks later. Bare feet, too. Not that he could see them. Not that he even looked up to see her at first.

"It's five a.m." Those were Iz's first words to Chazan, whom she didn't yet know was Chazan, or even Leo.

He glanced up as he again hit the carriage return. Not-quite-red hair. A stubble of beard on a sturdy chin. Noticeable ears, one with a mechanical pencil tucked behind it.

He didn't stop typing. His gaze remained fixed on the top page of a pile to the left of the typewriter, a typed movie script marked with penciled-in changes.

Isabella was used to waiting for men to finish whatever they were doing before acknowledging her, but she was cranky. Mannix had moved her into the studio's cottage himself in the middle of the night, not trusting the secret of her being in Carmel to anyone else. She'd balked at Mr. Thau's insistence that she come immediately—she couldn't possibly go that night, she'd claimed, when the truth was she was afraid—and Thau or Mannix or both of them together sent someone else first, or several someones. Now instead of heading to Beverly Hills for a final fitting, she'd hung her gown in the tiny closet of a six-hundred-square-foot cottage with plywood walls three hundred miles north of LA, with no real hope of wearing it to the Oscars and nobody to blame but herself.

The fire-shot clack and ding and zip of a typewriter had jarred her awake after just two hours of sleep, leaving her padding next door to find this man at a desk at the front bay window, shoulders curved in toward the paper as he typed madly away.

"It's five a.m.," she repeated. "I'm next door. I was sleeping."

"I do my best writing in the morning, in the quiet," he said without a pause in the clack of the keys.

Was that a trace of a foreign accent?

"Valentine's Day," he said. "Love in the air and all that."

"It's March," she said. "And there's nothing quiet about your typewriter."

Had he even heard her?

"Valentine's Day is *February 14*," she said. "And anyway, despite all the modern romantic blather, its roots are in a Roman celebration involving dogs and goats being sacrificed so men could whip women with the hides."

He did stop typing then.

"That's dark," he said with a quick glance to her as he pulled a sheet of paper from underneath a gold watch serving as a paperweight and grabbed that pencil from behind his ear. "The unexpected specificity: dog and goat hides. But are you sure you're old enough to know that?"

"They were naked and they were drunk," she said, trying to hold on to her crankiness in the face of him caring enough to write down what she was saying. She realized only then that she shouldn't be talking to her next-door neighbor or anyone else, she was supposed to do exactly what Mannix told her to do, which was to stay in the cottage so nobody but Mannix and Thau would know she was in Carmel.

The man leaned back in his chair then, tucking his pencil behind his ear again and fixing an appraising gaze on her. Eyes that were crescent-shaped, an unsentimental and intimidating brown. Intense but with a hint of something that read as hungry or angry or both. Intelligent. A little too confident.

"Those Roman women lined up for their beatings, believing the ordeal would make them fertile," Iz said, "and in a sort of sexual lottery, men drew their names from a jar to have however they wanted for the three days of the festival."

She crossed her arms over her thin robe and pajamas, thinking, *Sort of like Hollywood.*

"Oh, I see. From next door," he said, now folding the page of notes in half and hiding whatever he'd written, as if even those naked and drunk Roman women were now a disappointment. "We'll never get that past the PCA, will we?"

The Production Code Administration guarded the door between Hollywood and an audience's morals lest anything political or religious or sexual on film undermine society as the morally righteous liked to imagine it.

"Well, I'm Leo," he said.

In a better world, Iz would have known exactly who he was, but Leo Chazan had been banished from Hollywood well before she got there. And she was young. Young and inexperienced enough to think it was the acting and not the script that made a film great. Young and naive enough to think success was still, if just barely, in her own control.

March 1957

*B*ack entrances. Side doors. Secret elevators and servants' stairs. As Leo more sharply creased the folds of the notes he'd taken, resisting the urge to grab his camera, the desire to capture something about this girl standing at the Fade Inn door in her pajamas, he thought of Greta Garbo explaining her life to him in those words, with no idea that they described the way Leo too lived, always mindful of ways to get out of any place he found himself. Nobody had any idea of that side of his life even now, not here in Carmel and not back in LA.

LEO HAD COME TO HOLLYWOOD straight from Dartmouth in December of 1947, already with a studio contract to write screenplays—seven years of a steady paycheck to look forward to for the first time in his life. He'd just turned twenty-four then, if you could believe his French passport, which you couldn't; he was actually a day short of twenty-two, and he'd lived nothing of the charmed life his Dartmouth education and quick move to Hollywood suggested. But that was the life Garbo clearly assumed for him as, just a few weeks after he arrived, she threaded her arm through his and led him down Mabery Road toward the long, flat stretch of Santa Monica Beach. It had been so surreal, strolling on a sunny beach in Los Angeles with one of the world's most famous movie stars when just a few years before he'd been slipping through darkened streets, desperate to remain unseen and alive.

Leo hadn't met Garbo at one of George Cukor's luncheons, which he never went to and she no longer did by then, or over the Ping-Pong table at one of Salka Viertel's Sunday salons. Salka had introduced them privately just an hour earlier, over coffees and almond cake in her home, which was the closest thing to a home Garbo herself had—just the three of them before a roaring fire despite the sunshine on the lilacs beyond the glass doors. Garbo hadn't acted in anything in years; she would agree to do films, only to later drop out on one excuse or another. Still, Salka had in mind to write whatever role Garbo wanted to play, and she wanted Leo to cowrite it with her.

"You're talented and young and attractive, Chazan, and a little frightening to be honest," Garbo told him as they walked at the ocean's edge.

They were alone, their hostess left behind with the coffees and cake, and Leo was savvy enough to understand that this was intentional; even on a Monday there would be beachgoers who would recognize Greta Garbo and speculate about the young man chatting so intimately with her. Were Greta and Salka lovers? It had been a good fifteen years since the *Hollywood Reporter* outed Garbo as "ambidextrous"—the rag magazine's label for stars who were bisexual, homosexual, or lesbian—but the country had taken such an alarmingly conservative turn that everyone was being more careful.

"Yes, that's it, a little frightening," Garbo repeated. "It's your smile, I suppose. People will say it's the intense look in your eyes, but I think that smile of yours hides something I don't want to know."

WAS THAT WHAT DREW LEO to this girl in his doorway in Carmel now—a smile that hid something he didn't really want to know? She was hiding something, but then everyone the studio sent up to the cottage next door had secrets to hide. Everyone in Hollywood did. And even as he tried to ignore her, willing her to leave him alone to his damned writing, he was drawn to this girl who spoke so glibly of Roman celebrations involving dog and goat hide whips.

It wasn't her smile though. It wasn't the whole of her standing there, sleepy-eyed. It wasn't even the whole of her face. It was just the narrow slice of her eyes.

He looked away from her and stared out the bay window. Across the road, the ganglion stones of Hawk Tower twisted up into the dark mist, its lone hawk gargoyle invisible in the damp darkness but there still, stretching from the highest battlement as if to attack Tor House, across the garden from it. He listened closely to the crashing of the sea under the starless sky beyond them, understanding now what was missing from this script—not dog and goat hide whips specifically, but the underlying darkness he needed to make a story interesting, or even to make people laugh.

The minute the girl left, he started typing again, ignoring the loud thwack of the door slamming at the studio's cottage. His *e* bar hung up, the neighboring bars tangling with it. Hell.

He grabbed a cloth from the kitchen and grabbed his scotch bottle too. Back at his desk, he spilled a little scotch on the cloth and cleaned the misbehaving type bar with it, then that slug and the *o* too, both so fouled with ink that they were typing as solid dots. He wiped them dry and returned to the script, only to hit the end of the ribbon. And when he turned it around to restart it, it was twisted.

Damn it all to hell.

He straightened the ribbon, but his rhythm was broken and without rhythm there was no writing, none worth the paper spent, never mind the carbons.

At least the girl wouldn't be here for more than a few days. Nobody stayed longer than necessary in the studio cottage.

He'd thought he was done with the script, he was typing with the expensive carbons and onionskin so he'd have four copies without having to retype them all. He'd been telling himself it was fine, if not actually good, and so often fine sold better than good these days anyway.

If only that damned producer would pay him what he was already owed.

He rolled the page out of his typewriter, carefully extracted the carbons and set them aside, then crumpled the page and copies, knowing he ought to save them, to use the backs for making notes or typing drafts, but sick of the constant need to economize.

He pulled a volume from the shelves and let it fall open to a random page, thinking an unexpected poem might set him right again, Robinson Jeffers's long lines spooling out in rhythms like heartbeats or tides, the astronomical and geological sense of time, the wild beauty of this Carmel coast. This poem, though, was a dreadfully bleak few stanzas about a woman and her sons torturing a horse here on Carmel Point. "Apology for Bad Dreams," indeed. Bad dreams even when you were awake.

Hell and hell again: the ink from the ribbon and the carbon paper had smudged black-and-purple fingerprints where he'd touched the book.

He scrubbed the ink from his hands with a nail brush in the bathroom sink. Pulled on a jacket. Hoisted his typewriter with a single new sheet of paper in it onto one shoulder and stormed out. He grabbed the aluminum folding chair from the stone front patio with his free hand as he set off.

Tor House across the road was still dark, but the Hawk Tower window was lit now. The studio's cottage on his side of the road was lit too; the girl was pouring herself a coffee from the percolator. He followed the road around the corner and crossed Scenic Road to scramble down to the little cove on "this coast crying out for tragedy," all the while trying to shed the overhang of the poem and of the girl's haunting eyes. He set the chair in the sand and settled in, his back to the palisade's granite face and the cove sheltering him, the endless water ahead and his typewriter on his knees.

This was what people did in Carmel-by-the-Sea—what they'd always done in this place founded at the turn of the century by people who pitched tents while they built their own cabins to form a sort of summer camp for painters and photographers, playwrights and novelists, actors, scientists. From its first days, artists set up their easels on Carmel beach.

He thought of what the girl had said, those men whipping women with animal hides, and the women submitting, the women wanting this cruelty inflicted on them in the hopes of becoming pregnant. And he thought of the girl's eyes again. They weren't Margalit's eyes, exactly. They weren't the color of Margalit's eyes, which were as brown as his while this girl's were like the sea at its best, a stormy and turbulent gray-blue that, in sunshine, might be the bold blue of the sky that day he met Garbo. It wasn't the shape of her eyes either, or the delicate lashes or perfectly arched brows. It was the look in them, the dread and fear masquerading as something else. Flirtation. Flattery. The hope that if she smiled prettily enough, she wouldn't be hurt.

Margalit had died with that look in her eyes, no older than this girl. His doing, her death.

March 1957

The same typewriter, which had gone mercifully silent just minutes after Iz returned to the studio's cottage, began clacking away again about noon and was still going that first evening. Iz turned up the volume on the TV, a new model Motorola Golden Satellite with a Transituner so you didn't even have to get up from your chair to change the channel. *The Huntley-Brinkley Report, Danny Thomas, I Love Lucy*, and *Lawrence Welk*. She fell asleep to the damned clack and ding and was awakened again the next morning by it.

She was already sick of the damned television, the damned chair, the damned little TV table with its rickety legs, so she pulled out the Hitchcock script. She'd lost the role to Vera Miles, but with nothing better to do, she began rehearsing it alone, inhabiting the role of a woman not unlike her, who wanted to seem like someone she wasn't. Then Mannix telephoned.

"He can't see you this week," he said.

See her. She tried not to think about what that meant.

"He'll reschedule you for next week. I'll let you know when."

She looked to the bedroom at the back of the cottage, the little closet.

"I could come back now and return after the Oscars tomorrow night," she said.

She'd brought her Oscar gown with her just in case, hoping against hope for this kind of reprieve.

But no, with the Oscars not much more than twenty-four hours away, Mannix was far too busy to make the long drive up to Carmel to fetch her. And Mr. Thau wanted her to stay in Carmel in case anything changed.

"Stay in the cottage so you won't be seen," Mannix said. "One of my best men will bring you groceries." Leaving her wondering if her delay in agreeing to come up to Carmel was the real reason Thau and the studio were denying her a seat at the Oscar ceremony Wednesday, or only an excuse, a punishment for her hesitation to bend to their will.

"By the way," he said, "we just heard that Hitch's surgery has set everything back a month or more."

The very day she met with Thau, Hitchcock had gone into the hospital for emergency gallbladder surgery.

Iz said, "But Vera Miles already has the part."

"It turns out Miss Miles is going to have Tarzan's baby," Mannix said. "Benny will discuss the script with Hitch, but he won't entertain any role that calls into question your innocence."

Sexual innocence, he meant. It was fine if she murdered someone as long as she was a virgin when she did it. But if they were talking with Hitchcock about the details of the script, that meant he was interested. And his surgery would give Iz time to get back to Hollywood to take the role.

Yes, she did want a shot at this, she assured Mannix. Yes, she would show up exactly wherever and whenever he arranged for her to.

"The Jade Tree Motel," she repeated with a confidence she didn't feel.

She was to approach the motel from the back parking lot, on Torres. It would be dark by eight this time of year. A door tucked away behind the stairs in the corner on the ground floor would be unlocked. She was to make sure she wasn't seen, then slip in. If nobody was there, she was to wait.

She was hanging up the phone before she saw Leo standing at her own cottage's top-half-open Dutch door, watching her as she'd watched him. How long had he been there?

"I was rude to you yesterday," he said. "I've grown boorish, living alone. Could we start over? Dinner and watching the Oscars at the Fade Inn Wednesday?"

She looked down at the note she'd written while talking to Mannix: *The Jade Tree Motel. Room 101. Tuesday, April 2. 8 p.m.*— only the date changed from the note Benny Thau had given her in his office. She folded it slowly, hoping Leo hadn't seen it, hadn't heard.

"The Fade Inn isn't an actual inn, it's my cottage," he said. "The cottages here are all named to help people find each other, since most of the homes in Carmel have no postal address."

The Jade Tree Motel. There was no way to suggest that was the name of a cottage.

"What is this cottage named?" she asked to distract him.

He studied her without answering, and it was only later that she realized the studio's cottage had no name precisely because the people they sent up to stay in it did not want to be found.

"Nobody wants to watch the Oscars alone," Leo said, as if he could see past her closed bedroom door to her gown hanging in the closet. It was the most elegant thing she'd ever seen, designed just for her and fitted precisely, with a white tulle skirt and navy blue velvet top, as elegant as black but more innocent. The gown was floor length where the one Grace Kelly wore in *Rear Window* was tea length, but it had similar detailing where the bodice met the skirt lest anyone at the Oscar ceremony where she was supposed to have worn it fail to draw comparisons.

"That makes you uncomfortable," Leo said. "Of course it does. You're a good girl."

Making fun of her, the way men so often did.

"Well, I'll take you for a drive now, in broad daylight," he said, more command than offer. "We can be old friends before Wednesday's ceremony rolls around."

She hesitated, but who would recognize her anyway? She wasn't yet as famous as all that. No photo had run with the Hedda Hopper column, and A Little Summer Romance wasn't yet out. She could hide under a hat and oversized sunglasses. And she was so very bored.

MOMENTS LATER, ISABELLA WAS SITTING in Leo's yellow Buick Roadmaster, with the top folded back so that the damp sea air billowed her short wool coat and buffeted her hat. It was a chilly day even for Carmel, and the coastal fog was so thick on the Carmel–San Simeon highway that oncoming cars leapt out startlingly from nowhere. But she was going to be the next Hitchcock girl. She could feel it. All she had to do was get through the next few days.

The little cove Leo took her to was tucked into the rocky coast well off the main road. Hidden Beach. It was smooth stone rather than the white sand everywhere else here, and so shrouded in fog that she couldn't see past the cresting waves in one direction or the wooden stairs up the cliff in the other, even after she took off her dark glasses. They were sitting on a blanket, she in her coat and the unmemorable black felt cloche hat Mannix had her wear on the drive up from Hollywood, Leo with a sport coat over his plain white shirt and tie. He poured coffee from a thermos into china cups and set out a plate of shortbread as the waves washed toward them, each crest bringing with it a startling blast of water through a narrow archway carved into the granite outcropping behind her by centuries of waves.

She'd wanted to go somewhere she wouldn't be seen, but the solitude left her uneasy. What did she know about Leo . . . had he even told her his last name? Those eyes of his were compelling, but they weren't the blue she was used to looking into. And there was something not quite right about him. Was it just that nothing about him suggested he had any kind of means except his gold watch with its worn leather band, the camera hanging from an equally worn neck strap, and the car which, although top-of-the-line, was six years old? That car would have cost nearly as much as his shabby cottage. What did that say about him?

"I love your car," she said, for something to say.

He considered her without expression. "I bought her when I sold my first screenplay."

"A romantic comedy?" *Valentine's Day. Love in the air and all that.*

He fished a shell from the pebble beach and examined it, then handed it to her. His fingertips were stained a pale and disconcerting purple. "If you consider violent death romantic," he said.

She studied the shell for the excuse to look away: a perfect little egg-shaped thing not much bigger than his shirt-sleeve buttons, the chestnut of his eyes, its pure white underside rimmed with sharp little teeth.

"They shot scenes from *Rebecca* here," he said. "The Monte Carlo cliffs where Joan Fontaine first meets Laurence Olivier."

"Where she finds him about to jump?" she said. "Maxim de Winter and . . . "

A huge rush of ocean exploded through the narrow granite arch-way behind her.

"You can't come up with her name because she doesn't have one," he said. "She's never named."

"How extraordinary."

"Is it?"

He reached out and moved a strand of hair that had blown across her lips, then raised his camera—like all men, wanting her to look just so.

"I'd rather you not take my photograph," she said, lifting the cup to her lips with both hands and dipping the brim of her hat to hide her face, still with the shell tucked into her hand.

He lowered his camera only slightly.

"It's as if she only exists in relation to her husband," he said. "The second Mrs. de Winter who is never named."

Iz looked to the steps, barely visible in the fog.

"And you?" he said. "Do you exist only in relation to someone else?"

She tightened her fist around the sharp-toothed shell. Nobody knew where she was. Nobody but Thau and Mannix even knew she was in Carmel, and if she disappeared they would not own up to the fact that they had.

"I thought our friendship might go more easily if you're willing to tell me your name," he said. "Or perhaps you, like the second Mrs. de Winter, are a figment of Hitchcock's imagination?"

"Have I not—? I'm F— Isabella Giori," she stammered.

Leo considered her as another wave crashed behind her, the sweep of tide lapping closer. "Hedda Hopper's newest darling," he said.

"You'll hold that against me, I'm sure. I certainly would," she said, realizing too late that she ought to have stuck with Fanny Fumagalli, and trying to shake her discomfort with a bit of flirtation, the way she'd come to deal with men by habit. Was he surprised at who she was, or had he already known?

"And you?" she said. "Do you have a last name?"

In the silence that followed, she took another sip from the delicate china cup that did not belong on this wild and foggy beach.

Leo hadn't taken a single sip of coffee himself. The cookies too were untouched.

She shivered at the shadow of the milk scene in Hitchcock's *Suspicion*, what men did to women in order to drive moviegoers to theaters. Rochester, who kept his wife in the attic. The cruel and vindictive Heathcliff. Maxim de Winter, who murdered his wife and sank her body in a sailboat, although in the movie version Hitchcock dialed back the evil so that her death was an accident.

"You'll look different on film, Isabella Giori," Leo said so quietly that she could barely hear him over the waves.

"Nobody looks as good without the constant attention of hair and makeup and lighting," she said, feeling suddenly as inadequate as she had standing before Hitchcock in Grace Kelly's clothes and hair and crocheted white driving gloves.

"Don't they?" Leo said.

*T*he Fade Inn. That's how the discreet carved-slate sign beside the Dutch front door reads, the playful name Gemma's grandfather gave this barely-two-bedroom cottage overlooking the ghostly stone of Tor House and Hawk Tower and, invisible beyond them, the great white spray of Pacific meeting rocky coast. FADE IN—*the way every screenplay begins before it sets off on its own journey.* He taught her that. *It makes the starting easier, Cricket,* he said. *Two words to type, and then you're typing. That's how the miracle that is a movie begins, with eight fingers on eight keys and a single mind searching.*

Inside, the tiny front room has gone musty, ocean damp with traces of paper and ink, coffee, and chocolate. It's as tidy as always, his typewriter—that black metal beast of a thing with its forty-eight keys—still on his desk in the front bay window, the letter slugs ink-free and barely a dust mote on the type bars. A stack of clean white paper sits to the left of it, but there is not so much as a title page in the carriage. Nothing "by Chazan," as he always wrote his byline. Not "Léon Chazan" or even "Leo Chazan," but simply "Chazan." Her grandfather's name. Her mother's name. Her name.

Across the road, a door to a contemporary cut-granite-and-glass "cottage" beside Tor House and Hawk Tower opens, a yawning promise. *Point of No Return,* a new sign above the door reads.

She dumps her backpack and the paper sack with everything that was in her refrigerator when she left LA at four this morning (a bottle each of vodka and ginger beer, three limes, and a single carton of yogurt) and sits in the worn wooden chair. It feels wrong to sit in his sacred place, and yet with his ashes in hand—gray dust in an inelegant plastic bag sealed with a red zip tie, the way Gran was finally returned to her yesterday—it's as if she's holding him here the way he so often held her as he taught her to type on this very typewriter at this very desk. He lifted her into his lap and polished her little blue bifocals with his shirttail, then placed her chubby fingers on the keys and showed her how to reach up with her pinkie to type the *q*, her ring finger for the *w*. She learned her letters that way, and arrived at kindergarten believing the alphabet began not with A-B-C-D-E-F, but with Q-W-E-R-T-Y.

She stares at the typewriter as if the decades of shadow-letters pounded into its empty roller might provide answers that don't exist. It's 2018. February 26. A month and four days since Gran died here on the morning after the last weekend she spent with him. She needs to get on about this, to pack away his pots and pans, his shirts, his toothbrush and half-empty toothpaste, his razor and things even more intimate, things that will go to Goodwill or into the trash, impossible as it seems to be sending Gran's last pencil to a landfill. There are things here that need to be kept too though, and she needs to cast Gran's ashes off the point so he and Mom can surf the currents together to all the places he never managed to visit in his ninety-four years—a longevity he attributed to long daily walks, good company even when he was alone, and the absolute best of scotch.

Good company even when you're alone, it's a feeling that comes with doing everything you can to become whoever you want to be, even in your nineties, he used to tell her. But all Gemma wants to be now is her mother's daughter and Gran's granddaughter, to be loved again by them, to write that love onto the page like Gran did and have that to give to the world.

She rolls one of the clean sheets of paper into Ole Mr. Miracle, the black enamel keys with their white letters taunting her. She again looks out the bay window to Tor House. The charming little cottage would be the perfect setting for a romantic comedy, while Hawk Tower, made of the same stone and just across the garden from it, suggests the stuff of nightmares and horror films: Evil experiments. Candles lit against storms. Monsters who eschew daylight, sleep in coffins, terrorize.

Tor. A craggy outcropping. Gemma is a writer. She collects words. They comfort her except when they don't, when she's trying to write and they won't come, when she's trying to gather her grief back into the dingy little stone of her heart she hopes nobody can see.

She reaches over and unlatches the top of the Dutch door the way Gran did whenever he sat down to write. At Point of No Return, a cute guy in running shorts now stands stretching in the open doorway as a puppy circles his feet. He smiles and waves, leaving Gemma feeling the lift of this friendly gesture from anyone, much less a good-looking guy who bucks the current fashion for hypoallergenic doodle dogs in favor of the good old-fashioned chaos of a golden retriever who will shed all over everything.

She raises her hand slightly and waves back.

"Isabella!" the guy calls, his wave not meant for her.

Put your fingers on the keys, let the story begin however it will, Gran would tell her. *The bits inside you, they come best when they come slantwise, catching you off guard.*

Before she loses her nerve, she hits the green shift-lock key and types *FADE IN.*

Two words. Six letters. Three vowels. Not everyone starts screenplays this way now, but she does, because Gran taught her to.

She adds the colon. Releases the shift. Tabs across the page just to ring the margin bell, like she so loved to do when she was little. Swipes the chrome return lever.

Why has she never thought to add this delightful ding and zip as a computer keyboard sound effect?

She can almost hear Gran laughing now, riffing about the graciousness of death from the perspective of ashes in a zip-tied plastic bag in his funny yet respectful way that left movie audiences laughing even when they were scared to death.

Trust that your story will begin to make sense looking backward, once you reach the end of the first draft, Gran would tell her. *It's so much easier to revise than to start, so start anywhere, start exactly where you are.*

Gemma could do that, she could begin a scene right here: Int. Gran's Cottage - Day. Or she could put as dialogue on black screen what the guy just said to the puppy, "You good for this, Knicks?"—the dog named for the basketball team, Gemma guesses, which leaves her less enchanted. She could write what she sees and feels and does: Gemma watches the runner and puppy trot off, then returns to her empty typewriter. Puts her fingers back on the keys. Bangs her head against the typewriter roller in despair.

Eight fingers on eight keys and a single mind searching, but what is she searching for? Is that why she can't write anymore, because in the wake of losing first Mom and then Gran, she's lost her bearings? And Conrad too now, a different kind of loss.

She hadn't imagined as she drove up this morning that she was searching for anything except a real estate agent. None of the budgets she's penciled out shows a way to keep her Venice Beach bungalow and this cottage just big enough, Gran used to say, to host a favorite grandchild—favorite being no real honor since there was no other grandchild to claim Mom's attic bedroom or Gran's love. By the time Gran was her age, he'd already been nominated for two Oscars, while what has she done? And now she's orphaned at twenty-six, left alone to fade in at the Fade Inn with only the scrape of feet on stone somewhere beyond the cottage for company, the slow thump thump thump of the sea and—

"Cricket?"

The nearness of the voice startles her, leaving her exhaling, "Mom?", knowing even as she looks up that it can't be her mother's voice. The only way she can hear her mom now, and Gran too, is by replaying their last messages left on her phone. But only Mom and Gran ever called her Cricket.

Does Iz really remember this cold damp of the stone against her bare soles from that first morning she stood at Leo's half-open door, or is that an experience that became so familiar that her mind echoes it back to the beginning?

"I'm sorry. I didn't mean to startle you," she says to Leo's granddaughter, who looks up from his typewriter as if she's seeing the ghost Iz often feels she's become, her visibility faded with her youth. Gemma Chazan could as easily pass for sixteen as Iz could at her age, her skin so clear that she doesn't need the makeup she doesn't wear. Her long lashes blink blink blink behind eyeglasses the Monet blue-green of her eyes, this girl Iz knows is Leo's granddaughter but who clearly has no idea who Iz is. Not that anybody does these days, not until she introduces herself. And perhaps she won't. Perhaps she can somehow come to know Gemma without the overhang of expectation—this girl who so reminds her of her younger self, with the same awkward beauty that for Iz was a head too big for her shoulders, a too-wide mouth, big collar bones and small breasts, and that hair they changed.

"I heard the typewriter," Iz says, "and . . ."

And what? The noise woke her? She had a moment of imagining this girl was Leo, never mind that he's been dead a month now? The excuse she came armed with was that she would like to buy the Fade Inn if the girl means to sell it, but she finds herself unable to so boldly lie to this granddaughter of Leo's who is probably no better at recognizing a liar like her than her grandfather was.

"I'm so sorry about your grandfather," she says. "I'm Isabella Giori, from next door."

The girl tears up even as she peers at Iz now with unabashed in-credulity, the way people do. They expect the young actress frozen on film, not the grandmother-of-an-American-who-marries-a-prince that she is to audition for tomorrow. But grandmother is the only role Iz has been offered since she turned forty. Roger Moore was still playing James Bond at fifty-seven. Sean Connery—sixty-eight when Iz was just sixty—wooed a twenty-nine-year-old Catherine Zeta-Jones in a part Iz was "far too old" to play. But even this grandmother audi-tion would never have happened without Hugh Bolin. Hugh Fucking Bolin. But she's eighty-two now. She regrets every grandmother role she was too young-looking to be considered for or too proud to take. She wants to be someone again.

Leo's granddaughter blinks back her tears, saying, "Next door in Rose Cottage?" And when Iz tells her she's next door the other way, in Manderley, the girl quotes, "'Last night I dreamt I went to Manderley again,'" in a perfect mimic of Joan Fontaine introducing the crumbling castle of Hitchcock's *Rebecca*, its high walls ensnared in malevolent ivy, its shrouded rooms haunted by memory and tradition, expectation.

"You came here to write?" Iz says—the line too rushed, any director would tell her, but she doesn't want to give the girl time to wonder how her grandfather's next-door neighbor could be a movie star he's never mentioned, one with a name she recognizes even if she might never have seen Iz onscreen.

The girl sputters, "No. No, I'm just here to meet with real estate agents." She rolls the typewriter carriage. *FADE IN*: That's all she's typed. "I haven't written anything worth anything since Mom died last year," she says, a confession she clearly needs to make, and Iz is the one standing here.

Iz opens the bottom of the Dutch door and steps inside, tucking her guilt behind the shield of the girl's confused emotions.

The girl says, "I did think maybe up here . . . I'm looking for inspiration, I guess." She looks up through the window and says to the heavens, "I know, I know, Gran. Inspiration isn't something a writer waits for. 'Inspiration is something that sometimes visits a writer if she shows up every morning and puts her fingers on the keys.'"

Her laughter then is so familiar, although Isabella has heard it only once before, one long-ago morning when Leo's daughter arrived a day earlier than expected with this daughter of hers, this child Leo called "Cricket," who is no longer a child.

HOW CAN IT BE SIXTY years now since Iz first met Leo? Since she'd been awakened again that third morning—Oscar day of 1957—to the same clack and ding and zip of Leo's typewriter. Five a.m. Again. Did he mean to write an entire screenplay in the few days she would be next door? He'd returned her to the cottage unharmed the day before though, and if the rest of their conversation at Hidden Beach had been no easier than the discussion about the nameless Mrs. de Winter, he had at least capped his lens without taking her photo. They'd eaten the cookies and drunk the coffee, and when she said she had to get back, he replied, "Of course," as if he too were relieved.

She had again tromped over to his cottage to find him hunched over the typewriter, working so furiously as she stood in her pajamas and bare feet that she left without interrupting him. She returned to the studio's cottage and her Oscar gown in the closet. She gulped coffee she made in the percolator that wasn't hers. Pulled on warm clothes and her coat. Tucked her hair under the black hat, and set out into the cloaking darkness.

At the oceanfront road, ancient granite spilled down to a turbulent sea, each foamy peak and each spray of crashing wave against the rocky outcroppings below amplified and made mysterious by the meeting of moonlight and dark. The sky too. It was thick with stars you never could see in LA, where the streetlights dull the heavens.

It was not a five-minute walk to the end of the point, where the palisades plummeted toward boulders as high as rooftops. She scrambled down the steep path, then crabbed across the jagged and algae-covered rocks to the sea's edge, already imagining she might come out here early every morning. In this wild, peaceful place, at this wild, peaceful hour, she could know she was alone and unseen.

She could still change her mind, she told herself.

But she was under contract for six more years, and while the studio had an option to terminate her, she had no parallel right. She couldn't go back to Pennsylvania now either. She would have nowhere to go.

A huge wave crashed so nearby that it left her scurrying back, scraping her palms on the granite. To the left, at an estuary where a river broadened before cutting a path in the sand to reach the cove, three bright stars hung in a tidy line. The dark shadow across the cove would be Point Lobos, where Leo had taken her, where in *Rebecca* Maxim de Winter scuttled the boat holding his dead wife's—

She startled. Was that a man tucked in against the higher rocks not ten yards away?

She sat paralyzed, spooked in that way darkness makes you when you've lost the sense of its cloaking safety. She held her breath as if that might make her invisible. Had he been watching her all this time?

Maybe it was nothing, the light playing tricks, or her mind doing so?

She listened intently, hearing nothing but the crash of waves, and still she was left in the creepy shadow of Maxim de Winter scuttling Rebecca's boat.

A man emerged from behind the highest rocks.

He stopped and stood perfectly still.

She froze, too afraid to turn her back to him to get away up the slope.

He moved toward her slowly, deliberately. His body thin and hard. His face angular and shadowed. The stale smell of cigarettes already smoked.

He stopped beside her.

He looked to the sea, so still now that it seemed lifeless.

The fact that he had not yet looked at her was somehow more frightening than if he had.

In his hand: a flick of metal.

A flame dented the darkness. The crinkle of a cigarette, its tip burning an angry red as the flame was extinguished.

"The stars go over the lonely ocean," he said.

He continued across the rocks and up the slope then, his footsteps on the gravelly uphill path never faltering despite the protruding stones.

After a moment, the tip of red swung slightly back and forth up Scenic Road. It seemed such a long time before it turned up Stewart Way, where Isabella would turn to go back to the cottage.

A mist was coming in, extinguishing the stars over that lonely ocean. She pulled her coat tighter but wasn't warmed.

After he disappeared, she gathered her courage and picked her way back across the rocky outcropping, so much more precarious than the climb out. She barely breathed as she clambered back up the palisade and hurried toward the cottage.

She slammed the cottage door and locked it, then stood holding the doorknob.

A window lit at the top of the medieval-looking tower across the road, not with electric light, she didn't think, but with the eerie glow of candle flame.

She stuck her hands in her coat pockets, trying to get warm even still. Her fingers brushed against something small and hard and cold.

The clack of typewriter keys next door sounded again, only sporadically, but still she was comforted to know she wasn't alone.

She pulled the shell from her pocket, felt the perfect smoothness and the bite of its teeth. She would take it back to Los Angeles, she decided, as a reminder of this fear she might want to recall for the role in the Hitchcock film she was no longer sure she would get.

I . . . Would you like coffee, Ms. Giori?" Gemma asks, she doesn't even know why. She doesn't want company and she's slightly suspicious of this woman standing at Gran's door, although that's ridiculous, Isabella Giori is the famous one. She no doubt keeps a cottage here for the reason so many famous people always have, because there are no maps of where the stars live here, no celebrity bus tours. Bing Crosby. Beverly Cleary. John Denver. Joan Baez and, briefly, Bob Dylan. Doris Day owns an inn in town and lives near Clint Eastwood, the movie-star former mayor who turned the rat-infested Mission Ranch into a luxury hotel. Brad Pitt is now looking for a place.

And Isabella Giori is already responding, "I've given up coffee but I'd love a cup of tea. And I have fresh almond croissants, let me fetch them. Please though, call me Isabella, or simply Iz."

Minutes later they're settling into Gran's Adirondack chairs, Gemma trying to come up with something to say when she can't for the life of her remember the title of a single one of Ms. Giori's films. And Ms. Giori wrote one of them too, didn't she? Gemma read about it in an article about how Matt Damon and Ben Affleck writing *Good Will Hunting* together nearly ruined a friendship begun when they were ten and eight. Like Con and her, if you left out the "nearly." Writing together had been the end of them.

"Iz!" someone calls from up the road, the runner from Point of No Return returning. He scoops up his puppy and runs to join them.

His eyes are so near the color of his puppy's ears that he might have bought the dog to match—that's what Gemma is thinking when he catches a toe on Gran's stone walkway and pitches forward. She lunges into Gran's rosebushes to break the puppy's fall.

"Hey, careful there, sweetie," she says to this dog now licking her face, and licking it some more. It's probably a bit of croissant at the edge of her lips the puppy is after, but Gemma chooses to feel it as love. Puppies fix everything.

As the guy apologizes, Isabella introduces him as Sam Kenneally.

To Sam, Iz says, "I hope you don't mind, but I gave my croissant to Gemma Chazan here and kept yours for us to share." Then to Gemma, "He brings them every morning. I'm his excuse for the sugar sin."

He leans over and takes a bite of the croissant in Isabella's hand, then tears off another bite and feeds it to the puppy in Gemma's arms, whom he introduces.

"Knicks as in 'the New York Knicks'?" Gemma asks.

"N-Y-X, the disloyal Greek goddess of night who emerged at the dawn of creation to abandon me for the first new neighbor we meet, even as I try to entice her back with a bite of my croissant."

"My croissant," Isabella Giori corrects him. "Gemma is eating yours."

"You just said you kept mine for us to share!" He grins, then turns a sympathetic look to Gemma. "I . . . We sure miss your grandfather here."

Gemma rubs the puppy's soft ears, thinking *shift-N-y-x*, it would look pretty in courier font, that juxtaposed *y* and *x*.

The guy plops down in Gran's favorite Adirondack chair, like the ghost of Gran as a young man. "I loved *Eleanor After Dark*," he says.

"Oh! Thank you," she blurts out, surprised he's seen the little no-budget film she and Con wrote and Con directed. Yes, Gran would have hounded everyone he knew into seeing it or saying they had, but this Sam doesn't strike her as a film-festival kind of guy. Is he the one Gran met last spring, not long after Mom died? Gran was forever trying to improve on Con, as if Gemma might be this guy's type in some way other than if his blood too is O negative. O negative—the universal donor. She can share with anyone but can only accept exactly her type.

"The car scene, you filmed that with the car backing away from the actress?" Sam asks—something Gran might have told him, but she likes that he's someone who paid attention to Gran, and remembers.

"Then reversed it and sped it up so it looks like the car plows into her," Gemma says. She hadn't known then that Con was already sleeping with the actress, that Gemma's idea for improving the scene would leave everyone thinking her lover's new lover could actually act. And the role was Gemma herself too, in ways she would never admit.

Sam says, "The writing in *Eleanor After Dark* is brilliant. The double entendre in the title? The things Eleanor does at night, literally after dark, and in the darkness of her mind."

Which would have made Gemma like him even if he *had* named his puppy after a basketball team.

She realizes then that she left Gran's ashes on the counter. Is the zip-tied plastic bag far enough from Gran's old percolator, or will it melt? She offers to fetch Sam coffee or tea for the excuse to check, and demurs at his offer of help.

"'All right, black as my heart then, Cricket,'" he says. Gran's expression.

At the look on her face, he blanches.

"I'm sorry," he stammers. "I— You don't like 'Cricket'?"

Gemma blinks away the wash of fresh grief as she hands Nyx back to him. It's what Isabella too called Gemma, but Cricket—the memory of that little girl she was—has died with Gran.

"It's fine, it's fine, really," she says. And maybe it is.

Then Sam is exclaiming, "Your arm!" and before Gemma knows it the two of them are bumping into each other in Gran's narrow galley kitchen as Sam holds her arm, scratched from elbow to wrist by Gran's roses as she rescued Nyx, under the faucet. He gently washes the blood away, then presses a towel to her skin and has her hold it while he fetches antibiotic ointment and gauze and tape from the bathroom across the hall.

For no reason Gemma could explain, she tries to hide the bag of Gran's ashes, but there's no room in the silverware drawer, and the oven seems far too ominous even though Gran is already ash. She has the refrigerator door open when she clocks Sam watching her from the bathroom doorway.

He lifts an eyebrow. "Leo did always prefer cold to hot, but I'm not sure about the refrigerator—although there *is* ketchup in there as old as he was, so he'd be in good company."

His words are ridiculously silly—lines that wouldn't survive a decent writers' room—but Gemma laughs so hard she has to wipe her face with the cloth he used to clean up her arm. How odd that grief expresses itself in such opposite ways, through laughter and tears, and so often both at the same time.

"Point of No Return—that's a clever name for a cottage," she says as he gets her arm gooed up and gauzed, his pale lashes blinking over those amber eyes as if he's trying to see something inside her that even she doesn't know is there.

Sea View, Gemma remembers then. That was the name of the original cottage where Point of No Return now stands. It's bad luck to rename a cottage in Carmel, but Gemma guesses Sam's family or friend or whoever paid fourteen million dollars for it last spring, if the *Carmel Pine Cone* is to be believed, can afford to tempt fate. From this side, the place looks relatively modest: a single-story stone cottage, albeit with two garage doors where many cottages have none. But it's built into the cliffside overlooking the Pacific. From the oceanfront road, it has two high stories flanked by turrets, with floor-to-ceiling glass that folds away to an endless view—all hidden from here by the canopy of grand old Monterey cypresses and coast live oaks. And it has the most adorable "Carmel Dog Bar"—a hip-high stone hut built into the low wall on the oceanfront road, with nothing but a water spigot and doggie bowl inside it, so that any dog walking their owner along the coast can stop for a drink.

Sam pulls three fresh mugs and Gran's scotch from the cupboards—"the absolute best of scotch" she and Gran always shared on Oscar weekends. This weekend will be the first time she hasn't come up to Carmel to watch with him since her freshman year at UCLA, Gran always in his tuxedo and Gemma in an old prom dress of her mom's that still hangs in the chifforobe in the attic bedroom, the two of them making up titles for the scripts Gemma might write to win her own Oscar. "Your first Oscar," Gran always called it, as if she would win dozens.

"What do you say?" Sam says. "A toast to your grandfather?"

It's not even noon, but Gemma doesn't object.

As they step back outside, Sam whispers, "Look," pointing with the hand that holds Leo's scotch bottle. "On the gargoyle."

A young falcon sits there, as still as its stone hawk perch. The creature's dark eyes in its black head seem to be watching him, not as prey but as something in need of protection.

He sets the ashes in Leo's chair and takes the one next to Gemma Chazan while Nyx climbs back into her lap.

He pours a measure of scotch into each mug and hands them out, then raises his to the bird.

"To Leo," he says.

As Iz echoes him, Gemma says, "To Gran."

Sam throws his back. "Shit, that's awful," he says.

"It's 'the absolute best of scotch,'" Gemma protests, and she too throws hers back. "Gosh, that *is* awful. No wonder I only ever drink scotch with Gran."

Drank, Sam thinks, but he doesn't say that.

"Did you know Robinson Jeffers?" he asks Iz, using the full name although he thinks of him simply as Robin, the poet who built Hawk Tower with his own hands over a period of six years during which, stone by stone, he found his poetic voice. Sam tries to imagine doing that himself, apprenticing with the stonemason who built Tor House, then building the improbably high tower alone. He regrets now that he didn't talk much about the poet even to Leo, but he'd been trying to form his own idea of him first.

"Jeffers was an overnight success, and then he was nobody," Isabella responds, ducking Sam's question, although she's right. The poetry collection Robin wrote as he built Hawk Tower in 1925 rocketed him to fame, putting him in the company of Ezra Pound, T. S. Eliot, and Robert Frost. But by the 1940s he'd largely fallen out of favor on account of his criticism of World War II.

She's a little evasive, is our Isabella Giori, Sam thinks. And Leo's granddaughter is a little evasive too. She's prettier than he expected, her eyes behind the lenses as light as Sam's own and her skin even fairer where Leo was brown-eyed, his features less delicate. She has Leo's sense of humor though: A little wacky. More than a little dark.

Across the road, the falcon takes flight—a peregrine. Less rare now, recovering from near extinction due to DDT. The fastest creature on earth. As he watches, the young bird's chest still brown and buff as he catches the wind, he thinks of Robin's ashes and his wife's too buried with those of their first child, who lived only a day, in an unmarked grave on the Tor House and Hawk Tower property.

"'I built her a tower when I was young— / Sometime she will die,'" he says, quoting lines from "For Una," Robin's wife who married him only after her first husband refused to take her back.

"Well, that's dark," Gemma says, which makes them all laugh.

She says, "Gran would have appreciated the character contradiction, this cheery neighbor who runs with his adorable dog and yet quotes dark poetry. It's the contradictions that make a character interesting. He taught me that."

Leo. The first morning Sam woke here, he watched Leo Chazan carry a beach chair and some paper down to the little cove that Point of No Return overlooks. The man was in his nineties, but he set up the chair there, then returned again with his typewriter. *That* was an interesting character.

"Our good Mr. Jeffers wasn't a man who bent toward popularity," he says to Leo's granddaughter. "His poetry explores the physical beauty of this coast but also the human destruction of it. Cruelty.

Violence. War and murder and mayhem. Incest. Rape." Robin's *The Double Axe* was condemned as "a necrophiliac nightmare," although Sam doesn't tell her that. He knows others read Robin as dark, but he's drawn to the wonder and the joy in his poetry, "the infinite wheeling stars" and Orion ascending the winter heaven—words he'd first read in a book Leo loaned him. "Iz, I could see you as the model for his 'Medea,'" he says.

Iz says, "We love Sam despite his tendency to go on about his passions." Then to Sam, "At the risk of pressing your tell-me-about-video-games play button, do tell: What ex-lover do you suspect me of poisoning?"

March 1957

When Isabella heard the opening of the 1957 Oscar ceremony rather than the sound of typing coming from Leo's cottage, she hesitated. She was supposed to stay hidden for the entire week. But Leo knew she was here and yes, he made her a little nervous, but he *had* brought her home from the little cove without harm. And he was right: nobody wants to watch the Oscars alone.

He didn't look surprised to see her at his door a minute later, dressed in her Oscar gown. He simply invited her in and excused himself for a moment, leaving her to watch her reflection in his bay window, imagining her white tulle skirt swishing as she entered the Pantages Theater with the cameras flashing, her bare neck above her gown's navy blue velvet top draped with those pearls the studio had planned to borrow for her to wear, that had belonged to French queen Marie-Antoinette. When she first heard the shutter click, she imagined it was in her imaginings too, the press anxious for photos of "the new Grace."

"You can read it," Leo said, startling her. He'd changed into a smart tuxedo and was lowering his camera. On the television, Bob LeMond was welcoming everyone from outside the Pantages Theater and telling them, by the way, that they ought to buy Oldsmobiles. Leo reached past her for a few manuscript pages on the desk. "Here. Just the opening scene."

By Chazan, his byline read. Was that his last name? He hadn't answered when she'd asked at Hidden Beach, she realized only then.

The two pages she read as he poured them scotch were disturbing, never mind that the dog and goat hide whips had come from her. But the fact that he wrote creepy scripts didn't mean he was creepy. Hitchcock was the king of creepy, and she wanted more than anything to work with him.

Even if Leo sent the photo he'd just taken to the press, she couldn't be identified just from the back of her head and her shoulders and gown, she told herself.

They clinked glasses and she grimaced at that first awful sip.

Inside the Pantages, the Academy president proclaimed this the fiftieth birthday of the motion picture industry, its "golden jubilee," and introduced comedian Jerry Lewis, the master of ceremonies. If Iz weren't such a fool, if only she'd let Mannix bring her up to Carmel that night Mr. Thau told her to go, she would be smoothing her own gown into a seat between Kirk Douglas and Anthony Quinn while everyone speculated who she might be.

Leo had attended the Oscars three times, he told her, for a script he'd been brought in to fix but wasn't credited for, and two for which he'd been nominated but hadn't won. Films she'd seen. Films nearly everyone had seen. It was the kind of success most men would lead with: *Hi, I'm three-time Oscar nominee Leo Chazan.* He was broodingly attractive in a Bogart kind of way too—not her type, but she was all dressed up and with nobody else to tell her she looked beautiful.

It was just as well that the scotch was rotgut, she decided as she smoothed the tulle of her gown onto the sofa, conscious of her good posture and crossing her legs at the ankles, while Leo took the chair cornering her. The lousy scotch would keep her from drinking too much and making a fool of herself.

She set her gloved hand on the sofa arm, close enough to Leo's fingers lightly tapping on the chair arm between them that, if he had a mind to, he could reach out with his pinkie and overlap hers. He didn't though, and even when he waltzed her around the tiny room as the Academy orchestra played the Best Song winner, "Que Sera,

Sera," he held his body a proper ruler-distance apart. Still, she closed her eyes, feeling the warmth of his hand on the Grace Kelly detailing of her gown and imagining for a moment that she was dancing at an after-party, Oscar in hand.

"We have contenders for best actor and best supporting actor, Douglas and Quinn," she said as they sat again. "And Norman Corwin for writing *Lust for Life* too."

"Douglas has three children by two different wives," Leo said, the disapproval in his voice unnerving. "And Corwin met with O'Neil."

James F. O'Neil was with the American Legion, the self-appointed clearinghouse for getting your name off the blacklist. And Corwin was represented by Martin Gang, the top lawyer for those willing to inform on friends. But what could Iz say? Corwin had written the script that would likely be her first lead role if she didn't get the Hitchcock part.

Leo said, "The Academy changes its bylaws to deny anyone who is blacklisted an Oscar, so Corwin gets a nomination while Michael Wilson is stripped from *Friendly Persuasion,* a hell of a lot better film."

Iz took a gulp of the lousy scotch as, on the television, they cut back to the second presentation stage, in New York. *Friendly Persuasion* was eight years in the making, costing three million dollars and the good will of Gary Cooper, who grumbled about having to play a fifty-five-year-old father even though he was fifty-six and two decades older than his on-screen wife. The studio couldn't afford to have the movie boycotted and fail at the box office on account of a writer's politics.

Leo said, "Maybe this libel suit Faulk has filed will help break HUAC's stranglehold, but until then the only person left in Hollywood who can reliably manipulate his way around the Committee is Eddie Mannix."

Mannix. Iz took another slug of scotch, trying to mask her alarm at the sound of his name.

IT MATTERED LESS THAT THE stories about Mannix were true than that the stories about Mannix were told. He was a stereotype of what he was. Bulldog face. Big fat stogie. Central casting could not have done better. But he wasn't an actor. While he was officially the studio's general manager, he was, less officially, their fixer, the man in the shadows. He arranged executive sessions before HUAC. He arrived in ambulances with doctors, security guards, and wads of cash to sprinkle liberally at the bars where he picked up Spencer Tracy, to take him to sober up out of the public eye. He rescued Judy Garland from her drug benders. He arranged abortions for Ava Gardner, Bette Davis, Joan Crawford, and Jean Harlow—all of which would of course be denied. And after Harlow's husband died under suspicious circumstances, Mannix was on the scene hours before the police were called. If you were a bad boy in Hollywood, Mannix was your savior. But if you were any kind of girl, bad or good, the shadow of Mannix on your doorstep stopped your heart, and not in a good way.

They'd all heard the story of Patricia Douglas, a twenty-year-old who answered a casting call. She and the other girls who showed up to audition allowed themselves to be made up and put on a bus to a nearby ranch where the banquet hall and orchestra there were not, it would turn out, a set for auditioning. It was 1937, and while the Depression drove Paramount and 20th Century Fox into bankruptcy, Iz's studio had instead restructured their film rentals to double their profits, and the studio and producer Hal Roach were hosting a week-end getaway to thank the salesmen.

The girls were treated as party favors and, with five hundred cases of scotch and champagne for three hundred men, things did not end well. Douglas was held down and force-fed alcohol, then dragged to the back of a car, where she was raped by a salesman from Chicago.

Nobody had to be told that charging anyone at that party with rape would serve only to leave the girl herself as damaged goods, her reputation in tatters and any career hopes with it. That was the way the world worked. But Patricia Douglas was going to do it anyway. So the studio brought in Mannix, who employed Pinkerton detectives to track down and bully every other girl who'd been there into characterizing the party as good clean fun.

In the end, Douglas tried to kill herself.

But Iz wasn't hiding from Mannix. Iz was being hidden by him.

HAD LEO SEEN MANNIX DELIVER her to the cottage? It had been late at night, when nobody would see them. Mannix turned off the headlights before they turned onto the road, well before he got her suitcase from the trunk and keyed the door. They hadn't turned on the lights inside until they were sure the curtains were closed. Still, it was all Iz could think about as Jerry Lewis announced Deborah Kerr to present the Story Writing Oscar. Leo had worked in Hollywood. He might know Mannix by sight.

Iz focused on Kerr's dress, a gauzy thing with sparkles at her bosom and a neck as bare as her own. If she was a good girl she would be at the Oscar ceremony next year, Thau promised to take her even if she didn't have a nomination. His suggesting it now didn't mean it would happen, but it did mean he thought her performance in *A Little Summer Romance* was Oscar-worthy. She was on her way. All she had to do was exactly what Mannix told her to do.

"You know Mr. Mannix?" she said to Leo. Mr. Mannix, so Leo would assume she didn't know Mannix well, or perhaps at all.

Leo considered her as, on the TV, Kerr kissed Lewis on the cheek and Lewis responded with goofball ecstasy.

"Mannix sent me to the same cottage you're staying in," Leo said, "to give me time away from the press to testify, like everyone who shows up there these days."

"You named names?" The words an exhale, the question one nobody working in Hollywood asked anyone else.

He stared at her, his eyes as hard as that little shell he'd given her.

"The last script I sold," he said finally, "I had to drive all the way down to Santa Monica to be paid in cash literally handed off to me at a prearranged stroll on the beach. The producer was happy to have my script for three thousand dollars when just a few years ago he would have had to pay ten times that, but he couldn't risk anyone knowing I wrote it."

He'd been sent up here by Mannix to name names but had changed his mind and now he was blacklisted—that was what Leo was saying.

Iz started to say how sorry she was, already searching for an excuse to leave. The faintest suggestion that she was spending time with anyone on the blacklist could end her career.

But his attention had been caught by the television. He was intently focused on the screen now, longing bare in his face as Deborah Kerr began announcing the writing nominees. Was he in love with her?

Kerr accepted the envelope, already opened and with the card pulled out so she had only to read the winning writer's name. "*The Brave One*. Robert Rich."

Leo leapt to his feet, pulling Iz up with him and hugging her so fiercely that her feet left the floor. And as Kerr announced that the vice president of the screenwriters' branch of the Writers Guild would accept the award for Mr. Rich and a man charged up the aisle, Leo grabbed their glasses of scotch. He grinned like a boy who'd just caught a frog even as he was tearing up. He seemed such a different person.

"To Robert Rich," he said.

"Who wins an Oscar and doesn't show up to collect it?" she blurted out.

Leo laughed, and he clinked glasses with her again, and he wiped at one eye as if there were a bug there rather than some emotion he didn't want her to see.

"Even Rich himself would never have written his winning an Oscar into this script," he said, leaving her wondering if Rich was a blacklisted writer, or even if Leo himself might be Rich. That would explain the brooding man he'd been until this moment: a man who'd written a script that was an Oscar contender under somebody else's name. *Nobody wants to watch the Oscars alone*, he'd said. She'd assumed he was thinking of her, but she hadn't by then even told him her name.

She needed to leave, but it would be too cruel to leave him alone if he was Robert Rich, if he'd just won an Oscar and couldn't even tell anyone. And the ceremony was nearly over.

She looked to the bay window, devising excuses to draw the curtains, but there were none.

As Lewis introduced the lead actress award, Leo said, "She had a daughter with her first husband before she took up with Rossellini. Ingrid Bergman did."

The *Casablanca* star and Hitchcock favorite had become pregnant with director Roberto Rossellini's child while they were both married to others five years before, and the response had been brutal. She was denounced on the Senate floor for having "perpetuated an assault upon the institution of marriage." She was called "a powerful influence for evil" and much worse in letters that arrived by the bagful. Ed Sullivan cancelled an appearance. And Bergman—who was still box office poison, never mind the male stars who fathered out-of-wedlock children and still ruled the marquees—hadn't been back to Hollywood since.

"I understand falling in love, I do," Leo said as they were again implored to buy Oldsmobiles. "I understand that marriages sometimes fail. But I don't understand a woman putting her own needs ahead of her child."

Bergman's daughter from her first marriage, the subject of a vicious custody battle, lived with her father now, and never saw her mother. But that was the ex-husband's choice, to bar his daughter from seeing her mother. So few actresses managed to have children and a career. Yet the notoriously "difficult" Elizabeth Taylor, who'd just wed for the third time amid rumors she was pregnant with Mike Todd's child even before her divorce was final, was having a grand time in her four-million-dollar tiara and thirty-carat diamond ring. Todd was an important director. Nobody wanted to offend him by criticizing his new wife. And Taylor remained close to her ex-husband, who had allowed her to keep custody of their children. A mother without her child was a more horrible thing than a wife without her husband, her morals more suspect even if it wasn't her fault, even if she'd had no say in the decision.

"The winner . . ." Ernest Borgnine paused over the card in the envelope. "Ingrid Bergman."

As Iz silently hoped this Oscar might somehow help Bergman get her daughter back, the camera cut to the crowd. Some were applauding, but most sat stone-faced and angry, determined to judge, as Cary Grant hurried up the aisle to accept the Oscar for her.

"'Who wins an Oscar and doesn't show up to collect it?'" Leo said, echoing Iz.

"I'm sorry," he continued. "I shouldn't have gone on about all that earlier, about testifying. I shouldn't be trying to tell you what you should and shouldn't do. Everyone has already been named by somebody else anyway. And Mannix knows how to get you cleared with HUAC. You can trust him. You can do what he tells you to do."

March 1957

Could anyone really trust Eddie Mannix though? Leo wasn't sure anyone could trust anyone in Hollywood anymore. In the fall of 1947, just before he'd arrived, a list of who's who had gathered at Ira Gershwin's house to organize opposition to the HUAC investigations, which they saw as a witch hunt. Frank Sinatra. Rita Hayworth. Groucho Marx. Henry Fonda. They included fervent *anti*-communists who believed in the right to free speech and in the film industry itself, which was being brutalized by the right-wing press. The first "Hollywood Fights Back" show on ABC Radio that October had opened with Judy Garland, beloved Dorothy from *The Wizard of Oz*, insisting all Americans had the right to see any movie or read any book or magazine or listen to any program they wanted to. And the American public had been with them, opposing punishment for the Hollywood Ten by three to one.

But the prosecutors pushed on, and the people in the thrall of the red-baiters were far more fanatical than those who weren't. They wrote so many letters denouncing Katharine Hepburn that Spencer Tracy had to step in to rehabilitate her image, arranging for her to costar as his wife and the potential First Lady in *State of the Union*—as American as they could make her. Humphrey Bogart announced that his trip to DC to support the Ten had been a mistake. And the studios scrambled to get their stars out of the way, cutting a deal with HUAC to fire anyone who couldn't or wouldn't "clear his name" in exchange for the Committee refraining from attacking the studios themselves. Even the Actors Guild under Ronald Reagan and the Writers Guild too voted overwhelmingly to bar suspected communists from membership.

Leo had thought that would be it. Everyone thought that would be it if they just kept their heads down. But a second round of HUAC hearings began, with some of Hollywood's most famous brought to trial and imprisoned or forced to flee the country to avoid prosecution. Charlie Chaplin. Orson Welles. Dorothy Parker. Lena Horne. Hollywood's writers were particularly hard hit, the nearly five hundred writing under contract when Leo arrived pared down to one hundred by the time he was sent to the studio's cottage. That was late 1953. He'd been writing screenplays for six years. He never did know what changed, who named him, but he knew the moment he heard Mannix's voice on the phone that they were coming for him.

By then, he was living so many lies that it was hard to keep them straight, much less know which lie was the safest to cling to. He couldn't afford to have the FBI digging around in his past. He had no choice but to do whatever he needed to do to appease them. So he came up to Carmel at night, as Isabella had, although Mannix hadn't brought him; he was a writer and none of the writers in Hollywood were so identifiable that they couldn't drive themselves.

His executive session had been delayed a few days, which Leo had come to believe was intentional. They left you alone in the bleak little cottage with its plywood walls and dirty windows, lonely time in the shroud of Carmel fog to contemplate what your future would look like if you didn't testify. Leo went where he was supposed to go at the prescribed time, to tell them he wasn't a communist and never had been. If he was lucky, he would simply be asked to sign a statement recanting anything he might have said that they now labeled progressive. If made to, he would name some people who had already been named, to clear his own name like so many had before him. Then he would slip quietly back to LA and the rest of his life.

Two men in dark suits, white shirts, and dark ties had already settled at a round table when he arrived at the shabby motel room. One told him to take the seat in front of the tape recorder and microphone. The man was friendly enough, under the circumstances. He assured Leo the recording was only for their own records, and slid a Bible across the table. The other said nothing. Neither introduced himself.

Leo suppressed a frown as he set his hand on the Bible and swore to tell the truth.

"State your full name," the same man said.

Leo hesitated, trying to block out the images haunting him: The fear in Margalit's eyes. The snow on the mountaintop beginning to fall again as the real Madame Chazan turned back the way they'd come, with no idea that she too would soon be dead. But he couldn't close his eyes in this room with these men, it was too dangerous to show any hint of weakness no matter what he had done in the past or what he did here now, what he might or might not say.

The man fished in his pocket and pulled out a pack of Chesterfields, "the milder cigarette." The brand of Humphrey Bogart, Claudette Colbert, and Peggy Lee. The other simply sat, silently waiting.

"Your name?" the inquisitor demanded. "Surely that isn't a tough one."

The man leaned back in his chair, tapped a cigarette from the white pack with its fancy lettering and little gold crown, its bright red "Chesterfield" in plainer font on the bottom. He lit it and took a deep drag.

Leo leaned into the microphone as the smoker exhaled through his nose and the other man continued his silent, unwavering gaze.

"I plead the Fifth," Leo managed. Firm and solid. Not *I think*. Not *I want to*. Simply *I plead*.

The man leaned forward, the cigarette drooping so low that Leo feared it would burn the table. "For your name, son?"

Léon Chazan, Leo thought. Just say it. Say it and get this over with. Save yourself.

"What are you playing at?" the man demanded. "Don't you be wasting our time."

Leo did not meet either man's gaze. That was something he'd learned the hard way, to be careful not to look angry men in the eye lest they see it as a challenge to them.

He moved his hands from the table and set them in his lap, tamping down his fury. He couldn't afford to provoke them.

He thought of Salka then. Salka who, in pairing him with Garbo, set him solidly toward success even though Garbo backed out of that project, as she always did. Salka who, just months before, had been blacklisted herself and fled to Switzerland.

Léon Chazan, he told himself. It was the name he signed to every script he'd ever written: Chazan. It was the name he'd used to sign his contract, which the studio had just offered to extend at double the salary, with his agent telling him if he went freelance he could get north of fifty thousand dollars for his best scripts and absolute freedom over what he wrote. To say anything else here would be to throw away the life he'd so carefully built. But he didn't know what they knew and what they didn't. Where he came from. What he'd done and what he hadn't. Who he was.

"I invoke my Fifth Amendment privilege against self-incrimination," he said, keeping his gaze on his folded hands. "I respectfully decline to answer your question."

The place to start is Gran's bedroom, but Gemma feels like a trespasser as she stands at the bedroom door. She retreats to the kitchen, where she finds a box of Guittard bittersweet dark chocolate baking bars, a plastic honey bear, and a box of soy milk, unopened but past its expiration date, and anyway, she hates soy milk. She stares out the bay window to Point of No Return, wondering what Sam Kenneally is doing now, and whether he does what he does with a girlfriend, or even a spouse.

She sets the dirty mugs, still smelling of scotch, in the sink, and she plays a phone message from Gran, soothed by the sound of his voice, then pushes through the bedroom door.

The room is practically antiseptic, as if Gran knew she'd have to clear out his cottage and wanted to make the task easier. The bed is made, the closet doors closed. The door from the bedroom out to the backyard is unlocked, but that doesn't surprise her. Gran never locked his doors. A few pages sit face down on the little table next to the chair in the corner, with one of Gran's pencils and his reading glasses on them. She has a moment of thinking he's just gone out to pour himself a scotch and will be right back. But it's only an IRS notice. Gran is due a refund.

Do you want an autopsy? the policewoman had asked when she called to tell Gemma they had found Gran dead in this chair. No, there was nothing suspicious about a heart attack at ninety-four, she was just required to ask, she said. And Gemma couldn't face the prospect of Gran's body being cut apart, his brain and liver removed to be weighed and measured, his very big heart held in latex-gloved hands, set on a cold metal scale, described in scientific language that had nothing to do with the way he loved.

He's been gone a month, but there isn't even much dust on the dresser, a maple gentlemens' chest that had been covered with her mom's drugs and schedules for taking them, phone numbers for doctors, and thermometers the last time she was in this room, when what was ahead was months of treatment that would cure her mother, but ended up being only weeks and the rest of her life.

Now there are only two framed photos and an Oscar that reads:

ACADEMY OF MOTION PICTURE ARTS AND SCIENCES
WRITING (STORY AND SCREENPLAY—
WRITTEN DIRECTLY FOR THE SCREEN)
THE DEFIANT ONES
NATHAN E. DOUGLAS AND HAROLD JACOB SMITH
1958

She fingers the metal, golden and cold. A man, naked but without a penis. (There are jokes she could make about this, but they aren't jokes she could ever tell; even today, men who tell dirty jokes are funny as hell while women who do so are trashy.) One photo is of her and Mom at her college graduation, the other of Gran, not much older than Gemma now, with a friend.

She turns to the closet. It will just be clothes, while the dresser will be underwear.

When she opens the door, a pile of manuscripts topples and spills. They fill the shelf all the way to the ceiling. The piles on the floor reach the hanging rod where it's empty. Gran's shoes sit atop shorter stacks that reach to the few shirts and pants hanging on one side. The tuxedo Gran always wore on Oscar night hangs alone on the other side.

Emptying this place is going to be so much harder than she imagined.

She piles the fallen scripts back up and closes the closet. The underwear will be easier. Surely Gran was a boxers man.

In the top dresser drawer, she finds cufflinks, a bowl of coins, an empty ring box. A stack of envelopes rubber-banded together, the top one from her mother and postmarked Hanover, New Hampshire, which she can't bear to read now. And Gran's watch too, its leather band so frayed it will soon split in half. Patek Philippe. Two circles on the white face and two second hands, both perfectly still. Initials engraved on the back that aren't Gran's. His phone was returned to her along with his wallet with his credit and Medicare and Medigap cards, a smaller copy of the graduation photo and, oddly, a one-hundred-franc gold coin from 1929 that left a circular outline in the leather. But the watch is in this drawer still. He hadn't yet put it on the morning the paramedics found him sitting in the chair, already dressed for the day, with Gemma's number on the display on the phone in his hand. She'll never know whether he hesitated to wake her, or if he died before he could finish making the call.

She winds the watch. Sets the time. Puts it on her wrist.

The room is cold, or she is. She finds Gran's favorite tan cashmere sweater and pulls it on, breathing in the smell of him as the tears spill silently down her cheeks. She turns to the closet again, pulls out the tuxedo, and holds it close.

She's surprised to see a wall safe built into the closet where the tuxedo was hanging. Gran, who never even locked his door? The dial lock doesn't spin open on any combination Gemma can think of for the numbers of Gran's birthday, 12.22.1923. It doesn't open on any combination of her own birthday either. She tries several versions of her mom's.

Click.

Inside: An old camera with a roll of film still in it. The deed to this cottage. The title to Tubby. A copy of Gran's revocable trust that a lawyer has already told her leaves her everything. A French passport from when Gran was eighteen, his birthday listed incorrectly as December 2. And two more scripts: *Valentine in March by Chazan* (a terrible title, and titles are so important, but she feels disloyal for not loving this one) and *The Ghost of Hawk Tower* (a better title; she rather likes it). The latter has no byline but it's typed on Ole Mr. Miracle. *Drop the* m *for murder,* he used to joke because his m key struck slightly lower than the others.

If either of these scripts was made into a movie, she doesn't know it. Why are they locked up in a hidden safe?

She once told Gran she wondered if she would be writing if it wasn't Con's dream to direct. Gran had answered that if anyone was borrowing the other's dream, it was Con. *It's okay if your loves shape the loves of those you love,* he said. *It's okay if their passions shape yours. But you are who you are. Don't let anyone try to change that. And the people we love are who they are too. We can't change them. We have to accept them as they are.*

Gemma started the first screenplay she sold—the only one she's sold—up here one time she was visiting Gran. She'd finished film school at UCLA and was waiting tables, living a thousand miles away from her mom and going home only at Christmas. Gran told her to grab her laptop, and he handed her an old aluminum beach chair and threw one over his own shoulder, and he lugged his typewriter down to the sand with her in tow. He set Ole Mr. Miracle in his lap and started typing. When she only sat there, staring at a snowy egret perched on a rock out in the little cove and the fog bank fat on the horizon, his keys went silent. "Let go of the doubt," he said. "Trust yourself. 'Love your eyes that can see, your mind that can hear the music.'"

She started *Eleanor* up here too. She wrote most of it herself but gave Con cowriter credit, since the few times she pitched scripts without him, the men in the room just didn't recognize these "girls" and didn't think audiences would relate to them. Not that she's gotten a chance to pitch to anyone lately.

She takes the two scripts into the front room and settles in on the couch, with Gran's ashes on the coffee table beside a coaster as if to remind her to use it, and his sweater keeping her warm. *Valentine in March* begins no more promisingly than its title. It's got some funny bits, the same kind of funny Gran managed in his darker writing, but it's horribly dated; the male lead is not bad but the female is terminally 1950s. She sets it aside and begins *The Ghost of Hawk Tower*. This one is more like Gran. By the end of the first scene, a body falls from the tower. Or jumps. We're pretty sure someone is dead. The amazing thing about Gran's writing, though, is that what seems the unlikeliest is almost always what happens, convincingly. So maybe it's someone who lands on their feet and escapes. Or maybe it isn't even a body. Maybe it just looks like one.

THE LIGHT IS SOFT AND reddening by the time she reads the wonderfully twisty ending, the young debutante proving herself innocent even though she's guilty as sin and is getting away with murder. Gemma pours a measured shot of vodka and half a ginger beer in her mug. Gran has no lime squeezer, but she cuts a lime in half anyway and tries to squeeze juice from it. Why are the limes in her life never fresh? She puts half the lime cut-face-out in her mouth, leans over the cup and bites to juice it, then takes a sip of a disappointingly limeless Moscow Mule.

She pours out the drink and grabs the red-zip-tied plastic bag. "All right, Gran, let's just get this over with," she says.

But there is a family on the high rocks out on the point. Four raucous children. A mother sitting with her legs dangling from Flat Rock, the granite ledge where she and Gran released her mom's ashes, where she means to release Gran's ashes too. Can nothing go right here?

She walks on to the McGinnis steps and down to Memory Bench.

There is a secret mailbox underneath this bench, filled with journals and pens. People who know about it or happen upon it sit and write whatever is shredding their hearts, stories of love and romance, grief and heartbreak, anger and gratitude and hope and, so very often, lone-liness and memory. She pulls one out and reads a few entries: Someone is struggling with a girl who clearly doesn't deserve him. Someone is crushed that her best friend is ghosting her. Someone misses his par-ents, who have been gone nearly a decade, his siblings and grandpar-ents too. *I'm sorry*, she writes in response to that one, anything else seeming inadequate. She's never quite sure whether she's supposed to read these entries or if they're supposed to be, like in any other journal, private thoughts, but it seems to her that anyone writing in these public journals needs to say things they can't say to the people they love, and yet they want to be heard by someone. Rarely does anyone respond to her responses though. The journals are filled and taken away, replaced with clean new ones.

1992 THE MCGINNIS BENCH, a plaque reads. BOB • GERT • BOB, JR. Gemma traces a finger over the last writing on the plaque, LOVE, MARCIA. Is Marcia the one who fills the mailbox, allowing us to set down our cares in this beautiful place and find that even in our lone-liness, we aren't alone?

Across the little cove, one of those raucous children is atop the highest boulder—a perch Gemma first climbed when she was a shy, bookish fifteen-year-old hidden behind glasses, just moved to Grand Junction, Colorado, where her mother was to be a staff photographer for the *Daily Sentinel.* Con was as eyeglassed and friendless as she was back then; his father was a successful banker, but his mother was a mean drunk the family tried to hide. He was chewing his gum loudly at the library, and responded to her annoyed glance by offering her a piece. And when she told her mom over boxed macaroni and cheese and canned peas that night that she'd made a friend, Mom looked so happy that Gemma knew she would make it true.

She turns to a clean journal page and writes *I want to tell you about my Gran*, like she did after her mom died, and she fills a page with the way he made hot chocolate. He poured whole milk into a pan and set it gently on the stove. He broke off squares of good Guittard bittersweet chocolate and set one in each mug—always Guittard because Etienne Guittard was a Frenchman who brought his chocolate-making skills to San Francisco during the gold rush, so his chocolate was both American and French. *Like I am*, Gran liked to say. It was her job to crush the chocolate in the cups into little pieces. When the milk started to bubble at the edge of the pan, Gran took it off the stove, filled the cups, and squirted honey from a little plastic bear held as high over her cup as he could reach, to make her laugh. The warm milk melted the chocolate, but no matter how well she stirred there was always a pool of melted and gooey chocolate at the bottom that she could scrape up with a spoon or, when her mom wasn't watching, with a finger. That was the way they made chocolat chaud when Gran was a boy.

She doesn't know why she writes about the chocolate and nothing else, why she sits there for a long time with the journal open in her lap and the waves crashing on the point. The family is far enough away that she can't hear them, but she can sense the joy of being a child scrambling over the rocks at the edge of the ocean.

She clicks the pen open again and writes, *Who do I belong to now?*

She closes the journal then and sets it and the pen back in the underneath-the-bench mailbox, oddly comforted to know she's not the only lonely person in the world, or even in Carmel.

She's still sitting there when she hears something scampering down the sandy steps.

"Nyx!" she says, lifting the puppy, who carries her leash in her mouth.

"I'm so sorry," Sam Kenneally says. "Nyx spotted you and there was no holding her back."

"Your self-walking dog," she says.

"She's not my dog, I'm her human," he says. "She's letting me run off-leash."

Gemma stands, slipping the bag of Gran's ashes into her pocket, and she offers Sam the bench.

Nyx is tossing her head, drawing attention to the leash in her mouth, and Sam says it's time for them to go back too. "That's her way of saying she can walk us both," he says as he clips Nyx's leash back on. "I know you're a water dog," he says to the puppy, who is now pulling to go down past the *No Climbing on the Palisades* sign to the beach rather than up the steps to the road. "But we're not going to erode the slope here even if everyone else does." Then to Gemma, "And there's no getting the sand out of her fur at night. It ends up in my bed."

They set off together then, toward Point of No Return and the Fade Inn.

March 1957

Iz heard a knock on the studio's cottage door the day after the Oscars and cracked it open just enough to see Leo standing there, an aluminum folding chair slung over one shoulder and his typewriter tucked under the other arm. He wondered if she would like to go snorkeling, he said in his usual solemn voice, as if this were a favor he didn't want to do and he needed to get it over with.

"You snorkel with your typewriter?" she answered.

"I don't believe in waiting for inspiration, but I don't mind walking to it," he said. "I was writing at the beach. I just need a few minutes to make sure there's no sand in my typewriter, or brush it out if there is."

Iz was supposed to stay hidden. And Leo was a blacklisted writer whose friendship could destroy her. She'd already been out too; she'd waited for the Hawk Tower window to be lit, and still she'd been a little spooked at the point. But she was restless. And she was attracted to Leo. The truth was that even before she became Isabella Giori, she was a sucker for men who, in remaining perfect gentlemen, leave a girl uncertain where she stands. The truth was that something about being unsure whether Leo was attracted to her or not left her attracted to him.

And in a face mask and snorkel, nobody could tell who she was.

They hiked into a cove even more remote than Hidden Beach, with archways you could row a small boat through carved into the cliffs. Hundreds of seagulls and pelicans and cormorants perched on a massive bird-dropping-covered rock out in the water called, appropriately, Bird Island. And there was not a person anywhere.

"If you're still here next month, we could come watch the harbor seals birthing their babies," Leo offered. Then, pointing, "Look, right there."

Iz raised her binoculars just in time to see a spray of mist out past Bird Island.

"A gray whale," Leo said. "A devil fish, the whalers call them, because they're so aggressive when harpooned."

"Is she heading south? Back to Hollywood, like a movie-star whale!"

"She's pretty ugly to be a movie star—huge and mottled, with a knuckled dorsal hump covered with barnacles."

"A character actor whale then."

He laughed, and he said in a slightly less solemn voice, "She's headed north now. She heads south to Mexico every fall to have her babies, then brings them back in spring, a trip that can be fourteen thousand miles. But she has better sense than to stop in Hollywood."

Iz lowered her binoculars and looked out to the sea, which was smoothed over now. "I wish we could see her."

"We'll call her Miss Giori, the one who doesn't want to be seen."

He didn't look to her though, didn't put her on the spot, didn't question her secrecy any more than she questioned his.

"Do you know who lives across the street?" she asked. "In the house with the tower?"

"Jeffers? Only to nod a neighborly hello. I don't think he's published a poem in years. Certainly not a book."

So that was what the light in the tower was: a poet writing?

"His wife died some years ago now. Cancer. They say he knew about it, but never told her."

"How awful," she said, feeling the cast of the shadow-man from the point falling over this sunny afternoon. Why had she asked?

They stripped down to their swimsuits, donned masks and snorkels, and descended a stone stairway to the water. Leo dove in first and came right up to the surface.

"Just plunge," he said.

The water was so cold that Iz thought her heart would ice up and crack. She came up sputtering, saying she couldn't possibly stay in for even a minute. But after a few seconds, she emptied the water from her mask and blew it out of her snorkel, then stuck her face into a world of underwater boulders and valleys, white sand ocean floors and kelp forests, schools of fish, colorful anemones. Every sort of shell creature clung to the rocks and nestled in the crevices, beautifully craggy and ugly and alive, and magical. She dove under, swam down to touch the rough top of a starfish, the sharp shell of a mussel, the soft fringe at the mouth of an anemone. She touched as gently as she could. A larger creature—a whiskery-faced sea otter—edged away but didn't flee, as fascinated with her as she was with him.

She climbed back onto the steps, shivering after the few minutes she could bear the cold, still with her dive mask on and the snorkel in her mouth.

Leo, standing several steps above her, lowered his camera and recapped his lens. "Nobody will be able to recognize you behind the mask."

She wrapped herself in a towel, trying to get warm.

"So will you be?" he asked.

"Will I be?"

"Here next month?"

She looked to the smooth sea, the elusive gray whale so much more exciting somehow than the creatures more easily seen.

"I don't know," she said, although she did, really. She would be back in Hollywood, done with Carmel, in a week, or perhaps even days.

April 1957

After those first outings to Hidden Beach and China Cove, Isabella's days in Carmel fell into a pattern. She woke early to the sound of Leo's typewriter and walked to the point before sunrise, trying not to think of the poet and his lost child, his lost wife, his lost fame. She passed the rest of the days however she could until Leo finished writing and they set off to explore. They drove along the oceanfront road in Pebble Beach, where they walked down to see the beautiful old Lone Cypress clinging to the cliff, its old limbs cabled together and its trunk encircled in stone to help it survive. They drove south through Big Sur to McWay Falls, a tide fall that plummeted almost one hundred feet from a cliff directly into the ocean, and they stopped on the way back to watch the red rays of sunset stream through the keyhole rock arch at Pfeiffer Beach. Leo borrowed wetsuits—a new thing—and they snorkeled at Lovers Point in Pacific Grove and at the quarry that provided the granite to build the San Francisco Fed. Iz loved the lightness of her body in the water, the anonymity that came with a mask and wet hair, the beauty of the world beneath the surface, where no creature cared who she might or might not be.

She was risking her career, out exploring with a blacklisted writer, but she was twenty-two, she had no sense, and the risk made her feel alive.

Leo took pictures on their outings, but never more than a single shot, always from the same camera and with her face turned away or shadowed by a hat or hidden by snorkeling gear—film he said he would leave undeveloped and give to her. She could choose to remember these days or not, he said. Did he want her to say that of course she would want to remember?

For all his attentions, Leo never moved past their out-in-his-convertible friendship. If he had a girl, Iz saw no signs of her. But he never so much as touched her except to grab her hand if she was slipping on a wet rock, and their conversations tended to favorite movies, the Hollywood gossip, and all the speculation about the mysterious case of the missing Oscar winner, the whole fiasco an embarrassment for the Academy. Robert Rich had not been expected at the award ceremony because his wife was having a baby—but then there was no Mrs. Robert Rich in any maternity ward in all of Los Angeles, nor any Robert Rich in the Writers Guild. A Robert Rich who was a cousin of Frank King of King Brothers Productions, the company that had made *The Brave One*, was only a pretender. A writer not named Robert Rich filed a lawsuit claiming the story had been stolen from him. Even the *New York Times* was reporting "widespread rumors" that Robert Rich was a pseudonym for a blacklisted writer. "But of course the studio calls that ridiculous," Leo said.

Was Leo himself Robert Rich? Not all the information he brought her was in the news.

He showed up one afternoon with a thick bundle of manuscript pages rolled up and tied with a yellow bow. "I want you to have this," he said, "whether you decide to testify or not."

"To testify? Oh, Leo, I—"

"You can name me. It doesn't matter. I've already been named. It can't hurt me any more than I've already been hurt, and then you can go back to Hollywood and—"

"I'm not going to name anyone!"

Her words so loud with the little cottage so quiet, the TV and the radio silent. She'd turned them off when Mannix called just a few minutes before—to confirm that she knew where she was to go tonight, he said, but she knew there was more to it, that he had been calling to make sure she knew what was expected of her, and to make sure she hadn't lost her nerve.

Leo set the rolled pages on the little table. "I understand what you're going through, you know that, right? I stayed in this cottage. I was all set to name names. Even Arthur Miller—the world's most famous playwright—isn't beyond their reach. Even a Pulitzer Prize won't protect you."

When she didn't respond, he looked down at that script.

"I see," she said. "You want me to sell it for you."

"No! That's not what I—"

"Like this Robert Rich who fronted for you."

"For me? No, I—"

"For your 'friend.'"

She waited. She was so tired of men lying to her.

"It doesn't matter," he said. "Let's— Should we go snorkeling?"

"I have things to do," she said, giving him no choice but to leave when the last thing she wanted, really, was to be left alone to wait out the last hours before she was to be at the Jade Tree Motel.

THAT EVENING, NOT LONG BEFORE sunset, Iz hid under her black cloche hat and oversized sunglasses and set off for the long walk from the cottage to downtown Carmel-by-the-Sea. She took back streets, skirting the business district's restaurants and bars, its shops with their impossibly quaint names: The Hour Glass, The House that Jack Built, The Tuck Box. She made her way to Torres Street, to the back of a building that fronted on Junipero, and found the door just where Mannix told her it would be, tucked away behind the stairs in the corner on the ground floor. She looked around to make sure nobody was nearby, then slipped through the door—unlocked, as promised—into a small, nondescript motel room. She took off her dark glasses, her hat. She wished she were anywhere but here.

She sat at the edge of the bed, her back straight, her legs crossed at the ankles. She opened her pocketbook to confirm the paper bag was there where she put it.

It seemed an eternity before a click startled her.

She bolted up from her seat, turning toward the sound—not the door she was watching but one to the adjoining room.

A man loomed large and backlit, a shadow dressed in a dark suit and a plain white shirt, an unmemorable tie.

He removed his hat.

"All right," he said. Stern. Disapproving. She hadn't expected that, hadn't been prepared for that, hadn't quite imagined what it would be like to be here alone in this cheap motel room Mannix had sent her to.

The man motioned her to come through the door into the adjacent room. His face in the light was as angular as the man on the point, and larger.

The room behind him was large too, with a round table and chairs beside the bed. The bedspread had been removed, leaving only the sheet.

Had he done that himself? With his large hands that would touch her however he wanted, and she would have to let him.

If she didn't do this now though, if she wasn't back in Hollywood soon, someone else would get the Hitchcock role.

She couldn't catch a breath.

The man made an impatient little half sound.

She said, "I'm sorry, I can't—"

And she was fleeing out the door she'd entered, already pulling her hat on and tipping it lower, jamming her sunglasses back on despite the dark. She was hurrying back the same way she'd come, on the least busy streets.

April 1957

Leo knocked on the studio's cottage door the day after Isabella accused him of wanting her to front a script for him, an unfathomable risk for someone like her, something he never would ask. He was armed with sandwiches and a resolve to act as if that conversation hadn't happened. When she opened the door, he stepped in as if of course she would welcome his company, and chatted easily from the little kitchen as he measured water and grounds, turned on the cooktop, and set the percolator on the flame.

"Jeffers across the street is having a little gathering tonight," he said.

"You haven't told him who I am?" Alarm rising in her voice as surely as the rhythmic pump of hot water up through the grounds in the percolator.

"Told Jeffers? Well, no. I don't know him, really. I keep to myself here. But a friend from LA is going to be there, and I thought—"

She excused herself and disappeared into the bathroom.

He waited in the kitchen. The place was tiny, with only a thin wall separating the bathroom from the open kitchen, but all he heard was silence. He put the sandwiches on plates and set them on the coffee table. He set napkins beside them. Everything in the cottage was still in the same place as when he'd stayed here himself, when he'd shredded his future for nothing at all.

THE FADE INN HAD BEEN for sale then, when Leo first came up in 1953. It had been, like the studio cottage, a place without a name. Maybe it too had belonged to someone who didn't want to be found, he didn't know, but when he first saw it he imagined what a quiet place this would be to write. He couldn't afford the fancier places hanging out into the sea—Cabin on the Rocks and Butterfly House and Seaburst, all recently completed—but he was making enough money to afford the little cottage behind Tor House and Hawk Tower. He hadn't been able to inquire about buying it though. He was in Carmel to testify in an executive session, staying hidden in the studio's cottage, like everyone who came to testify did.

He returned to LA and the studio after he pled the Fifth, armed with a story to explain being missing. He was accomplished by then at weaving stories together into a life he never had lived. But nobody came by to hear it. He went to the commissary for lunch and collected his usual turkey sandwich and two tall glasses of fresh orange juice, only to find no empty seat at the table where the studio writers always gathered over clever stories of the type people who spend their days concocting clever stories can tell. He was left to pull a chair over and half squeeze in at a corner, eating off the tray in his lap. Had word gotten out that he'd gone to testify?

The next morning, when he arrived in Buttercup and greeted the same guard who'd smiled and lifted the gate to let him pass every morning for years by then, the man said,

"I'm sorry, Mr. Chazan."

Just those two words, *I'm sorry*, spoken by a man whose last name Leo didn't even know. That was how he knew he was blacklisted.

Back home, more stunned than he would have imagined, he found the lid of his garbage can askew, the contents rifled through. And after he gave up on trying to pass the uneasy day at a movie and left the Fox Westwood Village Theater, its dramatic white spire rising like the temple it was to this modern god of film, a man fell in beside him and flashed an FBI badge.

"Do you have time to answer a few questions, Mr. Chazan?" the agent said, lest there be any doubt that he knew exactly who Leo was, that he'd known that Leo was in that theater, that he'd waited for him.

Leo climbed into Buttercup and drove off, leaving the man watching him go. He knew as surely as the agent did that it wouldn't matter, that answers weren't what the man was after. The FBI simply wanted Leo to know he was being watched, that at any moment he could be seen—his world changed so quickly, just as it had been in France all those years ago.

He called about the cottage that afternoon and agreed to buy it sight unseen. And long before dawn the morning the sale was to close, he loaded Ole Mr. Miracle and a few things into Buttercup, leaving everything else behind once again.

What Leo earned after that, writing secretly due to the blacklist, was so little that he had to work constantly just to pay the mortgage. He could occasionally sell work under a friend's name, but he couldn't do that often without raising questions about differences in style or the volume of work those friends could produce. Sometimes he sold work to producers who knew he'd done the writing even if he'd put a fake name on the script, but that paid little because of the risk to them. Sometimes he could find an unknown friend of a friend who would front for him for a cut in hopes of breaking in to writing through Leo's work, but the pay for an unknown too was always low, and it became complicated when those unknown fronts started becoming known on account of Leo's writing; their family and friends would wonder why their names were on the screen and yet they didn't seem to have the income that would bring. And even when he sold a spec film, he couldn't communicate with anyone. No discussions with the producers, the director, the actors. No feedback. No give-and-take. If someone needed to be on set for changes during filming—and almost always, someone did—that person wasn't him, and maybe whoever it was respected his work or maybe they didn't, maybe they destroyed what little magic he managed to deliver.

He held on to his best scripts as long as he could rather than sell them, in the hope this madness would end and he could sell them for what they were worth. Most of the money he earned came from jobs he was quietly hired to do to fix somebody else's script, which meant a dingy motel room a few miles from the set and whoever had hired him running the changes back and forth so that nobody else would know, and such lousy scripts that only blacklisted writers were willing to tackle fixing them. He did draw the line one time, refusing to fix a script featuring a long-suffering mother whose son had become a communist. *He had always been too bookish*—some fool had written, along with, *His football star brothers aren't communists, they're war heroes*, lest anyone miss the point that people who read are dangerous, much better to stick to sports. Nobody went to that film. None of the anticommunist-rant films did well. *The Red Menace. I Was a Communist with the FBI. I Married a Communist.* Even the titles sounded farcical, and American moviegoers have a surprising nose for shamelessly moralizing crap. The studios knew those films would flop at the box office so they made them on the cheap, not for profit but to appease the fanatics in Congress—dues paid to gain more freedom for the films they wanted to make.

LEO SET TWO MUGS ON Isabella's kitchen counter, but hesitated to fill them lest the coffees grow cold. "It's an impossible decision, don't beat yourself up about it," he called out to Isabella, still in the bathroom, and finally the water ran in the bathroom sink and Isabella emerged.

He poured the coffees and took them out to where she settled on the couch in the little sitting room. He took the chair that cornered it, looking to the California Oak branching a craggy gray lace over the windowpanes. Across the road, Hawk Tower was a darker gray against a bank of fog caressing the point.

"You're in good company," he said. "Lillian Hellman locked herself in a ladies' room before she was called before the Committee too." It was at the request of the U.S. government that Hellman had visited Russia during World War II, but that didn't stop the

Committee from damning her for it. Lilly might easily have testified and remained working but as she said, *I cannot and will not cut my conscience to fit this year's fashions.* The first morning she testified, she was about to signal her lawyer that she needed a break when she saw from the clock that she was only sixteen minutes into a hearing that might last for days.

"Her refusal to name others cost her a one-million-dollar contract with Columbia Pictures," he said. A contract under which she would have written and produced four feature films—any story she wanted and with final cut control. That was nearly unheard-of for any writer, much less a woman. Now she and Dashiell Hammett were left penniless, living on the proceeds of a family farm Lilly had to sell.

"Did you go to jail?" Isabella asked so quietly that he could barely hear her.

He shifted in the chair. "My executive session was after the waiver doctrine had been confirmed by the Supreme Court," he answered, "so I knew the choices."

The choices were the same for anyone called to testify now: refuse to answer questions on the basis of your First Amendment right to free speech and go to jail for contempt; name names and maybe—*maybe*—continue to work in Hollywood; or refuse to answer on the basis of your Fifth Amendment right against self-incrimination and don't say anything about yourself so you don't waive your rights under it, and you could refuse to name names, which would leave you blacklisted but not in prison. He knew, when he sat across from those men, what the cost would be in refusing to say even his name.

"I'm not an ideological purist," he said. "I haven't done anything that would incriminate me, but I wasn't willing to go to jail for the principle of the thing, so I took the Fifth."

His words were true enough.

At Tor House, a woman in an apron and a wide-brimmed hat began cutting the first of the season's roses in the shade of Hawk Tower.

"Why do you think they came after you to begin with?" Iz asked.

"You mean 'Am I now or have I ever been a member of the Communist Party?'" His voice angrier than he'd meant.

Outside, the birds called to each other. The woman cutting the roses began singing into the rhythmic wash of the sea.

He met Isabella's gaze. It was like after the war, he thought. Back then, nobody had ever been a Nazi sympathizer. Now nobody had ever been a communist. But he hadn't been a member of the party. He'd never attended a meeting. He'd been so careful not to invite questions about who he was.

He never did learn who had named him or why.

"You'll be okay, whichever way you decide," he said more gently. "It's not your fault. It's none of our faults. We forget sometimes that even those choosing to testify—not even choosing, really, it's not a choice—they aren't to blame. The people to blame are the politicians like Richard Nixon and film industry grandstanders like Ronald Reagan who use this witch hunt for their own gain."

He stood and took his cup to the kitchen, topped his coffee although he hadn't yet drunk much of it. "I can still write," he said. "And I have savings enough to see me through for a while more if I'm careful, with no wife or child to support. I didn't even have a swimming pool to give up."

He turned back to her. "I may have to leave tomorrow," he said. "I may not be back for a few weeks."

Outside the window, Hawk Tower loomed even in the daylight, the windows unlit, as the woman who'd been cutting roses disappeared into Tor House, closing its plain brown door.

April 1957

Iz watched out her window that night as people gathered across the street. The whole place was lit up. You could see a woman playing a piano inside Tor House, at a window facing the sea. The windows in Hawk Tower too were lit, with people mingling on the lower of its two rooftop terraces. A thin, gaunt shadow-man stood there, his cigarette glowing brighter red each time he took a drag—Robinson Jeffers. The hard, angular figure that haunted the point. The candlelight in the tower window. His wife was already long dead from a cancer he did not allow her to know she had. He lived on without her, with only a lonely ocean of abandoned poetry. It's a dangerous thing for a star to defy the moral code of the audience his fame depends upon.

Or her fame. Isabella's own career had nearly been ruined before it started. She had gone along with everything the studio wanted, starting with dyeing her hair. She'd endured studio executives and doctors scrutinizing her: She didn't have hair on her face that needed to be removed—that was how they started. Her skin wasn't bad, nothing a little Nivea wouldn't address. But her nose was a little broad, that was what was "wrong."

"Just minor work," they assured her. She didn't need a major nose job like Carmen Miranda had. She didn't need her jaw and chin reshaped, like Marilyn Monroe. Just a slight narrowing of the bridge of her nose, like Elizabeth Taylor had after her face matured.

Iz hesitated, but her contract required her to undergo any surgery the studio wanted her to.

Afterward, they abandoned her in her little dump of an apartment in Studio City, with her eyes black and blue and her face swelling more every day. She peered through the slits of swollen eyelids to see an absolute wreck in the mirror, terrified that she'd ruined whatever looks she had.

She gained weight recovering inside, in bed, so after the swelling subsided and the bruising faded enough that she could cover it with makeup, she lived on spinach and tomato juice. Each morning, she reported to the studio for the daily mortification of stripping down to her bra and girdle until the scale registered the exact 118 pounds they wanted to see.

She took great care with her skin, trying not to panic at the sight of each little blemish.

She did not swear in public.

She did not show anger.

She did not date.

She hadn't loved the idea of making her film debut as Janet Leigh's little sister, but her contract allowed her no say in how she was cast and it wasn't a bad role. So she did her job. She worked on the role day and night, not just memorizing her lines until she could deliver them in her sleep, but trying to become that girl. Still there was one line that her tongue got twisted up in again and again. *It's a stupid superstition*—a simple line, four words that ought not to have been anything. But she had to deliver them in the only scene she had alone with Hugh Bolin.

Hugh was the kind of charming that left everyone in his orbit, men and women alike, feeling good about themselves. He was a few years older and already a great success, that was definitely part of the problem, being alone in the camera lens with someone like Hugh. When she delivered the line, an extra *t* snuck in, "It's a stupid stuperstition."

The director called "cut" and pointed out the mistake, and told her not to worry. "But get it right this time, doll." At the third time she flubbed the line, he began to mock her. By the sixth, he said, "Cut. Cut. Fucking fucking cut." Then, "Who is this girl? Can't we get some pretty girl who can say the lines without so much fucking drama?"

It was the first time Isabella had realized that that was all she was to him, some pretty girl who could easily be replaced. Her career was over before it had begun.

Hugh Bolin set a hand on Iz's newly blond hair though, and said, "Let's hear you say it, Al." The director's name was Albert. Nobody but Hugh called him Al.

"'Superstition'?" the director said.

"The whole line," Hugh said.

"'It's a stupid stuperstition,'" the director said.

"Exactly," Hugh said.

"Exactly what?" the director said.

"Can't you hear yourself? It's impossible. Nobody can say it."

Even speaking slowly, the director stumbled.

"All right, let's break for lunch," he said.

"Don't be an ass," Hugh said. "This is her first role. Tell her you're fixing the script."

The director looked at her then, and said, "Don't wet your knickers, doll. I'll get them to change the script for you."

"To *fix* the script," Hugh said. And when the director harrumphed, Hugh insisted, "Tell the *writers* not to wet their knickers." Then to Isabella, "Sit with me for lunch?"

By the time they'd eaten, he with his plate piled high while she took little more than the spinach and tomato juice she'd grown used to, everyone in the scene had a new script. And when the director gave them five minutes to learn it, Hugh said, "Really, *don't* be an ass, Al." Then to Iz, "Try saying that five times quickly, 'Don't be an ass, Al,'" and he laughed and guided her to a quiet corner to rehearse together until she was comfortable with the new line.

The revised scene was perfect on the first take.

"You look tired, doll," the director said to her after they'd finished filming for the day, and she was, she was exhausted. She hadn't been sleeping well, anxious about what she'd do if she failed here.

"Why don't you see Max on your way out," the director said. "He'll give you something to help you sleep."

Hugh took her by the arm then and said what they all needed was a stop in at Barney's Beanery. And because he suggested it, because he was going, even the director went.

Hugh was nothing but a gentleman all evening; he made Iz feel interesting, capable, an actress who belonged. He taught her to shoot pool while all the cast had a ball trying to say, "Don't be an ass, Al!" five times quickly, with even the director himself busting a gut. And when the evening was winding down, Hugh took her aside and told her to throw out the pills they'd given her. "They'll help you sleep to-night, sure, but tomorrow you'll need a little helper to get you through the drug hangover and they'll give you that too, and pretty soon you won't feel right without them. Pretty soon there will be nothing left of your beautiful young self."

Your beautiful young self. Iz had felt beautiful that night because Hugh said she was. She had felt young, too—naive, she saw now as she stared out the cottage window to the tower across the street.

It was late, and a thick fog had long before driven the Jeffers par-tiers inside. She knew she ought to go to sleep. She wondered not for the first time if she shouldn't have kept just a few of those sleeping pills she'd thrown out that night after she got home from Barney's Beanery. She felt less beautiful too. She felt tainted as she stood watch-ing a shadow figure atop the high Hawk Tower turret.

Was it Leo?

It was the curve of his shoulders, as if he had spent so long bent over his typewriter that he couldn't stand straight, although he had posture Hitchcock would praise. Now though his head was bent to-ward another shadow-person. A woman with hair as short as Miss Head's that day she auditioned for Hitchcock.

Or not a woman, but rather a thin man?

She watched, feeling wrong about watching, feeling she was ob-serving an intimate moment not meant to be seen by anyone, as piano music and conversation spilled from Tor House into the garden, into the night.

When Gemma and Sam and Nyx get back to the Fade Inn, Gran's Roadmaster convertible is in the driveway.

"I didn't want you to worry where Tubby was," Sam says.

Tubby, short for "tub of butter." Gran had told her a neighbor was keeping Buttercup (her formal name) in their garage and helping him get around. But Sam? The Roadmaster had always been beautiful in a faded-glory way, but now she belonged in the Pebble Beach Concours d'Elegance.

"You had her restored?" she says.

"Restored? No! You don't want to touch her. Original paint. Original rubber. Do you know how rare that is?"

"But she looks brand-new."

"The miracle of car wax, leather and carpet cleaners, and elbow grease," Sam says. He dangles the keys and nods at the red zip tie poking from her pocket. "Would Leo like to go for a ride?"

She hesitates, then says, "Don't make me drive."

SAM, WHO IS A TERRIBLE driver too, it turns out, asks for a tour of Gran's favorite places. She chokes up. Does she even know? The places Gran took her were the places she wanted to go: They walked along the ocean path to say hello to the fairies living behind the fairy doors tacked onto the tree trunks, miniature painted-rainbow doors with round crystal windows flanked by dried flowers and red polka-dotted toadstools, driftwood pediments, tree-bark awnings. They went tide pooling. Built sandcastles. Flew kites in the annual festivals they never did win. They made bonfires on the beach. Things she could easily share with Sam, but she feels that stingy chip in her heart again, that longing to keep the things Gran and Mom and she shared all to herself.

"Gran liked to visit 'the seasonals,'" she says—the decorations that pop up on the beach path and in the pocket parks and medians: St. Patrick's Day shamrocks now. Easter eggs next, with ceramic bunnies nestled on random tree stumps. At Christmas, a Santa cruises the sunny streets in a wheeled, horse-drawn sleigh, and someone leaves a box of ornaments underneath a pine tree in Mission Trail forest, beside a path made in the 1700s by priests from the mission walking to Monterey to say Mass. It's surprising what a delight it is to decorate a forest tree.

"How about dinner at his favorite restaurant?" Sam says. The invitation seems to startle him as much as it does her.

"Gran never went out to dinner," she objects for no good reason. All she has back at the Fade Inn is that carton of yogurt and the makings for a Moscow Mule.

"Nepenthe?" he says, and she pretends she misunderstood, that she thought he meant a restaurant in Carmel. Did Gran like Nepenthe?

The wind swirling around them as they head south down Highway 1 makes conversation blessedly impossible beyond the occasional point-and-shout: to the Carmelite Monastery, to Calla Lilly Valley, to the iconic Bixby Bridge. They're forty-five minutes down the road when Gemma's phone rings—the real estate agent she's forgotten. Sam pulls to a stop in a parking lot as she settles it with the agent: he'll get the key Sam tells her Isabella has and have a look around without her.

"You're not going to sell that place," Sam says after she hangs up, sounding like Con, as if he knows better than Gemma what she needs to do.

She smiles politely, unwilling to admit she has no choice but to sell this cottage that has been her grandfather's for sixty-some years, this home where her mother grew up, that is the only home Gemma herself has now, the only connection to Gran's life, to his writing, to the family she no longer has.

"I'm sorry," Sam says. "It's none of my business, of course it's none of my business, it's just . . ." He takes the bag of ashes by their red zip tie and leads her up a stairway to the restaurant entrance. "You don't think Leo will come back to haunt us?"

GEMMA IS AFRAID THE HOSTESS is going to cry when Sam introduces her as Chazan's granddaughter, something in the way he says it letting the woman know Gran is gone without Gemma having to hear it said. The woman takes them past the long shared tables on the patio, to a two-top with its own umbrella near the outdoor fireplace and its roaring fire. It's the only empty table, the one they save for movie stars and moguls, with its long view of the Santa Lucia range butting up against the ocean forever to the south, higher and more dramatic than in Carmel. The woman hands them menus and returns a minute later with drinks they haven't ordered.

"On Leo," she says. "Our Big Sur Bitter Ginger Shrub, his favorite."

She starts talking about the mudslides that were all over the news not long after Gemma's mom died, leaving this stretch of Big Sur reachable only by helicopter for eight long months. Food. School supplies. Medicines. It all had to be brought in by air. "Your grandfather called every day to order lunch and pay for it," she says, "to be held 'for pickup' after the new bridge was built. If it hadn't been for people like him, we wouldn't be here anymore."

The restaurant has been here since 1947, when the family who still owns it bought a little cabin from Rita Hayworth and Orson Welles, who'd bought it on first sight with the cash in their pockets on a drive from San Francisco to LA, then divorced not long afterward. The hostess doesn't remember when Gran started coming, she just remembers his phone orders after the storm and meeting him when the road opened again.

She takes their orders herself, and Sam asks her about playing some different music, "not now, but in a bit."

After she leaves, it's just Gemma and Sam across the little table from each other, his eyes not the gold of Nyx's ears, exactly, but the color of good maple syrup at the center and the edges with some mix of a dark goldenrod and something not-quite-green in between, and his full lips a color that ought to be a lipstick shade.

"This is not Gran's scotch," she says. Gran's "favorite" Big Sur Bitter Ginger Shrub is a vodka cocktail tasting deliciously of ginger and citrus and a hint of sage, more her kind of drink than Gran's.

"'Quaff, oh quaff this kind nepenthe,'" Sam says, "'and forget this lost Lenore!'"

"'The Raven'?"

"Poe borrowed 'nepenthe' from Homer. In *The Odyssey*, 'nepenthes pharmakon' is a magic potion given to the beautiful Helen by an Egyptian queen to banish sorrow and grief through forgetting. Some chance Homer's 'magic potion' was opium, actually."

"You know this from playing video games too?" Gemma teases.

"Playing . . . ?" He looks confused.

"Where 'Nyx' comes from?" Why is it so disappointing that he named his puppy after a character from a video game? "Isabella said you play—"

"Oh." He smiles and it's a nice smile, a guy-who-likes-golden-retrievers smile. "I do play them, but it's what I do."

"Like, for a job?" She knows people play video games competitively, but she's never met anyone who does. "You play, what, *Super Mario* and *The Sims*? And *Children of Chaos*, obviously."

"I— No. I *make* video games," he says. "Well, video *game*. So far just the one, just *Children of Chaos*."

"*You* made *Children of Chaos*? That's my fave game!"

He looks like she felt when he said he loved *Eleanor After Dark*. And when she asks how one makes video games, he says, "Video game, singular," and waves away the question—never mind that he let her go on and on about *Eleanor*, which maybe twelve people saw, while he created a game played by millions all over the world.

Their Famous Ambrosia Burgers arrive, and even before Gemma takes a bite, Sam leans toward her and says, "I miss the sound of your grandfather's typewriter."

She laughs. The words are so unexpected. "I was wishing this morning that I could make my computer sound like that!" she says. "Not the clacking, but the ding of the margin bell and the zip when you hit the return."

He can do that for her, he says. "If there isn't already an app for it."

As they tuck into the burgers, they fall into an awkward silence that leaves Gemma searching for something else to say, the way you do when you find yourself spending so much time with someone you don't really know but want to impress. He's cute. He's creative. He's funny and humble and nice. Gemma guesses he must have a cute, technology-savvy girlfriend to complete the set.

"Can I—?" he starts while she says, "Did you ever—?"

"You first," she says and he says, "No, you."

She says, "I was just going to ask if you ever played *Logical Journey of the Zoombinis*."

"The pizza trolls!" he exclaims.

"'More toppings!'" Gemma says in the voice of the game.

He used to play it with his sister, he says. "You didn't even realize you were learning, you were just having a ball guiding little blue creatures through puzzle lands. Sorting. Linking. Patterns and deductive reasoning. Hypothesis testing. Even algebraic functions. It's amazing what they did with nothing more than a 486/66 megahertz CPU, eighty megabytes of hard drive, and eight of RAM."

It turns out they had both contributed to a Kickstarter to fund a reboot of the game.

"God, what a geeky kid I was," he says.

She still is a geek: she's sitting with a cute guy in one of the most amazing spots in the world and she's talking about little blue creatures on a computer screen.

"Your turn," she says. "What were you going to say?"

He looks a little sheepish. "You can dance on the patio here—that's why the bleachers," he says, indicating the large stepped area covered with pillows, where people sit waiting for tables, leaving Gemma feeling guilty for having been seated ahead of them. "Richard Burton and Elizabeth Taylor danced here when they shot *The Sandpiper*—not that I've ever seen the movie, but that's what your grandfather told me. He could tango like nobody's business, couldn't he?"

"Gran?" She has only ever seen Gran dance to the Oscar Best Song nominees, and never a tango.

Sam stands and waves to the hostess, and the music changes as he offers Gemma a hand.

"We can't dance," Gemma says. "Nobody is dancing."

But already Sam is holding Gran's ashes in one hand while leading her out onto the empty bit of patio in front of the fire, showing her how to step and clap, to cross-step and turn. It's a line dance, so it isn't intimate or awkward. And as if everyone has been waiting for this, people climb down from the bleachers and abandon tables, missing dance steps and bumping into each other and laughing so hard it's contagious.

Sam passes Gran's ashes to her and she dances with the red zip tie in hand, remembering Gran holding her on his hip and waltzing her around his little cottage while Mom laughed, and Mom taking her from him, like she was cutting in, and dancing with her before Gran cut in himself and took her back. The song "When You Believe" from *The Prince of Egypt* was playing on Gran's television. Mom had let her stay up way past her bedtime. Oscar night.

"What I was really going to say earlier was thank you," Sam says as he takes Gran's ashes back for another spin. "You're as amazing as your Gran always said you were. Thank you for sharing him with me."

He smiles his golden-retriever-loving smile, and he says, "But you're not really going to sell that cottage," and she hears no demand in his words now, nothing of Con. Only the same hope she feels that she'll somehow manage to keep the Fade Inn.

"Because if I do, Gran will haunt me," she says.

"Also," he says, "if I know Iz, she's teaching Nyx to bite before that real estate agent shows up, so he won't be coming back."

Sam is sitting at his desk, which is ridiculous. He's drunk far too much between Leo's scotch, the Ginger Shrubs, and his own better scotch here alone in his office to do anything but wreak havoc on his new game. The bit he's working on, a passageway through the labyrinth inspired by the Jeffers poem "Fawn's Foster-Mother"—he can already hear Mads asking if he really expects anyone to figure out that they have to pick up a newborn fawn, take it to a human mother, and get her to feed the beast from her human breast. It's a heartbreaking moment, or it's disgusting, he doesn't know which, but the fawn is starving, the fawn will die without the human mother's milk. Humans, being human, have destroyed most of the natural world in his virtual one, a future Robinson Jeffers posited in his writing long before it was fashionable to care about the environment. A future echoed in a poetic tribute to Jeffers that Sam read, about Tor House and Hawk Tower being rented to "trillionaire non-literary folk" like him, the clear walk to the sea Jeffers once had now spoiled by places like this house in which Sam tries to create not poetry but only a video game that wants to be something like poetry but fails.

Never mind that, he pours another splash and sits watching in the dark as, beyond the window and across the road, Gemma Chazan emerges from the back bedroom with one of Leo's scripts in hand, her hair falling in waves to a sweater Sam recognizes as Leo's. She sets the script on the counter, only her torso visible now between the countertop and the hanging cabinets separating the little kitchen from the sitting room. In a video game, he would be the creepy guy who has to be discovered for the predator he really is and taken out with the weapon of your choice before you could progress toward the top of Hawk Tower. Not that he's in Hawk Tower. But he would be, if he were in his game. Of course, he wouldn't have a puppy fast asleep in his bed, the more sensible of the two, but then the only "cocktail" Nyx drinks is water from the bowl in the Carmel Dog Bar, which Sam loved keeping filled even before he had a dog.

So often late at night when he'd thought he'd done enough work, he'd see Leo in that bay window, writing screenplays half the night in his nineties, and he would keep working too, like he had with André that first year at Stanford when they were randomly assigned to a dorm room; Sam would think he'd studied enough, but with André still hard at work, he would keep working too.

One night toward the end of Sam's first month here in Carmel, he'd looked up from his work to see Leo watching him from his separately well-lit pretend world, with the darkness stretching between them. Sam nodded hello and turned off his light. Still, he sat there watching what he knew by then to be Leo's end-of-work routine. He pulled the last page from his typewriter or he didn't. He grabbed the pencil from his ear and made a few notes. He tidied the stack of pages beside his typewriter. He put his watch back on. He poured himself a scotch. That night, though, Leo didn't pour, he grabbed a second glass and the scotch bottle and he walked out his door and crossed the road and knocked on Sam's.

Sam watches Gemma throw ice in a glass and add a good dose of vodka from the refrigerator. She cuts a lime in half and tries to squeeze it by hand, then puts it in her mouth and leans over the glass.

It's foolish, he knows it is, but he grabs his scotch bottle and he leaves his dark office to find the hallway and the rest of his house lit so brightly that it will spill toward the ocean, annoying anyone out walking in the moonlight—something he's usually careful not to do.

He voice-commands "I'm leaving" so that everything on in the house will turn off, and he hurries across the dark street to knock on the Fade Inn door.

Gemma looks through the bay window to see who's here. "You've read my mind and brought me milk?" she says as she opens the door, drink in hand.

He offers the scotch, realizing only then that its top is still on his desk back in his office, and he's forgotten glasses. "Your grandfather and I used sometimes to nod to each other from our windows when we were both working late," he says. "Then one night he showed up at my door with a bottle of scotch, saying he was no damned good at moving from scriptworld to dreamworld, and would I like a nightcap?"

She says, "He only ever offered me hot chocolate sweetened with honey, and the milk has gone off."

"I have milk," he offers.

She says in a voice that is a perfect mimic of Nyx in *Children of Chaos*, "'That's it, milk,'" with the hint of Wallace from *Wallace & Gromit* that Mads had the narrator add to play up his unintentional echo of "That's it, cheese" from the iconic clay-animation comedy. Mads parlayed that two seconds of dialogue into so much free publicity and so much praise for Sam's "genius" that it left him feeling a fraud—a feeling Mads forbade him to admit.

They're outside her door then, Sam with his bottle of scotch and Gemma with a box of baking chocolate and a little plastic honey bear, when she says she's forgotten shoes. He stoops low and tells her to hop on his back, the way he used to do with his little brother, and for a moment he's blindsided by the memory, the fact that Noah will never be older than the fifteen-year-old boy of eight years ago. But Gemma can have no idea of that as she hands him the chocolate and honey and, before he knows it, has her hands around his neck and her legs tight around his waist, that old sweater of Leo's soft against the bit of Sam's neck between his collar and hair.

Yes, they are both drunk.

She's still on his back as they enter his living room with its wall of glass overlooking the sea, which is roiling in the moonlight, waves crashing on rock and no lights on in the room, so nobody can see in but they can see out.

"'Toto, I've a feeling we're not in Kansas anymore,'" she says in such a perfect Dorothy mimic that he half expects little Munchkins to peek up from the rocky cliff while a bubble floats in to deliver the Good Witch.

He sets her down in front of the wall of glass and cracks open one of the French doors on the balcony side of the dining turret so she can hear the waves without getting too cold. He bumps into her when he turns back, and he grabs her arm so she won't tumble, and then they are kissing, her lips soft, her mouth warm and wet.

He knows he shouldn't be kissing Leo Chazan's granddaughter, just as he knows he shouldn't have sat in the dark watching her, but there is no "shouldn't" in this moment. There is only him removing her glasses so he can better see her unbelievable eyes. Him pulling her sweater over her head, the T-shirt coming with it, underneath which is nothing but Leo's watch on her wrist, the gauze he taped to her arm not twelve hours ago, and moonlit skin.

There is only him, kneeling to circle her nipple with his lips, a soft moan which he thinks is her, and still the sound of the waves.

Her fingers in his hair.

Him unzipping her jeans.

His fingertip tracing the top of her lace panties that she would have put on for some other guy this morning, this Conrad who Leo didn't much care for.

He slides her jeans off, and his lips are on hers again, his hands cupping the soft skin of her breasts.

"Cricket," he whispers, or maybe he doesn't, maybe he only thinks it.

He takes her nipple between his thumb and middle finger,

pinching not quite enough to hurt her, or not much, as he drops his own jeans, his boxers.

He slides his hands under that lace.

And he is lifting her up onto him then, the way he has been trying not to think about doing since she climbed onto his back outside Leo's door. He's inside her, holding her against the window glass as the stars go over the timeless ocean, the lonely stars.

April 1957

Isabella had spent the day the same way she'd spent every day since she last saw Leo when he again knocked on her door. It was a week after that Tor House party she didn't attend. She left the cottage only for predawn walks to the point before Robinson Jeffers emerged from Tor House. She spent the long days and nights with her only company the radio and TV, trying not to worry that she would never get back to Hollywood. She rehearsed the part in the Hitchcock script she began to fear would, in her absence, surely be given to somebody else. She pulled the yellow bow off the script Leo brought, the Valentine's Day script, and, with nothing better to do, began working on that part too. She knew Leo must have gone somewhere—the sound of his typewriter hadn't awakened her since the day before that party, his shadow-meeting atop Hawk Tower—and that was just as well. Mannix had agreed to reschedule for her, but pointedly reiterated that if Iz was discovered up here, the studio would cut her loose.

The day Leo returned, she was listening to a radio bit about a new memoir by Alger Hiss, a State Department employee and supposed communist spy Vice President Nixon had made his name bringing down, who was now charging the FBI with "forgery by typewriter," claiming documents he'd supposedly passed on to the Soviets weren't typed on his typewriter but were instead forged to look like they had been. She should have just kept listening. She shouldn't have answered the door. But she was so tired of being alone.

"I thought you'd be gone by now," Leo said.

He didn't apologize or explain his absence any more than she explained her continued presence.

"This fellow in your script, he sounds a lot like you," she said, opening the door wider to let him in, then closing it behind him lest anyone see.

He said, "Does she seem like you?"

"I hope not! She's so compliant."

"Well," he said, a little miffed but trying not to sound it.

She ought to have said more gently that his female lead was more Doris Day than Katharine Hepburn. But of course Doris Day was big box office. Her film with Hitchcock, *The Man Who Knew Too Much*, was a huge success. And Leo's whipping-with-dog-and-goat-hides bit was funny now rather than gruesome, more appropriate for a romantic comedy.

"Did you see the Dalton Trumbo interview where he said Mike Wilson is the infamous Robert Rich?" she asked, comfortable conversational turf.

Trumbo was rumored to have written *The Brave One* as well as the Audrey Hepburn and Gregory Peck hit *Roman Holiday*, for which a British screenwriter was given the Oscar. He'd refused to own up to being the mysterious missing Oscar winner during the interview though, or to having written any particular film, although he did say that "somewhere between one and four" scripts he'd written under aliases had gotten Oscar nods.

"This works for the studios," Leo said. "It isn't in their interest to know who the real writers are, or to admit they do. They can cut anyone loose any time they want and get the same great writing at bargain rates while keeping their audiences happy that they've supposedly rid Hollywood of communists. They can call us in on a moment's notice to fix a script that any fool could have told them wasn't going to work, but now they're midway into filming, the financial clock is ticking the dollars away, and that's when they realize they have a problem, that's when they call me in, put me up in a crap motel for weeks on end without so much as a telephone so nobody will know the writer who is working twenty hours a day to save their damned film is good ole blacklisted me."

She poured him a bourbon, her drink but he clearly needed a drink. She poured herself one and sat next to him on the couch. That was where he'd been then, off fixing some script for little pay and no credit. She supposed he didn't have much choice but to take the job on whatever terms were offered. Even in Carmel, there were electric and phone and grocery bills to be paid. Even cheap scotch isn't free.

"God forbid I should slip something into a script that might in any way be seen to corrupt an audience's morals more than the rest of the crap they're serving up in theaters these days," he said. "But maybe this is all coming to a head. This Robert Rich business—even the *New York Times* is now saying sure there's nothing illegal about the studios hiring blacklisted writers, but doesn't the public have a right to know?"

It was one thing for a blacklisted screenwriter to say he sold scripts to the studios and quite another for the *New York Times* to call out their hypocrisy.

"'Silence on the part of the Association of Motion Picture Producers is not becoming under the circumstances,'" Leo quoted.

On the radio, they were now talking about Arthur Miller. The playwright had refused to name names a year earlier, saying he could not in good conscience bring trouble on people for what they might or might not have done a decade ago. Now a federal judge had ruled that he would have to stand trial for contempt.

"The trial will draw even larger crowds than Lillian's did," Leo said.

"They'll all want to catch a glimpse of Marilyn Monroe," she agreed.

As he drank down his bourbon and poured himself another, Iz thought of him atop Hawk Tower, his head bent toward that shadow-person. It left her uneasy, the two of them leaning so close together. It seemed so intimate, but maybe it was this, a clandestine deal being made for Leo to rewrite a script.

"Do you find her attractive?" she asked him.

"Monroe?"

Marilyn Monroe was gutsy: when Fox suspended her for refusing to do yet another stupid musical comedy, she took them on and emerged with her own production company and a contract paying her $400,000 to make four films of her choosing with any director she wanted. But it wasn't her guts you meant when you asked a man if he liked Marilyn Monroe.

"She's not exactly my type," Leo answered.

She sipped her bourbon, waiting, but he didn't offer anything more.

"Is he?" she asked quietly. "Arthur Miller? I know it's not uncommon, men who prefer men."

Lavender lads, the tabloids called them, under headlines like "Natalie Wood and Tab Wouldn't" after Natalie and Tab Hunter started showing up together everywhere.

"It doesn't matter to me," Iz said.

Leo didn't look shocked or offended. He simply leaned in and kissed her, awkwardly, his lips full and warm even if pressed together in the way of the movie kisses the Production Code Administration preferred, his calloused hands warm on her cheeks.

"I was sure you'd be gone. I thought you'd have testified in your secret session before these new hearings in New York began," he said, moving his hand to her waist. "I thought you'd be back in Hollywood—"

Alarmed, she eased his hand away and smoothed her blouse over her waist, unable to meet his gaze.

He stared at her, those uncompromising brown eyes seeing more than she wanted him to, sensing if not yet understanding the string of lies lurking beneath her silence.

She looked to the blank rectangle of television, thinking of Ingrid Bergman, who'd been the darling of Hollywood until she had Roberto Rossellini's baby. Remembering all of Hollywood sitting stone-faced as Cary Grant accepted her Oscar for her.

"You aren't up here to testify," Leo said, leaning away now, his expression shifting to confusion as the truth dawned on him. "You never have been."

On the radio, the announcers were crucifying Marilyn Monroe for refusing to denounce her husband when, if she'd denounced him, they would be crucifying her for that.

"You're not even up here to . . . to earn a role you want," Leo said, the softness gone from his eyes. There were only three reasons a girl like her might need to hide up here, and Iz wasn't in Carmel to testify or to sleep her way into a movie role.

"You're up here to have a baby?" he said.

She stood and went to the kitchen sink, turned on the tap, found a glass almost as an afterthought. To not have a baby. That was the truth of it. But she couldn't say it aloud.

PART II

February 1957

You *don't mean to keep it.* When Iz first told Hugh she thought she was pregnant, that's what he said, with no hint of question in his voice. If she meant to keep the baby, she would be on her own, that's what he'd been saying. Even if she chose to have the baby and give it up, she would be on her own for the time until it was born, and how would she manage that? She lived in a shabby one-bedroom walk-up in Studio City. She had no money, all she had was a seven-year contract with the studio that contained a morals clause allowing them to terminate her and end her career. She had parents back in Pennsylvania, but even if she might have been able to bear the shame of going home to have a baby, her father would not take on her shame and her mother wouldn't ask him to.

But an abortion was illegal. Criminal.

The actresses she'd known in New York had spoken about it in hushed tones. You could use a coat hanger, you just needed to break the sac. You would know you'd succeeded when fluid began to leak out. But if the coat hanger wasn't properly sterilized, and even if it was, you could end up with an infection that would make you infertile, you could puncture the wrong thing and bleed to death. There were drugs you could take instead, but they could kill you, or fail to work and, in doing so, leave you infertile. There were places where abortion was legal—Hungary, maybe, or some of the Scandinavian countries—but Iz had no idea how to arrange that and even if she had, she couldn't afford to fly to some country where she didn't speak the language in the hope of finding a doctor who would do it.

And the reason any girl could speak of it at all without worrying it would draw suspicion to herself was the frequency with which it appeared in the newspapers: article after article about people on trial for murder because they'd performed an abortion or had one. No amount of money or prestige could protect you. The papers reported with gruesome glee the story of a Philadelphia food-store heiress whose mother and two abortionists had been convicted, the abortionists sent to prison. Doris Jean, that was the girl's name. Such an ordinary name, and she'd been exactly the age Isabella was now, twenty-two. The girl had eloped with a policeman. She was married. She could have had the child in wedlock, but her parents helped her arrange an abortion and something went wrong and now she was dead.

"You haven't gone to anyone, have you?"—that was Hugh's first question. Iz didn't know any doctors in Los Angeles and she couldn't exactly start randomly calling for an appointment for a pregnancy test and expect to keep it secret. Still, his response startled her.

BY THE TIME IZ FIRST met Hugh, on the set of *A Little Summer Romance*, she was becoming practiced at turning away the attentions of men who didn't matter. She was less savvy about ducking those who could influence her career, but she navigated that with an air of innocence that allowed her to draw the line at going to bed with anyone. Hugh was married, but he'd had lovers, not that he said so. What he said was that his marriage had long been over. Had he used the word "separated"?

That was a conversation they had over a late dinner the Thursday night of their second week of filming, after Hugh had gotten the script rewritten for her and taught her to shoot pool at Barney's Beanery and warned her off the sleeping pills. He didn't take her to any of the places Hollywood usually went—the Brown Derby, where Harry Cohn of Columbia Pictures and Jack Warner of Warner Bros. had their own tables, or Musso & Frank, frequented by Bogart and Brando and Monroe. He took her to a tiny place well off the strip, where he told her over a table for two in a secluded corner near the fireplace that he'd married in college because she was pregnant and he was an honorable man.

He kept a photo of his daughters in his wallet, five-, six-, and seven-year-old girls who all favored their mother, their hair dark where Hugh's was nearly as blond as Iz's was by then, their features delicate, their faces small where his was movie-star large.

"Genevieve, she's the oldest, the bossiest," he said. "Faith ought to be an actress. And Clairey, she's the great organizer already. She'd make a first-rate producer if she were a boy."

"Or a studio head?" Iz said.

He laughed and said, "She's a pistol, that girl. If only she were a boy. But someday I'll have a son."

He ordered sweetbreads for Iz over her objection, and he spooned them into her mouth, which was surprisingly erotic. But he didn't even kiss her, as if he knew the trick to making Iz want anything was to leave her thinking it was something she couldn't have.

His attention to her on the set the next day was that of one actor mentoring another, with no hint of the sexual tension she'd felt at dinner. He flirted lightly with the makeup and wardrobe girls and more seriously with Janet Leigh. It was another week before he again paid Iz more intimate attention. The smallest gesture. He moved a strand of hair from her face, the way Leo had at Hidden Beach that first afternoon.

Hugh made Iz laugh. He was a good mentor and a good lover. And he made her life so much easier simply by being with her. She didn't have to forever turn away other men's advances. Their relationship was discreet, she preferred it that way, but she was Hugh Bolin's girl and he was a big enough star that nobody wanted to alienate him by bothering her.

She hadn't banked on getting pregnant. She'd been a virgin

before Hugh. She thought she was supposed to be. She hadn't understood why the blood on the sheets made him angry. She hadn't understood that when he said he loved her, what he meant was that he wanted to have sex with her, and that her having been a virgin laced the event with a responsibility he didn't expect or want.

Had she really ever imagined he might marry her? Had she hoped they could sort out a way to marry quietly and quickly? She would have said that she did, that she wanted what she was supposed to want.

In truth though, she wasn't ready for marriage. Marriage meant having a family, and a family meant being seen differently, not as a sexy young star but as a mother who left her children to be raised by somebody else just so she could have an acting career. A family meant taking off a year or more every time she was pregnant. Marilyn Monroe didn't have children. Katharine Hepburn. Audrey Hepburn. Grace Kelly left Hollywood to marry her prince. It wasn't a way for a woman to get ahead in 1950s Hollywood, having a child.

The truth was what Iz wanted back then were men who made her feel more attractive than she felt herself to be, who were available as lovers but not as loves so she wouldn't have to face the truth that she didn't want what women were supposed to want. She didn't want to become her mother, cowed by an abusive husband. She wanted to be the women she saw in her favorite movies: The hard-boiled reporter Rosalind Russell played in *His Girl Friday*, who was so strong and competent that even Cary Grant as her conniving boss and ex couldn't do without her, who left people walking out of theaters thinking differently about journalism and politics. The lawyer Katharine Hepburn played in *Adam's Rib*, the smartest person in the courtroom even when her husband, played by Spencer Tracy, was there. A woman without a thought of giving up her career, she was a professional woman and that was more than enough.

Not that what Iz might have wanted or not mattered. Despite everything Hugh had said about loving her, he would not be caught in a scandal. He had a reputation to keep.

He could deal with things though. That was what he said—that he knew how to "deal with it."

He gave her Mannix's private phone number. She was not to mention Hugh's name. She was not to admit that he was the father or that the father knew of the pregnancy. They might not help her if she'd told anyone.

Mannix and Thau were as unfazed as Hugh had promised. She hadn't told anyone, had she? Good. She wasn't to, not even her mother. The studio could not be involved if there was any risk of this getting out.

So the fixers had been called in to consider the options. They'd done all the considering, as if Iz were a thing they owned, which she supposed was the case. She had no idea even who "they" were, whether it was Mannix alone or Mannix and Thau or others too. All she knew was that it was arranged in a way that it would be difficult to prove anyone but her was involved. The cottage. The doctor. Even groceries, so she wouldn't have to risk going out and being seen. "We need to keep you out of reach of the press."

Nobody ever put a word to what they meant for her to do, but they did always refer to the person who was going to "take care of it" as "the doctor." She took some comfort in that.

She was to pay him herself: two thousand dollars, which was nearly a third of her annual salary. She'd withdrawn all her savings and added the bills to the brown paper bag of cash Hugh had given her. There would be no anesthesia, because that took too much time. She was not to ask the doctor's name.

The doctor might choose to create a cover story that their meeting was an affair should it ever come out that she'd been seen with him. That was his choice, not hers. She was to do whatever he wanted. She'd felt the creep of dread, understanding what was in their tone if not in their words: the doctor might choose to have sex with her, and she would have to let him.

If anything happened after the doctor had "seen" her, she would have to deal with that herself. Again, the tone relaying what the words skirted around: If she hemorrhaged or got an infection, she would have to find medical care if she could, and she would be alone in any legal repercussions. She was never to contact the doctor again. If questions were ever asked, the studio would admit to having loaned her the cottage "to recover from exhaustion," and nothing else.

April 1957

Iz woke again to the sound of Leo's typing, but muted. Not even 5:00 a.m. The day before, while she stood in the kitchen with her back to him, unable to sort out how to explain that she couldn't possibly have a baby, Leo slipped out the door without so much as a goodbye.

The Fade Inn door was closed this morning, and although when Iz knocked he stopped typing for a moment, he didn't answer. He returned to his typing, banging the keys harder. She could see him in the bay window. He could have seen her but he didn't look up. He couldn't fathom a woman giving up a child in any way, not Ingrid Bergman or anyone else. But "sixteen and innocent" can't be with child, particularly not with the child of the man who would win her sister's heart, even if it was only her movie-role sister. No actress paved her way in Hollywood by convincing an audience she was *not* the onscreen character they loved. No actress paved her way anywhere by having an out-of-wedlock child.

With no idea what else to do, Iz set off for the point, which was empty and dark when she reached it, empty and dark when she left again. Even the stars had abandoned this lonely ocean.

A low voice was murmuring from inside Leo's cottage when she returned. The radio. She knocked. She called his name. No answer. His desk chair, she could see through the bay window, was now empty.

She turned the knob. The door opened.

She called inside, "Leo?"

He still didn't answer.

On the radio, they were discussing the upcoming Arthur Miller trial.

Iz stepped in and called for Leo again. The lights were on, but if he was there, he was pretending not to be.

His typewriter sat silent on his desk. The waste bin beside it was filled.

The page in the typewriter read:

```
FADE IN:

EXT. HAWK TOWER - NIGHT

In darkness and silence, only the crashing
of waves, a body falls from the top of Hawk
Tower.
```

Nothing else.

Iz pulled a page from the waste bin. It included the same opening and another half page. She pulled several other pages, all beginning more or less the same way, sometimes a body falling, sometimes a woman, but all abandoned midpage.

Across the street, the light flickered in the Hawk Tower window. Jeffers was there, writing poems that would never be read. It was something Iz couldn't yet imagine, the weight of fame once had and lost.

She stared out Leo's bay window, as spooked as she'd been that first morning at the point. She half expected the body Leo had conjured on the page in the typewriter to fall through the early morning dark. Not forgery by typewriter, like Alger Hiss claimed. Murder by typewriter. That was what Leo did.

G emma's head throbs. She's thirsty as hell. She's lying naked in a canopy bed draped with twinkling fairy lights. Someone is asleep beside her. His shoulders bare. His face soft in the blinking light.

Not Con.

The room is in a turret, with six windows in an arc facing the sea.

Bits of the night come back to her: The dark quiet filled with the same ocean sounds she now hears. Sam's scotchy breath whispering *Cricket*. The cold plate glass on her back.

What has she done? She's never been with anyone but Con. She's never been like that even with him, standing naked in front of that wall of glass, not even thinking about who might see.

Sam rolls over, looks right at her. "Eliza?" he whispers.

He reaches out to touch someone in the space between them who isn't there, some other woman he's dreaming about after sleeping with her. He closes his eyes again, gives a little sigh of contentment.

Gemma feels like a human typo, and on a typewriter too, where any correction leaves a shadow of what was wrong.

She slips silently from under the covers, wishing she had something to wrap around her, to hide herself. She feels exposed and vulnerable and inadequate, nothing like the swimsuit models in the magazines who she knows are Photoshopped and airbrushed, but knowing and feeling are not the same thing, and guys never know that, guys think that's what she's supposed to look like.

She has no idea where her clothes are.

At least it's still dark.

She freezes, startled by a sudden rustling in the bed.

Nyx shakes, grabs a chew toy, and scampers down a step stool at the foot of the bed to follow her, with no regard for all the noise she is making. Gemma wants to shush her, but what if the puppy takes that as an invitation to bark?

Gemma tries one door, a bathroom, then a second bathroom, Nyx scampering along with her. When she opens a third door, a light pops on—shoot!—illuminating a walk-in closet with shirts on hangers, sweaters and T-shirts and jeans folded in the built-in cubbies and racks of shoes all so neat they might be for sale. She closes the door quickly to kill the light, but still Sam stirs again.

She finds the door to the hall, finally. Her glasses on the coffee table. Her clothes in a pile by that big wall of glass. It's early-morning dark, the stars fading. Her T-shirt is inside Gran's old sweater. She's still wearing his watch—4:08.

She pulls on the T-shirt and the sweater with it, her lace tap pants, her jeans.

She can't find her shoes.

But of course, she wore none. That was where this started, with her riding on Sam's back to make hot chocolate they never did make.

The room is so spare after she's collected her things—nothing but Sam clothes and the chocolate and honey, the still-uncapped scotch bottle, and a book open to a poem: *This place is the noblest thing I have ever seen. No imaginable / Human presence here could do anything / But dilute the lonely self-watchful passion.*

Nyx abandons her, then barks down by the bedroom door, leaving Gemma grabbing her chocolate and honey and hurrying to leave out the back before the puppy wakes Sam.

The first door she opens is a crowded closet of an office, its desk overrun with computer screens attached to a beast of a computer. She opens a second door—this one to a mudroom and, thankfully, the back door. But places like this with their fourteen-million-dollar views are always alarmed, aren't they?

Nyx reappears with a ball she drops at Gemma's feet. Gemma stoops to quiet her, petting her puppy ears and whispering, "I can't stay."

She's an adult. She doesn't even have a boyfriend anymore. She can sleep with whomever she wants, whenever she likes. But this is Gran's world, where you fall in love and you marry before you get in bed together, and when the love of your life dies in childbirth, you remain loyal to her for the next sixty years.

She slips out, holding the puppy back from following her. Mercifully, no alarm sounds. A moment later, Nyx appears on the desk in Sam's office window as Gemma hurries to Gran's cottage, where she hasn't even locked the door.

ALL SHE WANTS IS A shower, but when she pushes back the curtain in Gran's little bathroom to let the water warm, she's awash with the grief of Gran's crumpled shampoo bottle, his last sliver of soap. She blinks back tears as she collects cleaning supplies and garbage bags from the trunk of her car.

The shampoo and soap and washcloth go into the garbage bag first. She takes two aspirin and dumps everything else into the bag: Gran's toothbrush and toothpaste, his nail brush, the rubbing alcohol and the inky toothbrush he used to clean his typewriter, the gauze and antibiotic and tape Sam must have put back after he bandaged her arm, the single threadbare towel. Her tears spill over at the sight of the nasty old toilet brush, grieving for all the times Gran made this bathroom so nice for her. There is nothing left of all the supplies for taking care of her mom when she was dying. Gran must have cleared them out so she wouldn't have to see them and be reminded. So he wouldn't either.

She cleans the bathroom the way Gran would have done it for her, then collects the towels he kept for her from the chifforobe in the attic bedroom, turns on the water, and strips. Her reflection in the mirror:

too thin in the places she should be round, too round in the places she should be thin. She tears off the ridiculous gauze and tape and dumps them in the garbage. She sets Gran's watch on the bathroom counter—the one he wore every day and yet she never really noticed it. So much she never noticed, that she'll never have a chance to notice now.

Showered, albeit without soap, and dressed in the clean T-shirt and underwear and socks she packed in her backpack and the pants she wore up here, she attacks the tiny kitchen. The biggest surprise is a wad of several hundred ten-dollar bills dating from the 1950s in an old Folgers tin at the back of a top cabinet. She throws out almost everything from the refrigerator, including the ancient ketchup, leaving only some frozen chicken and walnuts in the freezer, the expired soy milk and her yogurt and vodka and limes.

The clothes in Gran's dresser and closet are not even Goodwill-worthy. How has it never occurred to her to bring Gran a new set of sheets or a new shirt? She hesitates over the tuxedo before stuffing it too into the bag. She puts the contents of the safe on the coffee table in the front room, which is when she sees a handwritten note clipped to the title to Tubby.

Gran has signed the title over to Sam.

How can she have left it to a stranger like Sam Kenneally to clean up Buttercup, to drive Gran to buy oatmeal, even to dance with him at a restaurant she didn't even know he liked? And she can't even call the guy to tell him Tubby is his. She can't email him. Note to self: in the future, consider sharing contact information with a guy before you have sex with him.

The note says Gran knows Gemma will think Sam already has everything. *But the things he has are just that, Cricket. Things. He needs a Tubby, a reminder that he is loved as much as he loves.*

Gemma begins crying then, thinking again that if only she'd stayed one more night she'd have been here that morning to call 9–1–1. But she'd rushed back to LA to be with Con, only to find he was leaving her. She'd left Gran to die alone in the room where her mother too had died—not of the cancer Gemma was so sure the immunotherapy would cure but, like Gran, of a heart attack, her mom's heart weakened by the cancer.

These tired old things aren't Gran, she tells herself, weeping big gobs of snot as she ties off the garbage bags and drags them outside, heaves them into the bins at the side of the house. He's in Tubby, yes, and Tubby won't be hers. He's in the Fade Inn, which she can't afford to keep. But he's in the photo of Mom and her on his dresser, too. He's in his scripts. He's in the things that fill his desk drawers, which she doesn't have the heart to empty right now, and in Ole Mr. Miracle with its forty-eight keys.

THE SUN IS RISING, FINALLY, but if Sam has emerged from Point of No Return to take Nyx for a walk, he's gone out on the ocean side, avoiding her. She takes Gran in his zip-tied bag out to the point, where the path down to the water is steep and slippery, the sandy dirt jagged with bits of protruding rock. The climb out to the spot where she and Gran let her mom go is over wet boulders. The tide is high, the waves crashing, with nothing of the sea green or bright blue of a sunny day as she sits on the hard granite, watching the churning white and steely cold, the sea without bottom. It will be so cold for Gran. It must be so cold for Mom. But maybe Mom is somewhere else, in a perfect blue-white cove on the Phi Phi Islands in Thailand, or on St. John's, or in the Seychelles—those places they imagined going together on freezing Colorado nights.

There are no rules for letting someone you love go, we'll let her go when you're ready. That was what Gran told her when she was reluctant to let Mom's ashes go. She wonders now if he would like to have kept her longer, kept her closer. Mom had been Gran's daughter for decades before she became her mother.

Writing kept me alive even when I was dead, Gran told her the night she drove up with the news she'd sold the script she began in the little cove here, as they shared a good dose of scotch—to celebrate her first sale or to commiserate, he wasn't sure which. That script hasn't yet been made into a film though, and they couldn't get funding for *Eleanor After Dark* either, she'd used money Gran had put away for Mom, that Mom had left her. But what else can she do but write? That's what she's thinking as, back at the Fade Inn, she puts her computer on Gran's desk and opens Final Draft. She's already applied to Sundance with an old script, but the deadlines for the Nicholl, the Page, and Austin are coming up.

Midmorning, she sticks the hard block of frozen chicken in a bowl of water to thaw for later, then tosses some frozen walnuts and honey in a bowl with her yogurt. She cracks a square of chocolate into tiny pieces and throws that in for good measure, then checks her email while she eats alone at the little table for two they used to make work for three.

Her director friend Michal from her UCLA cohort has emailed that two writers just left the popular *Royalty* TV show to develop a Netflix series, and he thinks she'd be perfect for their old gig. *My Gran died*, she writes back, her tears welling. *I'm in Carmel, getting his place ready to sell.* She wishes she'd taken Michal up on his idea to cowrite the script he's now developing for DreamWorks, based on an idea they brainstormed together. But she'd been too deep into *Eleanor*. And doing anything with Michal was complicated because of Con, who found Michal self-centered and boring, less talented and yet somehow more successful than he was, although he never said the "more successful" part aloud. *But I'll have my agent submit me*, she types, then deletes it and admits, *I don't have representation at the moment. You think there's any chance they might consider me anyway?* She does a search for *Royalty TV show*, pushing back the part of her mind that is screaming about princess shows. She doesn't even wait for the search results before she returns to Michal's email, copies the contact for the showrunner, and tosses her name in for the gig—writing carefully (she's a writer, they'll be judging her from the very first word) but sending it immediately, before she loses her nerve.

Her search page, when she returns to it, has at the top a photo of Isabella Giori looking elegant as she climbs from a limousine, captioned *Isabella Giori rumored to be the next addition to the* Royalty *cast.*

She looks up at the sound of rumbling outside to see a garbage truck pulled to a stop. The men hustle to collect Gran's garbage bins, to put them in place for the truck's mechanical arm to lift and empty.

She yanks the door open to call to them to stop, she's made a mistake, she can't throw out everything that was Gran.

Already the bin is in the air, the bags tumbling into the truck, its compressor pulverizing Gran's toothbrush, his last little sliver of soap.

The *Royalty* showrunner is a fiftysomething woman who goes by Sass and has seen Iz's movies, but does Iz mind if she has her read? Iz does mind, but she can't say that. She's too old now to be suspected of doing anything interesting, too formerly famous to audition. But she's no longer well-known enough to expect to get even a grandmother role without showing what she can do, it turns out, despite Hugh's promises, despite her going to see him again after all these years—for a grandmother role, for pity's sake.

She brushes her hand over the hard lump inside her brassiere, and does her best with dialogue that is frankly a bit meager but is almost certainly her last chance to act.

Sass asks her to read again with less irony, then with a little melancholy.

"Elegant—you've sure got that down," she says. "But I imagined it more . . . something."

Vacuous, Iz thinks. *Gentle. Old.*

Then somehow she's regaling Sass with tales of auditions long past: taking off her bra so directors could see her "with and without," screaming or crying or crawling on her knees, vamping and tramping, snitching and acting witchy and any other humiliation a director wanted to drag her through. All that scrutiny of her face, her hair, every part of her body, which was so young and beautiful then and yet all she saw were her flaws. It seems impossible that she can be so much more comfortable in her skin now, her creased and sagging belly and arms, her neck and jawline and face that fare slightly better thanks to a top cosmetic dermatologist. Is it that she's learned to live in the skin she was born in, more or less? Or is it simply easier to avoid criticizing herself when nobody expects to see something she never was, sixteen and innocent?

"One guy put me on a ladder with a camera shooting up my skirt and told me to think about . . . well, I'm sure you can imagine," Iz says.

"That is so Hollywood!" Sass says. "I'd like to say 'so old Hollywood,' but . . ."

Iz says she's glad to have women in leadership roles now. "It will change how we're portrayed in film and TV and, because of that, how we're perceived more generally." She stops herself from pointing out that the top "occupation" for women in film and TV is "royalty." This *Royalty* grandmother is the only role she is up for.

"Well, so what we're looking for here," Sass says, "is to make sure there's chemistry."

"A grandmother with a love interest?" Iz says. Then, to Sass's perplexed expression, "Chemistry . . . that used to mean an actress made the lead actor seem sexier. If he then wasn't able to make the filming schedule, I'd be out too."

Sass laughs. "Hollywood, and definitely not old. But no, by 'chemistry,' we mean that the whole cast needs to click."

It was too much to hope for: a grandmother with a good dose of spunk and a little lust.

Sass's phone rings, and she asks if Iz will forgive her for just a minute. "It's my coproducer, Clairey Bolin."

CLAIREY BOLIN. HUGH'S YOUNGEST. SHE'D been just five the day Hugh brought his girls to the set. It was part of what made Iz think Hugh was in love with her: he wanted her to meet his daughters.

They were on the umpteenth take of a scene that would have been a meet-cute if Hugh and Iz were meant to end up together romantically, Iz in a pleated white tennis dress, barefoot for no reason other than that the director had just made her remove her socks and shoes to better show her legs. The problem, Iz saw only years later, was the satisfied way Hugh looked at her in the moment before he turned to Janet Leigh when it was Janet he was supposed to love. They'd just had sex in his dressing room while someone knocked on the door, calling, "Three minutes."

By then, they were spending evenings together in an elegant suite Hugh kept at the Hotel Bel-Air, languid lovemaking preceded and followed by good food and wine and conversation about who they were now and about the making of movies but never about their lives before, all the past she wanted to leave behind. He made her feel surprisingly and casually sexy in his appetite for her, for those long nights and the shorter stolen moments in his dressing room, which joined hers through a secret door he told her had been put in for Clark Gable, "or perhaps it was Mickey Rooney," but she later learned was installed for Hugh himself.

She knew of course that Hugh had more than the occasional lover. And she knew he had daughters whose photos he carried in his wallet, a Russian-doll trio of fine-boned, dark-haired girls with nothing of Hugh about them except an unflappable sense of belonging where they clearly did not. Why did that make a man more appealing and a woman less so, to have children they loved?

"Daddy!" the girls shouted as they streamed onto the set out of nowhere, without adult accompaniment. No mother. No nanny or babysitter. Not even a driver. They raced to Hugh as if some great prize awaited the one who reached him first. There must be film footage somewhere capturing the moment. The cameras were running. She and Hugh had been at the base of the elegant stairway, waiting for Janet Leigh in her ballgown to step gracefully down.

"Cut. Oh hell, cut. Maybe we should just cut the damned scene altogether," the director said as the two older girls plastered themselves all over Hugh and he knelt to accept their excited exclamations of . . . Iz has no recollection what.

What she remembers is the littlest one stopping disconcertingly close to her and observing her so intently that Iz had instinctively stooped to the girl's level.

The girl had touched one of the pleats of Iz's tennis skirt as if it were magical, then the wide white headband and her newly blond hair.

"You're so pretty," the girl said.

Iz laughed gently and asked the girl her name.

"Clairabel Charlotte-Anne Bolin, but you can call me Clairey," the girl answered earnestly, the name as much a mouthful as Iz's name had been—Francesca Guilianna Fumagalli, better known as Fanny—before she was rechristened for film.

"Well, Clairey, I'm Isabella Giori, but you can call me Iz," she said.

The girl answered, "Mommy says I have to be respectful with grown-ups, Mrs. Giori."

Iz felt Hugh watching them as if they were two of the same thing in different sizes. "*Miss* Giori, then," she managed.

The girl leaned closer and, touching Iz's hair again, whispered, "Can I marry you when I grow up?"

THAT CHILD IS NOW IN her sixties; Hugh's youngest daughter, Clairey, has grown into a prominent television producer but is his daughter still. She had just left her parents' house with her mother when Iz knocked on their door two months ago now, after sitting in her car for an hour, waiting for the wife to leave.

"One of your daughters?" Iz said.

"Clairey," Hugh said, his spine straightening in pride at this daughter who made such a success of herself in a role he'd once imagined only for a son.

"It's been a long time, Iz," he said.

She stepped inside although Hugh hadn't invited her. She removed the gloves she'd worn to have something to do with her hands while she let the worry about what she might be here for fill his vain little heartless heart. She slipped the gloves into her coat pocket that held the cowrie shell. She hadn't told Leo she was doing this.

"You look well," she told Hugh, although in fact he'd aged shockingly. She'd seen him on occasion over the intervening years, but only across the room at the Oscars and industry parties, in glossy-magazine soft-light photos and, one memorable time twenty years ago now, at a screen test for, it would turn out, someone wanting to market "Isabella Giori and Hugh Bolin reuniting for the first time since her debut," a project that interested neither of them. She didn't think Hugh avoided her. He was Hugh Bolin. She didn't imagine it ever occurred to him that he needed to avoid anyone.

He'd aged in a way she didn't imagine having done herself, the way you don't much see the daily creep of life reflected in the bathroom mirror. He was still handsome though. Fit. His jaw firm enough for a man in his late eighties. But there was a patina of vanity there that she hadn't seen when they were together, her own shortcomings or what she perceived as such having blinded her to his arrogance. He'd seemed so much older when she was young, twenty-eight to her twenty-two. He'd been an established star.

Without invitation, she found her way past the curved marble stairway and into a great room where three mugs sat on a coffee table—the remnants of a morning spent with his wife and his favorite daughter, not that Hugh was the kind of father to admit having favorites. She slipped her jacket off and laid it across the back of a yellow-striped couch as she took in this home that was his even when they were together. A flat-screen TV hung on the wall where, back then, it would have been a black-and-white in a fancy console. A full-sized pool table was scattered with stripes and solids. That would be where he and his friends sipped bourbon and laughed about the actresses they'd bedded while a football game played on the TV and their wives and children were at Saturday matinees or children's birthday parties or the beach.

She chose a cue from the rack and chalked it, then set the little blue chalk square on the edge of the pool table with its scattered balls.

Had Hugh been shooting with his daughter before she left with her mother? She addressed the cue ball the way Hugh had taught her that night with the cast at Barney's Beanery.

"What can I do for you?" he asked finally.

She took a shot at the two ball, solid and blue. Sank it in a side pocket.

"I'd like to ask you a favor," she said.

She lined up a shot on the five ball, a pretty orange. She didn't sink it the first time, it bounced at the pocket but didn't fall.

She offered him the cue. He didn't take it. This was her game, she was setting the rules, even he saw that.

She lined up a second shot on the five, then looked at him across the table. "I'd like you to persuade your daughter to hire me for the new role they're adding to *Royalty*."

Was that a frown, successfully suppressed on his lips but creeping into his eyes, as he said, "Would you? That's interesting." Trying to sound amiable but unable to mask a hint of irritation. And when she didn't respond with anything more than a look, "Is this a request, Isabella, or a threat?"

She chalked her cue again. "A threat," she said, but warmly, as if she were only teasing.

He smiled that forced smile and said, "I'll simply call you a batty old loon, and who is there to disagree?"

She took the second shot, a gentle tap that sent the ball slowly over the edge, from felt tabletop into woven leather pocket, the last of the solids cleared.

"Chazan," she said.

"For fuck's sake, Isabella!" The stunned response out before he could suppress it, before he could turn away, pour himself something from a drinks cart and down it.

She watched his back, the curve of his shoulder toward the drinks cart as he poured himself another. Clearly his family didn't know, and how could he explain it to them now, after sixty years?

"It would ruin you," he said.

But without this *Royalty* role, what life did she have to ruin? She had no daughters who would feel betrayed. No spouse. She was no longer the one with the most to lose.

He said, "You can't imagine Clairey would hire you if there were any hint of this."

She circled the table, pushing back the memory of that little girl visiting her daddy on the set, and lined up a shot on the eight ball.

"I won't have my legacy tarnished by a scandal," he said.

"I don't intend for there to be any scandal," she said. "Do you?"

She studied the shot. The eight ball sat in the corner, ready to fall as easily as the five had on her second try, at the lightest tap.

"Nobody but Chazan knows?" he said.

She suppressed a smile as she took the cue and set it back in the rack, leaving the easy shot untaken.

"I'll let you finish the game," she said. "You and your daughter."

She took her coat then, and saw herself out, closing the door quietly behind her.

AS IZ HALF LISTENS TO Sass's side of the conversation with Clairey Bolin, she gets the sense they're partners in more than just work. She thinks of Leo's granddaughter too grown up now, and Sam. Other people's children. Iz doesn't really know Gemma yet, but she knows Sam well enough to see he's smitten with her— two young people who, without parents or grandparents to provide love, might welcome Iz in the role. But Gemma won't stay in Carmel. The charming and perfectly livable Fade Inn is a block from the ocean on Carmel Point; it will sell as a tear-down for two million dollars. And Gemma is a screenwriter. She needs to be in LA. There is too much "in the writers' room," too much fixing scripts on set and gigs gotten when someone bumps into someone at just the time they're realizing they need to bring in a new writer, or when they're a few martinis in at a cocktail party and receptive to a pitch from a pretty young woman like Gemma.

Without Gemma around, Sam will fall for some girl he works with in LA, because who else does he meet, working all the time like he does? Someone who will want to keep doing what she does like all the girls do now, and they'll have a family and Sam will have no time for Carmel.

And sure, Iz's own LA place has plenty of room to gather friends. It's a seven-bedroom gated estate with a separate guest house next door to Joan Fontaine on the "Bad Boy Drive" section of Mulholland, where Roman Polanski and Marlon Brando were once neighbors and where Jack Nicholson (notorious for throwing drug-and-alcohol-fueled sex parties during which he locks himself away in another room to write) still does. But LA isn't a neighborly kind of place. Everyone is too busy and everything is too spread out and the traffic is impossible. Even when you live next door to someone you're fond of, nobody stops in at a bakery and grabs pastries for the excuse to sit together and chat the way she and Sam do in Carmel.

Sass says as she hangs up, "It was Clairey's idea to audition you. She was at her dad's, watching an old movie of his you were in—and no, don't ask me what kind of egocentric guy invites his daughter over to make him dinner and keep him company as he watches his own old movies! I don't get it either."

She says they're scheduled to start filming again shortly. Two of their writers just had a pilot for a new show picked up, so she and Clairey are looking for replacements, but they have the first few episodes written.

Iz tries to say she's available whenever they might need her without looking like a girl who's never had a date on a Saturday night.

"Well, I've been asking all the questions," Sass says. "Is there anything you'd like to ask me?"

Iz brushes back the possibility she won't get this role.

"Are you really wedded to the name Wilma?" she asks.

"Like *The Flintstones*, right?" Sass laughs. "That's what I keep saying. How is *that* elegant? But Clairey Bolin, she is hella stubborn, I'm telling you."

April 1957

Iz again slipped through the door behind the stairs at the Jade Tree Motel and waited in the same dingy motel room, determined to stay this time, to have the doctor do what he had to do and get it over with. She opened her pocketbook. Took out the brown paper sack. Two thousand dollars. When the door to the adjacent room opened, she stood and walked through it and handed the sack to the same man who'd been here before.

He didn't say anything. He only nodded, which she understood meant she was to undress.

He told her to lie on her back and spread her legs.

She felt so vulnerable, with the slight roundness of her belly no longer hidden under clothes.

Without so much as a warning, he inserted the cold metal. She closed her eyes, trying not to think or to cry.

He made that same impatient little half sound, then pressed a cold stethoscope to her belly again and again, Iz's alarm growing at each cold touch of metal to skin.

"You little fool," he said. "You've made it more dangerous for us both."

He wrote something on a small notepad, tore the sheet off, and handed it to her—an address. "A week from Thursday. Four a.m. You're too far along for me to take care of it here, and I can't risk it at home until my neighbors are away. You'll need to have someone to take you home afterward. Don't tell her where you're going or why."

"But—"

"Park on the next street over. The house backs up to a small woods you'll cut through. There are stairs to the cellar at the back of the house. Make sure nobody sees you. Your friend waits in the car."

IZ HAD NO GIRLFRIEND IN Carmel to ask, no one in her entire life to ask, if truth be told. Still, she couldn't bring herself to ask Leo until the night before she was to go to the doctor's home.

"I don't have anyone else to—"

"Ask the father."

Hugh hadn't even been surprised that she was pregnant, and he knew exactly who to send her to. Was what he'd said about their unwillingness to help her if the father knew even true, or was that his way of keeping his name out of it? There had been nothing in his reaction of the desperation Iz felt. Still, with nobody else to take her anywhere at four on a Thursday morning, she'd called him. He'd raged at her for calling his home and insisted it was too risky for him, he might be seen.

Leo, when she didn't respond, said, "Mannix, then. He can fix anything."

Iz was still standing at the door, still holding the doorknob as if it might steady her against the dread that her future was already destroyed.

She might need someone to take her to a hospital if she hemorrhaged, and Mannix had been very clear that nobody from the studio would risk being implicated if things went wrong.

"Someone I can trust," she said.

April 1957

Someone she could trust. Isabella Giori was dead wrong if she thought he could be that person, for her or for anyone. Leo had failed even his own family. Nobody came to the United States with him. Nobody was here to meet him. He left nobody behind.

He slept his first night in this country on a warm subway grate, then in the New York Public Library, the librarian who'd helped him find a French-English dictionary looking the other way when she was locking up. It was weeks before he found employment; the factories producing war goods were closed to him because he was foreign, and other jobs because he didn't speak English. He was hired finally to usher at an off-Broadway theater, where he could listen to the same words being spoken night after night, and learn the language that way. He spent his days in the library memorizing words and staying warm until his shift, after which he would hide away until the theater was silent, then sleep on a bench backstage.

That was how he survived until he was discovered sleeping one morning by a refugee woman who'd left behind a palais in Vienna filled with art and jewelry and furs to flee to New York, where she lived in a small apartment she could barely afford on what she made cleaning the theater. She made up a divan for him in her tiny apartment, and she fed him and schooled him in the diction that allowed him to sound American. She enlisted the help of her friend Berthold Viertel to help him gain a place at Dartmouth. It was easier to gain admittance to a college in those days, with so many American boys off fighting the war. And at Dartmouth, he wrote a play that his professor sent to Peter Viertel, a former student who gave it to his mother, Salka, who'd written almost every movie Garbo had starred in since the 1933 *Queen Christina*, when Leo was a seven-year-old boy newly settled in France; Salka was the one who'd read about the Swedish Queen and suggested the role to Garbo, and although Salka had been an actress then and not yet a writer, MGM had paired her with one of their best to cowrite the script. Salka gave Leo's Dartmouth play to a friend, who arranged for Leo to come to Los Angeles. Screenwriters too were scarce because of the war.

How had he come to imagine, after that first year or two in Hollywood, that he had shed his past?

Leo had buried himself in his work, in the writing. It was a thing he did alone, for the most part. A place to hide. He did not look for romance, and when it occasionally looked for him, he turned it aside. He could barely convince himself he was Léon Chazan. It was not something he imagined he could hide from someone he loved.

When he first met Isabella, though—even as she stood there in her ratty robe spouting that bizarre bit about the animal-hide-whip origins of Valentine's Day—he'd had to fight the urge to tell her who he really was. He couldn't even say why. He'd been alone in the cottage for three years, maybe that was it, the long days spent being nobody, taking to nobody, hoping every morning that this would be the day it would end.

And all Isabella wanted was his help in doing that same thing he'd wanted of Margalit more than a decade ago now: to get rid of a baby that was not yet a baby, that was never meant to be. All Isabella wanted was for him to drive her to a house not far away, to wait while she had it taken care of, and to bring her home.

April 1957

It was still the frightening predawn as Iz hurried back up the cellar steps from the doctor's house. She caught a toe on the top stair, somehow managed to keep her balance, and hurried across the backyard and through the woods to where Leo waited in his yellow roadster, the top up.

He startled when she opened the door. "That didn't—"

"It's too late." The saying it aloud making it feel no more real. "He said he won't do it. It's too late."

LEO CAME IN WITH HER when they got back to the studio's bleak little plywood-walled cottage, to make sure she wasn't going to kill herself, she supposed. His voice was a warm murmur meant to soothe: Could he open the door for her? Could she hand him her key? Why didn't she sit on the sofa? How about some hot chocolate? And when he could find no chocolate, "How about a coffee?"

He brought coffee on a tray, with crackers on a little plate. He sat in the chair that cornered the sofa, poured her a cup, and placed it in her hands. He made sure her fingers were well wrapped around it before he let go.

The truth of her situation was washing over her like the relentless crash of waves outside. It didn't matter that she wasn't visibly pregnant yet, at least not when she was dressed, the doctor told her. Since he'd seen her at the motel, the baby had quickened, he was moving inside her even if she couldn't feel him. "To do this now . . ." he said. "Maybe you can find someone else to do it, but I will not."

She couldn't go back to Los Angeles, and she couldn't go home, and she was broke. Would she get back the money she'd given the doctor?

Would the studio allow her to stay in the cottage? That seemed as unlikely as them paying her under her contract for time she couldn't act.

But surely there was something else to do, some other doctor or something she could do herself.

Doris Jean. Once the name came to her, she couldn't push it away. The food-store heiress. Dead from a botched abortion at her own age, twenty-two.

She said, "I don't even have any place to stay, Leo."

He moved to the couch beside her, put his arm around her shoulder, and gently kissed the top of her head. They sat together like that for a long while, with no sound but the crashing of the waves as the world beyond her curtains lightened, another day begun.

The phone rang, and she answered it. She didn't think not to.

It was Mannix calling to tell her he'd just bumped into Columbia head Harry Cohn having breakfast at the Hotel Bel-Air with a gang from Paramount. They were going over the paperwork to loan Kim Novak to Hitchcock for the movie role for which Iz had eaten all those steaks.

G emma is spooning the last of the chocolate- and walnut-speckled yogurt, trying not to think about Sam but unable not to, when her email alert chimes. Jessica Pennyweather, a young agent she met recently, wants Gemma to send her the *Eleanor After Dark* script, or anything else that will show Gemma's best writing! Gemma is composing a response, trying to keep her excitement in check, when a second email from Jessica arrives. Would Gemma be game to write a sample episode for Darren Dunn, the *This Man* showrunner? *I think it would be a great gig for you*, the agent writes.

DARREN DUNN. GEMMA HAD INTERVIEWED with him the prior October, while she was still with her old agent, in hopes of landing a steady paycheck while Con got *Eleanor After Dark* launched. The showrunner had loved her sample episode and he too thought she'd be good for his gig, "Since I need to have a chick perspective in the writers' room, or so I'm told."

"Let's jump right in," he said, offering her a seat on his office couch and taking the chair cornering it.

She smiled a little, thinking she'd been Cricket for as long as she was anyone, she was an excellent jumper.

He asked who her favorite character on *This Man* was, and she picked the nerdy biologist—in the cast to tend to the lead character's ego, but so were all the female characters, and at least the biologist was smart.

Dunn said, "Toss out a line you'd like to hear her say."

"'And the Oscar goes to . . . Gemma Chazan!'"

He laughed, and he said, "But you mean the Emmy, right?"

"That line would be 'And the Emmy goes to Darren Dunn'"—the flattery a bit blatant, but he struck her as the kind of guy who liked to be flattered, and she did want this job.

He asked her the same question for her least favorite character, the annoyingly pompous father.

"How about, 'I quit'?"

He laughed again. This was going well, although she did have to bob and weave a little after a reference she made to the main character's somewhat more subtle sexism was met with confusion. The main character was him, of course it was, and the sexism unintentional and unrecognized. He really did need "a chick perspective."

Dunn moved on to trying to ferret out the stuff even he knew he wasn't supposed to ask, like whether she had children or planned to work after she did. "I want to be clear how hard my room works," he said. "Personal lives take a backseat."

"I'm good with that," she said. She's twenty-six. She doesn't see having children in the next several years. She wants to write. And it's a rare show in which the creative energy lasts beyond five or six seasons; Dunn would likely swap her out for a fresh voice if his show survived and she stayed that long, which she didn't imagine she would.

"I'm a hard worker," she said, "and there's nothing I love better than writing."

"Nothing?"

Did he pause a beat there? Was there something she missed?

"One a.m. Two. Three," he said. "We crash here as often as not."

"Note to self: bring a sleeping bag and a pillow to work," she said. "A toothbrush too."

"Great," he said. "Great. I just wanted to be sure you're up for whatever we need."

Then he was standing in front of her, dropping his pants.

She ought to have handled it better. She ought to have said something other than "Really, that's all you've got?"

The words just came out.

Within days, all her interviews were canceled, and her agent dropped her on the excuse Con would use a few months later, that she was "difficult."

She didn't even tell Con about losing the agent at first, but he so endlessly badgered her about how she could have blown the interview that she finally admitted that she blew it by not blowing the guy.

Con barely paused before he said, "It's Hollywood, Gem. Did you not want the gig?"—joking, but she didn't laugh.

"Seriously," he said, "you must have been . . . You give out mixed signals."

Telling Con had been almost more humiliating than that moment in Dunn's office. If he thought she must have done something to give the guy ideas, maybe she had. But exactly what kind of signal says, *Yeah, drop your pants so I can get this job?*

She knows Dunn is the one who ought to be ashamed, and Con too—Con who was already sleeping with the actress who couldn't act even while living with Gemma. But she doesn't suppose either of them is. She's sure Dunn's friends all picture her on her knees in that office, her body naked and pale, imperfect, even though she didn't do any of that, she just said what she said and walked out.

That interview was just weeks before Harvey Weinstein was outed by the *New York Times* for paying off actresses he assaulted. Just a month before the Me Too movement took off with a tweet of a screen-share of a phrase coined to help sexual assault victims know they aren't alone. In the last four months, other producers and actors and directors, news anchors, and radio hosts have been called out. An opera conductor resigned. A U.S. senator. *Time* named as its Person of the Year "The Silence Breakers." Just about every woman in Hollywood wore Time's Up pins to the Golden Globes last month. Already though there are questions and backlash: a hundred French women denounced the "overreach," and people are questioning why a movement to support black and brown women has been conscripted by famous white women while women of color remain largely ignored. And still Louis C.K. can say aloud as part of an "apology" that he thought what he did was okay because "I never showed a woman my dick without asking first," unaware of "the predicament" he put them in. Predicament. Such a sterile term for what Gemma felt in that showrunner's office, what she feels every time she thinks about it. Still, even with so many women now saying Harvey Weinstein sexually assaulted them—more than eighty in just these few months since the story broke—no charges have been brought against him. Each one of those women going through that humiliation, and going through it again as the world imagines them with that awful man, and for what?

GEMMA CRAFTS AND SENDS A careful response to Jessica Pennyweather's first email, attaching the requested *Eleanor* script and simply pretending she hasn't seen the second email asking for a *This Man* sample.

She hesitates over the keyboard here at Gran's then, trying to brush off the sense of Gran looking over her shoulder. It feels like he can see everything about her now. (That was how she used to picture heaven, as a place where you would know everything, and if you were a good person everyone in the afterlife could see that, and if you weren't, they could see that too. But ever since her mom died, she's seen that wouldn't be heaven, that would be hell. Even if you led a perfect life, you'd have to know all the wrongs done by the people you love.)

She types "Darren Dunn" into the search bar and hits the return, like a gambling addict at the slots.

If anybody has posted about Dunn in the last week, she doesn't see it.

She reopens the tweet that started Me Too, where every day there are new responses. She hits the quote-retweet button and types #MeToo—not for the first time, but she always deletes it without posting. Her experience with Dunn is nothing compared to so many, and he would just claim she's bitter that he didn't hire her. His mother, an actress Gemma admires, would probably be more hurt by the scandal than he would if anyone believed Gemma, which they wouldn't. He's somebody. She's nobody.

Out the window: Hawk Tower. Tor House. Point of No Return. Still no sign of Sam and Nyx.

She deletes the post and searches "Isabella Giori screenplay."

The first result is a film called *Double Deception*, for which Isabella received an Oscar nomination. Gemma adds it to her streaming queue.

She types "Sam Kenneally" into the search bar which, if she's honest with herself, is why she opened the laptop. Hoping to find what? Something in common beyond Zoombini-video-game-love? How *did* she end up in bed with him? Not even in bed. In against-a-wall-of-glass, where anyone might see. In again-on-the-couch. She doesn't even remember how she got to the bed of this guy who was dreaming about someone else while she was asleep beside him. While she was awake, and maybe he was too. Maybe he woke up and realized she wasn't Eliza, and closed his eyes again to pretend sleep, hoping she would disappear. For all she knows, he could be one of those arrogant technology guys, with eight children by eight different mothers, none of whom he bothers to see.

But Gran liked him. Gran left Tubby to him.

If Wikipedia has his birthday right, "Samuel Phipps Kenneally, American video game developer" just turned twenty-eight. No spouses. No children. He graduated from Stanford the year before Gemma finished at UCLA. He started developing *Children of Chaos* in his Stanford dorm room and brought it to market with classmates Mads Amesbury, now the CEO, and André Jackson, whose role in the company isn't stated and whose name isn't linked. They've had multiple acquisition offers from marquee game makers, but Kenneally isn't interested in selling. That last bit is according to Amesbury. Kenneally, the entry assures her, does not give interviews—although there does appear in brackets a notation that this fact needs to be sourced, as if it's that easy to prove a negative.

Gemma clicks on Amesbury's name.

Madison "Mads" Amesbury is not the geeky freshman roommate Gemma expects, but a woman. All-American gorgeous in a super-professional way: smooth chestnut hair framing a neck as elegant as Isabella Giori's, and intelligent brown eyes behind studious-looking glasses on a nose so perfect that surely it's not the original. Stanford graduate with an MBA from Stanford Business School. Like Sam, no spouse or children. She grew up in Pasadena, where she was a Rose Parade queen and a national champion in track and debate. Of course she was. She came up with their company name, SidewalkChalk—"A move that is credited with allowing the company to tap the female video-gaming market in a way no prior game has." Now twenty-five developers overseen by someone not named Sam Kenneally are working on an extension to *Children of Chaos* while Kenneally explores new game possibilities, but Amesbury "is quick to point out that no creative work is done without his approval." Amesbury does, clearly, give interviews, with this statement sourced in a footnote linking to a business site video.

Madison Amesbury looks even better in motion than she does in the stills, and she sounds smart. Gemma wants to hate her, but the truth is she looks nice. Gemma imagines that she too wore an eyepatch to correct a lazy eye when she was young, and made her way through grade school forever conscious that if something happened to her glasses she would be left unable to escape into a book.

GEMMA IS SITTING ON THE sofa, sorting through the piles of Gran's scripts and thinking she'll go with dry Shredded Wheat for dinner rather than the still-frozen chicken, when a red Porsche convertible pulls into Sam's driveway. All she can see is the driver's windblown chestnut hair as she points a clicker at the garage door and pulls in beside Buttercup. Last night suddenly has "foolish one-night stand" very clearly written all over it.

Gemma grabs her laptop again and googles "Sam Kenneally and Madison Amesbury."

Her message center lights up with an incoming email from Jessica Pennyweather: *Hi, Gemma! This is Peony. I work with Jessica. She so enjoyed chatting with you the other day, but she's inundated and won't be able to take you on. Good luck!*

Even a new agent with almost no client list isn't willing to represent her.

She closes the email, leaving her staring at a screen full of search results with, at the top, a photograph of Sam and Madison Amesbury in that red Porsche against a backdrop of strip malls she recognizes as Lincoln Boulevard, just blocks from her Venice Beach bungalow. The convertible top is up. Amesbury is driving. Sam, in the passenger seat, holds a golden retriever puppy. The caption reads, *SidewalkChalk founders Madison Amesbury and Sam Kenneally bring 'Nyx' home for the first time.*

Sam is startled when the door from the garage opens beside his desk, so immersed in creating his game that he didn't hear Mads pull in.

"You look dreadful, I hope that means you've been working," she says as she stoops to pet Nyx, then pets Sam too, rubbing his shoulders that way she does so that his tension drains away. "You *are* working?" Not demanding, but hopeful. "If we don't have a new game to turn over to the team soon, we're going to have to start letting people go. Or we can pay their quarter-of-a-million-dollar salaries while they spend their days on their surfboards."

"None of them surf," he says.

She boxes his ears, but gently. "Really, Sammie, come back to LA. You're allowing your whole life to be consumed with regret. And you go to the dark places when you're alone. You know you do."

He considers this. Mads is always certain even when she's dead wrong, but really, when has she ever been wrong?

"Hawk Tower is here," he says. "The inspiration . . ."

Mads pulls him up from his desk chair and leads him back to the kitchen. She opens one of the good chardonnays she stocks the wine refrigerator here with, and they sit on the couch where Gemma fell asleep before he carried her into his bedroom. He wants to ask Mads, who has always been more casual about sex, if she ever slipped out after a night with a guy without so much as leaving her number. But he knows what it means, he's not an idiot.

He thinks of Gemma half waking when Nyx, already in the bed, licked her face. Of how soft her hair was when he stroked it, saying, "Shhh," the way his mother did when he was a kid, and the way her lips parted just a little as she settled back into sleep.

"Sam?" Mads says. "You with me?"

She's sitting still, not multitasking like she usually does, but waiting patiently. It's her secret weapon in business as well as in love: she can let the silence sit there until someone else fills it. Sam thinks she's going to wait him out again.

Instead, she says, "I miss you, Sammie. Everyone at the office misses you. *André* misses you, although don't tell him I said so."

André, who'd arrived alone at their Stanford dorm room freshman year with a suitcase, a plastic bag of bedding and towels, and a bus ticket stub, while Sam came directly from the San Jose jet center with a whole entourage of family and twenty boxes of things they'd brought from Connecticut on their private plane. Sam had learned more from André than from all his classes combined. About what it meant to have a spot in a university like Stanford, a thing nobody should squander. About how to work hard for something you wanted. About how to be a friend. By the time they graduated though, André was the one who had everything: a place at UCLA medical school, near his family, and a future as the neurosurgeon he'd arrived at Stanford intent on becoming. And Sam had nothing. Everyone—his parents and grandparents, his big sister and his little brother—went down in his mother's plane on the way to his graduation.

André was the one who saved him back then. André and Mads. André woke him the morning of graduation, with Sam's gown already pressed along with his own, and Mads there with him.

"This isn't just honoring you, it's honoring your folks too, your family," André said. "And maybe you won't ever regret it if you don't walk the stage, I don't know, man. But you certainly won't ever regret it if you do."

He handed Sam the gown, and slacks and a white shirt and tie, too.

"He can't wear your tie," Mads said.

"Sammie here is the only one who turned up here with a tie," André said.

"He can't wear *that* tie," Mads said. It was the one André always looped over their doorknob when he was with a girl, poking fun at Sam's prep school past.

André just looped that tie around his own neck and fetched another one for Sam.

At the ceremony, André fell in behind Sam in the diploma line, responding to Sam's pointing out that he was a J, not a K, simply by straightening the knot in that damned doorknob tie and then Sam's tie too. And when the dean called André's name and he didn't mount the steps, everyone looked to where he stood with Sam, a six-foot-six Black guy, easy enough to find. The dean set André's diploma aside, and after he called Sam's name a few minutes later and Sam mounted the steps, Sam felt André's hand on his shoulder. "I've got your back, man," André whispered. "You're never going to be alone."

You're never going to be alone. It was pretty much the same thing Mads said to him on the first anniversary of the plane crash. It was already evening when she knocked on his door. She made him shower and dress. She'd brought the makings for risotto and a good bottle of wine; she liked a good chardonnay even then.

"If you stay holed up doing nothing," she said, "even the memory of them will be gone."

That was when he showed her what he was doing, the only thing that passed the time in a bearable way, which was the work that became *Children of Chaos.* She was the one who pointed out to him—not until later, when the game was nearly done—that the characters were his family. There was his father in Aether, his mother in Hemera, his sister in Philotes and his brother in Oneiros, his grandparents in Hesperides, Moirai, Geras, and Eris. "Gods and goddesses," she said. "Immortals." Leaving him trying to shrug off the idea that he'd put his sister, who had always been his best friend, in the heart of Philotes, the goddess of friendship in Greek mythology and in his game.

And when he resisted the idea, when he said if he'd put his family into his characters, why hadn't he put one of them into Nyx, Mads stroked his hair the way she always did just when he needed someone's touch.

"Surely you know that Nyx is you, Sammie," she said so gently. "You've parked yourself in the person of a goddess so nobody will think to look for you there, sure, and I won't give away your secret. But Nyx is you."

And when he suggested maybe Nyx was Mads, she kissed his cheek and said simply, "No, this one is for your family, and you are Nyx, the first child of Chaos, who gives birth to all the others. Maybe I'll be part of the next game, but this one is for them. Your way of remembering them. Of making the whole world remember these people you love so much. And the whole world will, Sammie. I'm going to help you make sure of that."

Mads had done that, too. She was in graduate school, she didn't have time for anything, but she sorted out what he needed to do to bring a game to market. And when he couldn't do it, she did, she made *Children of Chaos* the international sensation it became. Their first meeting with a game distributor, she'd made Sam promise to let her do the talking. *It will disarm them, dealing with a woman, and I'm a better negotiator than you are.* If she set a hand on his leg, that meant he should keep his mouth shut. And after the introductions, she put her hand on his thigh and left it there. She did the talking even as they demonstrated the game, and they walked out with a letter of intent that left SidewalkChalk complete ownership of *Children of Chaos*, which the buyer would distribute nonexclusively for their game device for a relatively small percentage of sales. She asked nothing of him in the process. She didn't even ask him to do a single interview. Yet she did nothing without consulting him first, nothing he didn't want her to do. She wouldn't even take any equity until he stubbornly refused to sign the company's incorporation papers unless she took a big piece, and André a smaller one that could break any tie. And at no point in that process did she share even with André the truth she'd shown him, that the game was his way of keeping his family alive after they died because of him.

"I LOVE YOU, SAMMIE," MADS says now. "You get that, right? I know you feel alone in the world sometimes, but your family is in Manhattan Beach now, waiting for you to come home. I'm your family."

"I know, Mads," he chokes out, wishing they were still in college together, Mads and André charming his visiting parents over dinner at Osteria or Reposado or Evvia. Wishing he and André still lived together, even in that tiny dorm room with twin beds they barely fit in and an industrial bathroom shared with forty other students, even with all the hours he spent finding somewhere else to hang out when that tie warned him off their room. But neither Mads nor André really understands what it's like to be left alone when you're only twenty-two and have no idea who you are.

"I know, Mads," he repeats, more surely now. "I love you too."

"Nothing is the same without you," she says. "Even André is turning into a grump."

"After I get some purchase on this new game, I don't think I'll spend as much time here," he says, a small concession. "But I need to be able to climb to the top of Hawk Tower and sit there at night, see those stars Robin writes about."

"You've gone then? You were supposed to let me know so I could give the Jeffers Foundation a heads-up."

He hasn't gone yet.

"Remember that dress you wore to that thing last fall?" he asks.

"What thing?"

"The charity thing with the singer, where we first met Iz."

"The Monique Lhuillier!" she says. "I love that dress. It's too bad you can't wear the same dress twice."

Her superpower is to wait out anyone. His defense is to change the subject before she realizes he has.

Not much later, when she's cooking dinner—the one night a week she gets to so leave her alone, she's told him often enough that he believes her—he grabs the last book of Jeffers's poems Leo lent him, for the excuse to see Gemma, and sticks his head in the kitchen.

"I have to run across the street for a minute," he says.

Mads says, "You can have two minutes rather than just the one, and there's plenty. Invite Iz!"

Nyx looks up at him as if she expects him to tell Mads that Iz is in LA for an audition and it's Gemma he's going to see. He doesn't say anything.

THE LIGHTS ARE ON INSIDE Leo's cottage. The coffee table is piled with screenplays, with one on the sofa. He doesn't see Gemma, and maybe it's the hope she isn't there that allows him the courage to knock. She's just not that into him, he gets that, he knows there is no other explanation for why she left in the middle of the night.

She emerges from Leo's bedroom with another stack of screenplays, sets them on the table, and answers the door.

"I'm sorry, last night was a mistake, I understand that," he says, and he pauses, hoping she'll say it wasn't, which she doesn't. "I just— Your grandfather—"

He steps back a little, feeling exposed in the porch light. God, he can't start crying now.

He hands her Leo's book. "I wouldn't even know who Robinson Jeffers was if it wasn't for him."

She isn't following. Of course she isn't. She has the lost look of a character from *Children of Chaos* wandering into the world of the new game he's working on, *The Ghost of Hawk Tower*. Even the color bleed is on a different scale. He must have been a jerk in a way he didn't realize or doesn't remember. A drunk idiot jerk who goes to dark places.

"I just miss him. Leo. Your grandfather."

Gemma closes the door on him, and he thinks that's it, he's alone again, everyone gone on account of him stubbornly insisting on Stanford when his mom and dad would have had him choose Yale, where they met and where, when the engine failed on the way to his graduation, they would simply have pulled over and arranged for another car to pick them up. That was something Leo and he shared: the toxic cocktail of loss and guilt. *You can laugh or you can cry,* Leo told him. *You only have the one life though. How do you want to spend it?* Leo spent his writing stories—important stories with important themes that, nonetheless, also made people laugh.

Leo's door opens again and Gemma thrusts something into Sam's hands. "Gran signed Tubby over to you."

"Tubby?" he says, confused.

She just stands there, her eyes the blue-green of fading cilantro, anger flecked with grief. Part of him feels defensive. Part of him feels deserving. Part of him thinks he needs to remember this look, he needs to use it in his new video game.

What had he been thinking?

"Your dinner is ready," she says coldly.

"What?"

He registers Mads's voice, then—Mads standing in the door-way across the street, backlit so he can't see her face, but he knows that tone.

Nyx, wagging her tail, circles from the road's edge to Mads and back as if she wants to come to Gemma and him but can't leave Mads behind. When Sam turns back to Gemma, she's already closing the door on him again, a solid and final thunk.

April 1957

The knock on Isabella's door—Mannix coming back to tell Iz one more thing, she thought—was instead Leo. He eyed the bags of groceries Mannix had brought her.

"You can't stay inside for six months," he said.

She kept her back to him, wiped the tear that had fallen on the peanut butter jar.

"He wants the baby," Iz said.

"Mannix?"

"The father."

"So you're going to marry him?"

She pulled a loaf of bread from the paper sack. "The father and his wife," she managed.

That was why Mannix had come himself this time, to tell her Hugh wanted the baby. He would provide three hundred dollars a month for her to live on until she gave birth if she kept her pregnancy secret, and he would cover the medical expenses. Iz wouldn't be named even to the wife. Hugh would, she supposed, just say they'd adopted. Even if there was some suspicion that the baby was his, it wouldn't hurt his career. The child would have one of his parents, a father and a mother and those three little girls, sisters who would adore him. The life he'd have with Hugh would be so much better than life with an unmarried and destitute mother.

But the studio couldn't be seen to be hiding her if she were found out. Mannix had brought her groceries enough to last a week, but by the following Friday she would have to find another place to live.

She said to Leo, "This way, I'll know the child is being raised by a good family."

"A father who cheats on his wife."

"A father who loves his children."

And what choice would Hugh's wife have? She couldn't leave Hugh. She would be left with nothing but the shame of being divorced.

Iz opened the jar of peanut butter to have something to do with her hands, to steady herself, but the smell made her nauseous, as so many smells did.

A Little Summer Romance would release without her, she supposed. It wasn't a film that could be held for release in the fall. There would be a big party for the opening, with Hugh's wife there by his side. Or maybe not, maybe his wife was hidden away so that when they showed up with a baby this fall nobody would know she hadn't given birth.

"Maybe I can even see him grow up," she managed. "Not to know him or for him to know I'm his mother but—"

Leo said, "That won't end well for anyone."

She recapped the peanut butter and put it back in the cabinet.

"You should move into my place," he said. "Now, before the speculation about the mysterious woman in the unnamed cottage begins in earnest. I'm a recluse and have been for years, long enough for people to lose interest."

He'd thought this through even before she had. Leo too lived a secret life; he knew what it was like to need Hollywood more than it needed you. And, yes, Iz brought her trouble on herself, but she was paying a price Hugh Bolin would never be asked to pay. Even Hugh's wife would bear more of the shame than he ever would if the fact of this baby became public. A woman who couldn't keep her husband from straying was nearly as reviled as the woman who strayed with him. But the husband? He was just a man, doing what men did.

Leo said, "I don't have much. I live pretty modestly but . . ."

Iz looked around the little unnamed cottage: the chair and rug and lamps that belonged to the studio. The dishes. The bed. She was sitting on a sofa that belonged to them, next to the only thing in this cottage the studio hadn't bought, including her.

"You would do that?" she asked him.

Had that one kiss meant more than she imagined? What was he asking?

He said, "It's what people do, good people."

He steepled his fingers and touched his lips to his thumbs. "I wasn't born Léon Chazan," he said.

LEO WAS BORN IN GERMANY. He was German, but he was with his family at their villa in France when Hitler was made chancellor in 1933, when Leo was barely seven, and they never went back. They pulled what money they could out of Germany. They weren't destitute. But when the war began in September of 1939, his father was required to report to a French internment camp. He was German. He might be a spy for Hitler, never mind that he'd fled the Reich because he was Jewish. And after the Germans took over France, the family lived under the fear that Leo's father would be deported from the French camp to a German one. They lived as quietly as they could, in hopes the fact of a family of German Jews living in a villa in the countryside might be kept secret.

Leo wanted to join the Maquis and fight with the French, but he was only thirteen when his father left, and his family needed him. He was sixteen when he began to deliver Resistance newspapers, biking out late at night to collect them at a drop point and distribute them throughout Aix-en-Provence, tacking them up in public to spread the word that people *were* resisting the German occupation and to give others ideas how they could do so themselves. His mother had asked him not to do it, she'd explained to him the danger it would put them all in.

"The danger will never end if we don't stand against them, Maman," he answered, although that wasn't the whole truth. The whole truth had something to do with being a bored teenaged boy wanting the thrill, wanting to be someone, and it had to do with Margalit too. But his mother hadn't objected further, not even to say that "them" was his own countrymen, that he was German, perhaps because he no longer was. Germany had stripped all its Jews of citizenship. He had never been French either. He was a boy without a home.

His mother slit open a seam in the waistband of his trousers, slipped in a one-hundred-franc gold coin, and sewed it back up again. "Don't ever use it unless you have to," she said, and she hugged him fiercely, and she said, "I love you. Remember that always. I love you."

She'd known even then, he sees now, that his action would bring the Nazis to their door.

He arrived home one night to their villa being ransacked as Nazis stood guard. What stopped him before he got too close? Some sense that none of his family was there, that the soldiers had come for Leo and, not finding him, had taken them.

He slipped back to the newspaper drop point to wait there until the next night, the arrival of the one person he knew he could trust.

His contact in the Resistance—Jacques, although that of course wasn't his real name—took him in and sent a message through his underground network, and they waited. Word came back that his family had been deported immediately, sent to a German camp. His father too had been deported from the French camp to Germany.

The night after they learned his family was gone, a woman about his mother's age showed up unannounced—or unexpected by him, anyway, although of course Jacques must have arranged it—and within minutes Leo was leaving even his own name behind. He was allowed to bring only his father's watch, which Jacques safety-pinned to Leo's underwear lest it draw attention, and the gold coin still sewn into his waistband, that nobody else knew was there. He left carrying a passport with his photograph carefully inserted where some other boy's had been, a French boy born December 2, 1923, two years and twenty days older than he was. Léon Chazan.

The woman led him west, taking local trains and back ways. She didn't know his real name and he didn't know hers. He called her Maman, as she'd told him to, and she called him by the name on the forged documents. She might have been his own mother. She wasn't young. But she led him up the Pyrenees, several days in the freezing cold, to the Spanish border.

From the mountaintop, she pointed him to a guard hut.

"You'll show them your passport and state your name—Léon Chazan—and nothing more," she said, "and they will, I hope, allow you to cross the border and escape into Spain. I believe they will."

She handed him enough Spanish pesetas to find his way by train to Portugal, enough Portuguese escudos for passage on a ship to the United States, and three U.S. half-dollars for when he arrived. She said the documents and travel had all been arranged in the same name, Léon Chazan. And she turned back toward France.

He called to her to wait, but he didn't even know what he needed to know, so he simply asked her who had arranged this, who he owed his life to, along with her?

"I don't know," she answered, "and I wouldn't tell you if I did."

"Your name?" he asked. "You can tell me that."

"One can't tell the Nazis what one doesn't know, even under torture. You will be safer in Spain, but you won't be truly safe until your ship docks in America."

And when he asked if she could at least tell him who this person he was supposed to be was—"Who was Léon Chazan?"—she hesitated, reaching one hand unconsciously to her chest as if to make sure her heart was still in place.

She said, "Leo enlisted the day he turned seventeen and died at Dunkirk five months later, as France fell to the Boche."

"HER NAME WAS BERTHE CHAZAN," he told Isabella. "Léon Chazan was her only child. I learned that after the war. She somehow found the strength to hand over the future her son would never have to a stranger, a boy she would never see again."

He intertwined his fingers with hers and sat with the sound of the waves crashing on rock beyond the tower across the road and, nearer, early-morning birdsong, remembering how he'd produced the French passport that identified him as Léon Chazan at each checkpoint and border, a falsehood that through repetition began to seem true even to him. He made his way to Portugal, where ships were still leaving Europe. He traveled in steerage, where he slept the deep sleep of relief despite the hard bunk and the snoring men everywhere, and the farting and belching, the vomiting from seasickness, the men screaming out in their night terrors, and the threat of German torpedoes sinking the ship. The hope had been to make it to the United States, and it was only after he arrived that he realized he had no idea what to do here. Was he to give again the name of Chazan, or could he tell people who he really was? He was afraid they would know he wasn't Chazan, but he had no other identification and he was more afraid that if his name didn't match his passport, he would be sent back. He's not sure even still how he made his way to that library. He supposes his experience would have been different if his passport had been German rather than French, or stamped with a red J identifying him as Jewish.

"'It's what people do when it comes down to it, good people: they help each other,'" he told Isabella. "That's what Madame Chazan told me. 'We do it in memory of those we loved and could not help.'"

He turned to Iz then, blinking against the creep of tears but feeling steady and sure. "Am I now or have I ever been a communist? I don't know. What I know is that at sixteen, when I was distributing Resistance newspapers, most of the writers were communists. Much of the Resistance was communist. The woman who helped me escape across the Pyrenees was a communist to whom I owe my life."

"I'm sorry," Iz said. "I didn't . . ."

"You don't have to decide now," he said, his finger on the face of the watch his father had given him just before reporting to that French internment camp in order to keep his family safe. His family had still had valuables then. They were lucky. They had gotten their wealth out of Germany when Jews could still do so.

"You have family," Leo said to Iz. "Of course you do." He hadn't thought of that somehow, he'd imagined she was as alone in the world as he was. "You'll go back home?" he said. "To be with them?"

April 1957

"If you marry a blacklisted writer, your contract will be canceled and you'll be through," Mannix insisted.

Did Iz love Leo, or even like him? Mannix hadn't asked. He didn't care. It didn't occur to him to be concerned about anything but the profit the studio could make on her and what might jeopardize that. And what choice did she have? She couldn't face the prospect of going back to who she used to be—not Isabella Giori with the romantic life story the studio was even then creating for her, but Fanny Fumagalli from that dreadful Pennsylvania town that was so much smaller than her dreams, where her father, on the news she'd gotten her first nothing role in theater, called her a harlot for wanting to parade herself in public, and her mother bowed her head in defense against his anger. Even if Iz could bear to go home, her father would refuse to allow her to and her mother wouldn't defy him. And there would be no way to keep her pregnancy secret there.

"I'm not marrying Leo," she told Mannix. Leo, who was always a gentleman, who never even responded to anything beyond friendly affection. "I need a place to stay and it doesn't matter who I live with. If I'm discovered pregnant, I'm through in Hollywood."

A FEW DAYS LATER, AS Leo was helping her pack her things, a news flash interrupted on the radio: Joseph McCarthy was dead. He'd drunk himself to death, but they didn't say that, and Leo said it wouldn't matter. HUAC had been doing its work years before McCarthy made his name taking the credit, and it still would.

Very late that same night, Iz and Leo slipped her suitcase and her Oscar gown on its hanger out through the bedroom window, crossed the yards, and entered the Fade Inn through the back door into Leo's bedroom. With the lights off so that nobody could see in through the bay window, they crept up the narrow stairs to a tiny attic bedroom with a single window in the eaves and nothing but a twin bed and an old chifforobe in which she hung her gown. The window was small and high, but still Leo draped a blanket over it before he turned on the light.

He'd brought up everything she needed: a pillow and blanket, bedside table, lamp, washcloth and towel. "Do you prefer to bathe at night or in the morning?" he asked, and she said morning, re-solving to get up early since she couldn't imagine bathing naked in the little bathroom with Leo awake in the bedroom on one side of it or the front room on the other, or in the little galley kitchen just feet away. She gave Leo the first of Hugh's monthly three hundred dollars and said she knew drapes would be expensive but they'd need them downstairs. His expression—she hadn't realized until then what writing in that bay window meant to him, that it was his way of showing the world they could drag him through hell but they couldn't stop him from creating the stories that would terrify them while, at the same time, breaking their hearts.

She tried at first to make herself small and unobtrusive. She bathed and dressed quickly, edgy about the possibility of Leo walking in on her, with no lock on the bathroom door. She walked out to the point well before dawn to allow him morning privacy too—the only time she left the cottage, not wanting to risk being seen and remem-bered. But simply to use the bathroom she had to go through the tiny cottage's front room where Leo worked, and she had never had to go to the bathroom so often before. She took to putting a tissue in the toilet bowl to quiet the sounds, beginning to think this was as terrible an idea as Mannix had warned. But over time, they became used to each other's rhythms. Over time, it became too much trouble to feel so very self-conscious. She overslept one morning and, faced with the choice of going downstairs in her robe or dressing first and then undressing in the bathroom to wash up, she chose the robe. Leo only smiled and asked if she felt okay, he'd been starting to worry that she was unwell.

"I've never been so tired in my life," she said.

"That's the pregnancy," he said, leaving her wondering, as he made her coffee and toast even before she bathed that morning, how he knew anything about pregnancy. Had he had a wife and children? If so, where were they now?

She settled in gradually, filling the long hours while Leo wrote by reading in the little attic bedroom—books he checked out from the library downtown, old scripts of his, magazines he bought when he went to run errands or buy groceries. She pored over the weekly *Carmel Pine Cone* with its local news about school bond issues, new building plans, and disputes about homeowners bulldozing the verbena-and-sea-daisy carpet on the dunes to improve their views. She perused the "From a Librarian's Notebook" column for new books Leo could check out for her, and the gossipy "Pine Needles": Mrs. Marie Short had taken the Tolerton house at Big Sur for the summer and installed a telephone so friends wouldn't drive down only to find she wasn't in. Bing Crosby was back home in Pebble Beach. The guests at "Mrs. Grace Howden's At Home on Sunday" were treated to an impromptu singing of the Marseillaise on the D-Day anniversary. And of course Iz read everything she found about the Arthur Miller trial, which ended in his conviction on May 31. The hours crawled by each day until Leo finished his writing and drew the new drapes, and they made dinner together and listened to the news, watched the TV, talked about the world outside the cottage and, eventually, about more personal things. But always, when the night was over, they climbed into separate beds. If Iz sometimes wondered if Leo might ever kiss her again, he never did, he seemed never even to think about it or remember he had.

She very occasionally spoke with Mannix, and sometimes waited in the shadows if Robinson Jeffers was at the point when she arrived, but she was alone in the world, except for Leo. He kept to himself in Carmel, and he never mentioned her during his Sunday phone calls with his friend Nedrick Young, when the long distance rates were low, or in his occasional calls with other blacklisted friends, often to offer them jobs they needed even more than he did.

He put Hugh's three hundred dollars in a Folgers can, refusing to use it for anything even though money was tight. He sometimes disappeared at night in the roadster to take whatever he'd just finished to whomever he'd sold it to, or for a few days to work on films or television or perhaps even radio programs he wouldn't tell her about lest he put those employing him in danger of losing their jobs. She didn't think what he was doing was illegal, precisely, but she lived in the shadow of Hawk Tower, the reminder of Leo at that late-night meeting atop it, two heads bent in conversation not meant to be overheard.

THE BIG REWRITE GIG LEO took a month after Iz moved in would, he thought, have been bad enough in the usual crap motel, with nobody to have a coffee with in the morning, nobody to talk to or laugh with. He hadn't realized how lonely his life in Carmel had been before Isabella showed up. But this time, there wasn't even a crap motel. Gary, the director who hired him, showed him to a makeshift bedroom and office in a windowless storage room behind the set, where he could work only at night lest his typing be heard. On jobs like this, he usually revised scripts at night and slept in the days, but it was impossible to sleep with the second AC slapping the clapperboard at the start of every take and Gary blowing a cork when the lead actor again missed his mark, people tripping on cords and toppling lights more often than you would have imagined. Even using the john was off-limits in the daytime lest he be seen, although Gary did leave a tired metal bucket in one corner of the room. The only company of any kind Leo had was after even the crew had left each evening, when Gary brought him sandwiches and chips and coffee enough to last the night, along with the pages, and early each morning when he returned to collect the changes. Gary was a friend though. He was taking a risk, hiring Leo. He didn't like this any more than Leo did, Leo could see that. Gary was caught between some rock and some hard spot, even if Leo didn't know what it was. Maybe HUAC was coming for him.

On the fourth morning, Gary came into the storage room and closed the door. "Where's the magic, Leo?" he asked. "Have you lost the magic?"

Leo considered his own ungenerous response, then said it anyway. "This script is a plotless piece of dialogue drivel that cannot be saved by me rewriting the few lousy scenes you haven't yet gotten around to filming."

Gary stared, then laughed. "Hell, you think the script is bad, you should see what the actors are doing with it. You'd think that dialogue couldn't be made worse, but trust me, it can."

"At least my name won't be on it," Leo said, and Gary laughed again.

Leo's pay, it turned out, was coming out of Gary's own pocket, a last attempt to salvage a film the studio had given him no choice but to do. He couldn't explain a motel bill.

"Just three more days?" Leo asked.

"We lose the location this weekend to some church having a weeklong retreat. Talking in tongues and the like, I'm told."

"Maybe you could film that and stick it in to liven this script?" Leo suggested, and they both laughed.

"All right, the truth is I can sleep anywhere," Leo said. On the cold stone at the Resistance newspaper drop site after the Nazis had taken his mother and David and Margalit and the baby from the villa. Burrowed into a snow drift in the Pyrenees, Madame (whom he did not yet know was Berthe Chazan) insisting they lie together for warmth, and stroking his head when he cried at night. In a garbage heap in Spain, the distant barking of Nazi tracking dogs driving him to that exhausting night. In the locked loos of trains and the crowded steerage of the ship, the New York subway grate, the chair in the library, the theater bench, and even the relatively more comfortable divan after he met the actress who took him in out of pity or kindness or simply some sense that this was one thing she could do, one person she could help in a world that needed so much help.

When he got home from that writing job, Isabella had left the second three hundred dollars from Hugh Bolin on the kitchen counter. He put it in the Folgers coffee tin with the first three hundred, and redoubled his resolve to sell something for enough money to last him as long as she stayed.

ALFRED HITCHCOCK PRESENTS BEGAN THAT night as always, Hitchcock appearing in silhouette from the edge of the screen and walking into his self-portrait line caricature to the tune of "Funeral March of a Marionette." A minute later, the famous director appeared sitting at a desk with his arms crossed and the knot of his tie slightly crooked, saying "Good evening" with Hitchcockian glee and asking the audience beyond the TV screen whether they believed in ghosts. "No, of course you don't," he said.

Leo wondered if they might stop haunting him if he believed in them, his ghosts.

"My mother's name was Rebekka," he said to Iz. "After Rebekah from the Bible, who some think is as self-centered and evil as Hitchcock's Rebecca, because she was barren for twenty years."

"Leo," Iz said.

"But she was loyal to her husband," he said. "She was generous and kind. She sent her son off to keep him safe, knowing she would never see him again."

It was nearly thirty minutes later, they'd watched the show through to the end, before he managed, "My father was named Jacob," and he began telling her their names: his grandparents, Otto and Inge and

Heinrich and Yennj, uncles and aunts and cousins, none of whom had survived the war. It was surprisingly soothing, to say their names.

"No brothers or sisters?" she asked, her voice gentle.

"My brother David, he was just eleven, a boy still," he choked out.

The second hands on the watch that had been his father's moved relentlessly forward. Tick. Tick. Tick.

"What was your own name, Leo?" Her voice now a whisper.

He stood and went to the television, turned it off.

"I wanted to enlist after I got here," he said, still with his back to her. "To go back and fight. But I didn't know what would happen if I was found out to be living under a dead boy's identity."

He stood there, staring at the gray square of silenced screen, feeling her attention on him. Kind. Caring.

"Leo?" she said.

He turned to see her sitting there, ready to listen, the way Margalit had always been when he went to her for advice.

"To be anyone other than Léon Chazan now would dishonor the boy whose death allowed me to live," he said. "And his mother, who was arrested on her way back down the Pyrenees, for helping me escape."

Berthe Chazan, who had saved him. She could have safely waited out the war in her apartment or her villa or wherever she lived, he didn't even know. But she was caught helping him escape and she was sent to Gurs, a concentration camp in southern France where she, like so many, died of hunger or disease or beatings or suicide, nobody cared, there was no record of why or how she died there, only that she had.

June 1957

One evening after spring folded into summer—after Iz had given up her own clothes for Leo's larger shirts, white cotton so well-worn they felt like cashmere, and a single pair of tab-waisted $2.87 maternity slacks from the Sears catalog—she was surprised to find Leo handing her a script.

"It's not done but I have a good draft," he said.

She took the pages upstairs and curled up in her bed and began reading: FADE IN: EXT. HAWK TOWER - NIGHT.

It was the script he'd tried to start after he first learned she was pregnant, all those pages she found in the trash. *The Ghost of Hawk Tower.*

It was awfully dark, thick with the menace of evil unchecked, like so many of Leo's scripts. The opening left her particularly uneasy, feeling the same dread she had that first morning on Hidden Beach with Leo, and the next morning when the shadow-man startled her in the darkness at the point. The script was steeped in the creepiness of Hawk Tower, where in the opening scene a body falls from the top.

"Hitchcock ought to direct it," she told Leo after she'd read the whole thing. "It has everything every Hitchcock film ever made has, right down to the dreamboat of a girl who might be evil or might be good."

"Hitchcock can't make a film written by Chazan," he said. "Not even Hitchcock takes on HUAC. Any front I could get to sell it would be paid nothing, after which some hack writer would be brought in on one excuse or another to gut the magic from the thing. Or even if the magic survived, like with *The Brave One*, the Oscar would have another writer's name on it."

"That *was* a fronted script, then?" Iz asked.

She'd come to believe over the months since that Oscar ceremony that first week she was in Carmel that Leo knew far more about the mysterious case of the missing Oscar writer than he would admit.

"Did you write it, Leo?" she said, keeping her voice soft, not accusing but simply caring, wanting to celebrate him if it was his script that had won. "I'm trusting you to keep my secret. I think you can trust me with yours."

He smoothed the first page of his script, and she saw in the motion that he held no real hope it would ever be made.

"That one is not my secret to keep," he said.

"What would you change here?" he asked.

"In your screenplay, Leo?" she stammered. "I'm not a screenwriter."

"You remember that scene in *Rear Window* where they see the husband with his missing wife's handbag, and Grace Kelly points out to Jimmy Stewart that a woman wouldn't leave her favorite handbag behind?"

"'And the jewelry . . . Women don't keep their jewelry in a purse, getting all twisted and scratched and tangled up.'"

"You can't image someone named John Michael Hayes came up with that line, can you? So what would you change here?" And when she still balked, "This is just a first draft. I'll have lots of changes of my own."

Iz's first thought was that the ending wasn't quite right, but she couldn't think why and that seemed too big a criticism for what really was a compelling script. What did she know about how a creepy movie should end? What she knew was how to play a part, how to deliver a line, how the wrong words could trip you. Stupid stuperstition—say it quickly, five times. So she skimmed the script, found one of the lines that she had stumbled over when she first read it, and admitted she thought it could be better. To Leo's probing why, she said she didn't know, it just felt wrong on her tongue.

She and Leo talked about that one line for nearly an hour, with Iz trying a dozen different ways she might deliver it, intonations and gestures, sitting and standing and pacing, perfectly still, agitated—none of which felt convincing. "I guess . . . I just don't think very many women can be this blunt and manage to remain liked," she said, "much less loved."

"Ah," he said. "I see that. I do."

He put a pencil in her hand then, saying, "What do you think she would say?" And they spent the rest of the evening talking about the script.

"I miss this," he said. "Collaborating."

"It's always a collaboration, making a movie, isn't it?" she said. "The costumes and the music, the camera angles and lighting."

"And the actors," he said. "I have to leave room for the actors to bring what they have to a role, but there has to be enough character in the writing. I meant collaborating with other writers though. My characters are so real in my head that sometimes I need a writer friend to help me see what hasn't yet made it to the page."

She asked why he left Los Angeles. There, he would have the company of other writers, blacklisted and not.

"The Feds don't leave you alone there," he said. "At first, they just knock on your door, and you can pretend not to be home. But then you walk out of a movie theater or a market and there they are, just wanting to ask you a few questions. And the people you thought were your friends, they cross the street when they see you coming. My friends with children . . . how is a child supposed to understand why nobody will play with him?" The question so heavy with grief that Iz saw deep in his eyes a boy who must have had great friends in France until Hitler made having a Jewish friend untenable.

"Nobody up here even knows who I am," he said. "Nobody bothers me."

She rolled the mechanical pencil between her fingers, the cold metal. "That sounds awfully lonely, Leo," she said.

He looked away, to the desk and the typewriter, the drawn curtains beyond which Hawk Tower would still rise into a sky that would be red and orange and yellow and blue all at once in the late, summer-setting sun.

"I never imagined it would last this long," he said. "I thought in a few months, maybe, I'd move back to LA and pick up my life again, and I'd keep this place as a getaway. I've been living a day at a time for four years now, forever sure the blacklist will end tomorrow or next week."

He said, "It felt like such a miracle, *The Brave One* winning the Oscar, even though it wasn't mine. All that 'mystery of the missing Oscar winner,' the implication that it was wrong not to honor the real writer, blacklisted or not. It felt like the beginning of hope that this will end."

EVENINGS AFTER THAT, THEY DREW the curtains and went through the *Ghost of Hawk Tower* script, not just reading but talking about how she might inhabit the parts. He ran ideas for edits by her and encouraged her to pencil in changes, and talked to her about character and setting, dialogue, plot. She started paying more attention when they watched television, noting Lucille Ball's slightly bawdy tone, focusing on the word choices. Outrageous. Naive. Singing at the top of her lungs, oblivious that she was ruining the song. Calm Ethyl, and funny Fred. Ricky, with that Cuban accent. Droll. Patient except when he wasn't. Always gentlemanly. Iz began to jot down her thoughts about Leo's script even in the daytime. He said he loved her gentle humor, and she was too embarrassed to admit that the bits he thought were funny weren't bits she meant to be.

He taught her to type too, leaning over her shoulder to repeatedly hit a little green "Tabular Key" till he reached the center, then backspacing several times. "Press the shift with your left pinkie and hold it," he said. "Now the *I* with the middle finger of your right hand."

She did so, but the striker barely hit the paper, leaving the faintest *I*. "Press harder," he said.

"I *was* pressing hard." Sounding cranky, which was one part morning sickness that often lasted all day, and a bigger part being cooped up in the cottage.

She pressed the *s* under her left ring finger, the *a* under her pinkie. Leo showed her how to reach down for the *b* and up for the *e*. And there it was a few keystrokes later, her name in the center of the fresh white paper.

He reached around her and rolled the paper down so her name disappeared under the typewriter tape, then tabbed toward the center again, backspaced once, and told her to type a *b*.

"Now the *y*." And after she'd typed that, he said, "Excellent," reminding her of Hitchcock when she'd laughed at his elevator joke.

She rolled the page up:

by

Isabella Giori

She said, on impulse, "I could front for you, Leo."

That was the moment she first felt the baby kick, this child who would play football in college, like Hugh had, she found herself thinking before she stopped herself, before she resolved that she would not imagine any life for this baby. He wasn't her baby. He would always belong to another family. And she was glad for that. She was glad to know the baby would have a good life, and she would too.

The small of Iz's back and her feet are complaining after the day trip to LA; she had stopped by her LA house on her way from the airport to Sassy Claire Productions, but stayed only long enough to change and have her hairdresser and makeup gal do what they could before her grandmother-role audition. Gemma though is sitting in one of Leo's Adirondack chairs, looking like she needs a friendly lift even more than Iz needs her pajamas and a double dose of bourbon.

The girl spent the whole day trying to sort through Leo's scripts, there must be three hundred in his closet, she tells Iz. "I half expect to find the play he wrote at Dartmouth here." And when Iz offers to share the leftover curry in her refrigerator, "Would I turn down a chance to hang out with the next *Royalty* star?"

There is, Gemma tells her, a photo in the online *Hollywood Reporter* of her arriving at the glamorous new offices of Sassy Claire "to discuss the terms under which she might agree to take" the elegant-grandmother part. Is that her agent's doing, or Hugh Bolin trying to make sure she gets this role?

"I *am* starving," Gemma says. "The chicken breasts I pulled from Gran's freezer—"

"Don't you dare eat those!" Iz says. "They probably predate talkies."

Gemma, as they dig into the curry, says, "I'm sure it's great, *Royalty*, but girls raised on princess shows? Of course they end up thinking the goal in life is to marry a guy with a title, never mind that he probably hasn't done anything since his fortunate birth."

"This princess . . . Think Harvard and Yale," Iz says. "A bad-ass lawyer and human rights activist."

"But beautiful too, right? Heaven forbid we should be exposed to an ordinary-looking princess."

"She's too busy trying to get attention for issues like educating girls in Afghanistan to brush her hair; her minders are always trying to brush it for her," Iz tells her. "And the prince packs the lunches and drives the kids to school. The showrunner is a woman and so is her coproducer." But she knows Gemma is right. Princess—it's still the most popular "career" path for girls and women in film and TV, never mind the women's movement.

She says this audition was a Sunday tea compared to the old days, and she tells Gemma about eating all those steaks for Hitchcock.

"He changed your lipstick how many times?" Gemma asks, laughing as Iz hoped she would.

Gemma spoons a mouthful of curry. She's wearing Leo's watch. Iz wonders if she knows where it came from, what it means that it has survived.

"Gran left Tubby to Sam," Gemma says.

There is hurt in her voice, of course there is.

"His girlfriend seems nice," Gemma says, but nothing in her tone says she means it, and her expression reminds Iz of Nyx. Gemma and Nyx look a lot alike, now that Iz thinks of it, except that Nyx doesn't wear glasses. Or clothes.

"Mads? Do you think she's a girlfriend?" Iz says. "They spend a lot of time together in that little office, staring at computer screens."

They both look across the street to the window that is Sam's office, the room lit but empty.

"Con and I worked together," Gemma says.

Worked. Past tense. Well, Leo never did like that boy. *Con, an apt name,* he'd once told her.

"When Mads spends the night at Sam's," Iz says, "one of the guest room lights is often on." All right, she's a busybody. But that isn't necessarily a bad thing. And the relationship between Mads and Sam is something she hasn't quite worked out herself.

IT'S THANKS TO MADS THAT Iz knows Sam. Well over a year ago now, Mads was on Iz's favorite LA morning show along with producer Kathleen Kennedy, talking about the nonprofits they championed, Girls Who Code and Force for Change. "Put 'Mads' together with 'gaming company executive' and everyone expects a man," Mads was saying when Iz turned it on. "You see a lot about who people really are when you catch them off guard, let me tell you." Iz, still in her pajamas in her LA kitchen, had finished her oatmeal and was about to turn the show off when Kennedy asked if Mads's cofounder was one of the horse-racing Phippses. "Gladys Mills Phipps? The Seabiscuit breeder?" Kennedy said. She had been one of the producers on the movie.

"Sam and I were classmates at Stanford," Mads said, as if that were an answer.

Iz would have said it was the young woman's evasiveness that piqued her interest, but of course it was that coupled with the Phipps name. The Phippses of Connecticut who, in 1957, trained to San Francisco to adopt a baby they had never seen.

Given how successful SidewalkChalk was, it was surprisingly hard to find much about Sam Phipps, whose full name was actually Samuel Phipps Kenneally. He'd grown up in Connecticut, yes, but the Connecticut phonebook was surely full of Phippses. Still, Iz followed SidewalkChalk on Facebook, and when they posted about a Girls Who Code fundraiser they were hosting in Beverly Hills, she bought tickets—a good excuse to get all gussied up, she told herself.

She hadn't even had to find Sam to try to meet him at the dinner. Mads came to her table. She'd seen Isabella's name on the guest list, and her idea of a perfect evening was homemade soup and an old movie, she said. Sam, who was with her, wore a tuxedo. Mads wore a Monique

Lhuillier gown, and she was charming—not in a calculated way exactly, but in the way Iz supposed she would have to be to succeed in a man's world. Perhaps Iz recognized a bit of herself in the girl, perhaps that accounted for her uneasiness at first. But Sam, he was a dear from the start, shy and unassuming. He didn't stay long, but Mads pulled up a chair and spent half the night talking about Isabella's old films— "Don't you hate it when they colorize black-and-whites?"—and about the envelope fiasco at the Oscars that had all of LA abuzz, *La La Land* announced as the best picture winner when *Moonlight* had won. And when Mads called Iz later that week and suggested coffee, Iz didn't say she'd driven up from her LA place to her cottage in Carmel just the day before and was tired from the long drive. She suggested a coffee shop on Sunset Boulevard the next morning, and she got in the car and headed back.

They'd become something like friends by the time Mads and Sam, in Carmel for a friend's wedding, dropped by her cottage one Sunday morning on a whim.

Iz, who was having coffee with Leo in his Adirondack chairs, introduced them. "Madison Amesbury. Sam Kenneally. This is my friend Leo Chazan."

"*The* Chazan?" Mads said.

Sam was so taken with Hawk Tower that morning that Leo fetched one of his books of Robinson Jeffers's poems and read him "Orca," about sea lions and cormorants, the "wind-straked ocean," and human destruction of the Earth—a topic Sam was so passionate about that Leo loaned him the book. Something in the way the boy accepted it left Iz wondering if he wanted it for the poems or for the excuse to see Leo again. Leo had that effect on people. He made you feel better about yourself.

Sam and Mads both returned the following week, Sam with a ticket for one of the regular Saturday tours of Hawk Tower. He returned Leo's book, saying he was enjoying the poems so much that he'd bought a copy for himself, and a Jeffers biography too. He was surprisingly well-versed already in the life and words of this poet he'd never heard of six days before.

As Sam crossed the street to join the tour, Mads told Iz and Leo, "He's been working forever on a game to educate players about the dangers of global warning. It hasn't been going well."

And when the place next door to Hawk Tower came on the market a few months later and Sam bought it, Mads explained that this was how Sam worked. "He can't do anything, and then he finds some little way into what might be something and he jumps in with both feet. I hope the water here is deep enough. God knows he needs the distraction of work."

"LEO HAD A SAFE?" IZ says after Gemma explains that's where the title to Tubby was, already made over to Sam.

"I know, right? He never even locked his *door*. But there's a safe in his closet, with his will and the house deed and the car title. Some scripts. An old camera with film still in it."

Iz takes a bite of curry, a creep of unease shooting up the back of her exhausted and crepey neck. The evening has turned full dark, the fog that had threatened her landing at the Monterey airport now thick and cloaking. She is suddenly glad of that.

"The scripts he was nominated for?" she asks, because she can't ask about that film, and even if she could, Gemma won't know what the photos are, the film is still in the camera.

"Two I've never even heard of," Gemma says.

Isabella's mind buzzes then with all the ought-not-tos—all the things she's done that Leo would have told her not to if he'd known—as she listens to Gemma talk about the two scripts Iz herself already knows by heart.

One minute Nyx is standing beside Sam in the morning sunshine, her head drooping in disappointment as Mads's car disappears around the bend, headed back to LA, and the next the puppy is darting across the street and slipping into the slightly open front door at Leo's.

"Nyx, you moron," Sam says as he takes off after her.

He can see through the bay window that the front room of the cottage is empty. He knocks lightly on the door jamb and softly calls, "Nyx?" Bad puppy. She doesn't come. "Gemma?" he whispers. Then a little louder, "Gemma?"

He enters tentatively. Nobody in the front room, where Leo's ashes sit beside his typewriter, still sealed in that plastic bag. No Gemma in the kitchen or the bathroom or bedroom. No Nyx. He peeks into a door that is slightly ajar in the hallway: a narrow stairway. "Nyx?" He creeps up the stairs and into a slope-ceilinged attic bedroom where Nyx, her little tail wagging, watches Gemma, who sits cross-legged on a high twin bed. She has headphones on. The bed is scattered with a camera and several scripts, one of which she is reading. The tinny sound he's hearing is "Friend Like Me" from Disney's *Aladdin* at a much higher volume than that song ought ever to be played.

He's scooping up Nyx to slip out with her when Gemma gasps, "You scared me to death!" She pulls out one earpiece, splashing Robin Williams singing "to help you dude."

Friends like me, he gets it, friends with benefits and all that. He supposes it was easier to slip out before morning than to have to share coffee. He supposes this Con fellow she's been dating forever must be something like André, who is a human sea stack, a neurosurgeon who devotes his life to saving lives, and what can Sam say to that? Look at me, I make video games? Not even *games*. Just *game*.

Gemma removes the other earpiece and turns off the music.

"I'm sorry," he says. "She ran off and your front door was ajar, nobody answered and I thought . . ."

The way she considers him leaves him feeling a bit like a puzzle she's not sure she wants to solve.

"Is that your camera?" he asks as if he isn't trying to head off a goodbye he doesn't want to hear.

"It was Gran's," she says. "There's still a roll of film in it."

"I have a darkroom," he volunteers.

OF COURSE SAM HAS A darkroom, that's what Gemma is thinking that evening as she eyes the contents of the chifforobe in the attic bedroom: her puffy vest and her Oscar dress that was her mom's prom dress, a vintage black fake-silk spaghetti strap sheath that is clearly overkill for developing film and sharing a quick bite of leftover risotto before printing the shots. She pulls on her same black jeans, the cleanest of her two shirts, and her sweater, which is still fresh enough since she's been wearing Gran's. Why does she care? Sam has a girlfriend. But there's a little part of her that remembers feeling more comfortable with herself that night than she's ever been. With Con, she always felt like the fifteen-year-old she was when they first met. Flat-chested. A little chubby. The skin on her round face forever broken out. Her lenses thick. Not a girl who could be comfortable naked in front of that wall of glass, not even caring who saw. Maybe even wanting to be seen.

She opens her phone and listens to a saved message—"It's Mom! Just calling to say I love you. No need to call me back."—then heads across the street.

It takes a moment for Sam to answer the door. Of course it does.

The house is huge, with the living spaces at the far end, by the ocean view. She follows him to the room with the glass wall and the ocean view, the back wall of which she sees now is covered with floor-to-ceiling bookshelves, endless spines uninterrupted by photographs or mementos. The kitchen is even more impersonal: clean marble countertops, white cabinets, a Viking range, and a sink. What looks to be a large pantry door is a huge side-by-side refrigerator, nearly empty. Another is a wine cooler filled with wine.

He asks what kind she'd like—listing a gazillion choices, like he's imagining himself a sommelier who can pour the wine and leave. She says she might just have water.

"Sparkling or still?" he asks, which makes her laugh.

"Tap," she says.

"I have a confession to make," he says. "I do have a darkroom, but I have no idea what to do with it. I found a photo lab in Monterey that will develop the film overnight though. I can take it there tomorrow and pick it up the next day."

"My mom was a photojournalist. I've been agitating film since before I could talk," she says, trying to hide her relief that she won't have to put this film in his hands.

"Really?" he says. "Okay then. It's downstairs." He says the sellers left the chemicals and everything because the movers wouldn't take them and he didn't care. Why doesn't she make sure she has everything she needs while he puts the risotto on to reheat?

"If it were just me I'd microwave it, but while I can lie convincingly to Mads, if you can't . . . Let's just say she'll know the first time she meets you that I ruined her risotto by microwaving it."

He says it lightly, as if Gemma couldn't possibly be bothered that he, like Con, so casually lies to someone he loves.

She turns to Nyx, the puppy named not for a basketball team as she'd first thought, but for a goddess who lives at the ends of the Earth and drives through the night sky in a horse-drawn chariot. Nyx, who loves with reckless abandon, never pausing to worry whether she'll be loved back. Gemma photographs her sitting attentively as Sam spoons risotto into a pan.

"I hope you have enough leftovers for three," she says. And before she even realizes what she's doing, she takes a shot of Sam laughing. He has such a warm laugh. It's not a liar's laugh, is it?

"One shot left," she says. "I'm sure there's a way to rewind an unspent roll, but—"

Sam takes the camera, scoops up Nyx and sets her in Gemma's arms, and shoots the three of them.

"My dad used to love taking selfies like this in the days before phone cameras and selfies were a thing," he says, already rewinding the film.

There is an intimacy in the statement. Gemma is left sure he doesn't talk much about his dad, that he's opened a little bit of his heart to her that he doesn't often share.

DOWNSTAIRS, A ROOM BELOW THE plate-glass window room and nearly as big is filled with a Pac-Man arcade game, an Atari Home Pong hooked up to an old TV, an original Sony PlayStation, a Nintendo 64, and gaming consoles Gemma doesn't even recognize, along with shelves of old video games. French doors open to the patio and fire pit, the Carmel Dog Bar, the palisades down to the sea. There's a gym and several bedrooms down here too, all empty except one in which a Stanford ball cap and jumbled exercise clothes clutter the unmade bed, one running shoe toe peeking out from under the pile. She finds at the end of the hall, finally, a darkroom her mom would have loved, everything built-in and top-end. You could print a poster from a negative here.

By the time Sam joins her—without Nyx, whose fur would float about and ruin the film—she has the film canister, bottle opener, scissors, developing tank, and chemicals all organized and measured. Everything in order except her thoughts. She asks him to hold the scissors before she turns off the light and pops open the film canister, awash with the memory of her mother's voice in the dark teaching her how to do this. She cuts the film leader, Sam's fingers brushing hers as he passes the scissors. She feels in the dark for the nubs and slides the film in, then twists the reel to pull in the rest of the film.

Sam says, "You know how to do this, right?"

She shivers at the sound of his voice in the dark, just as she had when he'd whispered "Cricket" that first night.

She cuts off the spool and twists in the last of the roll, places the reel in the tank, and closes it, sealing the film away before she tells Sam he can turn the lights back on. She passes the time she needs to develop and fix and wash the film by asking questions about his gaming room, then hangs the film in the drying cabinet.

WITH THE CHANDELIER DIMMED IN the charming dining turret, Gemma can see out the maple casement French doors to the balcony and the sea. They're eating while the film dries, Gemma trying to think of something to talk about other than whether Nyx is under her chair because she's here or because this is where Madison Amesbury sits. Sam's answer to the question she comes up with—"Where did the idea for *Children of Chaos* come from?"—sounds like a story made up by someone with something to hide. No wonder he doesn't give interviews.

The timing of what he's telling her puts the start of the game not in his dorm room but rather after he finished college, with Mads important to it in some way he's skirting around.

Mads's risotto is, as advertised, delicious. Rose Parade queen. Champion runner and debater. Top-notch businesswoman who makes the best risotto Gemma has ever tasted, reheated no less. There might be a role for Gemma in Sam's life, but it won't be the love interest of the leading man. If this were a script Con and she were writing, she would shorthand this scene as "Mads's unfortunately excellent risotto," and Con would laugh.

BACK IN THE DARKROOM—THE SOFT jazz that was playing during dinner now on here too and the red glow of the safelight casting its eerie spell—Gemma sets the enlarger and projects the first frame onto photographic paper: A woman in a ballgown standing at a desk, her shoulders bare and square and beautiful. The desk is Gran's, the window she faces the bay window at the Fade Inn. Is she reading the page in Ole Mr. Miracle?

"Who is she?" Sam asks.

"'Reading from top to bottom . . .'" Gemma makes a clicking sound to mimic the sound of Grace Kelly turning on the lamps in *Rear Window*, "Lisa" . . . Click . . . "Carol" . . . Click . . . "Fremont."

"Who?" Sam says. "Although whoever it is, I do like the voice."

Why do you do that? Con asked Gemma some months before he broke up with her. *Why, whenever I get anywhere near your heart, do you push me away?* And when she said she never pushed him away, he mimicked her mimicking some movie line, to which she responded that he was a terrible mimic. Why had she said that? The bickering had begun when they started working together, each with a different idea of what they should write. It had grown worse over the course of making *Eleanor After Dark*, with all the money her mom had left her on the line and Con so angry sometimes that he stormed out. But that was the first night he didn't come home. Gemma imagined him walking the beach all night. She imagined him, in his anger, taking a curve too fast on Sunset Boulevard and killing himself. It never occurred to her to imagine him climbing into another woman's bed until he told her he had.

"She must be my grandmother," she tells Sam.

"From the 1950s?" Sam says.

It's old film in an old camera. Black-and-white. The dress doesn't help date it more precisely. It's a classic style, strapless black bodice with a fuller white skirt.

Sam says, "It looks like the dress Sofia Carson wore at last year's Oscars. Mads was obsessed with that dress. She wanted it for a charity thing we were going to. The designer wouldn't duplicate it exactly, but she did something similar."

Rose Parade queen. Champion debater. Business mogul and master chef who rocks a twenty-thousand-dollar dress while Gemma wears yesterday's dirty shirt and jeans.

She hangs the photo to dry and starts on the next frame. This one is far less elegant, and pretty funny. It's a girl in a bathing suit, wearing a dive mask and snorkel, hunched forward as if she's trying to keep warm.

"Is it the same person?" Sam asks.

"Maybe?"

"Could she be younger here?"

Gemma peers more closely, thinking maybe this one is her mom.

They go through the same process, printing frame after frame of what increasingly seems to be the same woman, or perhaps girl—none as elegant as the first photo. When they get to the last three shots, Gemma says they don't need to develop them, but Sam insists.

Nyx.

Sam laughing.

Selfie of the three of them. Not on Lincoln Boulevard. Not in a red Porsche convertible with the top up. Not taking Nyx home together for the first time.

BACK UPSTAIRS AFTER GEMMA HAS hung the last print to dry, Sam asks if she'd like dessert. "Leftover flourless chocolate cake made by Mads," he concedes, "but I do whip the cream myself." And already he's sliding the wall of glass away with a click of a button and offering her a separate chair facing the view and a cashmere throw to keep warm, which makes staying feel less awkward. He seems to sense how unsettled she is by those photos, how much she fears being left alone to try to understand them.

In the chairs with the cake, just as she is beginning to feel self-conscious about how seen they will be by anyone walking along the sea, he says, "Hey Google, turn off all the lights." The whole house goes dark then, leaving them in the stillness of the salty-damp air and the night sounds: the steady thump of waves, the hoot of an owl from a tree just outside, a responding hoot from farther away.

"I never met my grandmother," she says. "Even Mom never knew her. She died in childbirth."

Outside the window, a creature streaks by, gone almost before Gemma knows it's there.

"It's not my mom," she says. "The snorkeling photo—those aren't Mom's legs."

They sit watching the spray of sea in moonlight, the stars in the near sky disappearing toward the horizon. A fog coming in.

"You can't tell who she is," he says softly. "Not in a single one of those shots."

In every photo, the woman has her back to the camera, or a mask and snorkel on, or her head dipped forward so that a hat hides her face.

Sam says, "Why would he never photograph her face if she was his wife?"

Leo opened the Sears catalogue one evening in late June, suddenly hopeful. The Supreme Court had just overruled labor leader John Watkins's contempt conviction for refusing to name names. Arthur Miller's lawyers were already filing for a reversal of his conviction. The battle wasn't over—the HUAC Chairman was demanding the Supreme Court "take just one minute out to determine what communism is," and vowing to pass legislation "even the Justices will understand"—but a sword had been drawn by a Court far more difficult to strip of arms than anyone on the blacklist.

"Pick something, a dress to go out in?" he said to Iz.

"To go out in?" Iz balked. "I can't go out."

"The press is reporting on Elizabeth Taylor's maternity clothes as if they're Oscar gowns," he said. "It's not such a taboo anymore for pregnant women to be seen in public."

The taboo wasn't what Isabella was concerned about though, he knew that. She didn't want to be recognized. But people didn't even see pregnant women, they either looked away, embarrassed, or were unable to see past a pregnancy to the woman. And Iz's body was as changed as Margalit's had been, her face fuller and softer too, not less beautiful but less dramatic. He couldn't say any of that though. She would take it as having lost her looks. She would worry she would never get them back. And as much as Isabella didn't want to be seen now, she was a woman who needed to be.

"Your movie isn't out," he said. "People don't yet know who you are."

She said, "A *Little* Summer *Romance?* It will have to come out soon."

The studio had delayed the film's release on the excuse of changes required by the Production Code Administration, but the truth was Benny Thau was in a tough spot. He couldn't launch his new star if she wasn't there to take her bow. If he was going to release *A Little Summer Romance* before Isabella returned, he would have to downplay or eliminate her role—a simpler thing than Iz would imagine, if she imagined it, which Leo hoped she didn't. They would remove the "introducing Isabelle Giori" credit and edit most or all of her scenes out of the film, perhaps reshoot a few. That's what was really going on, the studio was buying time while they explored stripping Iz's part.

"They'll just change the title," he said. "'A Little *Fall* Romance.'"

He said, "Nobody knows you're here. Nobody is going to see that movie after it's released and think, *Wasn't this new actress that pregnant woman we saw months ago in Carmel?*"

"Who would we say I am?" she asked.

"Who will ask?"

She said, "I could dye my hair darker. It's shocking what a difference hair color makes."

DOES SHE, OR DOESN'T SHE? the magazine advertisement for a new Miss Clairol at-home Hair Color Bath assured readers, because no nice girl would dupe a man into finding her attractive by coloring her hair. Cheats and harlots and whores and every girl acting in the movies— that was who used hair color, and the movie stars went to discreet hairdressers every two or three weeks lest they get telltale roots. Leo had gone all the way to Salinas to get the unremarkable light brown Iz chose from the advertising photos. "I'm pretty sure the clerk at the register assumed I was an escapee from Soledad Prison looking to disguise myself," he told Iz.

He opened the bright yellow Clairol box and they read the instructions together, nervous about the process now that it was in their hands. An acrid smell filled the little bathroom as they mixed the dye.

Iz sat in her robe at the tub's edge with a towel over her shoulders, her back to him, and he took a brush and lifted a lock at the nape of her neck, buttery soft in his fingers.

Gently, his mother used to say. He had forgotten that until this moment, forgotten that as a boy he used to love to brush his mother's hair. That was before France, in the home in Germany they hadn't imagined they would never return to.

Leo didn't even have to close his eyes to hear his mother's voice, even after all these years. His mother, sitting his sister on the sofa in the French villa and setting a Limoges cup in her hand—real coffee, an unfathomable luxury. His father had been in the French internment camp for over a year by then.

"You're young, Margalit," his mother said. "Sometimes young women have pauses in their menses. You don't get enough to eat. Of course your menses have stopped."

His sister wasn't so young, though. She was two years older than he was, and he'd been with someone himself even before his father had gone off to report to that camp. It had been exciting, and frightening too even as it happened, no less frightening the second and third time, with the risk of being caught. Then his father said he was sorry he would have to give up his schooling and his friends, but he would have the run of his father's library, he should spend at least five hours each day reading whatever he chose, learning whatever he wanted to. And as his father had taken his watch off and secured it to Leo's wrist—one of the last times that he would feel his father's touch—he'd known that first love of his was over almost before it had begun.

His sister told them then about the German soldier she had been secretly meeting.

"You'll stay here in the house," their mother said. She didn't ask whether Margalit loved the boy or whether she might marry him. She said, "We both will. The boys will get whatever we need."

His mother would claim the child as her own. She hadn't said so, but Leo understood that was what she meant. His mother would take the shame of the child on herself. There would be no explaining the baby as legitimate, with his father in the camp.

LEO TURNED ON THE RADIO, Elvis Presley "All Shook Up" in love, as Iz pinned her hair into a bun, exposing the vulnerable nape of her neck. She pulled a single lock from behind the delicate curve of her ear for the test—hidden so they could cut it out if this went poorly. He coated the lock with the dye and noted the time on his watch with its two second hands.

As he stepped back, he caught his own reflection, his eyes dark with the pain he'd once imagined he might leave behind. It had been years since he'd really touched a woman's hair, since Garbo, he supposed.

He filled the percolator from the tap and added the grounds, took two cups down from the cabinet, and watched the liquid in the glass-bubble top of the percolator rise up in increasingly darker shades, like Isabella's hair. *Yes, that's it, a little frightening,* Garbo had said of his smile that day on the beach, and she'd stopped walking, and he saw then that they were being watched. It had been instinct, him taking a lock of her dark hair between finger and thumb and twirling it, meeting her gaze. He kissed her or she kissed him, it didn't really matter, what mattered was that they kissed, gently at first and then more passionately, his fingers running through her hair. That had been different though, a performance. He hadn't really touched anyone in such an intimate, vulnerable way since France.

He handed Iz one of the coffees, then wiped the test strand with tissue, noting the time on his watch, and showed her the strand. He parted her hair in multiple places then, as the directions suggested, pinning it up with bobby pins as, on the radio, Tab Hunter sang "Young Love."

"Do you think that's true, is there really only one girl for every boy?" Iz asked quietly, thinking, he supposed, of Hugh Bolin.

He said, "I don't know."

As he listened to Tab's voice, surprisingly deep for someone with such boy-blond heartthrob looks, he wondered if he himself had ever been in love, or if Isabella had, or even Tab Hunter. Tab sang so convincingly about it, but if there was only one person for him, it was not Dorothy Malone or Debbie Reynolds, to whom he'd been romantically linked in the press, but Anthony Perkins. Tab dominated the marquees despite having been described in magazines years earlier as attending "limp-wristed pajama parties," and was now rising to musical fame with this love song that presumed all love was heterosexual. If you were good-looking enough, everyone saw what they wanted to see.

When Leo was done pinning Iz's hair, she looked like a creature from *Science Fiction Theatre*. He pulled on rubber gloves and squirted the dye all along the part lines, then unpinned her hair and ran his fingers through it over and over again as if he might find, after each additional touch, that he was in love with her and she with him, the one love Tab Hunter sang about.

"The Monterey Symphony Guild is hosting a garden party gala at Bing Crosby's place next week," he said as they waited for the dye to take. "I could get us tickets."

"We can't stand alone at a garden party, refusing to mingle," she said, raising her fingers nervously to her head.

He took a tissue and wiped her fingers, lest they stain.

"I wish I could go snorkeling," she said. "But I don't suppose there's a wetsuit in this world that would fit me now."

He washed her hair for her afterward, running his fingers through it to have again that human touch he hadn't experienced in any real way since that last night in the mountains fifteen years ago, with Madame Chazan's body spooned with his, protecting him from the cold.

Iz looked so different afterward—no longer the woman he'd imagined as the lead in *The Ghost of Hawk Tower*. He wasn't sure anymore who she was. Was that the hair color, or was it something more?

"Fanny Fumagalli," she said to him. "That was my name before."

Not her real name, but her name before. Like him.

While she disappeared upstairs to dress, he collected the little box he'd tucked at the back of his top dresser drawer and paced back and forth as he waited. Had he ever paced before? Did anyone really pace in real life, or was that just Cary Grant in a comedy, doing it for a laugh? But he couldn't sit still.

"Iz," he said when she came back down, her hair still wet. "I brought you . . . I wanted to . . . I thought you might . . ."

He tendered the ring box. "People will assume you're my wife," he said. "Nobody here knows me. Nobody knows I'm not married."

She took the box and opened it, tears welling in her eyes. He was sure she was going to object, but she simply took the plain gold band from its velvet pillow and slipped it on her finger.

"All right," she said. "Thank you."

LEO WALKED IZ ALL THE way along the oceanfront to the end of the beach and back in the soft light of that evening. When she stumbled on a bit of broken road, he caught her arm to steady her, and he found he liked that, holding her arm, keeping her safe. It was a warm night too, without the usual June gloom of Carmel.

After they passed the Frank Lloyd Wright house, they took the stairs to the beach and removed their shoes, and walked along the water with the cold sand squishing through their toes. The water was even colder, but still there were children playing easily in the surf. Holes dug in the sand, and piles that wanted to be castles. Dogs on leash rather than running free, on account of the rabies scare. Further along, two women stood painting at easels set in the sand, facing a sky that was now red and blue and golden all at the same time, the sun shooting rays through gaps in the clouds at the horizon, then slipping away again. A kite string rose high toward the shore, the kite steady as its long tail danced as gayly as the boy whose father helped him hold it. Had Leo ever flown a kite? He couldn't remember.

An old man coming from the other direction smiled at them as they passed, seeing them as a couple, soon to be a family, just as those people on Santa Monica Beach a decade before believed him to be

Greta Garbo's lover just from a moment like this, two people holding hands, chatting, with no real intention of romance. People tended to believe what they thought they saw. In that moment, he imagined he might believe it himself.

After that first walk, Leo started looking at the *Carmel Pine Cone* with Iz every Thursday after he finished writing, and they often walked to the town bulletin board packed with flyers for local events. They went to see *The Man on a Stick* at the Golden Bough Circle Theater, a play that made them both laugh. They went to the movies: Spencer Tracy and Katharine Hepburn in *Desk Set* at the Carmel Theater. *The Spirit of St. Louis. Funny Face.* They walked almost every evening after dinner, sometimes stopping for cones of ice cream at the Carmel Bakery and licking the melting chocolate, always chocolate, on the way home. He would often take her hand—just for show, like that kiss on the beach with Garbo. He was depleting his savings, but he didn't care.

One evening he took Iz all the way to Nepenthe, an hour down the coast. He wanted to take her dancing, he couldn't even say why except that she seemed so sad that day, uncertain as her body got away from her that she would ever get it back, or that she would ever get back to Hollywood. He guided her around the patio with the other dancers, doing the easy line dances. He thought when the music turned to "Young Love" that she would want to sit out the slow dance, but she put her left hand on his shoulder, and he took her right hand in his left, and they pulled closer as they danced until, before the final words about devotion were sung, the child growing inside her was nestled up against him, and Isabella's head, smelling of that soap that was not his mother's lavender, was nestled in his neck.

"Thank you," she said in the silence after the final drum brush and piano note, and she kissed him on the cheek.

As they left just after that, having stayed far later than he had intended and mercifully seeing nobody who might recognize either of them, he wondered if he might ever settle into this kind of life, with a home and a family, someone to care for, even to love.

It's 4:30 a.m. The shadow of Hawk Tower out the little attic window stands against the starry sky—the last thing Gemma has seen so many nights here, the last thing her mom would have seen every day of her childhood, and now this cottage will be sold to someone with no memory of them. She pulls Gran's sweater over yesterday's underwear and T-shirt she wore to Sam's and then to bed, and she goes downstairs, still wondering if the woman in the photos now drying in Sam's darkroom is the grandmother who died giving birth to her mother, or some other love of Gran's, or someone else entirely. Is the camera even Gran's?

Gemma never knew either of her grandmothers. They were just these vague ideas, grandmothers. She knew other people had them, but she never did. What Gemma knew, growing up, was that her mom was her mother and Gran was the closest thing to a father she would ever have. He was a screenwriter until he wasn't, then he was again, but he was never as successful as he might have been if he hadn't been blacklisted all those years. He loved her. He loved her mother. He loved her grandmother so much that he never loved another woman again. He raised Mom alone, here in this little cottage, and she grew up to became a single parent too, a photographer who kept no photos of her own mother. But Gemma understands that. Her mom had, in being born, caused her own mother's death.

She knows Gran liked that she was trying to be a writer. She knows that he didn't like that she wrote with Con. "Eight fingers on eight keys and a single mind searching"—that was what writing was to Gran, not something you did with anyone else despite the current trend of gathering writers in a room to come up with something that will offend absolutely no one. And she knows Gran's favorite poet was Anne Sexton. That feels, somehow, like the most intimate thing she knows about him. Everything else is less about him than about who he was to her.

I would like a simple life yet all night I am laying screenplays away in a long box. Is there poetry in a screenplay? *My immortality box, my lay-away plan, my coffin.* Like Sexton, Gemma would like a life in which it's good enough just to drink hot chocolate. But like Sexton, and like Gran too, her ambition bird haunts her nights, chipping little bits free from her heart and shaping them into words.

She makes a cup of hot chocolate with the expired soy milk, feeling seen as she's backlit by the refrigerator, and not in a good way. But who else is up at this hour? And Sam doesn't seem like a "lonely self-watchful passion" kind of guy, he's light and funny. He took Gran's ashes dancing—which, okay, does seem slightly less humorous after he slept with her just hours before his risotto-making girlfriend arrived. But what does she know about what guys think about sex? Friends with benefits and all that. He's no different from anyone she knows, really. The difference is that she'd never slept with anyone but Con, that she'd imagined the night with Sam was something more than it was.

She opens Final Draft on her computer, cursors over the "Fade In:" button, and taps. The screenwriting program drops the phrase in where it belongs without any need to tab or backspace or worry about typos. But no words follow. She tries again with a fresh sheet of paper on Gran's typewriter. *FADE IN.* Two words. Six letters. Three vowels. *It makes the starting easier, Cricket.* She adds the colon. Feels the thump thump thump as she tabs across to sound the bell before the zip of the return lever. Still, no other words come.

She gives up trying to write and snuggles into Gran's couch, weaponizes the remote, scrolls through her queue. She's thinking she'll have to cancel Gran's internet and cable and streaming when she sees *Double Deception.*

Isabella wrote an Oscar-nominated screenplay at the age of twenty-two. Gran wrote two by the time he was her age. Does she just not have the talent?

A lot of people less talented than you write and *direct,* Gran used to say over her objections that only sixteen women have ever won writing Oscars, not a one in the last decade, and that female directors have an even harder time not because they lack talent (women make up half the cohorts at places like Sundance now) but because while men get distribution with Disney and Sony, women are left to independent companies with little money and clout. Gran was sure Gemma's talent would win out, that she would be the next Kathryn Bigelow, but even Bigelow had to best a man whose budget was twenty times hers to become the only woman ever to win a feature-film-directing Oscar. And whatever talent Gemma might have has gotten her nowhere. Now she can't even get in the doors.

Double Deception begins with a view through a windshield to a dark, empty road. Instantly ominous. A lighthouse comes into view, its beam sweeping toward the windshield, then blinding the screen to white. Then we're in the lighthouse, metal steps and an old rope handrail spiraling upward, the walls chipped brick and peeling paint. We pass a window with a view of the keeper's house, which is dark. We circle up faster and faster, the camera juddering all the way—a great effect, Gemma thinks. It adds to the dizziness, the dread. Who is this? What is happening here? We haven't seen a single person on-screen yet.

We reach a landing with portal windows and bolts in the ceiling that must anchor the light. We continue juddering up narrower stairs into a dark room filled with the looming shadows of the light works, then on up to the lantern room, where the light casts a long, distorted shadow of a person, or perhaps two people standing one in front of the other, moving out to the lantern gallery. And just as the shadow becomes a silhouette at the rail, we cut to a body falling.

Gemma hits the pause button and turns on the light despite how visible it makes her. Something is wrong here, this is too familiar. She digs through the piles of screenplays on the coffee table until she finds *The Ghost of Hawk Tower* and, with it in hand, watches the next scene, Isabella Giori in a debutante ballgown and white opera gloves making an entrance on the arm of a slightly menacing young man.

The film isn't set in Carmel, and a lighthouse stands in for Hawk Tower. The dialogue is snappier in places. But it's the script in her hands, isn't it? The opening scenes are so similar. The body falling. The debutante ball. They are so like Gran's script. Or not Gran's? The script is typed on his typewriter with its dropped *m*, but the pencil edits on it aren't Gran's and the title page doesn't say "by Chazan." It doesn't credit anyone.

She turns off the movie midway through the debutante ball scene and pulls on her jeans and socks and shoes. She feels uneasy as she steps out the door into the darkness, Hawk Tower a looming shadow. She tells herself not to be silly, it was only a movie, the terror isn't real. And the sky is already lightening.

She walks to the point and climbs out onto Flat Rock. The sunrise is just beginning to redden the notch behind Carmel River Beach and the waves are swirling close enough that if she opens the bag and up-ends it at arm's length, Gran will settle into the sea. She pulls the little half gloves Gran gave her for her last birthday from her vest pockets, soft cashmere that covers her wrists, her palms, and her fingers to the first knuckles, but leaves her fingertips free. It's amazing how much warmer they make her feel.

An even bigger wave crashes, the spray dampening her face as the first bright ray of sunlight shoots from the river valley, just the tip of the sun. She scoots back a little. Thinks to move Gran back too, but if he's washed away maybe that will be a sign it's time to let him go.

You are not going to damn me for eternity to a red zip tie. Gran's voice in her head now. *This thing will never biodegrade.*

"If you're going to haunt me, Gran," she says, "the least you could do is give me some advice."

My advice? My advice is if you're serious about letting me go, bring scissors, for Pete's sake.

For Pete's sake. Such a Gran expression, she thinks as she climbs down from the rocks before she gets drenched and instead circles around to Memory Bench. She fishes a journal from the mailbox and finds several warm responses now to her bit about how Gran made chocolat chaud. She wants to respond that their responses make her feel less lonely, but they don't really. And it feels like any dishonest word here, even offered in kindness, doesn't belong.

Sam hurries along the curve on Scenic toward Gemma when he sees her at the mailbox bench, Nyx pulling the leash the whole way. He slows midway down the steps, wanting not to seem uncool, but Nyx keeps pulling.

Gemma exclaims, "Nyx!"

She unhooks the puppy and lifts her into her lap, leaving Sam holding the leash with nothing at its end. In a video game, this would mean something, this would be a metaphor and a clue. Or maybe it wouldn't. Maybe it would be Sam's moment of self-deprecatory humor Mads has in mind to include in every game they produce, like Hitchcock's movie cameos but with the twist that everyone gets to laugh at him. It was as effective in *Children of Chaos* as Mads predicted, the moment where the player is on the swings and, with no warning, a cartoon Sam pops up, nobody can avoid plowing into him and knocking him down. But he pops back up like a bobble-head when they swing back, and eventually the players see they have to jump off the swing after they topple him to proceed. *Free press*, Mads said. *Something everyone will want to talk about, to show they're in the know, and it's terrifically ironic, Sammie. You're in the way of your own game.* When Sam suggested they include a cameo for her too though, she said, *No, I'm too pretty. Guys never laugh at pretty girls for fear they'll offend them, and women never laugh at things guys don't find funny, not with guys around, anyway.* A classic Madison Amesbury line that ought to have sounded conceited, but Mads really does feel her beauty works against her. She does everything she can to look professional and serious, from the suits she wears to the geeky eyeglasses she doesn't need, not cute ones that match her eyes like Gemma's, but dark things shaped like Einstein's reading glasses. When Mads started wearing them in high school on a dare, she began winning debate tournaments without, she swore, changing anything else.

The end of Leo's red zip tie is peeking out of Gemma's jacket pocket. He thinks about saying something about Leo, but can't figure out what it might be.

Gemma says, "Have you ever seen any of Isabella's movies?"

He takes the question as an invitation to sit and talk with her, not so much because he thinks she means it that way as because he wants her to.

"I was just watching *Double Deception*," she says. "I only watched the beginning, but it was super creepy. Like the movies my Gran wrote."

"His movies are amazing," he says, realizing only as he says it that he's actually only ever seen one, with Mads. What an idiot he is. He spends his life on science and fact, oblivious to the art and poetry around him. Jeffers's *stars, fool-proof and permanent, / The birds like yachts in the air, or beating like hearts.* Leo's films, and Isabella's too. He's never seen any of Isabella's films. But then he doesn't suppose they've ever played his video game.

He thinks about the game he's working on, and a line from the poem he read this morning for inspiration: *She whispered to me, 'Orion is winter.'* The poem, about a girl who seduces her brother, is full of ghosts. As so often with Robinson Jeffers: Orion and ghosts.

"Did he really say what you said when we were dancing at Nepenthe?" Gemma asks. "My grandfather? About me being amazing?"

He catches her neck in his elbow and gives her a noogie, like he used to give Noah, then feels like an idiot for doing that too.

"And here I am, waiting for you to walk across that water," he says. "He swore his granddaughter could trip across the tops of the waves to Point Lobos and back by the time she was twelve, never mind the chop. That wasn't you?"

THEY WALK BACK ALONG THE coast together, pointing things out to each other: a snowy egret perched on a rock; two boys fishing; a fierce wave covering a huge sea stack, leaving little waterfalls streaming down it—Robin's "streaming shoulders" that Sam added to his idea file over Mads's objection that they can't require players to simply sit still for a moment and admire seawater streaming over rock. She trusts him. They trust each other. It's what makes any relationship work.

Gemma stops to examine a bit of found art laid out on the tree stump in the little cove in front of Point of No Return: three small shells, a tiny bouquet of pink and blue wildflowers, a large foxtail, and a small bit of driftwood holding down a single piece of paper. "It's a poem written in French," she says. "'Je t'suivre un poème?' I … follow you a poem?"

Je t'ecris un poème, it says, the writing nearly illegible and the small *e* written as if it were a capital. He saw it the morning he first met Gemma. But he doesn't say so. He too wants the line to read *I follow you a poem.*

Gemma takes a phone photo of the poem and puts it back under the driftwood. They cross the road then, and let Nyx sniff around the Carmel Dog Bar before heading up the stone steps he almost never uses, favoring the Point of No Return back door and the possibility of bumping into Leo and Iz, and now Gemma.

They forgo his balcony view to sit in Leo's Adirondack chairs and look through the now-dry photos they retrieved from his darkroom.

"They have to be from the 1950s," he says. "By the 1960s, Jeffers had sold some of his land, and cottages would have been going up where, in this photo, Tor House and Hawk Tower stand alone."

The girl in the photos looks so young, and they were clearly taken here in Carmel, which meant Leo would have had to be in his thirties at least. Leo with a teenaged girl? It's just not something Leo would have done. And the girl in those photos wasn't struggling financially the way Leo has told Sam he was in his first years up here, after he was blacklisted. The dress in that one photo—it looks as expensive as Mads's Monique Lhuillier.

"Maybe it isn't even Gran's camera," Gemma says, her focus to the sky over Hawk Tower as a murder of crows raucously alights from an enormous Monterey cypress, one of the thousands of saplings Robinson Jeffers planted here on what was once a bare, windswept point. "If it isn't my grandmother," she says, "I'm not sure I want to know who it is."

He considers her. There is more she has to say, and he wants to know it, he wants to know everything about her.

"My mother gave me a father who loved her, who was going to marry her," she says, her eyes behind the glasses moist. "Who would have loved me and been a wonderful father if he hadn't died before he even knew there was going to be a me. But I had to know more, so I went looking. I didn't even tell Mom I was doing it, I didn't ever tell her that I had. What I found though . . ." She strokes Nyx's puppy ears. "What I found was that my father was a soldier who died in a helicopter crash, not a war hero but simply a casualty of a training exercise gone wrong. And it turns out that when he died he left behind a wife who imagined herself happily married."

He says, "I'm sorry."

She shakes her head. "She had no idea of my mom or me until I showed up at her door, this eighteen-year-old brat who drove down from UCLA to San Diego to find answers she didn't have. Answers Mom clearly didn't want me to have."

He says, "You didn't mean to hurt that woman."

She says. "But I took her loving husband away from her just the same. And for what? My family was Mom and Gran. They both loved me so much. Why did I ever think I needed anything else?"

"Is that what you were doing, though? Looking for more? Or were you just trying to better understand your mom?" And when she doesn't answer, he says, "My mother was looking for her biological mother when she died. She had this idea that she was poor, that that was why she'd put Mom up for adoption. I don't think Mom wanted to confront her or even make herself known. I think Mom just wanted to provide for her, to give her the financial security she'd given Mom by giving her up." Realizing only as he says it that it's true, and one of the very few things he might do for his mom now that she's gone.

"Mads thinks—"

They turn at the sound of steps on gravel, Isabella crossing her driveway to join them before he can say that Mads thinks he ought to take a cue from Leo, he ought to let go of the past and focus on the future. Mads loved Leo, and she loves Isabella too. She likes to imagine they might have been late-life, octogenarian lovers. She couldn't tell whether Leo was in love with Isabella, she said, but Isabella was definitely in love with him. All those years, and he never remarried. And Iz never married at all.

While Gemma fetches coffee and tea, Iz picks up the photos.

"They're from a camera Gemma found here," he explains.

Iz studies the top photo, one of the woman in a hat, then one of the snorkeling photos. She smiles, amused—it's a funny photo—then sets these two on the bottom of the stack and goes through the photos one by one, pausing for a long time on the last one, the one in the dress in front of Leo's desk.

"Her face isn't shown in any of the photos," he says. "If it was Gemma's mother or grandmother, why wouldn't Leo have photographed her face?"

He can't quite tell what Isabella is thinking, whether she thinks he's ridiculous or she thinks he might be right.

"Gemma doesn't want this woman to be Leo's mistress?" She studies him for a moment, as if she knows exactly what Gemma wants but is less sure about him, then wipes the little table with a paper napkin and lays the photos down. She takes the pastries and small paper plates from the bag and feeds a bite to Nyx, who has been patiently watching her but already knows begging from Iz doesn't end well.

Gemma emerges with three mugs in hand. She too feeds a bite to Nyx. The dog is going to get fat.

Iz flips through the photos again then. "Lordy, your grandfather was a charming man, Gemma," she says. "But he would never have had an extramarital affair. Your grandfather was loyal to those he loved."

Iz had an increasingly harder time getting comfortable enough to sleep at night. She worried what would happen when the baby came and yet so wanted to get it over with. She had a recurring nightmare: It was opening night of *A Little Summer Romance*. She was in a theater seat with Mannix sitting beside her and all of Hollywood with them, the stars of the show and the studio heads and the press. The film rolled with the theater lights still on, and there she was on the screen, but she didn't look sixteen and inno-cent and elegant. She was pregnant and the audience was gasping, everyone turning to her with the same angry faces they'd offered Ingrid Berman's Oscar win.

The nights when Leo was away on a job or to sell a script were the worst. She could pass the days reading and making little notes in Leo's scripts, and she even started a script of her own, which was dreadful, she was sure, but still it was fun to write. In the quiet of the little cottage in the misty Carmel darkness though, every sound felt like the possibility someone would discover her here. Every hum of car wheels on pavement might be the press. What sounded like a shutter continuously clicking outside her window was only a tree branch in the breeze. The sound of footsteps in the early morning might be any-one, and although she knew it was Robinson Jeffers, she never could shake the fear that it might not be.

Well before dawn that September first, she heard a car slowing on the road outside. Leo was in Hollywood, staying in a motel under an alias so that anyone who might want to buy the Valentine's Day script he was trying to sell could contact him through their studio switchboards. She opened a gap in the blanket over the attic window to peek outside. No car lights. But was that the click of a car door? Like the quiet click of the door on Mannix's car that night he brought her to Carmel, that more often than not explained the night sounds. Someone arriving at the studio's cottage only to disappear days later without ever being seen.

But someone was at the side of the house, she was sure of it, sure she heard almost-silent footsteps on gravel. Was someone peeking through the window downstairs? Some sleaze reporter from one of the Hollywood rag magazines who'd sussed out the real reason *A Little Summer Romance* wasn't out yet? Hugh Bolin and Jennifer Leigh were in full view of their cameras, but where was this Isabella Giori whom Hedda Hopper had created such a stir about?

Was that a door creaking open? There was no escape if she were found up here.

She crept down the stairs and opened the door at the bottom just a crack. The room looked empty, silent.

She slipped from the stairway, moving as quietly as she could toward Leo's bedroom, to the back door and escape.

She opened the door to his room.

A dark shadow stood right there, just inches away. A cold hand on her arm.

"Isabella." Leo's voice. "I'm sorry, I was trying not to wake you."

THEY MADE COFFEE AND RETREATED upstairs, where Iz sat on the twin bed and Leo in the chair at the card table where he'd set up his typewriter for her to practice while he was away. Her new gold ring clinked against the warm porcelain of the coffee mug, the wedding ring that was only a costume, a prop, another role she played.

"You look pale," Leo said. "You haven't been eating, have you? You need to eat more. Surely you ought to be bigger by now."

Neither of them had any idea how big she should be though. She didn't have a doctor to ask. The studio had given her a number to call when the baby was coming but not a name or anything about who it would reach. A doctor or perhaps a midwife would come deliver the baby and issue a birth certificate in "the proper names," by which they meant Hugh and his wife. And Iz was being careful not to gain too much weight. The studio had quietly suspended payments under her contract on the excuse of the morals clause and would, as its terms allowed, add that time to the end after she returned. But she would have to return promptly. She couldn't have too much weight to lose.

"I have some good news for you," Leo said. "Columbia just suspended Kim Novak."

"She's already been loaned to Hitchcock. That was decided in May."

"She was promised a long vacation, so they've been waiting, and now she's refusing to report for filming unless Columbia renegotiates her contract."

Novak's contract still had five years left on it. She was only a year older than Iz, a model who'd played an extra in a couple films before she was discovered. But it wasn't the first time she'd defied the studios. Unlike Iz and everyone else, Novak refused to change her name. She had agreed, finally, to go by Kim rather than Marilyn only because it was hard for anyone whose last name wasn't Monroe to claim to be a Marilyn anymore, even though Monroe's real name wasn't Marilyn but rather Norma Jeane. But even after Harry Cohn insisted nobody wanted to see "a Polack," Novak insisted that her name was her name, and would always be.

Leo said, "So that opening for 'the new Grace' may still be up for grabs."

Iz wasn't due for another month though, as near as she could tell, and Hitchcock was to begin filming any day now. Jimmy Stewart would have other obligations. He couldn't stand at the ready while they found another actress. And Novak was represented by the William Morris

Agency, who would know how to play the hand they held without losing the pot.

"Tell me about the trip, Leo?" she said.

LEO'S FIRST TWO DAYS IN Los Angeles, he got no takers from the studios, so he called in a chip from a fellow he'd helped years before, a writer nobody would hire before Leo began editing his scripts, teaching him. The man called from his home that night to tell Leo he couldn't contact him anymore, not even to leave an alias and a number.

"I hoped you might be as generous with me as I've always tried to be with everyone," Leo said with as much dignity as he could muster, a gentle reminder that didn't rub the writer's nose in the fact that he'd still be nobody if not for Leo's help. People on the defensive were rarely as generous as Leo now needed him to be.

"Leave the script on the bench in Palisades Park where we used to eat lunch, and disappear. I won't stop if I see you," the man said, and he clicked off before Leo could ask when.

Leo had barely set the least smudgy of his carbons on the bench, the script pages secured with two rubber bands in each direction, when two people scooted it aside and sat talking for a long time. They stood again, finally, and continued up the path that ran the whole length of the palisades shadowing Santa Monica Beach from the pier to Salka's old place on Mabery Road. Someone else sat and picked up the script, looked at it long enough to read the first page and set it back down as if they couldn't be less interested. It had been nearly three hours, Leo watching surreptitiously from a distance and about to give up and retrieve it, when someone on a bicycle scooped it up without even seeming to. All Leo saw was his back, a man with dark hair and medium build who might or might not have been the fellow himself pedaling up the path.

The following evening the phone rang in Leo's musty motel room. He took a deep breath, half hoping it was Iz calling, but knowing he had to hope it was the friend.

"I'll buy it outright for eight hundred. I'm doing you a favor. I doubt it will ever be made."

Leo sat on the tired bedspread covering the lumpy mattress, thinking he ought to try to talk him into more but afraid to risk losing the deal, even such a lousy one. He reached down to scratch the bed bug bites on his calf, then made himself stop.

"Yes, sure," he said.

He ought to have said thank you, not because he was grateful but to keep this line open in case he was ever this desperate again. But he couldn't bring himself to thank the fellow for robbing him blind.

"An envelope will be taped under the same bench," the man said and, again before Leo could ask what time, hung up.

It took Leo forever in rush hour traffic to get from his cheap motel in the valley to Palisades Park, only to find a couple sitting on the bench, watching the sunset. The woman said something. The man responded. There was tension in the short exchange. The woman rose and walked away. The man stood watching her for a moment, then followed.

Leo grabbed the bench before anyone else could.

He sat on one end and quickly felt around underneath it. No envelope.

Another couple approached. Could they share the bench? It was such a beautiful sunset.

"I have friends joining me," he said, looking about for someone he might claim as his friends, then simply ignoring the couple in hopes that sitting beside a hostile man wouldn't appeal.

As they left, he slid to the middle of the bench and sat with his legs sprawling, making it awkward for anyone who might have the idea of joining him.

After a few moments, he reached under the bench in the middle. No envelope. But it could be anywhere. It could be taped along the back edge, where it was harder to reach surreptitiously. It might not be there yet. It could have been taken by someone else.

"Do you have the time?" someone asked, startling him.

He checked the watch that had been his father's and answered, "Seven," hoping the man would drop an envelope of cash before he wandered off again. The man did not.

People were walking by now, eyeing him the way people do when there are limited seats and one person is taking space that might be enjoyed by four.

A policeman approached, making him nervous. How would he explain it if the officer found eight hundred dollars in an envelope taped under the bench?

Leo kept his head down. Opened the newspaper he'd thought to grab on his way out of his motel room. The policeman slowed. Leo was sure the man could smell his fear. He stopped on the path just before the bench.

Leo felt it would be less suspicious to look up than not to.

The policeman, too, had stopped to take in the sunset, the sun coloring the sky yellow and orange as it dipped toward an ocean that, down here, lapped unremarkably up to the wide, straight sand beach below, with nothing of the arc of the bay or the dramatic crash against rocky shore that made the Carmel beaches so stunning.

After the policeman said good evening and walked on, Leo waited, the minutes ticking by slowly from 6:57, which had been the exact time when the passerby had asked. When Leo looked up again, the sun was low, glowing alien red through a fog rolling in.

He looked around again to make sure the policeman was gone, then reluctantly moved to the end of the bench, sure that the moment he did so someone would join him.

The envelope was there, leaving him to wonder how long it had been and how lucky he was that nobody else had discovered it first.

The moment he stood, someone else was there, asking if he was leaving.

He waited until he returned to the motel to count the bills, but the money was all there. He used some of it to pay as he checked out

a few minutes later and climbed back into Tubby for the long drive
back, not wanting to spend another night in that dank room even if
he'd already paid for the privilege and would have to drive through the
night to get back to Carmel.

"THE MONEY SHOULD BE ENOUGH to see us through this if we're careful,"
he told Iz. By "this," he meant her giving birth. He was not going to
leave her again until she had the baby, although he couldn't have sworn
whether that was for her sake, or if he simply couldn't bear to humiliate
himself like that again. "As Albert Maltz said of Edward Dmytryk, 'He
has not now made peace with his conscience, he has made it with his
pocketbook and his career.'"

Dmytryk, one of the Hollywood Ten, had fled to Europe rather
than serve time, then spent four months in prison before changing his
mind. After he named names, he directed *The Caine Mutiny*, which
lost all seven Oscars it was nominated for to Elia Kazan's *On the
Waterfront*. Kazan, like Dmytryk, had at first refused to name names,
then capitulated. By then, most of Hollywood had turned against
those on the blacklist.

Eight hundred dollars for a script even that hack could sell for ten
thousand or more. The experience had been even worse than that
week Leo spent fixing that script for Gary, living in that closet on the
set. There had been nothing of his heart in that, it was just a job fixing
someone else's mess. This was his own work. This was who he was.

The first Monday morning in October, Iz and Leo went to The Tuck Box for breakfast. She'd seen an ad for the little teashop in the *Carmel Pine Cone* and been charmed by the idea of choosing among its whimsical and beautiful teapots. Leo held the odd-shaped gray door of the fairy-tale building open for her, and held her chair.

"May I have the cow teapot?" Iz asked. She'd loved the picture of it in the advertisement.

The waitress pointed to an old lady at another table already holding a spotted cow by his tail as tea spilled from his mouth. "How about the elephant?" the waitress suggested.

Iz said that would be lovely and Leo chose a red ladybug with a yellow head. "But could we have coffee, please," Isabella said.

"Sorry, ma'am, but the teapots are only for tea," the waitress said.

Iz and Leo looked at each other. Coffees, they agreed. Yes, mugs would be fine. They ordered food too, and a few minutes later, the waitress set the elephant teapot in front of Iz and the ladybug in front of Leo, and poured. Coffee. She smiled and put a finger to her lips.

The buttermilk waffles were delicious, Iz was just forking a second bite of them and nodding at what Leo was saying about the opening scene of her script, which she'd finally worked up her nerve to show him, when she felt the first slight pull at her stomach. Was she imagining it? She didn't say anything to Leo. She didn't know what to say. She wanted to get this over with, to have it done and get back to her life. But she was terrified. She had no idea what to expect. Back then, a girl relied on what her mother told her, what her dearest friends might have talked about if they had children, if they even remembered any of it, which they mostly didn't because the drugs made you forget. And Isabella's mother was not a woman who would talk to her daughter about childbirth before her wedding day. Isabella's friends were actresses like her, who wouldn't risk the truth of a pregnancy coming out.

The second contraction came perhaps an hour after they'd walked back to the cottage. Leo was at the typewriter. Iz was upstairs, trying to work what Leo had said into a better opening scene.

At the third contraction, she called the number Mannix had given her. She said as she'd been instructed, "I'm the friend." Not Mr. Thau's friend. Not Mannix's friend. A friend of nobody willing to be named.

A voice she'd never heard before. Male. Judgmental, she thought, but perhaps that was her own judgment against herself. "How often and how long?"

And when she told him, "Don't call again until they've been a minute long and four minutes apart for an hour."

The contractions remained far apart and not very strong all day and into the evening, but that night, they started getting stronger and longer, closer together, Isabella's body taking over, leaving her nothing but pain and panic and dread.

LEO, TIMING ISABELLA'S CONTRACTIONS ON his watch, called the number again. He handed the phone to Iz since she was supposed to be alone, then held her hand even more tightly as they awaited the doctor's arrival. He wasn't sure whether his grip was meant to comfort her or to steady himself, to stave off memory and guilt.

His sister had been just a child herself when she had her child, he saw that now, he understood that. And he'd done everything his mother had asked him to back then, both during the pregnancy and at the birth. He boiled the water and brought the rags, all the while trying to appear less terrified than he was as Margalit screamed. But he never did take her hand. He'd spent the long months of her confinement hoping she would lose the baby, and even as she was giving birth, he hoped it wouldn't survive. He couldn't bear the shame the child would bring on his family. It was a shame nobody yet knew of; they'd been so careful about that. But the baby, once born, would have to be explained, and his mother claiming it as her own in order to save Margalit's reputation would be his shame too. His father had left them all in his care.

It was only after the birth that he began his involvement with the Resistance. If his sister could put them at risk for nothing at all, surely he could do so for the cause of victory over the Nazis—that was what he told himself, what he told his mother when she asked him to explain where he disappeared to at night. He had been so lonely, living in the country with only his mother, his sister, and his little brother, and now a baby who kept them up all night. Slipping out to deliver Resistance papers brought him into contact only with a man named Jacques who wasn't, he knew, even really called Jacques, someone he'd met simply by lurking in the shadows because he could do that, he was good at moving about unseen and he loved the way it made him feel, like he could do anything. The man had surreptitiously posted a Resistance newspaper early one morning when it was still dark and even the Germans were warm in their beds, and Leo, who was not yet Leo, had surprised him with his presence, his heart pounding as exhilaratingly as it had that night he'd had his first taste of love, or of sex, anyway.

Margalit's child had not yet been a year old, just beginning to call their mother "Mama" and Margalit herself "Gaga," when the Nazis came for them. He didn't suppose that the German soldiers who took them off were fooled about whose child she was. Perhaps one of them recognized his own features in her face, and maybe he'd been surprised or maybe he hadn't, maybe he'd known Margalit was pregnant and simply refused to own that the child was his.

After they were taken away—his mother and sister and brother and the baby—Leo told himself they would all be together, with his father too, and the grandparents and aunts and uncles and cousins who'd stayed behind, they would all be together back in Germany without him, although he knew on some level that men and women sent to the camps were separated, that they were worked until they could no longer work, then left to die where they'd fallen, or shot.

It wasn't until after the war, though, that he learned that the baby whose name he had never spoken would not have survived the day they arrived at the camp, that she would have been taken from the arms of his sister or his mother, he would never know which, and handed to some stranger to be carried to her death. That his beautiful sister had been assigned to a brothel, made available solely to the Nazi SS until she managed to slip a knife from the clothes of one of them while he was sleeping and plunge it into her own neck.

He told himself as he held tightly to Isabella's hand, as Isabella cried out in pain just as Margalit had, that the past was past, that he lived on for his parents, for his family. He lived in a new world where there was no Hitler, no mass roundups or camps. But Hitler had been dismissed in Germany until he wasn't, until forty-nine days after he was installed as chancellor, he opened Dachau to imprison those who opposed him. Persecutions could turn quickly darker. A society set free of the bonds of civility to air its grievances devolves into a mob more rapidly than most imagine. People with good intentions who stand silent in fear for themselves allow a mob marching on the excuse of righteousness to trample everything in its path, and in the path of the leader whose purposes it serves.

He told himself that the leaders of the anti-communist witch hunts here in America had not yet reached the White House. President Eisenhower seemed a good man. He'd led the world to victory during the war and was now promoting a new civil rights act. But Vice President Nixon had made his career championing the red scare, and now a decade into it, fewer stood in its path than at the beginning. Leo couldn't see how it would end.

G emma hands Sam the *Ghost of Hawk Tower* script and explains that each slug line marks the start of a new scene. If he just imagines it as directions for a movie, it's not hard to follow. "The script is interlineated," she says. "You can read the handwritten changes or not, it doesn't matter."

He says after reading for a few minutes, "This isn't all that different from the game I'm working on. The Hawk Tower setting is even the same, although in a video game, if you had to throw an unarmed person off the top of a tower to progress to another level, that would be sick. And not in a good way."

"Great. You don't have to read the whole script, I just wanted you to have the feel of it," she says as she points the remote at the TV.

There, in the credits, is Isabella Giori.

"She got Oscar nominations for both acting and screenwriting for this one," Gemma says.

They watch for maybe ten minutes, until the body falls from the top of the lighthouse and Isabella appears on-screen in her debutante gown and white opera gloves. Gemma pauses the movie there, trying to imagine herself in a dress like that and glad for her own clean underwear and shirt—thanks to those old ten dollar bills she found in the Folgers can here and a quick pass through one of the little shops in town.

"So what do you think?" she asks.

"You mean, is this movie the script I was just reading?"

"You think so too, right?"

"What's Hawk Tower in the script is a lighthouse, but other than that, sure. So far. Body falling from a height, that's definitely the same."

"The script was in Gran's safe."

He looks at the script, which has no byline.

"The film credit is Isabella, but it's typed on Gran's typewriter." She shows him a dropped *m*. "Do you think she fronted it for him?"

"You could ask her?" he says.

"If she hasn't already admitted it and had the credit restored, why would she now?" she says. "She didn't win either Oscar, but this film made her career."

And the marked changes aren't Gran's. That's what she can't sort out. Maybe they remade the film, or were going to, and Isabella borrowed Gran's typewriter to update the script?

They watch for another hour before Gemma grabs the remote, saying, "Was that her, in that gown again but from the back?" as she rewinds and freezes on the strapless dress and bare shoulders and back.

"Isabella?" Sam says, confused.

"In Gran's photos."

Not photos, even. Film Gran left undeveloped in a camera he kept for half a century.

She hits play again and they watch more closely, vacillating between thinking the woman in Gran's photos and this young Isabella up on the screen could be the same person and thinking they aren't.

"The shoulders in the photo could be Mads's shoulders as easily as Iz's," Sam says. "They're beautiful and fine-boned and square like hers. There isn't anything really to distinguish them."

Gemma shrugs off the irritation of Sam's risotto-making, Rose Parade queen and champion runner girlfriend having perfect shoulders to go with her perfect nose and hair.

"If it's Iz, why didn't she say so?" Sam says.

They give up and watch the movie through to the unsettling end, until Isabella herself is revealed to the audience but not to the prosecution as the murderer, until she says, "I can't say that in public, no decent woman can say that," refusing to testify against the suspected murderer, leaving the prosecution no witness to call.

"She literally gets away with murder," Sam says.

"While exonerating the man who is to be prosecuted for her crime!" Gemma hates to say it, but it's better than any of Gran's films. What she wouldn't give to write a script like that.

Iz is just home from dinner at Mission Ranch with old friends from Hollywood when she catches sight of Leo's TV paused on a shot of her in that dress Hitchcock himself designed, with her hair the exact shade of blond he wanted it to be. The TV goes dark. Iz ducks into her cottage and watches through the window as Gemma emerges with Sam and Nyx, heading the way Sam has improbably taken to walking Nyx every night. He comes out his back door and cuts through the Tor House garden to scramble down to the road and the ocean—the long, hard way around to the same place the steps from his own balcony would take him. This route has something to do with a computer game he's designing, Iz gathers. Traveling this path to gain a sense of what it's like to be in a place you don't really belong and yet leaves you feeling at home.

As they disappear through the gate, Iz impulsively slips over to Leo's cottage. She hasn't been alone here in decades, not really, not even the morning Leo died. The last time, she supposes, was when Leo left to sell that Valentine's Day script (which never was made into a movie, so maybe the writer who paid Leo eight hundred dollars really was doing him a favor). That wasn't long before the doctor handed the baby to Leo in the attic bedroom, saying to him as if Iz weren't there, as if Leo rather than she had been the one to endure all those hours of labor without anything for the pain, "Better if the mother doesn't get attached. I'll confirm that the child is healthy and issue a birth certificate."

Confirm to Hugh, he meant. Issue a birth certificate in the names of Hugh and his wife.

"He'll come in the morning for the child," the doctor said, still addressing Leo.

After he left, Iz turned away and closed her eyes. She supposed the doctor was right that it would be better if she didn't see or touch or name.

Leo took the baby downstairs, where cans of formula sat on the kitchen counter and the drapes were pulled. He settled in on the sofa, where she could hear him with the child but couldn't see them. "Hey, you. You're really something, aren't you?" he said in the warmest voice she had ever heard.

Now moonlight splashes the coffee table piled with Leo's old scripts, all the joy he gave the world through his writing long after that same world shunned him, and shunned him again. The script she has come for is abandoned on the couch Leo and she used to sit on, not the original couch but a replacement of a replacement. The cover page, she can see even in the moonlight, doesn't include "by Chazan," who was both Léon Chazan and wasn't.

She inhales deeply, the scents of lemon cleaner and of Leo, the slightly musty smell of old paper, the ink of his typewriter ribbon, his scotch, and she takes the script and slips back into the once unnamed cottage that is now her Manderley.

G emma zips her vest against the cold as they pass the Doris Day steps, heading for Memory Bench. Even before Sam sits, he reaches into the little mailbox and pulls out the journal in which she wrote about Gran's chocolat chaud. She takes it from him as if of course he means it for her. Could she bear to have him read about her private grief, much less right in front of her? He pulls out another journal, and they settle in, with Nyx on the bench between them.

She tries to read a few responses someone has left to her own journal entry, while Sam writes in the moonlight, but the light is too dim to make out the faint words and she doesn't want to use the light of her phone, so she just sits there, pretending to read. Nyx nuzzles her hand, and Gemma sets it on the puppy's head and gently pets her, which seems to be what Nyx wants here, what Gemma herself wants, what anyone sitting on this bench must want.

Sam clicks his pen closed, then recites the poem he's put down there in tidy handwriting, "Carmel Point" by Robinson Jeffers. It's about the beauty in the granite here, as safe as "the endless ocean that climbs our cliff," and how we need to "unhumanize" ourselves and become more like the natural world we were made from. "'As for us: / We must uncenter our minds from ourselves,'" he says.

The hoot of an owl mixes with the ocean sounds. Another owl responds.

"I lost my whole family," he says. "A plane crash on their way to my graduation. Mom and Dad. Eliza and Noah. Grandpa and Grandma and Papa and Nan." He sets a hand on Nyx's neck, rubs it. "Even the puppy they were bringing me for a graduation gift."

Gemma's and Sam's hands settle against each other's just at the outside. She wants to say something comforting, but she can't imagine what. Eliza, the name he called to in his dream. Not a lover but a sister he'll never see again except in the lucky moment of a dream he will always wake from.

"Mom was an experienced pilot. Grandfather too. But they hit a flock of geese on takeoff out of Columbus after they picked up Papa and Nan. They're buried back in Connecticut. I don't know why. That was home, I guess. And there was no thinking then, really. There was just numbly going through the motions, nodding yes or no to the choices Mads and André put in front of me. They did everything. I couldn't, so they did."

Gemma thinks of the name he gave his place here: Point of No Return, the moment when your fuel source will no longer get you home again, when you have no choice but to head somewhere else.

"I know we've just met, Gemma," he says. "We're not like Mads and André and me, but if there is anything I can do to help you now . . ."

Gemma begins to weep then. She doesn't even know why. She wants to tell him about the night she and Gran scattered Mom's ashes onto the ocean from the very rocks they're overlooking, clambering down to the point by flashlight, and Gran ninety-three too, she had no business asking him to come with her but it had seemed so important to let Mom go here, at this beautiful rocky point. She wants to tell Sam how they took a flask of Mom's favorite bourbon, how they toasted her with it, then poured the last of it over the granite where some of her ashes had blown back and landed, so that the love that was her mom could float all over the world and yet always be here for her too. She wants to share this and let it go, the way she guesses everyone who writes in these journals wants to. She wants to uncenter her mind from herself.

Sam sets a hand on Nyx's neck and laps his pinkie over Gemma's.

He doesn't say anything. He doesn't ask why she's weeping or try to stop her. He allows her whatever it is she needs here.

After a moment, he opens the journal, clicks the pen, and begins to write again. Maybe it's another poem, or maybe these new words are his own, and maybe he's writing for himself or maybe he's writing in order to give her space to. That's what she does. She leans forward to get a pen from the Memory Bench mailbox, and she opens the journal again, this time to a fresh page, and she writes that she has Gran's ashes in a plastic bag with a red zip tie, that she talks to him and he talks back to her, but he seems only to want to make her laugh.

She needs to let him go here, to join her mom. But if she can't keep the cottage, they will be so far away. How will she ever be with them?

They sit like that for a long time, side by side in the darkness, writing their own words, unburdening their hearts.

Gemma closes her journal and looks out to the moonlit point, imagining her mom's long legs, still alive and younger than she remembers them, emerging from the sea, the water running from her skin as she makes her way onto a white sand beach across the ocean, a place where the sun is shining and children are digging in the warm sand. Mom walks up to a little girl with blond hair and freckles, blue bifocals and a blue bucket, a red plastic shovel, and she kisses the top of her head, and the girl looks up, and the girl is her.

Sam takes the journal and pen from Gemma's hands, and he puts them and his too back into the mailbox, and he pulls Nyx into his own lap and moves beside Gemma so that his thigh against hers warms her. He sets an arm on the bench behind her, not exactly touching her but providing comfort. Nyx lays her chin on Gemma's thigh as a wisp of fog passes before the moon, shadowing it for a moment before moving on and allowing the moonlight to bathe them again.

"Something about this place," he says. "This sand. These rocks. The ocean crashing against them sometimes, and other times just gently lapping. It's not so much that the loneliness goes away here as that I can think of them, I can remember them."

October 1957

Two days after Iz gave birth, the doctor showed up with a birth certificate for a child whose name was listed simply as "Baby" and whose mother's name was not Isabella Giori or even Fanny Fumagalli. A baby she'd never seen herself, although she heard Leo tending to her, feeding her, changing her diapers.

"Who is she, the mother listed here?" Iz asked the doctor.

Mary Smith.

"She's your savior," he said. "Be grateful for her, and don't ask."

"But no father," Iz said. "And no baby name."

Mannix had called her by then to tell her Hugh would not take a baby girl. "He already has three daughters," Mannix told her.

Genevieve. Faith. Clairey. They all looked like their mother. If the baby had been a boy, Hugh would have taken him and loved him. He so wanted a son. But a daughter . . . What if she looked like Iz? What if even his wife could see her eyes in the child's, her nose that had been fixed only slightly, her jaw and neck and collarbone? What if his daughters could see their baby sister was so different from them?

"You'll have to keep her for another day or two while we arrange something else," Mannix had said.

Another day of Leo tending to the baby in the back bedroom while Iz stayed in the attic, where she'd bled so heavily at first that she was sure she was hemorrhaging. Another day of her breasts, wrapped tightly the way the doctor showed her, feeling every sound the baby made.

"The papers are all in order for the child to be adopted," the doctor said when he showed up with that birth certificate. "This is what has been arranged, to protect against the scandal you'd be caught up in were your name attached to the child. That's all you need to know. Someone will come for the baby tomorrow, to take her to an orphanage until parents can be found."

"An orphanage?" Iz said. "But for how long?"

"WHAT WOULD YOU HAVE ME do, Leo?" Iz asked when he questioned putting the baby up for adoption. The baby fussed a little, asleep in Leo's bedroom. The child could sleep through Leo's typing, but she woke to the sound of Iz's voice, as if she understood that Iz meant to abandon her.

"The only thing I can do is act," Iz said. "I would have no way to support—"

"You could marry me."

"Oh, Leo, don't—"

"I mean it. Marry me."

She looked away, to the curtains covering the bay window, Ole Mr. Miracle sitting silent on Leo's desk. "But you don't love me."

The days at those beaches, and snorkeling. Even watching the Oscars together, Iz in that gorgeous dress. He admired her. Perhaps he thought she was beautiful. He did, yes. She saw that from the way he photographed her. And yet, except for that one kiss on the couch in the studio's cottage, he was unfailingly the gentleman.

"Your baby would have a father," he said. "I would have a family." His dark eyes sincere.

"But, Leo, you could—"

"I would always be loyal to you, Isabella. I swear I would."

In the other room, the baby made a noise. Leo looked, listened until the cottage was quiet again.

"We can have the doctor issue the birth certificate in our names," he said. "Nobody will ever know I didn't father her."

"The doctor—"

"He'll do it for a price, the same way he does things for a price for Mannix and the studio. He'll list me as the father."

"But he'd know about it. The doctor would."

"He's not likely to offer up that he knowingly falsified a birth certificate—which he's already doing. He'll have every reason to choose to believe I *am* the father. And who would say I'm not?"

October 1957

All that long night before they were to come for the baby, to take her to the orphanage, the typewriter clacked away downstairs. Somehow the noise didn't wake the baby. She woke at night only when she was hungry. Surely she wouldn't be long in an orphanage, Iz thought as she lay in bed trying not to hear the sounds of Leo warming a bottle. Surely the child would go to a good family, to have a better life than Iz could ever give her.

The studio wouldn't even portray her as having had a baby on-screen, and even Ingrid Bergman was ostracized from Hollywood for years for becoming pregnant by a man not her husband—and she married the father. Would this be different if Hugh could marry her? The studio could still use the morals clause to cancel her contract, or choose to use her only in smaller roles, but they wouldn't want to alienate a star like Hugh. It didn't matter though. Hugh was not going to marry her. And she wasn't Ingrid Bergman. She wasn't Ingrid Bergman and she would never have a chance to be if she kept this baby.

But it was one thing to give the child over to Hugh, to know she would grow up in Los Angeles in a life Iz could imagine, with every privilege. A father who would love her. A mother and sisters and grandparents. Cousins and aunts. What if her adoptive father was abusive, as rigid and unforgiving as her own? What if her adoptive mother was meek, or even cold?

Iz woke to the sound of Leo's typewriter again, or still, and the phone ringing. The baby made no sound, but she was there in the smell of the cottage, in the way Iz listened even when she couldn't hear her.

The door to the attic bedroom opened. Leo knocked at the base of the stairs and called up, "Telephone."

Iz came down, still wearing the old shirt of Leo's she slept in, still feeling overwhelmed, thinking Hugh ought to be overwhelmed too, but Hugh would be thought crazy to consider giving up his career to raise this child.

The receiver sat on the desk by the phone. Leo had disappeared into his bedroom, where the baby slept.

"A family has been found," Mannix said. "An excellent East Coast family."

Someone who knew someone who knew someone, with at least one of those someones and perhaps all of them being Mannix or perhaps even Mr. Thau. They were already making arrangements to come to San Francisco, where Mannix had arranged for the baby to be given to them, far away from Los Angeles and Hollywood and any connection to Iz.

"We think it would be easiest to keep this quiet if you keep her until they arrive," Mannix said. "It will probably be a week or two."

When Iz hesitated, Mannix said. "The baby will grow up with every privilege. You won't need to think about her ever again. All you need to do is get yourself back in shape so we can get you back in film."

IT WAS THIRTEEN LONG DAYS before Mannix called again—the day before the adopting parents were finally to arrive in San Francisco. Iz assumed that was what he was calling about, but he was going on about the new Hitchcock film.

Iz was cranky. She was sitting at Leo's desk, peering through a gap in the closed curtains to the empty road and the gardens at Tor House, the burly stone of Hawk Tower, the early-morning sky a relentless gray. Was this Mannix's way of telling her the couple from Connecticut had changed their minds? What would she do then?

"Listen to me, Isabella. You're not hearing what I'm saying. I'm saying Hitchcock read your script and he wants to do it."

"Kim Novak is already—"

"It's a great cover story for where you've been too. The press will eat it up: budding starlet writes the role of a lifetime for her big break-out movie."

Iz peered out through the crack in the drapes again, afraid to ask what Mannix was talking about—what script?—lest she dissuade him from salvaging her career.

"He's a man who wants who he wants," he said, "and now he wants your script and he wants you to play the lead."

Her script?

"You're going to loan me to Hitchcock?" she said. "That's what you're saying?"

"But we have some issues with the script ourselves," Mannix said. "Mr. Thau isn't thrilled that you sent it to Hitchcock without talking to him about it first. He has your reputation to protect."

She might have laughed, but Mannix was serious. Her reputation: young, virginal. It was, she understood, his way of saying that the studio would stay with her as long as her out-of-wedlock child wasn't discovered. If word got out, they would cut her loose. But all she had to do was appear to be as good a girl as they portrayed her to be.

The baby began to cry as Mannix spoke again, Iz's breast barely responding now as Leo began to coo to her.

"I'm sorry," she said to Mannix. "What did you—"

"He too has some changes he wants to discuss with you. It's a great script, but that doesn't mean it can't be better, and he's used to being very involved. He often writes much of a script himself."

"Hitchcock?"

"He's at his place in Scott's Valley, Heart o' the Mountain. They're shooting with Stewart and Novak up in San Francisco. He wants you to meet with him late this afternoon. Can you get there? It's not much more than an hour up the coast. Chazan has a car? I'd take you myself but there isn't time."

"For changes?"

"Notes on your script, yes. This *is* what you wanted, right? Why else would you have sent it to him? Get yourself dolled up—Hitch likes his women pretty—and get on up the coast. Wear a girdle and a loose dress. That will cover a lot of sins, and your legs and your shoulders and arms look terrific. You're bustier still? But that isn't a bad thing. Call me when you're leaving, and we'll let him know when to expect you. Take your things with you. He'll likely invite you to spend the night, and if not we'll get you a room up there. You'll need to come straight back to LA afterward, to get Mr. Thau's thoughts on the script."

October 1957

Of course Hitchcock wants to make it. That's why I sent it to him," Leo said in a low voice, so as not to wake the baby.

When he'd heard Isabella hanging up after talking with Mannix, he'd given her the new carbon of *The Ghost of Hawk Tower*, and made them coffee and oatmeal while she read the new ending. Nothing else had much changed, except that new twist which it seemed had been there all along, waiting for him to see it. It was already set up. He'd needed to make surprisingly few changes in the rest of the script to make it work. And when he'd finished it and reread it and knew it was right, he'd typed a new title page with her name on the byline and mailed it from the post office in Salinas when he went to buy baby formula and bottles and diapers.

He ought to have told her he was sending the script to Hitchcock, but he knew it would make her uneasy, and he could bear neither to send it over her direct objection nor to refrain from sending it.

"I can't take your script, Leo," Iz said. "I can't pretend your work is mine."

"The new ending will leave everyone talking," he said. "It will set you free to play any kind of role you want."

Which was why he'd changed it. Freeing himself in this small way by freeing her. Hitchcock would make the movie, and Leo himself would know it was his own work. He didn't need to have the world know it was his, he just needed the world to be moved by it, to be changed, to see life a little differently. To see death a little differently too.

"It's the perfect role for you, Iz," he said. "And you heard what Mannix said: Hitchcock has read it. He wants to do it *with you*."

"Oh Leo, there isn't an actress in this world who wouldn't want this part. You could—"

"We wrote it together."

She'd been there to read and comment, improve, but more than that, he'd started the script with her in mind. He'd at first been unable to get beyond that opening scene, written in anger just after he'd learned she was pregnant. He had the idea of who he thought she was in mind, the ending the one he thought she should have, but he hadn't really known her then, before she moved in with him. It was only with her overhead as he worked that the words came.

"We made it the perfect part for you," he said, "and this is the way to make sure you get to play it."

He took their cups into the kitchen, refilled them from the percolator, and set a fresh cup on the little table in front of her.

"You said it yourself, Iz: it's already 'a Hitchcock film.' At its center we have a common man dropped into nightmarish circumstances, just the way Hitch likes. A man with a guilt-ridden childhood that ripples into the present on Freudian dreams. An enchanting blonde . . ." He touched her darkened hair, which he'd come to prefer. "An enchanting blonde Hitch can long to control and yet be daunted by. Voyeurism."

"Surveillance," she said. "Distrust of authority."

The baby stirred, as she so often did at the sound of Iz's voice, but didn't wake.

"An unhealthy dose of sexual fetish," he said. "Violence of the type Hitch can never resist. And a bit of cross-dressing, which fascinates and repels him, or so he would have us believe."

"Paranoia," she said.

"And shame and more shame and more."

"And murder."

"A nice, polite murder steeped in the repressed emotions of a nice, appropriately respectable murderer."

She grinned. "Murderess. I love the new ending."

Yes, he wrote that for her. She would like to imagine committing murder. He rather liked imagining it for her.

"But Leo, I can't possibly bluff my way through talking to Hitchcock about the details of your script."

It was one thing to fool Mannix, who had no idea what it meant to write a script, and another to fool Hitchcock—she was right about that. And if Alma was there, so much the worse. Hitchcock's wife was a writer too, equally brilliant and far less gullible when it came to attractive blondes.

"This will just be to negotiate a price," he said.

"Mr. Thau has already done that," Iz said.

"Thau has?"

"That's what Mannix said. He said under my contract, I'm theirs for $150 a week."

"For your acting," he said.

Leo looked to the script now in his hands, the byline "by Isabella Giori." The single carbon. He'd sent Hitchcock the original. He'd typed it fresh, incorporating the last of Isabella's penciled changes and some of his own added as he typed, and the new ending.

"You'll be fine even if it *is* notes," Leo said. "Hitchcock is a friend to those of us who find it difficult to work in Hollywood these days. He's quietly insisting Norman Lloyd be hired as a producer for *Alfred Hitchcock Presents.*"

Lloyd, like Leo, was blacklisted.

Leo wrapped Isabella's fingers around the script. "I have one thing I would like to ask you for, not in exchange but . . ." He took a deep breath, setting hope aside. "But let's talk about that after you get back."

He took a sip of his coffee, down to the grounds again already, but he never did mind the grounds. If you had grounds in your cup, you were drinking real coffee. He never took real coffee for granted.

"Now, I believe if you look closely at your contract, you'll see it covers your acting but not your writing. And your contract has been suspended for all the months we've been writing this script. They haven't paid you a dime."

"I can't afford to alienate the studio."

"What do you imagine they'll do, Isabella?" he said. "Cancel your contract to pay you $150 a week when they've just agreed to loan you out for a thousand a week and pocket the difference?"

"A thousand a week!"

She was so smart, but so young too, still so pleased by a thing like a cow teapot, so inclined to underestimate herself. She was nearly as young as Margalit had been when she had her baby, and as easily taken advantage of. He had been so young too, he sees that now. But he ought to have taken care of them. He ought to have found a way to keep his family safe. He ought not to have put them at risk.

"The studios profit from loaning talent," he said to Iz. "That galled Hitchcock when he first came to Hollywood. When David O. Selznick brought him over from England, he was already Hitchcock, but he had the same standard seven-year contract everyone did."

Seven years because that was as long as the studios could legally bind anyone.

"He did *Rebecca* with David, but after that success David figured he could make easier money loaning Hitch out at a multiple of what he was paying him, and that's what he did for the next five years. Hitch did do *Spellbound* and *Notorious* with David, but only after David made a boatload loaning Hitch out for a half dozen other films."

He said, "The studio has as much to gain by loaning you to Hitchcock as you have in being loaned. Now, if I were you, I wouldn't give this script to him for less than twenty thousand dollars—"

"Twenty thousand! That's— I barely make twenty thousand dollars in three years."

"It would be worth seventy-five, maybe even more, if I weren't blacklisted." It was the best thing he'd ever written. "And you don't have to be scared you'll be caught fronting it. You'll keep that money, so there will be no trace for it."

"I can't—"

"You can. If Hitchcock has notes on it, that's fine, you can—"

"But really, Leo, if Hitchcock is already pushing to employ a black-listed producer—"

"If what I've heard about Norman Lloyd is true, that's the battle Hitch has chosen."

If he put his name on this script, that would open a second front, and nobody needed that.

"Now listen to me, Isabella. Don't let the fact that Hitchcock has notes frighten you."

Hitch was a particular brand of fanatic about control.

"All you need to do is listen. Better for a writer not to respond, not to defend her writing. Listen and write down what he says and nod prettily." Hitch did love a pretty girl. "Then bring the notes back to me. Tell him you'll need ten days to make the revisions."

"But what if he wants major changes, Leo? Or even a complete rewrite?"

He would, or he would think he did. Hitchcock didn't prefer full scripts. He "dictated" his pictures, he often said, by which he meant he liked to start with nothing more than an idea and a writer with whom he could thrash out a story for days on end, and drink with while he did. He liked to throw out random ideas for scenes the writer would then have to block out and shape into a story. He claimed not to read the endings in his source materials lest he get so saturated in them that he couldn't discard what he needed to—never mind that he struggled miserably with endings. And a brilliant ending was what made a good script into a great one. The "inevitable surprise." The best stories in any form—film or books or TV, short stories, perhaps even nonfiction—gave audiences unexpected endings that left you feeling you ought to have seen them coming, but didn't.

"Ten days," he repeated. "I can do anything in ten days."

And he wouldn't do much anyway, no matter what Hitch thought he wanted. This script was what it was meant to be, it was perfect for Isabella, and he wouldn't change it into anything else.

"What about the new twist?" Isabella said. "I love the twist, but the studio hates it. That's what Mannix was saying. Mr. Thau doesn't think the ending is right for my 'image.'"

"Hitch will battle the studio to keep the ending, so you won't have to. Not that he won't have thoughts. He will and they'll all be wonderful, and you'll write them down and bring them back here, and we won't likely use any of them because as wonderful as they'll be, they won't be right for this script. But Hitch, having proposed them, will believe he's the source of 'the Hitchcock imprint' this script already has. And anyway, I can do anything in ten days."

The baby fussed in the back room, but again didn't wake. Leo was relieved to find that Isabella's breasts didn't let down at the sound, or not so much that the milk leaked through the pads she'd fashioned for inside her brassiere. Alma would understand what a wet spot on a dress meant even if Hitchcock didn't.

"Just meet with Hitchcock," he said. "Keep your options open. Wear the yellow. You look good in the yellow and it will make an impression: yellow dress, yellow car."

She smiled a little, and she said, "I thought Tubby was 'buttercream.'"

He laughed and he said, "Wear the *buttercream* dress. Now, if Thau's name comes up for any reason when you're talking with Hitch, you refer to him as 'Benny.' You understand?"

"It suggests I'm his equal."

"Or his better. Young and gorgeous yes, but smart too. Ambitious. Confident."

"Ambition is not generally a plus in a woman."

"It will be for Hitchcock, and for Alma too. Don't underestimate Alma."

He then said, "Now, your hair." He'd gotten the hair dye the same day he went to the post office to mail the script to Hitchcock. "I'm afraid Hitchcock does prefer a blonde."

October 1957

An unpaved but oiled dirt road on Hitchcock's Scotts Valley property wound through an ominous cathedral of giant redwoods, leaving Isabella in shade so thick it might have been evening. If she were watching herself in a movie, creepy music would be playing, and she would be sitting in the theater seat urging herself to turn back, nothing good would come from going forward. Her grip on Tubby's steering wheel loosened only as she pulled to a stop at a Spanish-style white stucco home with a red tile roof and arches everywhere, so different than she'd expected. No darkness. No mystery. Just a landscape of hilltop beauty that appeared to stretch uninterrupted all the way to Monterey Bay.

She tried to shake off the feeling of being daunted as she pulled on the proper white gloves she knew Hitchcock loved and rang the front bell. The people who'd visited the Hitchcocks here were legend. Joan Fontaine's and Olivia de Havilland's mother helped find the property. Grace Kelly visited with Prince Rainier. Ingrid Bergman, when she was still spending time in the U.S. Jimmy Stewart. Cary Grant.

Iz touched her re-blonded hair, all that bleach Leo had used on it. *You don't have to decide anything yet, I know it's impossible to decide about anything now,* he'd said as he washed her hair afterward, and she knew he meant about the baby, but what choice did she have about the baby? She would be a miserable wretch if she gave up acting. She'd been a miserable wretch before she found her way to it. She had no other way to support herself, much less a child. The child would be so much better off with the family from Connecticut, a wealthy couple who wanted a child and couldn't have one, who would provide the child with the kind of family everyone would like to have.

She shoved her white-gloved hands into her coat pockets even though it wasn't cold now that she wasn't in the windy car. The perfect little cowrie shell Leo had given her that first afternoon at Hidden Beach was there. She'd forgotten it. As she took her coat off so she'd make a good impression in her buttercream dress, it seemed a good omen, that shell.

Hitchcock's daughter, who wasn't much younger than Iz, welcomed her into a house filled with music, something with strings playing so delicately that surely it must be Mozart, and the faint smell of cigars. Unbidden, she imagined her own baby grown into a teenager as this teenaged girl took her to a sitting room where Hitchcock was mixing drinks at a drinks cart.

"You'll need a martini after your drive, Miss Giori," he said, speaking as slowly and deliberately as he did on his television show. "Very dry—it's the only way to drink a martini, isn't it? Two jiggers of gin and a quick glance at the vermouth."

He was dressed, which was rather a relief. Mannix had warned her that he sometimes greeted guests like her, with whom he was discussing a script, in tailor-made silk pajamas and a dressing gown. He seemed an odd mixture of confident and shy here, away from a movie set. Not quick to meet her gaze although she'd seen him take her in as she'd entered.

"Thank you for seeing me, Mr. Hitchcock," she said. "And yes, a martini would be grand."

She didn't want to disappoint him by asking for anything but a martini, and she would take no more than a polite sip anyway. Even stone-cold sober and with all the time she'd spent reading drafts and contributing little bits as Leo wrote this script, it was going to be hard enough to convince someone as clever as Hitchcock that she had written it.

He handed her the drink, saying, "It's very nice to see you again." A kind way of letting her know he remembered those dozen steaks she'd cut into for him.

"Would you like to see the rose garden before we sit down to work?" he asked.

She said she would love to, eager to do just about anything that might make him like her enough that he wouldn't want to find out she was a fake.

He asked his daughter to take the drinks out to the veranda and let her mother know they would join her in just a few minutes. Iz breathed more easily despite the tightness of her girdle, knowing Mrs. Hitchcock would join them. She understood that Hitchcock had formed some sort of obsession first with Ingrid Bergman, then with Grace Kelly, although he had by all accounts remained close friends with them. She supposed he, like most men, was much better behaved in the company of his wife. And Leo had told her the two of them frequently worked together on the scripts he cared most deeply about, that Alma joining them would be a good sign.

As his daughter left, Hitchcock said, "It's just 'Hitch,' without the 'cock.'"

Iz smiled prettily, remembering Leo's advice that when you looked at Hitchcock, you'd best think of the strange little schoolboy inside him who smelled of the fish from his father's shop, who was made to stand at the end of his mother's bed every day and recite his sins.

On the way out to the rose garden, Hitchcock stopped at a hall closet to lift the needle on a record player. He slid the album into its paper sleeve and album cover, and tucked it into its particular slot in his extensive music collection. And the rose garden was as tidily kept as the record collection, all whitewashed brick paths and garden walls laid out with geometric precision, with white statuary and square plots of roses rich with fall blooms. This man who clearly ate and drank without restraint, exerting little control over his own person, seemed to need everything else to be just so.

He was keen to show Iz a mosaic hanging on one of the stone garden walls, two white birds outlined against a blue so vivid it might have been stained glass in a church. It was, he said, created by Georges Braque. "He was the French artist who, with Picasso, began the Cubist movement," he said, and he shared a bit about how he'd come to own it, leaving Iz feeling as if she'd stepped into a TV episode of *Alfred Hitchcock Presents*.

ALMA SAT ON A WICKER couch on the porch, Leo's script in her lap. She and Hitchcock were such an unmatched pair, he almost rounder than he was tall and with his ironic face, she with a tiny dancer's body and a face that, in repose, was slightly severe. But Hitchcock was known to say there were four people who were his most important collaborators, one a film editor, one a scriptwriter, one the mother of his daughter, and one a miracle cook, and their names were all Alma Reville.

"Well, what do you think, Mother?" he asked her.

Alma answered, "I think Miss Giori is very talented for a woman who has never written a screenplay before, or very generous, or both." Her face transformed as she spoke, into something softer and kinder.

"Here, sit by me so you can see the pages as we chat," she said to. Iz. "I'm Alma, by the way. And I like you already. Hitch and I both do. We like talented women and we like people who are willing to risk their own good fortune to help others. May we call you Isabella?"

"Yes, of course," Iz said as she settled in beside Alma, smoothing her dress not so much for the dress's sake as to assure herself that the girdle was there, that it would keep her looking more svelte than she felt. She understood from Alma's few words that the Hitchcocks suspected she might not have written this script, and that she wasn't to tell them if she hadn't.

She said, "Mrs. Hitchcock—"

"Alma," she insisted. "Now, the mood here is brilliant, dark and mysterious. The writing is quite accomplished."

Hitchcock interjected, "So many writers don't understand that there is no terror in the bang, only in the anticipation of it." He took a seat in a chair, sitting bolt upright. "There is plenty of anticipation here."

"Thank you," Iz said, marking the words in her mind so she could take them back to Leo.

"Of course, we have some thoughts," Hitchcock said.

"The dialogue is good already, thank heavens," Alma said. "Hitch doesn't prefer to write dialogue."

"It isn't that I don't prefer it," Hitchcock objected.

Alma said to him, "I was being polite, Hitch." Then to Iz, "Hitch is notoriously dreadful at dialogue."

"I think in pictures rather than words," Hitchcock said. "Now, Benny Thau tells me you are free to revise the script immediately and start filming next month?"

Iz said she was available for acting whenever the studio said she was, she was bound by contract for that. She gathered her courage then, hearing Leo's voice in her head.

"I don't know what Benny and you might have discussed about the screenplay," she said, the familiar "Benny" feeling awkward, but Leo was right that the more formal "Mr. Thau" would suggest a weakness that would cost her. "But my contract with the studio is for acting, not for writing."

Hitchcock looked to Alma, who smiled. She liked a woman standing up for herself.

Alma said, "Thau was going to sell it to Hitch for thirty-seven thousand dollars."

Iz tried to hide the shock she felt at this number. Leo had told her that if he weren't blacklisted and were selling it himself, he might get even more, but it was nearly as much as the studio would pay her for the entire five years left on her contract.

She said, "And yet it isn't Benny's to sell."

Hitchcock's eyes widened slightly, the only sign of his surprise. Iz wanted to turn to look at Alma beside her, but she dared not look away from Hitchcock, she dared not give any of the ground she'd just taken.

He said, "I will make you a star."

Iz sat quietly waiting, watching, as Hitch and Alma shared a glance that allowed Iz to adjust ever so slightly, so that she could see Alma too, if only just.

"If it were written by anyone with a name," Iz said, "you would pay seventy-five thousand or more for it."

Alma's eyes were suddenly livelier, she clearly relished a good negotiation.

"We felt thirty-seven was generous for a first-time writer," Hitchcock said.

The couple exchanged a longer look.

"Perhaps we could find our way to forty?" Alma said.

"I suppose we might do," Hitchcock said.

Iz sat quietly, waiting, as Leo had coached her to do, to let them talk themselves up.

Alma nodded ever so subtly to Hitchcock. He didn't exactly smile, but there was something in his expression that suggested he might actually be pleased.

He said to Alma, "We might find another ten, mightn't we, if Miss Giori would settle for fifty?" Then to Isabella, "I'm afraid I must hold on to enough of our budget to do you justice in wardrobe."

Iz smiled prettily again, at Alma first this time and then at Hitchcock. "All right then," she said as she pulled the notepad and pen Leo had given her from her pocketbook, prepared to write down every word they said and take it back to Leo.

Hitchcock tucked a finger to his eyelid, stifling a laugh, Iz thought, and he said, "It will give me no small amount of pleasure to tell Mr. Thau that a beautiful young woman has bested him at his own game."

Alma said to Iz, "He'll do no such thing. He knows better than to put you in such an awkward spot." Then, "Shall we start with the setting, Hitch?"

"Mr. Jeffers will be disinclined to have half of Hollywood trooping through his dear little home," Hitchcock said.

"I'm afraid so," Alma said.

"And we've been so long here shooting 'The Living and the Dead,' although it's beautiful here of course," Hitchcock said. "There is a point not far from the Jeffers place with a remarkable moving cypress tree we're able to film both on location and for the close-up in the studio." He grinned, looking to Alma to collect her appreciation for this little joke he was making about the tree, which wasn't real of course, but only a prop they trucked to the location.

"'Vertigo,'" Alma said.

"Pardon?" Hitchcock said.

They were all three distracted for a moment by the arrival of a delivery truck somebody else quickly attended to.

"We're not calling it 'The Living and the Dead' anymore; we're calling it 'Vertigo,'" Alma reminded him. Then to Iz, "Your setting, Isabella . . . Hitch is itching to travel after we're through at the studio. And he's gone off towers."

"That particular tower went off me," Hitch said. "We found the perfect tower for 'Vertigo.'" He glanced at his wife to make sure she saw he had the film title right this time. "But before we managed to get the scenes filmed, they tore it down."

"Dry rot," Alma said.

"It's only a movie," they said at the same time, and the two of them laughed easily together.

"We've had to resort to using a painting to add the tower to the movie," Alma said.

"A taller tower," Hitchcock said.

Iz smiled, amused and yet fairly certain their exchange wasn't meant so much for her amusement as for their own.

Alma patted the script. "So for this one, Hitch would prefer a lighthouse. We've learned of one high up on a cliff in Minnesota, Split

Rock Lighthouse, which we understand will look quite dramatic if shot from a boat on the water below."

"No, the lighthouse at Montauk Point," Hitchcock said.

"I thought you preferred the one in Minnesota."

"Minnesota will be terribly cold, and if I use Montauk Point, I can stay at the St. Regis and eat at 21."

Alma said to Iz, "You'll change the setting to Montauk," not exactly a question but not exactly not. "We can arrange for you to travel there if you need to see it."

Iz said she would think about whether she would need to see it, and Alma smiled knowingly.

They spoke for quite a while then about other changes both specific and general. Iz wrote frantically the whole time, not questioning or objecting but simply nodding and taking notes.

"You can take a first crack at changes," Hitchcock said. "Then we'll put our heads together back in Los Angeles and go from there?"

Iz said, "Yes, of course."

"You'll stay for dinner?" Hitchcock asked. "They've just delivered the first of this season's spiny lobsters. They are so much sweeter than a Maine lobster, aren't they? And we can have a guest room opened. It will be far too late to drive back to Los Angeles tonight."

Iz hesitated, then said, "I'm going only as far as Carmel. I have a friend expecting me. But dinner would be lovely, thank you." Glad the offer was for lobster rather than a steak. Or twelve.

October 1957

Iz found Leo still awake when she arrived back from seeing the Hitchcocks, and the baby was down, the house quiet.

"Fifty thousand dollars," she whispered, and they laughed quietly together. They laughed and laughed. Iz laughed so hard that she cried, which was the relief, those tears.

"They called it dark and mysterious, the writing accomplished," she said, and she went through the specific praise the Hitchcocks had heaped on the script. The notes, she said, weren't much, really. They boiled down to Hitch being antsy to be in New York. "He wants to set it at a lighthouse in Montauk, at the far end of Long Island."

Leo shrugged. "I can work with that."

She handed him the script and the notebook in which she'd written while she was with the Hitchcocks, and he poured them each a scotch while she slipped upstairs to peel off the damned girdle. She put on one of Leo's shirts even though she could wear her own clothes again. When she came back down, Leo was sitting at one end of the couch, the script in his lap. But he wasn't reading it.

She curled up on the other end, facing him. "What is it, Leo?"

"Would you consider naming her Rebecca?" he asked.

She looked away, to the closed door between her and the sleeping baby that would never be hers. "I can't name her."

"After my mother? With *c*'s rather than *k*'s, so she'll fit in better here?"

"I can't keep her, Leo."

"We could together."

She looked to the drawn curtains. Hawk Tower loomed beyond them, but she couldn't see that, she was safe here in Leo's little cottage.

"You deserve someone you love, Leo. A good man like you, you deserve to fall head over heels in love. I wish I were that person for you, but I know when a man is attracted to me and you aren't, I know that, I see that."

"We would be a family. Rebecca would—"

"You deserve your own family. You can't toss your future away on account of my mistakes."

"I . . . I don't have a way to have a family, though."

"Not now, but—"

For a moment, there was no sound but the waves against the coast and the baby stirring before she settled back into sleep.

She. A daughter Iz had never seen, a daughter she never would see.

Leo said, "I know it would be . . . not what you want. Not the love you deserve. But I do love you. And I would be a good father. We could . . . Mannix could fix it to look like we were married before you got pregnant and . . . and you could go back to acting, and after a while if you want, after you're a big enough star, we could get a quiet divorce."

A quiet divorce. What kind of life would that be for Leo, spending his best years with someone he knew he wouldn't grow old with? What kind of life would it be for her, or even for the child?

"I know it's not ideal, but a big-enough star can survive a divorce," he said. "Elizabeth Taylor was divorced before she was twenty. Zsa Zsa and Lana are each thrice divorced, Marilyn twice. And nobody would know, Iz. Nobody knows."

Nobody but her, that's what he was saying, how he was telling her who he was, who she'd known on some level he was since that night she asked if it was Marilyn Monroe or Arthur Miller who was his type. His kiss that night had never been real, it had been a stage direction for a role he'd written for himself, a role he'd likely been playing most of his life. That awkward kiss had allowed him to hide behind the man he knew she would assume he was, a man who had kissed her and found something wanting in that kiss, something less than satisfying that she would take as her own shortcoming.

She said, "The Committee . . ."

HUAC poked into every corner of a life. They went through people's garbage.

"I don't live in LA," he said. "I don't live in New York. I live here in Carmel, where the FBI doesn't bother to look. And even if they did, there has never been anyone, not since I came to America. There's nothing to find."

He poured his loneliness into his writing. He made it sad or he made it funny or he made it both at the same time. He made it something that others brought to life, actors and actresses, directors, producers, cameramen and costume departments and crews. He took the love he didn't feel he could have, or perhaps even should have, and he made art from it.

"You don't have to decide now," he said. "Think about it. Tell Mannix you need a few days to decide what to do, and think about it."

"They're coming for the baby tomorrow." The Phippses from Connecticut. "They're on a train from New York that arrives in San Francisco tomorrow."

"We'd be a family, Iz. Your baby would have parents who love her. We don't have to decide anything beyond that. If you meet someone— *when* you meet someone . . ."

"You could still act," he said. "You could still do *The Ghost of Hawk Tower* with Hitchcock. It's a good script. He won't want to let it go."

"It's not that," she said.

But it was that. It was all of it. If she married a blacklisted writer, she would never be the new Hitchcock girl. She would never be anything. The studio would cancel her contract, and she'd be through.

He said, "Will you let me, then?"

"Will I let you . . . ?"

"I could raise her myself. She could be my daughter."

When she didn't respond, he said, "You have a choice to make, and it won't help anyone for you to make a choice that will leave you bitter, or even angry, I understand that. You're young. You're ambitious for yourself. Of course you are. This was not something you meant to do. This was a mistake that happened. A mistake you don't have to let take away the life you want. Nobody is asking that of Hugh Bolin. You don't need to ask it of yourself. But it's different for me, Iz. I wasn't sixteen even when I was sixteen. I'm in my thirties now. And I am who I am."

He waited, then said so gently that she almost couldn't hear him, "And you are who you are, Isabella. You've already made the choice to give her up. You said you could give her away if you knew she would be with a good father."

"A good family."

"I would be a good family. I promise I would. You were going to put her in the care of the man who fathered her simply because he did, and his wife you've never met. Now you're going to put her in the hands of strangers. You *know* me. You *know* I would love her. That I would do anything for her. Let me be her father? Let me be her family?"

PART III

I thought you'd be thrilled," Isabella's agent says. "This *Royalty* grandmother—These major roles don't come along often, Iz, and it's the perfect part for—"

For a washed-up old actress like me, Iz thinks, although she knows her agent doesn't think of her that way, as the kind of sweet old grandmother she so long eschewed. Oddly, her agent thinks of her as rather a heroine of some sort. Iz supposes she confuses her with the roles she's played.

"I am thrilled," Iz says.

"*More* thrilled. You *do* want this? Don't ask me to call them up and say you've changed your mind now that they've made up theirs."

Iz should be grateful, she knows that. When anyone writes about the span of her career, they'll say she went from "sixteen and innocent, and yet somehow elegant" to "eighty-six and innocent, and yet somehow elegant." Young virgin to sexless old lady.

There *is* an elegance to this sweet old grannie role though, at least there is that. And there were some wonderful roles in between, starting with *Double Deception*. In those brief few years in the fifties and early sixties, the great actresses could open a film as surely as the great actors could: Grace Kelly, Doris Day, Jane Fonda. Nobody could assure a lousy script would make a profitable film, but they could assure people would buy tickets on opening weekend, they could open as well as the fellows. That had ground to a halt with the new cinema of the 1960s, films like *The Wild Bunch* and *Easy Rider*, all about the male perspective. Iz thought at the time it was just her, she was getting too old. But looking back on it she sees it was more complicated.

The dear sweet if elegant old grannie. Would they keep Iz if her past came to light now, the scandal of unwed motherhood? Clint Eastwood had welcomed a surprise daughter into his family and it hadn't hurt him, but the mother's name has never been revealed. It's different for a woman. A woman can't claim she didn't know about a baby. And maybe that mother's own family doesn't know about that daughter Eastwood fathered even today. Maybe the mother refused to meet her, maybe she never told her spouse or their children, and didn't want to admit now to living a lie. Or maybe she was famous and didn't want whatever reputation she'd built for herself undermined by the news she'd given up a child. A man could embrace an out-of-wedlock child as a sign of his virility. A man could claim never to have known, like Eastwood had. But even now, in this age in which women have children out of wedlock and raise them as single parents, a woman who gives her child over to be raised by someone else is seen as unforgivably selfish, shameful, unmotherly.

Would the new attention on Iz that would accompany a late-life comeback make it more likely the truth would surface? But Mannix died a few years after he first brought her up here, and Benny Thau too has been dead for decades. Both the doctors, the one who wouldn't do the abortion and the one who delivered the baby, were older men, and that was sixty years ago. Even Leo is gone. And Hugh isn't telling anyone.

"They're so keen to have this grannie be sweet," she says to her agent. "Boring as hell. Named Wilma, for pity's sake!"

"Do you hate the name that much? Clairey Bolin is wild for it. But she does love your idea of Wilma having a love interest. She and Sass both do. They might even want her to be a player—against stereotype, flip the script—if you're good with that? It would be a much bigger role."

"You're kidding."

"Can you live with Wilma? Clairey thinks the nod to *The Flintstones* will work well both for the comedic undertone and . . . Wait. She sent this to me to share with you." She puts Iz on speaker so she can pull up an email, then reads, "'Wilma was not just elephant vacuum cleaners, pelican washing machines, and gravel berry pie. She's beautiful and she's modest, but she doesn't hesitate to knock out crooks with her stone purse. She sold that pie recipe to a supermarket chain, so call her an early role model for female entrepreneurs. And she was a journalist too. Remember the spoof of *The Mary Tyler Moore Show*? Wilma's editor was Lou Granite!'"

Like Lou Grant, Mary's boss in the first TV show that centered on a career woman.

"Clairey uses an exclamation mark there. She says, 'Wilma Flintstone is this super smart character whose women's groups are the bedrock of Bedrock.'"

Iz laughs, still a sucker for a good pun, or even a bad one.

"She and Sass both love your idea of creating a modern-day live-action Wilma with as much smarts and spunk. They think it's just the kind of thing *Royalty* needs. And they promise they won't give you a cigarette-girl past unless you want it, unless you have something clever to do with it."

WHEN IZ KNOCKS ON THE doorjamb at the Fade Inn's half-open Dutch door, Gemma looks up at her from Leo's coffee table, now piled with scripts.

"You got the part!"

"But I just heard myself."

Gemma shrugs. "Your door was open. My door was open. I couldn't tell what you were saying but I heard you laughing. I thought you'd be happier!"

Iz tenders the bag of pastries Sam dropped by just before her agent called. "I am happy, but I'm also a little nervous. I'm not sure I can even pretend to be as interesting as they expect me to be."

Gemma considers her in a way that shows she's at least a little surprised at this. Does she not understand what it's like to need to pretend to be better than you are?

Gemma returns to searching the piles on the coffee table, saying, "You won't believe what I found here. I think it's your original script for *Double Deception*. I found it with Gran's scripts, under a different title. Now what did I do with it?"

The Ghost of Hawk Tower. Iz shouldn't have taken the script. She should tell Gemma she has it. She should give it back to her. But she's never been good at giving up what she wants.

Gemma says she'll find the script later, and they settle into Leo's Adirondack chairs, already talking about tomorrow's Oscars as they wait for Sam and Nyx to finish their morning run and come share the pastries he dropped by. *The Shape of Water*, with thirteen nominations, is expected to dominate the awards. But what is expected to take center stage is the lack of diversity in the nominees again, and now Harvey Weinstein and the sexual abuse that appears to be rampant in Hollywood.

"Gosh, this is the first year since I started college that I'm not going to watch with Gran," Gemma says, the longing in her voice heartbreaking. And when Iz invites her to watch at Manderley, Gemma suggests watching together here, at the Fade Inn.

They're well into concocting a snack menu to go with Leo's lousy scotch when Sam joins them, not sweaty from his run like usual, but showered and dressed. He's half in love with Gemma already. Does he see that? Does she? Their glances meet, but neither is willing to risk being seen wanting without being wanted, when any fool who isn't named Gemma or Sam can see they both want the same thing. Leo would have spun this moment into a fantastic movie script, Leo would have audiences shouting at the screen, *Somebody kiss somebody here, for Pete's sake!*

Sam hands Gemma a photograph, saying, "Sorry, I found it on the floor in my hallway. We must have dropped it when we brought the photos."

The photos.

Iz sits quietly, letting the moments captured on film roll over her. That first outing to Hidden Beach, when she asked Leo not to take her photo. The funny and fascinating day he first took her snorkeling. That gown she could have worn to the Oscars the next year, but she never did wear it again. She still has it though.

She was beautiful then, she can see that now even in this photo that doesn't show her face. She knew she was, and yet she never felt beautiful. She felt people were seeing an Isabelle Giori who wasn't real.

"The photos are of me," she admits, knowing that surely Gemma has realized this on some level. "From the summer I first met your grandfather. I don't know why I didn't say so before."

Gemma sees it's true. That look in her eyes. A different kind of doubt forming itself into questions Iz can't answer.

"No, that's not true. I do know," Iz manages somehow through an unexpected wash of grief; she will never see Leo again. "It's not something I ever talk about, though."

She looks to the rough stones of Hawk Tower, the smoother stone-work of the house that is now a museum but was once a home, the garden where the ashes of Robinson and Una Jeffers and their baby daughter are buried.

"The studio sent me up here," she says. "To have an abortion." Which has the advantage of shutting down any questions they might want to ask, the truth that hides the lie.

Town is so crowded when Iz and Gemma go for Oscar-watching provisions that they park all the way up by the Forest Theater. They talk nonstop as they shop, but it's only after they're walking back to the car that Gemma says, "You knew Gran for a long time then?"—the beginning of the questions Iz tried to duck.

"I knew him, and then we didn't see each other for ages," Iz says. "Then I bought the cottage from the studio."

"You didn't have an affair with him?"

Iz meets her gaze. It's an odd place to have such an important conversation. They've just turned right on Torres. They're about to pass the motel that used to be called the Jade Tree. Iz never comes this way, but Gemma set off uphill from Bruno's Market and here they are.

"I did not," she says.

"Why did he have those photos of you then?" Gemma asks.

Her frank blue-green eyes will not be lied to.

"Your Gran was kind to me when I needed kindness more desperately than you can imagine," Iz says. "He woke me up with his typing one morning. That's how we met. I don't know why he came to like me. I don't think I'm very likable, and I certainly wasn't back then. Maybe he *didn't* like me, but he rescued me. I think it was his way of being thankful for the people who rescued him during the war."

She shares what she knows then about Leo's family being taken by the Nazis while he was out delivering Resistance newspapers, and the woman who led him over the Pyrenees, to freedom and safety and a future lived under the name that had been her son's.

"There are so many questions I never asked Mom or Gran," Gemma says. "I didn't want to make them rake up whatever it was that made them so sad.

"Maybe that's Gran's real name on the Oscar on his dresser?" she asks. "Smith or Douglas? It's a writing Oscar for *The Defiant Ones*."

That Oscar that wasn't Leo's but ought to have been, that he kept in his bedroom, just for himself. Iz remembers that ceremony, sitting in her own seat as Elizabeth Taylor read the names of Smith and Douglas as nominees for *The Defiant Ones*, then Isabella's own name for *Double Deception*—the crowd murmuring all the while on account of the fact that Taylor, who'd had the whole world's sympathy after Mike Todd died in a plane crash four weeks after their daughter was born, was by then having an affair with Eddie Fisher, who was married to Taylor's own matron of honor. In the tabloid feeding frenzy, Debbie Reynolds was a victimized innocent and Taylor a home-wrecking slut.

"Smith was real," she tells Gemma. "'Douglas' was a pseudonym for your grandfather's friend Nedrick Young, who was blacklisted."

When *The Defiant Ones* won the New York Film Critics writing award, the fact that 'Douglas' was Young leaked, and the Academy, faced with the prospect of having to deny him the Oscar, voted finally to allow the awarding of Oscars to blacklisted artists—although still they awarded that Oscar under Young's pseudonym. 1959. A dozen years after the blacklist began. Years in which writers of films like *An Affair to Remember* and *The Bridge Over the River Kwai* were denied credit for their work. And still it didn't end. *Inherit the Wind, Spartacus,* and even the 1966 film *Born Free* were all written under pseudonyms.

"By the time I met him, your Gran had been Léon Chazan for half his life," Iz says. "I think it was easier for him to be that man, to have that new name and that new life that didn't remind him every moment of the family he lost. But he *might* have used his real name as an alias."

Iz herself has been Isabella Giori for so long, and yet she still feels vaguely ashamed that her own Oscar doesn't say Fanny Fumagalli. It sits on a table in the entryway at her estate in LA, always with flowers from her gardens: roses from April to December and sometimes into January, camellias starting in the fall, magnolias from her trees in winter, and in the spring, azaleas and tulips, lilacs, and her favorite fox-gloves she has planted every year since she bought the place, although she supposes she never will again. A wild display to draw attention, so that every guest and every delivery person she opens her door to, every plumber who comes to unstop her toilet, will see her Oscar beside the vase and know she's someone. Even after all these years, she needs to be someone she never has been.

"Those photos, Gemma . . . I suppose your Gran kept them for me, in case I ever needed to understand who I was then. I think he understood that—who I was—even though I didn't really understand myself. Sometimes I don't even now.

"I was just about your age when I got pregnant," Iz says. "Younger even." Four years younger, but young people seem to stay younger these days. "Back then, an out-of-wedlock child . . . it was stigmatizing not just to the mother but to the child too."

She makes herself look to the door behind the stairway at what used to be the Jade Tree Motel. "That door there, that's where I first went to meet the doctor," she says. "Abortions were illegal then, so it was dangerous for him too."

"I'm sorry," Gemma says. "You don't have to talk about it. I wouldn't want to either."

Iz sets off walking again, Gemma beside her. She hadn't meant to say anything more, but the words bottled up for so long tumble out in a rush: foolishly sleeping with her costar, whom she doesn't name; meeting Mr. Thau in his office; driving up to Carmel with Mannix in the middle of the night; sitting in that motel room as the adjoining door opened.

They're back at the Forest Theater where, instead of getting in the car, they climb to the top row of seats, when Gemma tells Iz about a showrunner who exposed himself as he was interviewing her.

"He trashed my reputation before I could have said a word about him," she says. "Not that I would have. It was before Me Too. Any woman who said anything was assumed to be disappointed and bitter and seeking revenge."

She tears up, but wipes her eyes and looks out across the treetops of Carmel all the way to the ocean.

"Nobody will hire me now," she says. "It's sort of . . . It's not the same at all, of course, but I can imagine how Gran must have felt. Even when nobody would hire Gran though, he still wrote."

Iz gently moves a lock of hair from Gemma's face like Leo did that first day at Hidden Beach, a gesture she saw as presumptuous if not downright menacing, but was meant to comfort, she sees that now.

"Don't think your grandfather didn't feel despair too," she says. "It's impossible to face injustice without some amount of despair."

Gemma considers her. "Did you ever think about marrying the father and having the baby?"

"He was already married," Iz admits.

Gemma says her mother was engaged when she got pregnant, to a man who died before Gemma was born but, it turned out, was already married. "He was never my father," she says.

And when Iz asks if she might feel differently if he were alive, she looks frankly through those glasses that match her eyes and says, "You mean, like Mom and Gran lied to me my whole life and he lives next door or is the postman, the guy at the chocolate shop? If he were alive that would mean he spent all these years not wanting to know me, choosing some other thing as more important than Mom and me. I sure don't need a father like that."

Iz shifts on the hard bench seat, looking to the stage and the trees and the point, which seems so far away.

"I feel like I should be braver than I am," Gemma says. "I feel like I should file a complaint against that showrunner, but I know he'll just deny it."

This is what Gemma is up against. That showrunner is making some studio a lot of money, and she isn't.

"Your Gran's friend Nedrick Young brought a lawsuit against the blacklist that your Gran declined to join," Iz says. "These are personal decisions—the battles we choose when they don't choose us, and even when they do.

"I don't suppose you have a way to prove it?" Iz asks.

"Dang, and I had a phone with me! I should have pulled it out and taken a shot of him."

Iz laughs. "A dick pic!"

Gemma says, "You better not let Gran hear you say that! 'Language, Cricket,' he was forever reprimanding me, leaving me pretty much unable to swear even now, in an industry where swear-words are punctuation. 'It sets you apart, Cricket, not swearing in a world where everyone does.'"

Iz says, "The dick and his dick."

How ironic it is: For Leo, it was refusing to name names that was the brave thing to do. For Gemma, it's naming a single name.

"I can't keep Gran's cottage without a job," Gemma says, "but a room full of writers isn't 'eight fingers on eight keys and a single mind searching.'"

Cricket, Iz thinks. *Oh, Cricket. Why do women hold themselves to such impossible standards?*

"When your Gran started, there was no television to write for, no writers' rooms," she says, "but he wrote under contract with a studio, the movie scripts they needed at the time."

Gemma nods. "The rooms are so male," she says. "Not even men. Boys. If Harvey Weinstein hadn't been such an ugly man, I'm not sure this new Me Too movement would even have taken hold."

Iz laughs. She's never heard anyone say this out loud. Harvey is such an ugly man, but nobody is quite sure yet whether he's truly dead or, like the titanium skeleton in *The Terminator*, he'll rise again.

"I'm going to scatter Gran's ashes off the point tomorrow night, after the Oscars," Gemma says, looking as surprised as Iz feels at the statement. "Will you come with me?"

Iz can't sort out a way to say no that doesn't require an explanation Gemma doesn't want to hear. And the truth is that what Iz is thinking is *I'd like that, Cricket,* only stopping herself because she feels she would be betraying Leo to use that love name again.

"I'd like that, Gemma, if you're sure you want me there," she says. It feels like one last thing she can do for Leo.

Gemma plays just the beginning from one of Gran's phone messages, *Cricket, I love this new script!* and one from her mom simply saying, *I love you. Call me when you can,* then opens Twitter to the bookmarked tweet. Sixteen words—"If you've been sexually harassed or assaulted write 'me too' as a reply to this tweet"—with a screenshot of a text suggesting that this might be a way to give the world a sense of the magnitude of the problem. She opens a reply and types "#MeToo." Five letters. Two capitals. One hashtag. Not a single space in which to pause. She hits post. Not naming anyone. Not sharing details. Just adding her voice. That is, she realizes now, the point. To say this does happen, it happens far more often than anyone wants to admit it does. Like with the journals under Memory Bench, this lets others know they aren't alone.

She borrows Tubby from Sam to take Gran for one last ride. She sets his ashes on the dash so he can see out and Gemma can see him and she sets off, still thinking about that showrunner, torn between calling him out before he ruins some other poor writer's career and deleting her tweet. She parks and goes into the beautiful old library where, for as long as she can remember, she could choose any book she wanted and check it out with her own library card. She stops at the Carmel Bakery for a triple-dip ice cream cone, one scoop each of Mom's butter pecan and Gran's chocolate with her own rocky road on the top in case she can't finish it all, then eats the whole thing. She lingers at the Center for Photographic Art, started by Ansel Adams,

Cole Weston, and Wynn Bullock when her mom was just a girl, where one of the exhibits, "Artists as Teachers," shows arresting images of a hand taking a cell phone photo of a guitarist; a naked woman in child's pose set against a cascade of scattered sheet music and bits of female faces old and young (mouth, nose, a single eye, a strand of hair); and a blurry image of a woman walking toward the sea's edge, her footprints behind her in the sand.

"This one reminds me of Mom," she says quietly, to Gran.

And yourself.

"And myself."

She talks to Gran as she carries him by his red zip tie along the cliff above the crescent of beach at China Cove. "The harbor seals will be here soon, to have their babies."

"Another few weeks," a woman says, startling her.

She surreptitiously slides Gran's ashes into her vest pocket and makes polite conversation with the woman and her friend—roommates in law school forty years ago, they tell her. Gemma tells them she's a screenwriter, and perhaps because one of them is now a novelist who understands how hard it is just to write, they don't ask if they would have seen anything she's written.

"My Gran was a screenwriter too," she says, and she tells them he was an Oscar nominee, and then he was blacklisted. "I'm working the history into a screenplay," she says, realizing only as she says it that it *is* what she's doing, or trying to do.

And after they exchange names, the nonwriter says, "Your grandfather is *Chazan?*" and they both want to tell her "one quick story" about watching one of Gran's already-old-even-then movies in a theater in Ann Arbor when they were in law school. They're laughing so hard that it's impossible to follow what they're saying, but Gemma understands the memory that binds them. That's what a movie or a book, a good story, can do. Eight fingers on eight keys, and people all over the world laugh or cry, people all over the world look at others a little differently, with more compassion and sympathy, forgiveness.

At Memory Bench not much later, she pulls a journal from the under-the-bench mailbox and flips to her last words about Gran's ghost only wanting to make her laugh. Someone has replied that sometimes laughter is the best medicine, to which someone else has responded *Cliché*. Gemma wants to tell whoever wrote that to stuff it, but there is no room for vitriol in these journals, they're meant to be a safe space, and really, what a sad life that writer must lead, needing to denigrate someone trying to give support to someone else in a journal where everyone is anonymous. Like all those people who are nasty online, where anonymity keeps them from having to face who they really are.

There are two other short responses followed by, in tidy handwriting, a poem, "Love the Wild Swan" by Robinson Jeffers. Gemma feels naked, exposed. Sam has read her most private thoughts.

She reads it through to the end, fourteen lines that begin with the writer hating his writing, *every line, every word*. The poem is written slightly slantwise, so that its turn away from bullets and mirrors and self-hate catches her off guard. She reads it again, lingering on the familiar lines near the end: *Love your eyes that can see, your mind that can / Hear the music*—Gran's words that first time he took her to write at the beach. It never occurred to her that those weren't his own words, his way of encouraging her. It never occurred to her that they might be words borrowed from a poem written by his across-the-road neighbor, that Gran would have turned to himself. It never occurred to her that Gran too must sometimes have struggled for words.

The next entry in the journal says simply, *I feel a love story starting here.*

It's only as she reads the full entry and those that follow that she realizes the writer isn't writing about the love in the poem, or even about the love between Gran and her, but about romantic love. Short responses build off each other to make a collage of a love story written by the pages passing through the under-the-bench mailbox from one writer to another. It starts with an entry in which two strangers meet through a journal tucked in this mailbox. A dozen or more different handwritings describe moments the lovers share, some of which Gemma guesses are made up, but most of which read like moments remembered, written by people who perhaps were lonely but, on opening this journal and reading the words here, were drawn back to some happier time. In the last several entries, the strangers, now lovers, are standing out on the sand together, just at the water's edge. Maybe there are chairs or maybe everyone stands. Maybe the bride wears a wedding dress and train and veil or maybe she is barefoot and in blue jeans. Maybe they are both wearing tuxedos, or dresses, or bathing suits. Each writer in this journal wants to write their own ending, their own happiness.

Is it the photos that provoke the memory, Iz wonders, or is it the set of Gemma's shoulders as she climbs out of Tubby and returns to Sam's door with the keys. Are all young people so oblivious? Iz supposes she was. Of course she was. Leo is perhaps the only person she has ever known who wasn't. Leo who found wisdom as a sixteen-year-old returning to a home that wasn't really his to find his family already gone. He'd always known what he left behind when he climbed over the Pyrenees and into Spain. A family he would never have again.

That was what he had been asking of Iz when he asked for the baby. The baby, not her baby. The baby who was never meant to be hers, whose future was in her hands.

I would be a good family, Leo had said. Not just a good father. A good family, all by himself. Mannix could fix it. The doctor could fix it. They'd already arranged to list another mother on the birth certificate, so there would be no way to trace the child back to Iz. They could add Leo as the father.

But there was so much Iz didn't know about Leo, and what she did know wasn't always comforting, that's what she kept going over as she lay awake for what seemed all night that night after she'd met with the Hitchcocks, as Leo's typewriter clacked and dinged downstairs.

His financial situation was precarious. His livelihood depended on others fronting scripts for him, leaving him with little income even for what he could sell. She would give him the money from Hitchcock, she would figure out a way to do that, but federal tax rates alone on that much money were seventy-five percent. With a child, he wouldn't be able to travel, to take jobs fixing scripts. If it came out that he was using a front, he would no longer be able to sell scripts either, leaving him with no income at all. With him, the baby would have none of the advantages the couple from Connecticut would provide.

If Leo was a U.S. citizen—was he?—it was under a false identity. If he was caught, he could be imprisoned. He could be deported, and where would he go? He had been stripped of his German citizenship during the war and never had been a citizen of France. The real Leo, whoever he was—the son of Jacob and Rebekka—was Jewish too, which so often meant closed borders, even U.S. borders closed during World War II without anyone admitting they were. And closed doors even in Hollywood, where most of the men who made and ran the movie industry were Jewish and yet country clubs and even neighborhoods remained unwelcoming.

And if Iz put the baby in Leo's hands, the child would never have a mother, Iz did understand that. She didn't know exactly what Leo's life was, but she knew that if she didn't marry him, if he wasn't marrying the baby's mother, he would never marry. The decade of the 1950s was a different time. Same-gender sex even in private was a crime in every state. As late as the 1990s, a court gave custody to an absentee father who'd served time for murdering his first wife, finding him a more fit parent than the child's mother simply because she was lesbian. And in the environment of the blacklist, the FBI could destroy Leo simply for being who he was. Where would that leave the child?

THE NEXT MORNING, IZ WOKE in the attic bedroom to the sound of the waves crashing just the other side of Hawk Tower and Leo chatting with the baby as he did something—changed her diapers, she figured from the smell. His typewriter was silent, his work set aside for the child.

"It's okay," Iz heard him say. "You're just tired."

It was already eleven. Iz hadn't slept, and now she'd overslept. Mannix would arrive in just an hour to take her back to LA. The doctor would be here at the same time to take the baby. She didn't know whether he was taking the child up to San Francisco, where the parents had arrived last night, or some other arrangement had been made. She wasn't allowed to ask questions.

She got up and began packing, all the while listening to the sound of Leo taking such sweet care of the baby that would go to a family from Connecticut who might be good people or might not, Iz would never meet them, she would never know. He was gently singing in the front room, not a lullaby but instead that Tab Hunter song about there being only one love in the world for anyone. Iz imagined him rocking the baby in his arms as he sang. After a few minutes, his voice moved slowly to the back bedroom, where he would be laying her on his own bed, with pillows all around the edges even though it would be months before there was any threat of her rolling over, much less rolling off.

Iz was in the shower and out again, dressed and ready to go, before Leo emerged from the bedroom. Her single suitcase and her Oscar gown on its hanger were by the bedroom door.

Leo handed her the script. He'd worked on Hitchcock's changes all night and finished the revised script that morning. "Not long after Rebecca's second bottle," he said.

"Rebecca," Iz said. Iz hadn't given her a name, hadn't wanted to name her, hadn't been able to name her, knowing she wouldn't keep her, that whatever name she gave her would be only for the moment. But Leo had already named her in his heart.

"I'm sorry," he said. "I didn't—"

"If you kept her, Leo, you wouldn't be able to . . ."

He watched her for a long time, the only sound the surf against the shore on the other side of Tor House and Hawk Tower.

"I've lost one family already, Isabella," he said. "There is nothing I wouldn't give up to have a child. And . . . and this is a love I can express, a love I will never be shamed for or have to hide."

Would that be enough love for a lifetime? A single daughter?

He said, "Are you sure you don't want to . . . to try together?"

Iz wanted to say she would, she wanted to be that person, but she wasn't and would never be.

"If you kept her . . ."

If she gave him the child, how would he explain being a single father?

People had seen them together, though. It would be easy enough to leave the impression she'd died in childbirth, of anesthesia or hemorrhage or infection, it wouldn't matter, nobody would ask.

"If you kept her, maybe I could . . . not be her mother, I would be a terrible mother, but—"

"Allow her to think her mother is simply a family friend? I don't think either of us could lie that well, Isabella."

It would be unfair, even she could see that, to risk a child ever learning that the woman who gave birth to her was right there and yet refused to be anything more than the most casual part of her life.

"We would have to give up our friendship," she said.

He said simply, "Yes."

She couldn't raise a baby herself. She hadn't meant to have a baby and, since left with no choice, she'd always planned to put this baby in better hands than her own. What she hadn't planned for was to become so close to a man who understood her, who made it okay for her to be herself. A man she would have fallen in love with if only he would love her, whom she perhaps was in love with even though he didn't. A man who would be a wonderful father, a wonderful family to this baby all on his own, just as he had been to her these last months.

She said, "What would you have had me name the baby if she were a boy?"

He considered her. He seemed to want to tell her and yet not at the same time.

"Samuel," he said finally.

Samuel, a first name without a last name, like when they first met.

It's long before dawn, but Sam sees the lights on in Leo's cottage, he sees Gemma with a cup of coffee in hand. She's already dressed. Is she up early, or has her grief kept her up all night, the way his sometimes does even still? She isn't writing, she's watching television, that *Royalty* show Mads loves.

A few minutes later, he's standing at Leo's door with a thermos and two collapsible beach chairs in sling bags thrown over his shoulder, a candle and lighter in his pocket.

"It's me, it's Sam," he says as he knocks gently, so she won't be startled.

She's wearing Leo's sweater, which smells of him and her both now, of the love they shared.

"You want to see something special?" he says. "I promise, you won't regret it. Put on something warm."

She pulls on her down vest and the adorable knit beanie. She doesn't grab Leo's ashes, and he doesn't ask her to. As they cross the street, Nyx is standing on Sam's desk, looking out the window. The house is dark except for a light in his office forgotten in his haste on seeing Gemma. Nyx barks her funny little bark.

"There is going to be dog hair all over my keyboard again," he says.

He leads Gemma the same way he always goes, through the gate at Tor House, but instead of going around Hawk Tower, he goes to its entrance, slides the key in, and turns the lock to this tower Jeffers built with his own hands, hauling the heavy granite up piece by piece from the cove.

"Are we allowed to be here?" Gemma whispers.

"It's okay. Mads got me the key."

The new game Sam is working on is set here, or in a world inspired by this, and by Jeffers's poetry, but he doesn't tell Gemma that. He doesn't tell her he's had the key for months but has never used it, that when he's here in Carmel by himself, he thinks he'll wait for Mads, and when she's here he thinks he wants to come alone. He's not sure what he's afraid of. Perhaps the ghosts Jeffers warns of in his poetry? In "Ghost," his ghost doesn't mean to hurt anyone. *"I am just looking / At the walls that I built."* But in "Tor House," his ghost is something darker, buried deep in the stones stacked with his own hands, like Sam's own ghosts if Mads is right, and she always is. Ghosts buried so deeply in what he creates that he doesn't see them there even as he visits them.

"Mads arranged it," he says. "Really, there is nothing she can't do."

The door creaks open into two rooms, one largely belowground. Inside, he lights the candle he's brought so Gemma can see, so he can see himself.

Gemma gasps at a hawk over the window, perched in attack. Real, but dead and stuffed. Another kind of ghost.

The rooms are cramped, the stone walls thick and damp, the feeling less cozy than claustrophobic. Creepier in the dark than they were in daylight. You can see how Iz or Leo or whoever wrote that screenplay would imagine someone being murdered here.

There is no electricity in this tower. There never has been. There is an oil lamp in the ceiling, but he doesn't try to light it, or even pull it down.

An outside stairway provides an easier way up to Una's floor and would have the advantage of starlight, but Sam wants to take Gemma through the secret stairway inside the tower, stone steps so narrow that even Gemma, small as she is, has to turn sideways, leading with her left shoulder. He feels like a kid on a grand explore. Yes, this is definitely going to work for the setting of his new game. He hasn't figured out yet what ghosts will haunt *The Ghost of Hawk Tower*, but that will come to him on a long run, or while he's reading poetry, or just as he's telling Mads this game isn't working, that he's going to have to shelve it and do something else. Something in the act of telling her he can't do something always makes it untrue.

The second-floor rooms are all rich paneling and gothic windows, a stone fireplace with a wooden mantel carved with hawks and a fragment of Latin, *ipsi sibi somnia fingunt*—words from a poem by Virgil which, taken alone, seem to mean *they create their own dreams*. We create our own dreams; there is nobody else to do it for us. And so much of reaching for our dreams is feeling ahead in the dark, in the company of our ghosts.

When Gemma turns toward the sound of the sea, he moves the candle with her, to a separate little turret room surrounded by windows, big enough only for a single chair.

"This must be where Jeffers wrote his poetry," Gemma says.

It isn't, though. Sam too likes to imagine Robin looking down from this window to the little cove where Leo used to write. He likes to imagine Robin watching as storms roll in from the ocean, as "the old granite breaks into white torches the heavy-shouldered children of the wind." But Robin made this tower for Una to have space to be whomever she wanted to be, away from the chores and the children, with friends slipping up the secret stairway to join her. Robin wrote with his back to the sea. He worked upstairs at Tor House and, when his pacing overhead ceased for too long, Una banged on the ceiling that was his floor to bring him back from the darkness that haunted him as he wrote.

Sam imagines Robin did come here after Una died, to visit her ghost. But maybe he's invented that. Maybe he wants Robin to be like him.

" 'Je t'écris un poème / Artiste disparu,'" he says. "'I *write* you a poem.'" The French poem they found on the stump just below them, in that nameless cove. "It was a tribute to Robin, a poem written in his memory."

The look in her eyes, more green than blue here in the dark reflection of candlelight on stone: Why didn't he say so when they were first reading it?

"The only screenplay I've ever sold, I started writing down in that cove," she says. "Gran took me there to write with him."

He stands beside her, looking out the narrow center window to the dark sea, the white crash of water against dark rock, thinking not *screenplays*, but *screenplay* singular. Like him, not video games but video game. It's daunting, having done a thing only once. You are left uncertain that it isn't a fluke.

SAM LEADS GEMMA UP ANOTHER stairway, past two portholes salvaged from shipwrecks that look to the sea they were retrieved from, and through a cramped and bare third floor that leads out to a walled stone patio.

"A parapet," he calls it.

"A battlement," she says. "We could defend ourselves from attackers by shooting arrows through those gaps."

From here, impossibly steep stairs—with nothing more than a weathered chain to hold—ascend to the turret's top. It's dark, and even in broad daylight when he was here on the public tour, he was sure he would lose his footing and plummet the three stories to the ground. But from the tiny terrace up there you are in the heavens, or that was how it felt to Sam.

He can hear in Gemma's silence that she's thinking about that body plummeting from this tower in the movie script.

"Careful even when you get to the top," he says.

When Sam reaches the top himself, Gemma is lost in the view.

"'The stars go over the lonely ocean,'" he says, both the title of the poem and his favorite line from it, although he always wants to invert the words, he wants it to read, "The stars go lonely over the ocean."

The dark sky is clear now; the moon that was up last night is down and the stars are as thick as the colored sprinkles atop Eliza's and Noah's birthday cakes, the cherries in the pies his mom made for his own birthdays since he never liked cake. The sea air is moist and cold on his skin, and so earthy he can almost taste it. The stone is wet with the night dew, so they need to move carefully.

There is just enough room to set up the two chairs, which Sam has never used. When he removes the first from its bag, it pops into shape so suddenly that it startles him. Gemma grabs his arm so he doesn't lose his balance, then laughs her beautiful laugh.

They sit, taking in the ocean and the sky and the stars and all the more distant beauty, yes, but also Leo's cottage and Isabella's, and his own where he can just make out the shadow of Nyx's head now poking up over the seat back of a dining chair in the nearest window, a backlit shadow looking toward their voices. He silently sends her apologies: *I can't risk bringing you up here, pal; I can't lose you.*

The crash of surf and the occasional call of a frog somewhere. A flutter of wings. The steady in and out of Gemma's breath beside him as the rest of Carmel sleeps.

"Why do you lie to her?" she whispers.

He has no idea what she's talking about.

"To Madison," she says.

"Mads?"

Has he told Gemma he does that? That when Mads asks how the game is coming, he makes it sound like he's further along than he is?

"That's not lying exactly, that's telling a future truth," he says. "She gets me to say things so I'll be committed to making them true."

When Gemma doesn't respond, he opens the thermos, replacing the smell of stone and earth and ocean with the sweet scent of choco-latey milk. He pours a little into the lid that serves as a cup and hands it to Gemma. She takes a sip.

"It's made with honey," she says.

"And Guittard chocolate."

He doesn't have a second cup.

"We can share," she says.

And that's what they do. They sit together, passing the warm cup back and forth, refilling it from the thermos each time it's empty. Orion is in the sky, the three bright stars, and he imagines Robin sitting up here, watching it just as he is, and composing poems in his head. *Giant Orion, the torches of winter midnight, / Enormously walking above the ocean.* Or *In an hour Orion will be risen.* Or Sam's favorite, from "Tor House," *Orion in December / . . . strung in the throat of the valley like a lamp-lighted bridge.*

He's seen that from Carmel Point, Orion in the throat of the valley, where Carmel River comes through.

Gemma says, "Con used to lie to me."

Before Sam can respond, she sits up, suddenly alert. "What's that?" she says. "That light." She's pointing to the horizon. "See it? Is that an airplane?"

A pinpoint of light, bigger and brighter than any of the stars, races across the sky.

"That's the International Space Station," Sam says.

They sit watching it for a moment before Gemma raises her hand a little and waves.

"Hey, up there," she whispers. "I know you can't see us, but we're thinking of you. Safe travels, friends."

The Space Station fades into the horizon, the distant mist. It will circle again in ninety minutes, but they won't be able to see it again even if it passes overhead. It's visible only in the moments before dawn and after sunset, when it catches the sunlight and reflects it into a dark sky. Sometimes you can see it several nights in a row. Sometimes it's weeks before it reappears. Here in foggy Carmel, it seems to Sam a small miracle each time.

"I wanted to be an astronaut when I was a kid," he says.

"Why didn't you?"

"I don't know."

"You could take us all into space through a game," she suggests.

He considers this.

"I didn't like to be untethered from the earth even as a kid," he says. "My mom grew up flying with her dad." Together, they taught Eliza to fly and they wanted to teach Sam too, but he was always nervous in the air, as if he had some premonition.

She hands him the cup, and he takes a sip of the warming chocolate.

"Did you ever want to be anything other than a writer?" he asks.

"No, but . . . Not instead, but also. I'd like to direct too. I'd like to be able to keep that kind of control, to make sure what shows up on the screen is what I wrote."

"Why don't you?"

She says, "I don't know."

She takes the cup from him, takes a sip.

"Because Con wanted to be the director," she says.

What an idiot he is, falling for a girl who's been seeing the same guy forever.

He says, "'In the very place where you loved / lived / and put into words the things of my heart.' Those are the next lines." The poem, he means. The one on the stump. "I saw it when I ran that morning we met," he explains. "I took a photo of it, like you did. I don't speak French but I put what I could decipher through a translation program." He'd done it after coffee with her that first morning, after the falcon perched on the gargoyle up here had flown away. "I also got 'I follow you a poem' at first. I'm not sure I don't like that better."

"I'm trying to start a script for a movie I want to set here," she says. "Right here, at Hawk Tower. But I can't get any words."

"I'm setting a game here," he admits. His secrecy about his work is his own need, the need to keep his emotions locked down tight, he sees that now. "I have so many ideas swirling in my head, but I can't get them organized."

Not instead, but also—Gemma's words that describe what he too wants to accomplish. Science and poetry. The past and the future.

What we will do not just with this Earth we live on, but with this wide expanse of universe we have imagined for all time but are only now beginning to know. Could he weave Robin's poetry about this Earth into a space exploration game? Would a gateway through this tower out into the universe provide what he's been missing? Like Robin's poetry, reaching to Orion.

"That's why I wanted the key," he says. "So I can see this at night, see what Robin saw here in the dark."

"Uncenter your mind from yourself," she says.

"Yes."

"Does Madison like it up here?" she asks.

"Mads doesn't really get involved in the creative side of what we do," he says.

He's never brought her up here. She's never asked him to.

Gemma says, "But you're . . ."

He wants to say *I'm what?* but he takes a cue from Mads and simply waits.

"She has a clicker to your garage," Gemma says. "There are photos of the two of you all over the internet."

"Mads and me?" He laughs. "You mean like—"

"In tuxedos and ballgowns," she insists.

"Well sure, I mean, when it's a black-tie event," he says. "The thing is, André refuses to wear a tux, and Mads refuses to commit to anything beyond the most casual of relationships with a guy who won't wear one. Which isn't about the tux, of course."

She says, "You share a *dog.*"

The look in her eyes—if there is one thing he's learned from Mads, it's the look when a woman knows he's telling something less than the truth and not getting away with it.

"Mads told me she was getting Nyx for herself, but . . ."

But Mads knows him better than he knows himself. His parents were bringing him a puppy for graduation, it was the only thing he wanted. Would Mads ever have loved him? But Mads was with him at the cemetery in Connecticut when he buried his family, and maybe he never would have fallen in love with her even if she hadn't been, maybe she never would have fallen in love with him, he'll never know. She's too wrapped up in that time for him to ever risk losing her. And she's André's girl even if she still isn't ready to marry him, even if André is forever asking him to tell Mads one thing or another, leaving Sam insisting that if André can't fight his own battles with a woman half his size, Sam sure isn't doing it for him. Mads is André's girl and has been for as long as Sam has known her, and he would never risk losing André either. Mads is right though, he realizes. (Well, she usually is.) He's had this idea that the shape of shared genes is what matters, but his mom and dad, his grandparents, his siblings are all gone now. Mads and André are his family now.

"Nyx—Nyx is Mads back-dooring into my life the one thing she thought might . . ."

Might allow him to love again.

"I love Mads, I do," he says. "I owe her so much."

He looks to the sky again, to the line of three bright stars. He'll take the world to Orion, the Greek hunter known since the second century, since Ptolemy—how has this not occurred to him before? Not in the next game, but in this one, in *The Ghost of Hawk Tower.*

"I will always love Mads," he says. "But I'm not in love with her."

Gemma turns toward him then, her expression softer. He can't see the color of her Monet eyes in the dim light, but he knows that color beyond her glasses lenses, somehow both changeable and steady.

Great Orion, whose belt / Is studded with three nails of burning gold.

Orion, who could walk on the waves.

He fingers a strand of her hair, tracing the long wave of it down her neck, and he kisses her gently, the way he ought to have that first night. She tastes of milky chocolate. She isn't drunk.

She holds her breath for a moment but doesn't look away.

The sky has started to lighten, the sun rising. He removes her glasses so he can better see her eyes, and kisses her again.

They sit quietly together then, not saying anything more as the sky moves far too quickly from black to gray to red to orange. They sit sipping the shared chocolat chaud and listening to the hoot of an owl somewhere, watching a falcon spread its wings dark against the new-sun bleed of color as the day begins.

Rebecca Chazan," Iz repeated. "Do you have a middle name for her too, Leo? Have you given her one in your heart?" And when he shook his head, she said simply, "Leave her as just that, will you? Rebecca Chazan?"

Like him, Léon Chazan, who left his life behind and started again with nothing more than a borrowed name.

"Rebecca Chazan," he whispered, as if the name were sacred, his mother's given name and the surname of the mother who gave her son's future to him.

Iz said, "We have to arrange it with the doctor."

He said, "Yes."

"The couple coming from Connecticut, I don't know how—"

"There's another child the doctor delivered on the same day, to a teenaged mother, the mother named on Rebecca's birth certificate. It was a way to keep your name off any paperwork he would have to file. You were sleeping, you were exhausted after giving birth, and the doctor wanted an answer."

She nodded. It was what she would have agreed to herself, to let a girl she had never met claim her baby as a twin to hers in exchange for somebody paying her medical bill. That was what the doctor had proposed. Leo didn't believe the other mother knew anything about it. He thought the doctor just wanted to be paid twice. But he hadn't asked questions. He'd simply paid the bill.

"That other mother's baby was also to have been put up for

adoption, sent to an orphanage until parents could be found," Leo said. "Same date of birth. Same mother listed on the birth certificate. The couple will have exactly the child they came for."

And Leo would have the child he already loved.

AS THE DARK CAR THAT was Mannix pulled into the driveway of the studio's cottage, Iz put her dark glasses and hat on, and took her suitcase and the dress. She was to leave Leo's through the back door, circle through the studio's cottage, and quickly duck out to the car in which Mannix would drive her back to LA.

"Thank you, Leo," she said, glad that her glasses hid her pooling eyes. "Thank you for everything."

He took her by the shoulders then, and removed her glasses. "Just show them who you are," he said. "That's all you need to do." He kissed her cheek then, and turned her toward the bedroom door, beyond which was the back door exit to the rest of her life.

She pushed the bedroom door open. She focused on the floor, on the few steps to the back door. It was better this way, for her never to see the child.

She opened the door to the outside. It was a glorious day. Shining sun. The sounds of a feisty sea. Dozens of pelicans flapping their prehistoric selves across a blue blue sky to places she would never go.

She set her suitcase down. Set her gown across it. Her hat. Her glasses.

She went to the bed. Looked at Rebecca sleeping on her stomach there on the soft, clean sheets, surrounded by pillows enough to protect the Seventh Fleet. A soft blanket over her. Pale rounded cheek with just a hint of eczema near her mouth, the other cheek pressed to the bed. Her thumb dangling loosely from her slightly parted lips. Wisps of blond hair. Eyes closed. Long, pale lashes. Her little body moving just slightly with each breath.

Iz leaned over the pillows and kissed her forehead, feeling the warmth of her delicate skin, breathing in the yeasty-sweet smell of her.

"I'm sorry," she said.

She hurried to the back door then, donned her hat and glasses, lifted her suitcase and gown and crossed the backyard to enter the studio's cottage through the bedroom window Mannix had opened.

A moment later, she slipped from the nameless cottage that would, years later, be named Manderley, and climbed into the car, carrying only her suitcase and her Oscar gown.

Iz has pulled every string she can to get Leo honored in the Oscars In Memoriam, but who is she anymore? That's what she's thinking as a retro version of the 2018 awards begins, black-and-white and with the almost-square aspect of old television footage—like that first time she watched the Oscars here at the Fade Inn—and with a fake-1950s voice overlay and contemporary stars cut in. There's Meryl Streep watching herself inside the theater but in old-timey footage, the announcer saying she's been nominated for twenty-one Oscars but "her most important role is that of mother to her four children"—followed by a quick "Just kidding, she doesn't even know their names!" Iz cringes as everyone in the theater laughs. Streep became a mother just weeks before the release of *Kramer vs. Kramer*, a mother-guilt film for which (ironically) she won the Oscar, when Isabella was already forty-five. Streep's generation, freed of the Hollywood system with its seven-year contracts and studio control, could choose to play complex women who did not need to be seen as virginal to be loved by the American public, who perhaps didn't even need the public's love.

"You know Leo was wild about you, Sam," she says, trying not to think about the fact that every year the Academy snubs people, often those who were once on the blacklist everyone wants to forget. "He never thought blood was blood," she says. "He thought love was love." It's something she can give Sam, something she would know as Leo's friend. And Sam is the one who put Leo's ashes front and center, with the best view of the TV.

They're dressed formally, Gemma in a black dress she swears she's worn every year since she first came up to watch the Oscars with Leo—a prom dress of her mother's, she says, leaving Iz imagining Leo greeting some boy at the door and making polite conversation while every bone in his body wanted to tell the boy to treat his daughter right. Sam is wearing a tuxedo, a different one than he wore that first night she met him in LA, with Nyx in a bow she keeps trying to shake off. Iz might have worn the Oscar gown she wore that night with Leo. She's vain enough to make sure it still fits every year. But it's a young woman's dress. She no longer has the arms to carry off sleeveless and her neck couldn't be made beautiful even with Marie-Antoinette's million-dollar pearls. She wears a simple sage-colored, floor-length sheath.

Jimmy Kimmel launches into a bit about Oscar being the most admired man in Hollywood. "Look at him. He keeps his hands where you can see them. Never says a rude word." He talks about Harvey Weinstein being thrown out of the Academy, the importance of movements like Me Too, and the success of movies like *Wonder Woman* and *Black Panther* in a Hollywood which once believed neither women nor people of color could open a superhero film. "The reason I remember that time," he says, "is because it was last March."

Iz and Gemma and Sam laugh. Everyone laughs.

"Things are funniest when they're also true—Gran taught me that," Gemma says.

Sam says it's not so different in the video game world: Mads is one of very few women at the top. "It makes such a difference. Boys are gaming daily and their perceptions of gender are being shaped as much as the girls' are. It's weird; the early days of video gaming depended on so many women. Carol Shaw—she pioneered the use of algorithms to create continuous landscaping on a machine with only 128 bytes of RAM. But now . . ."

"At least we have our superhero doggess," Gemma says.

"Yeah, let's just say Nyx was a boy dog until Mads demanded to know what the hell I was doing naming a boy dog after such an amazing goddess. I was in the doghouse for months."

Iz laughs at the silly pun, she does, and so does Gemma, as Kimmel goes on with a tone of seriousness underlying his humor that suggests this year might really be different despite there being again not a single female director nominee.

"We have to dance!" Iz says when one of the best song nominee performances begins, something from *Coco*. The three of them hop up and join hands, dancing in a circle with Nyx weaving around their feet, Gemma and Sam singing along. Even after the performance gives way to a commercial, they keep singing over each other, songs from other animated movies Iz has never seen. They sing an entire song about a princess, for pity's sake, but Iz does like the line about nobody telling them where to go or that they're only dreaming. And she loves the way they collapse into laughter after Sam manages to hold the last note of that song even longer than Gemma does, then buries her in a hug.

"Gosh, Sam, I thought you were going to suffocate me," Gemma says, still laughing as they finally break apart. "I thought if I survived, I could use the moment in a script! Gran's ashes and their red zip tie. Nyx brushing against our legs. And a detective questioning you as you try to explain that you didn't mean to kill me. Murder by Affection."

And she laughs again, the way Leo was forever laughing to keep himself from crying, all that emotion Leo channeled into his writing, to make others laugh, and cry too.

When the In Memoriam finally begins, Gemma takes the ashes, and Iz takes her free hand. Sam joins them on the couch and Nyx nuzzles her puppy head right up against Leo's red zip tie to the train of photos of the recently deceased. Singer Chuck Berry. June Foray, who voiced both Rocky the Squirrel and Natasha from the *Rocky & Bullwinkle* cartoons and more other characters than you could imagine, often without credit. Producer Allison Shearmur. The French actress Jeanne Moreau, who was honored by Cannes and BAFTA and who, shortly before she died,

said she felt abandoned because she could no longer act. Both Roger
Moore and Sam Shepard receive the rare honor of audio clips, Moore
introducing himself as James Bond, and Shepard telling a young Jessica
Lange that she is a movie star now, "You give them what they want, you
can get anything."

And finally, Chazan.

They play a clip of Leo speaking too. It's from a recording he
put together when Hollywood Ten Dalton Trumbo was dying. Leo
hadn't been the mysterious Robert Rich who never picked up his
Oscar for *The Brave One.* That had been his friend Dalton, who had
written that script when he was so destitute that he was suicidal.
He sent it to the producers with a letter begging them to pay him
money he was already owed. His Oscar remained unclaimed until
the president of the Academy personally delivered it in 1975, shortly
before Trumbo died.

"Dalton said there were no villains or heroes, no saints or devils,
there were only victims," Leo is saying on the television. "Well, he was
wrong. Dalton himself was a hero. He was the brave one. His example
kept so many of us writing when we might have given up."

Fifty thousand dollars. That was what Hitchcock paid Iz for Leo's
The Ghost of Hawk Tower script, knowing the money would go to
someone on the blacklist even if he didn't want to know exactly who.
Iz cashed the check and left enough to pay the taxes on it in her account. She put the rest in a box, all that money in crisp new bills, and
she drove up alone one night and set the box just inside Leo's door,
which he never did lock. She didn't even leave a note. She knew he
would know what it was. She knew he wouldn't want to accept it. But
she couldn't take any more from him than he'd already given her.

If Iz had been caught fronting that script, it would have ended her
career. But she hadn't been. She wasn't. She claimed to have written
it and nobody ever questioned that after her afternoon with Hitch and
Alma on their Heart o' the Mountain porch. And that movie made
her career.

Is it that fairy tale she can't let go of? The memory of those years when she was a star, all that attention she took for granted, that she now wants back?

Leo had worked all night that night after she met with the Hitchcocks, and he took care of the baby too. He could do that. He could juggle writing and a child. And he'd wanted Isabella to know he could.

February 1958

Just a few months after Iz returned to Hollywood, she was an Oscar nominee for the first time, best supporting actress for her role in *A Little Romance*, which the studio had released the week she returned to LA, with "Summer" removed from the title. The movie was a huge success at the box office, but she lost the Oscar that year and the next too, when she also lost the writing award she didn't deserve, both for *Double Deception*. But the third year she was a nominee, in 1961, she took the Oscar home to her LA house and set it on that table in her entry hall, next to a huge vase of flowers the studio had sent. So she was a bona fide movie star before she first returned to Carmel.

She borrowed the cottage from the studio for a single night in September of 1962, five years after Rebecca was born. She slipped in quietly just after midnight, as she had that first time, although this time she drove herself. Mannix had had several heart attacks and was wheelchair-bound by then, and this visit had nothing to do with him.

She woke early the next morning, if she slept at all, and she watched out the window. It was dark at first, not so much as a single candle lighting Hawk Tower. Robinson Jeffers had died early that same year, four years after he published his last new poem, his death improbably followed by a rare snowfall in Carmel.

The Fade Inn as the light came up, finally, looked the same, but better, more cared for. Where Leo had had that single tired lawn chair on the front patio, four Adirondack chairs now sat. He'd planted roses too, young but healthy and blooming.

A neighbor emerged from the house beyond Leo's and set off walking. Another came by with a dog on leash. And finally, Leo emerged, smartly dressed in a jacket and tie, holding Rebecca's hand easily as he set off with her for her first day of school. The little girl looked up at Leo and said something, and his response left her laughing with her whole body, her little feet in her new Mary Janes skipping, kicking her gingham dress up as she went. Leo skipped with her, the vented back of his suit coat flapping. He was her father. Whatever it cost him to raise her, he would make the same choice again. Whatever he did or didn't tell her about the woman who gave birth to her was his choice. Iz was not her mother. Seeing them together in that moment, she understood that she wasn't, and would never be.

After Leo and Rebecca disappeared down the road, Iz climbed in the car again and drove back to her house on the Bad Boy Drive section of Mulholland in LA.

It was nearly thirteen years before she returned to Carmel. 1975. She came up twice that year, first to watch from behind the studio cottage window as Rebecca appeared in her cap and gown and drove off to her high school graduation, with Leo. That week's *Carmel Pine Cone* ran a list of the graduates, from which she learned that Rebecca Chazan was headed for Dartmouth. It was the last Ivy League school to admit undergraduate women, a place where fraternity pranks had pledges sliding letters detailing vulgar activities "required" of coeds under every woman's door, where the winner of an annual fraternity-song competition—judged by one of the deans—was ten verses of insulting, sexualized attacks on women. But it was Leo's school, and it would be Rebecca's too.

Two days before Dartmouth classes began that fall, Iz returned to Carmel. She had no idea whether Leo had already left to fly with Rebecca to New Hampshire, or if he was driving her all that way, or even if they had left yet. But she knew Leo. She knew he wouldn't put Rebecca on a plane by herself, that he would want to get her settled in her dorm room, meet her roommate, get her sheets and towels, a small refrigerator, a coffee maker and books and a winter coat. He would want to see enough of her new life to be able to imagine it. And it didn't matter to Iz how long she stayed. She was between parts. At nearly forty she was for the first time nearly always between parts.

She waited and watched as she had at Leo's so many years before, when he'd been away for writing jobs. And when he pulled Tubby into the garage three days later—he'd flown with Rebecca, then, from Monterey or San Jose or San Francisco—she took the bottle of his lousy scotch she'd brought and knocked on his door.

This was why she'd come this time, not to watch Rebecca leave but to be here for Leo when he came home alone, just as he had been there for her when she arrived alone eighteen years before. She knew he would be so proud of this daughter who had been his since she was born, really, and always would be, but that letting her go would break his heart.

"I thought you might like some company today," she said.

He hugged her then, and held her tightly, and said, "Thank you." He wasn't talking about the scotch or her company, although he was glad for both.

If anyone asked how they knew each other, they could say he was working on a screenplay for her, they agreed as they poured the scotch. The blacklisting days were over, finally, even if the havoc they wreaked was not. He was writing as Chazan again.

"We can say we're calling it 'The Ghost of Hawk Tower,'" he joked.

"I always liked that title better than *Double Deception*," she said, "but 'The Ghost of the Montauk Lighthouse' doesn't have the same ring."

"You were as amazing in that movie as I knew you would be," he said.

"I've never had a better part."

They sat outside in his Adirondack chairs, the first time they'd been together in nearly eighteen years, but they didn't even say much. They had dinner at the little table they'd eaten at all those years ago, where Rebecca had eaten breakfast and lunch and dinner all her life, done her homework, played checkers and gin rummy and Monopoly with friends. Where Leo's daughter filled out those college applications that were the beginning of her leaving him.

Just as they were saying good night at his door, Iz asked Leo about the cottage. "The studio will sell it to me if I want it," she said. She'd gotten, as one of the terms of the contract for her latest film, an option to buy it. "I would keep my LA place," she said. "I wouldn't come up when Rebecca is home. But I won't buy it if you don't want me to."

He looked at the threshold for a moment, the bottom half of the door that had divided them the morning they first met as wide open now as the top. "You should give the cottage a name," he said. "You should call it Manderley."

She laughed and laughed, which was one part the unexpectedness of his words, and a larger part a need not to cry, not to take this loss that was Leo's and make it anything to do with her.

"It's still the same one-bedroom, six-hundred-square-foot cottage it's always been," she protested. "Plywood walls. Single-pane windows."

"Call it Manderley," he repeated. "It makes you laugh. It will make us both laugh."

And she imagined it would. She imagined naming the little cottage might wash away a history she supposed she'd meant to take on as a hair shirt, all the young women sent up to Carmel for all the wrong reasons, for secret rendezvous they thought would pave the way to a future in film or for abortions or, during that dark period of the blacklisting, men and women both sent to name names in an awful attempt to clear their own, which could only ever have resulted in tarnishing.

Iz stayed three more weeks that visit, and the next time she returned, it was to a cottage she owned, with Manderley painted on the little Dutch door.

She would come up regularly after that, staying for weeks or sometimes a month, never imagining a future in which Leo's Rebecca would not outlive him. During Rebecca's lifetime, though, Iz was never again in Carmel when she was, except that one December when Rebecca arrived unexpectedly early to surprise Leo for his birthday, with her toddler daughter in tow.

"Cricket, my Cricket!" Leo had exclaimed when he opened the door to see them. Iz had never heard him happier.

After the three of them disappeared into the Fade Inn, Iz took the cake she'd made, already studded with an abundance of unlit candles, and climbed into her car and left.

Iz watches the Oscars In Memoriam move on to Jerry Lewis, who hosted that first Oscars ceremony she watched in this room all those years ago, and died in August. "Might as well like yourself," he says in the clip. "Just think about all the time you're going to have to spend with you."

Iz sets her free hand on the couch arm as if Leo might overlap his pinkie with hers, feeling the warmth of Gemma's hand too and wondering what made her knock on the Fade Inn door the morning Gemma arrived. She'd known Gemma would come eventually. She'd imagined that if she were here—she prefers her cozy Manderley to the big, empty LA house even now that Leo is gone—she would simply close the door to her cottage and leave, as she'd done when Rebecca surprised Leo for his birthday all those years ago. Was it curiosity, or longing, or sympathy for the girl arriving with nothing but a backpack, looking at the empty cottage with the same dread Iz felt when Mannix first brought her here? Gemma had looked no older than Iz had been then, and as alone.

"Almost nobody will ever know his first name, will they?" Gemma says as the next Oscar presenters are introduced. "Léon." She smiles and says, "I wonder if he just used 'Chazan' because 'Léon' is too much trouble. The only way to add the accent with a typewriter is to backspace and type an apostrophe over the *e*, or pen it in by hand."

"Like my friend André," Sam says.

"Who refuses to wear a tux," Gemma says. "Léon. Even in Courier font it will never look as beautiful as it sounds."

Iz says, "The single name, Chazan—it was the way your grandfather honored them both: the first Léon Chazan and the boy's mother who gave Leo her son's future and sacrificed her own life for him."

Gemma asks if her grandfather ever told Iz what his name had been before he escaped France, and she answers, truthfully, that he had not.

On the TV, they're awarding best adapted screenplay to James Ivory for *Call Me by Your Name*, a title that reminds Iz of Leo, who wasn't born Chazan, or even Léon or Leo. As Ivory, now the oldest Academy Awards winner ever, begins to cane his way to the microphone, they cut to clips from his movie, teenagers at a dance.

"How did any of us survive being teenagers?" Gemma says.

BE GRATEFUL FOR HER, AND DON'T ASK, the doctor had told Iz when she'd asked about the mother listed on her baby's birth certificate. That girl hadn't survived being a teenager. But had the girl ever even existed? Had there really been a teenaged mother who gave birth that same day? Iz hadn't wanted to question that. She'd so wanted to believe some other woman would put her name on that certificate so she didn't have to. And Leo had wanted to believe it too. Everything he did, she sees now, was Leo wanting to believe he could keep Rebecca. He paid that poor teenaged mother's medical bill when the doctor asked him to, using Hugh's money they'd kept in an empty Folgers can because Leo refused to use it to take care of Iz. He might have given all Hugh's money to that other mother, but she'd died in childbirth, or that was what that doctor told Leo. It hadn't made sense even at the time: If that girl really did die in childbirth, when had she agreed to give her name as the mother of Iz's child? Leo had known that doctor was lying about something from the day he turned up with that birth certificate, but he didn't know what, didn't want to know, didn't even tell Iz.

He kept the rest of Hugh's money in that Folgers can, which he dipped into occasionally over the years when he would hear of a child in need, sticking a few bills in an envelope and mailing it anonymously. He paid Isabella's own doctor bill himself the night she gave birth, even before they sold that script. He couldn't really afford it, but Iz couldn't pay it without using that money from Hugh, and Leo wanted her to have a clean slate, to know she didn't owe Hugh Bolin a thing.

The money Hitchcock paid for *The Ghost of Hawk Tower*—that Leo had rightly earned and Iz had tucked inside his door—he deposited that slowly over time into an account for Rebecca, and he invested it well. It paid for her college, with enough left last year to cover the experimental medical treatment that the insurance company wouldn't cover, that might have saved her, but didn't. The little that was left over he gave to Gemma to make *Eleanor After Dark*.

Mary Smith, the most common name in the country, and the doctor's signature an illegible scrawl. When Iz had first heard Sam's name, she'd thought of that family from Connecticut who were going to take Rebecca. The Phippses. She wondered if Sam might be that other mother's child, a child of the baby Mannix gave to the couple from Connecticut in Rebecca's place. It was preposterously unlikely, but she told herself he might be and she might help him somehow now—a small thanks for Mary Smith saving her all those years ago by claiming Rebecca as her own. She told herself that was why she went to that SidewalkChalk charity event, hoping to meet him. But the truth is Rebecca had died just days before, without ever knowing Iz. The truth is, she supposes, that she was looking for some connection to Rebecca, some way to imagine a life that might have allowed Iz to know her somehow, someday. The truth is the Monterey County records from the 1950s might include dozens of records for children born of a mother named Mary Smith, who might have been a woman of any age and any name, married or not, wealthy or poor, poised to be "the new Grace" or to go to college or to marry some man who wasn't the father of that child. A woman who might, like Iz, have wanted to keep the fact of an out-of-wedlock birth secret, who might have reasons to keep it secret still.

ON THE TELEVISION, JAMES IVORY says, "We've all gone through first love," then adds, "I hope." Leaving Iz wondering if she has. She has had other lovers since Hugh, of course, but she's never been in love, never married, never imagined a whole life with anyone.

Ivory thanks the directors and the actors, and his "life's partners": Ruth Prawer Jhabvala, who wrote for them, and Ismail Merchant, whom he describes only as their fearless producer for more than fifty years. If you didn't know it, you would never guess Merchant was the love of James Ivory's life, that even a decade after his death, Ivory doesn't publicly acknowledge their relationship because Merchant, an Indian citizen from a conservative Muslim family, kept their love private. It makes Iz think of all Leo gave up to raise Rebecca: The possibility of true love. A partner he could climb into bed with every night. Maybe share an Oscar with. And of the loss to Rebecca too, who might have had two parents, two fathers who loved her. Gemma might have had a second grandfather, free of the need for every family to look the same.

"If it isn't about the tux, what is it about?" Gemma asks Sam, and when he responds with a confused look, she says, "With Mads and André? You said last night that it wasn't about the tux."

She strokes Nyx's ears, waiting.

"It's about Mads being afraid André won't love her if she lets him see who she is, I think," he says. "But André . . . He's known her since she was eighteen. He knows her in ways she doesn't realize he does. Like I do. Like the three of us know each other."

The way Leo knew Iz, she sees now, and she didn't really know he did, either. The way, when you're that young, you're less accomplished at hiding yourself than you become, maybe because you don't even know who you are yet, you don't know what it is you need to hide.

"SidewalkChalk . . . that's who Mads is—a smart and talented person who wants to make a difference, the person she wanted to be when she first put on those fake glasses," Sam says. "Maybe she's ready to take them off? That's really all André needs: for Mads to love herself enough to risk loving a guy who refuses to wear a tux just because she wants him to."

Nyx, as if she's been listening and understands better than either Sam or Gemma does, nudges Gemma's arm.

Gemma hesitates, then repeats, "Risk loving him."

It's always a risk, loving someone: you lose them one way or you lose them another, or they lose you. But unless you take the risk, you lose at the beginning, without the benefit of loving or being loved.

On the TV, Jodie Foster and Jennifer Lawrence are announcing the best actress nominees—only one of the five nominees as young and classically beautiful as all the women had to be in the 1950s. The male nominees tonight were older too, three in their fifties, but older men winning Oscars is nothing new.

Frances McDormand, with her new Oscar in hand—her second, at age sixty—asks every female nominee in every category to stand. All night, almost no women of any age have taken the stage.

As all these women who didn't win stand and everyone begins to clap, McDormand puts all of Hollywood on notice that these women too have projects that need funding.

And Iz is standing with them. She's clapping. She's seeing that she ought to have been leading all along in whatever way she could. This is the path she chose, for the right reasons or the wrong ones, what does that matter now? But she ought to have done better, she ought to have brought other women along. Maybe she couldn't have made a difference. Maybe making noise would have resulted in her being denied parts in which she could at least appear to be a stronger woman than she was, parts that provided role models for the next generations even if they were examples she didn't live. But if she had tried to do more, maybe young women like Gemma would have an easier time now.

THEY WATCH THE AWARDS CEREMONY through to the last, until *The Shape of Water* is named best picture. Iz mutes the TV as the camera pans the Oscar crowd she was once a regular part of. She considers her words carefully. Iz has spent all these years choosing her career over loving Gemma's mom, and Gemma too, Gemma would think. Not wanting to know them. Choosing some other thing as more important than them. That isn't the truth exactly, but it isn't not. She's owned the cottage next door to Leo for decades now though. This is something one old friend might have told another late one night over a glass of scotch.

"Your mother was named after your grandfather's mother," she tells Gemma. "Your great-grandmother's name was with two *k*'s, R-e-b-e-k-k-a."

Gemma's eyes blink blink blink, and Iz braces herself for one of those movie lines Gemma hides her emotions behind.

"I always imagined it was from the Hitchcock movie," she says. "I thought Gran must have had a hand in writing it."

"For Pete's sake, Cricket!" Iz says, the way Leo would have, as if she's just quoting him rather than using this love name herself one last time for this granddaughter who is his and not hers. She laughs as she says it too, the way he would. "Your Gran was only a teenager when that movie came out!" she says.

She says, seriously now, "Your name, Margalit, was the name of your grandfather's older sister."

Gemma dips a finger behind her lenses to wipe her eyes, but doesn't take her glasses off. "'Margalit' means 'pearl,' Gran told me," she says. "'Gemma' from 'gem.'"

Like her mother and her grandfather, no middle name. Just Margalit, a loved sister's name. David, a brother. Otto and Inge, and Heinrich and Yennj. Jacob and Rebekka. And their brother, their grandson, their son Leo, who was not born Léon Chazan, but who survived.

Iz pulls from her bag the final shooting script for *Double Deception*, with "by Isabella Giori" typed on the cover page, along with the draft under the title *The Ghost of Hawk Tower* that she stole from this cottage, and she hands them both to Gemma. "These properly belong to you," she says. "They were your Gran's. I took the original script. I don't even know why. I fronted the script for him."

"You did?" Gemma looks at her like she's some kind of hero she never has been.

These young women, they need someone to look up to, and they have to make do with the likes of her, a pretend hero created for film by men and under their command. But it's close enough to the truth, and as much of it as Leo would want Gemma to know. When the Writers Guild was restoring credit for scripts that were fronted, Leo wouldn't ever allow her to request that script be credited to him lest it leave Rebecca with questions that, if answered, might cause her pain.

"It benefited me more than your Gran," Iz says, making herself a promise that she'll do her best from now on to set the kind of example in real life that she's only allowed herself to do in film. "It got me a part with Hitchcock, who could make a star back then. And the Oscar nominations. It lost the writing Oscar to Harold Jacob Smith and 'Nathan E. Douglas,' a pseudonym for your grandfather's blacklisted friend Nedrick Young. I'm sure that's why that Oscar was left to your Gran, because *Double Deception* would almost certainly have won if he'd given it to a man to front, but I needed the part and your Gran knew giving me the script was the only way I would get to play it. The studio I was under contract with, they wanted me to be someone I never was."

Iz pauses. She's the only person who knows the truth about Rebecca now, just as she's the only one who knows the truth about how Leo died. Pancreatic cancer. Metastasized to Leo's liver and bones and brain before it was discovered. He was already in pain, already exhausted, although he put up a good show even with her. *A few weeks, maybe a month, and longer won't be better,* he told her. *I can't put Gemma through that again, not so soon after Rebecca.* It hadn't been a year since Rebecca had died.

Iz supposes they're all thinking of Leo now. She's thinking of the script he wrote and gave to her. He wrote it, but he helped her make it her own too, the exact part she wanted to play to launch her career. He did it from the first moment he gave it to her to read. He put that pencil in her hand and urged her to add her own thoughts, to revise it with him so that it wasn't just his, but theirs. He made the script with her help, and put it in her hands, knowing she could make something of it that he never would have been able to. And with his help, she had a child, and she put that child in his care, which was going to be so much better care than Iz could ever have given her. Even then, Iz could imagine Leo sitting Rebecca in his lap, telling her about what he was writing, letting her press the typewriter keys. She could see he would always put his daughter first in a way she never would, that he was generous in a way she never was, a better parent than she could ever be.

As Iz is still watching the camera pan the Oscar crowd, Gemma turns it off and grabs her vest.

"All right, Gran, are you ready for this?" she says. Then to Sam, "Iz and I are taking Gran to the point."

He nods. He seems to understand that Leo isn't coming back. That Gemma has to do this right now, before she changes her mind.

He looks like he wants to join them, but he only takes Leo's bottle of scotch and hands it to Gemma, saying, "There's not much left, but he'll want a nightcap."

Leo always did like a nightcap, Sam is right about that, Iz thinks as she ducks into Manderley for her coat and more sensible shoes.

As she emerges again, Gemma is calling out to Sam, who has already crossed the street, "Would you like to come with us?" Clearly surprising herself as much as she surprises Iz.

"Now?" He pulls Nyx closer.

Goodness, how Leo loved that boy. Leo saw himself in that boy, of course he did. Both orphaned when they were so young, left to make families out of love rather than blood.

"I would," Sam says. "I would for myself but . . . I was so lucky to know your grandfather these last few months. I was so lucky to feel his love. But you both, he loved you for so long. I think he would want you to do this alone, if that makes any sense? But how about dinner tomorrow? Or lunch? Or breakfast?"

Gemma is relieved, Iz thinks. She says sure to doing something tomorrow, why doesn't Sam call her in the morning? And she heads toward Iz.

"I need your phone number!" he says, and Gemma calls it out to him, and a second later her phone rings, him telephoning so she'll have his number too.

Iz and Gemma head for the point then, Iz with a glance to the top of Hawk Tower, remembering that night of the Jeffers party, Leo's head tilted toward someone whose identity she never has learned. Not a lover, though. He'd told her there wasn't anything for the FBI to find and that was what he meant, no lovers, and she believed him. He left the next morning too, or maybe that very night, and was gone long enough that it had to have been a friend arranging for Leo to write something for someone—a friend who understood that Leo's writing kept him alive.

"I'M SORRY TO ASK YOU," Leo had said when he asked her to help him die. "I know I shouldn't ask you. I'm not afraid to die, Iz, but I'm afraid to die alone."

It wasn't illegal to assist someone with suicide in California any-more, but Leo didn't feel he had the time to deal with the bureaucracy required by the new law, and he didn't want to risk Gemma finding out that his death was something she might have delayed. He got Gemma to come up that last weekend only he and Iz knew would be his last, two days Iz spent in LA. But Iz joined Leo in his cottage long before dawn the morning after Gemma left, bringing a cup of coffee for each of them. The Folgers he liked. She made it at Manderley and took it over to the Fade Inn just before five in the morning, careful not to confuse the cups.

He sat in the chair in his bedroom and she sat on the edge of the bed, and he typed Gemma's number on his telephone so she would know he was thinking about her at the last, this girl to which he had been grandfather and father both.

"You're sure?" Iz said, wanting him not to be, wanting even one day more with him.

"I'm old enough that nobody will question an early-morning heart attack," he said, and she heard in his voice what he wasn't saying in words, that he'd saved his last days for Gemma.

She said, "And I'm too old for anyone to suspect me of doing anything interesting," because sometimes a laugh will do when you need to cry but can't.

It was, they joked, a script Leo ought to have written.

He took a first sip from his cup, the coffee laced with the foxgloves from her gardens in Los Angeles, the first early blooms.

"But we'd never have gotten this past the Production Code Administration," he said, and they laughed at who they had been that morning they met, two lonely souls ostracized from the only life they knew how to live.

When he began to feel unwell, she helped him finish the coffee, then sat on the floor beside his chair, holding his hand as his pulse grew increasingly erratic.

"I've had a good life, it turns out," he said. "Thank you for trusting me." And his last words, "I had such a perfect weekend with Gemma."

Even after his heart no longer beat, Iz sat there, not listening now but instead saying all the things she ought to have said when he was alive but understood he didn't want to hear.

"Thank you for saving me, Leo. Thank you for accepting me for who I am, and for helping me accept myself."

"I love you, Leo," she said.

"I've loved you since that first spring," she said. "But I suppose you know that and always have."

She kissed him on the forehead then, and slipped out the back door again with the two cups in hand.

At Manderley, she fed the rest of the foxgloves down the disposal. Such beautiful flowers, and so dangerous. She supposes that's why she loves them, why she planted them.

She ran the cups through the dishwasher three times, just to be sure: once before she walked out to the point in the predawn darkness; then as she carefully cleaned her whole cottage when she returned; and a final time just before she called the police to say she was concerned about her next-door neighbor, might they do a wellness check?

AS IZ AND GEMMA MAKE their way toward the point, a light is now on in Hawk Tower, the same candlelight Iz used to see there sixty years ago. It can only be Sam. Iz doesn't know if Gemma notices. She doesn't point it out to her. She supposes Sam has told himself he's just there to work on his game. Or perhaps he's more honest with himself than she is. Perhaps he knows he means to climb to the top, to watch over them as they let Leo go.

At the sharp turn toward Carmel River Beach, she and Gemma scramble down the path, holding their dresses up. Iz's legs are cold as they pause at the spot where Robinson Jeffers spoke to her, the only time they ever spoke, that morning she watched the tip of his cigarette swinging along the dark road back to his tower and his single candle flame, his poetry. He was long dead before she bought Manderley, but still she feels she knows the man. Is that through his poetry, or through the shared experience of fame lived and lost, or simply through that first frightening moment, the stars going over the lonely ocean and the lonely light of his window across the road in that predawn moment when she too was so alone?

She and Gemma climb all the way out on the point, beyond the high granite boulders all the teens love to climb. The waves crash around them as they stand on the shelf of rock Isabella has taken to coming out to sit on in the month since Leo's death, imagining him here with Rebecca already. The moon is out, a waning gibbous, the great mass bright but with a dark edge to it.

Gemma has brought scissors. She slides the blade under that red zip tie and cuts it. She pauses, clearly not wanting to toss the hard plastic strip into the ocean, much less in this sacred place where Rebecca and now Leo too will spend eternity.

Iz takes it from her and slips it into her coat pocket with the cowrie shell so that when Gemma is done here she will be done, she won't have to decide whether to keep a red zip tie that has nothing to do with who her grandfather was.

Gemma takes a big slug of his dreadful scotch straight from the bottle, then hands it to Iz, who takes a good slug too.

As Iz lowers the bottle, Gemma is watching her.

"Gosh," she says, "for a minute, I thought you were my mom."

Iz feels herself holding her breath. She can't tell Gemma who she is now, not in this moment. Not ever. She has to hope Gemma will never learn. How could she make her understand that the promise she made to Leo never to tell Rebecca, right or wrong, was a promise she kept for Rebecca's sake? A promise she needs to keep always now, for Leo, who knew he was dying and chose to take this secret with him. He was Rebecca's father, Gemma's grandfather. The decision was his alone whether to share the history of how he came to be. And perhaps he's right. Gemma is Leo's grandchild in so many ways. She doesn't want to live in the past, she wants to jump forward always, Leo's little Cricket. She wants whatever is ahead.

Gemma says, "Mom and I used to come out here together at night sometimes when I was a kid. I was allowed to climb to the top of that high rock in the daylight, but never at night."

Iz says with as much humor as she can muster, "Do not think you're going to climb it tonight, not with me here. Never mind in that dress!"

Gemma laughs, and Iz thinks maybe Leo was right, too, about leaving his granddaughter with the last memory she has of him being a good moment, a moment of laughter rather than grief.

"Thank you for coming with me," Gemma says. "I meant to do this alone, but I don't think I could have, really. And you feel like part of Gran's family."

Iz says, "I'm not sure what I would have done, who I would have been, without your Gran."

Gemma says, "Yeah. Me too."

She reaches into the plastic bag and pulls out a handful of ashes, then hands the bag toward Iz. Iz takes a handful too.

"I want to say something," Gemma says. "But I don't know what to say."

"'Ich würde an meinen Geburtsort zurückkehren,'" Iz offers. I would go back to the place I was born. "'Je retournerais là d'où je viens.'" I would return to the place I came from. Lines from *The Ghost of Hawk Tower*, which became *Double Deception*. Germany. France. Leo tearing out a piece of his own heart and placing it so carefully into his script.

"He loved you so much, Gemma," she says.

Gemma tosses her handful of ashes and they watch as a wave catches them and draws them down into the sea. "I love you too, Gran," she says.

Goodbye, Samuel, Iz thinks. It's a coincidence, she knows that, but it seems a good omen that Sam's name is the one Leo left behind. A name Leo never shared with Gemma, and he was her grandfather, that too was his decision. A name that now might change the way Gemma looks at Sam, and new love is such a fragile thing.

Iz tosses her handful, only to have half of it blow back right into their faces, leaving them sputtering and instinctively wiping their lips.

"For Pete's sake, Gran!" Gemma says, and she laughs and Iz does too.

They take handful after handful then, letting Leo go in great bursts.

Finally, Gemma upends the bag and taps out the last sprinkle, then squats and rinses the bag in the sea at their feet.

Iz takes the scotch bottle and empties it over the rock so that the ashes that have landed there are mostly washed away. Anything left of Leo will join the sea when the tide rises, as it always does.

It seems the moment, so Iz squats beside Gemma with the perfect little egg-shaped shell not much bigger than Leo's shirt-sleeve buttons, the porcelain chestnut of his eyes, with a pure white underside rimmed with hard little teeth—this talisman she tucked into her bra right next to her heart, to carry with her to every audition and every set every day since that afternoon with the Hitchcocks.

"Look," she says as if she has just found it, in the process wetting it with the sea.

Gemma takes her glasses off and wipes the sea spray from them, then takes the little shell and examines it in the moonlight. Iz feels herself breathe out, sure now that Gemma will keep it, that she will have it long after Iz is gone. That it will carry Leo forward in Gemma's life just as it carried him with Iz in hers.

They sit together, dangling their legs over the edge. As the feisty surf mists her calves, Iz feels a little like the girl she was when she first arrived in Carmel. The girl she thought was a woman already. She was so young then, far too young for motherhood. Twenty-two going on sixteen. She can't take any credit for Rebecca, much less for Gemma, but neither of them would have been on this Earth if she hadn't been that foolish young girl. A girl Leo had always, in his gentle way, urged to forgive herself. *We have to accept the loves we love as they come to us,* he'd once told her, or perhaps more than once.

Can she call what Leo and she had love? A different kind of love, but she supposes he was the best love of her life.

And she was loved too. She sees that now, as she reaches into her pocket, feels the grit of the small bit of ashes she held back, that she tucked into her coat pocket when she extracted the shell—a grit that will be there for the rest of her life. Forgiveness—that wasn't his to give. That is hers alone, to forgive herself.

Back at the Fade Inn, Gemma changes into her jeans. She takes a pencil from Gran's desk—which she hasn't emptied and now imagines she won't—and tucks it over her ear. She rolls a fresh sheet of paper into Ole Mr. Miracle, and types *FADE IN:*. If she can write and sell something quickly, maybe she can scrape together enough to keep this place.

Out the bay window, Hawk Tower and Tor House and Point of No Return shadow the starry sky. She leans over and opens the top of the Dutch door to the bracing sea air and the sound of the waves.

She hits the return—zip—and hits it again, then types *Int. Hawk Tower - Night.* Seventeen letters. Five vowels. Two short hyphens that, on her computer, would leap together into one lovely em dash.

There is no poetry in a computer keyboard, no eyeballs that never shut, Gran liked to say, forever invoking Sexton although he himself wrote only screenplays and never, as far as Gemma knew, penned a sonnet or a sestina or even a cinquain.

She turns the roller back so that she's at the top of the page, above *FADE IN:*, and tabs to the center. Centering text is so much harder on a typewriter than on a computer. She can almost feel Gran's fingers on hers on the backspace, teaching her how to do this.

She starts to unlatch Gran's watch she's been wearing the last few days, then pauses. She adjusts her glasses and pushes the typewriter to the back of the desk. She throws on her vest, grabs her laptop, and heads out the door.

At the tree stump overlooking Gran's little writing cove, she zips up her vest and pulls the half gloves he gave her from the pockets before she climbs down the path and sits right down in the sand, leaning her back against the granite palisade.

"Gosh, it's cold here, Gran," she says. "How do you do this?"

I'm sorry, I can't hear you. Your mother and I are traveling the waves together, the way you like to imagine us.

"Safe travels, Gran," she whispers to herself. "Safe travels, Mom."

She sets her fingers to the keys then. Eight of each.

She opens a new blank screenplay and taps her trackpad to add *FADE IN:*. She scrolls down to the title page icon and taps to open a title page. She centers the text with another tap, then types *The Ghost of Hawk Tower*. Nineteen letters and four spaces. Six vowels. Eleven backspaces on a typewriter. She finds she misses that little formality. But the capital G looks as pretty in the laptop's Courier font as in the typewriter's. The *w*'s too, and the *t*'s.

When she hits the return, she's startled by a sudden ding and zip. She laughs. Sam must have done something to her laptop during the Oscars, while she was in the bathroom.

His house up above the palisade is dark but there is no reflection upstairs, that big wall of glass must be open. Is Sam out on the balcony? She waves, with no idea whether he's there, whether he can see her any better than she can see him.

Nyx barks her funny little bark. And with the sound as a guide, Gemma can just make out the faintest shadow on the balcony that might be Sam waving back.

She puts her fingers on the keyboard again. Centers the text. Types *by* and hits the return, sounding that delightful ding-zip again.

She hits the shift key with her left pinkie and reaches down with her right first finger for the M, the way Gran taught her. Her left pinkie on the *a*.

It takes the shortest moment to type *Margalit*, her name that was the name of Gran's sister she'll never know, but who was important to him, a way to honor him. Then *Chazan* with its beautiful, unusual *z* tucked comfortably in the middle. "Gran's name. Mom's name. My name."

Isabella unfolds the one-page speech she's written, strikes the thanks from the end and adds instead a single sentence. She folds it up again, all the while watching and hoping as the hosts joke into their microphones. It's that kind of year at the Oscars again. Greta Gerwig was snubbed as the *Barbie* director and Margot Robbie for playing the lead—while, ironically, Ryan Gosling was nominated for playing Ken. *Oppenheimer,* which has thirteen nominations, had fewer than twenty women in almost a hundred speaking roles, and no female lead. But neither one of those films will be the one to take this Oscar.

As they begin to read the nominees, Iz sits forward and lifts her chin. Yes, even at nearly ninety, a woman the whole world now thinks of as a grandmother, she can't entirely let go of her vanity. She smiles her best smile as the camera pans, feeling Gemma's gloved hand in hers tighten. She sets her free hand on the navy blue velvet at her chest as Octavia Spencer reads the final nominee. The gown still fits, and it's still the most elegant thing she has ever seen, with its white tulle floor-length skirt and the Grace Kelly–in–*Rear Window* detailing now replicated on the diaphanous tulle shawl draped over her arms. The pearls she's wearing are not the Marie-Antoinette strand the studio had arranged to borrow almost seventy years ago for her to wear with it, although when she was asked about them on the red carpet, she left the impression they might be. That was Gemma's idea for a little joke on the world—Gemma in the black sheath that was once her mother's prom dress, that she wore every time she watched the Oscars with Leo.

Iz's mouth tastes of the lousy scotch from the flask Sam, on the other side of Gemma, brought. *For good luck.* She fingers the little bit of ash enclosed in the smallest square of plastic wrap and tucked into her strapless bra right next to her heart, where she'd always tucked that hard little lump of cowrie shell before every audition. Lordy, she wishes Leo were here.

So quickly, the last clip has been shown—Sandra Hüller in *Anatomy of a Fall* insisting, "Your generosity conceals something dirtier and meaner"—and Melissa McCarthy is opening the envelope and saying, "And the Oscar goes to . . ."

Gemma's hand in Iz's squeezes even more tightly, leaving Iz regretting the white opera gloves they're both wearing, keeping them from being skin to skin.

On stage, McCarthy pulls the card from the envelope. "Margalit Chazan, *The Ghost of Hawk Tower!*"

Sam lifts Gemma off her feet in his enthusiastic hug as André and Mads cheer wildly. Gemma smiles so humbly that everyone watching can see she didn't expect this, which of course will make them love her all the more. Best Original Screenplay.

Your granddaughter is so like you, Leo, Iz thinks as she too hugs Gemma. Gemma has taken his title and even his setting and made from them a wonderful romantic comedy that is also about the blacklist, that is the same mix of funny and dark that Leo wrote, and yet completely Gemma's own. A film with a lot of heart and an adorable dog whose name happens to be Nyx.

"The speech," Gemma whispers. "Tell me you brought it, Iz?"

Iz puts the folded paper into Gemma's gloved hands, the speech Iz wrote because Gemma couldn't bring herself to do it. Iz couldn't have remembered her own name when she was up there if it hadn't been written down, she told Gemma when she gave it to her. Iz had thought, really, that her writing a lousy speech for Gemma would move her to write a good one herself. But Gemma only read it and said, *You bring it, Iz, I don't want to jinx myself.*

Gemma now lifts the hem of that old black prom dress and ascends the stairs to the stage and McCarthy and Spencer and the Oscar she has just won. She accepts congratulations, then takes the Oscar and sets in on the podium, and unfolds the speech.

Don't read the last line, Iz wants to shout.

Gemma reads the list of people Iz wrote down for her: the producers and actors and everyone who helped her turn her script into this film she also directed. She thanks all the friends who saw her through UCLA film school. "Particularly Michal, who ought to be listed as a cowriter but he wouldn't have it, and heck, he already has two of these." (*Hell*, Iz had written.)

"My friend Mads, too, for keeping me in good risotto while I was writing this script," she reads, "and her husband, André, for getting her to marry him so Sam would have nobody left to marry but me." Everyone laughs, Mads and André and Sam loudest of all. Iz still has no idea how Mads got that extra ticket for André after Iz gave her her own plus-one. She really can get anyone to do anything.

Gemma lowers the paper and says, "I want to thank the amazing Isabella Giori, aka Her Royal Grandmotherness"—which is definitely *not* written on that paper but does make the crowd chuckle—"For so very much, including writing this speech for me."

As the crowd laughs again, sure she's joking, Iz knows the camera will be panning to her own tear-streaked face, but she doesn't even care anymore.

"*No really*," Gemma insists. "It's ironic, right? The writer who can't write lines for herself?" She reads from the paper again, "And Sam, my anchor . . ." she looks up and pauses, so all eyes are on her as she delivers the line ". . . in a good way, mostly, although there are days . . ."

This gets a bigger laugh than Iz imagined when she wrote it, but the delivery really was terrific, and Oscar crowds tend to be generous with the laughs.

"And most especially, the late, great Chazan, known to me as 'Gran,'" Gemma says, and she reads the titles for the two early films Leo was nominated for, *The Little Girl* and *Down the Lane*. "And *Double Deception*, which Gran wrote but was credited to Isabella Giori, a credit I'm happy to tell you the Academy has now restored to Gran," she reads. She looks up from the paper and ad-libs, "You're the best, Iz," then returns to reading the longer list of scripts Leo wrote under other names, credits that Iz is also working with Gemma to get restored.

Gemma raises the Oscar then—a direction Iz wrote in brackets in the speech. The statue is in her left hand, the wrist with Leo's Patek Philippe watch—those two circles on the white face and the two second hands and his father's initials on the back—worn over her proper white glove. The J for Jacob, a man interned somewhere in France even before the Germans invaded. It's the only jewelry Gemma wears tonight other than her wedding ring.

She reads on, "This one—" She stops and looks at Iz, and laughs, then says in a perfect mimic of Iz's own voice as the murderess in *Double Deception*, "'I can't say that in public. No decent woman can say that.'"

This one is going to be the first of many, if the ghost of my Gran has any influence—that's how that last line Iz added to the speech just minutes ago reads. But Gemma is right. A man or even a woman as old as James Ivory when he won his first Oscar might get an ironic laugh from the line. A young man might get an indulgent laugh or even an approving one. But coming from a young woman like Gemma, that line would be seen as arrogant. Still, Iz wants Gemma to think it, to realize this is just the beginning, and to know how proud Leo would be.

Gemma is surveying the audience, she isn't quite finished. The chime sounds. She's about to get the hook, they are about to cut to a commercial.

"This one," Gemma starts, and she looks upward to the heavens and, before they turn off the mic, presses that Oscar to her heart. And she says in the quietest, most respectful voice, "This Oscar, Gran, belongs to you."

AUTHOR'S NOTE AND ACKNOWLEDGMENTS

If you've ever been to one of my book launch parties, Dad was the guy forever refilling your champagne glass. Mom was the reader I counted on to tell me when a book wasn't finished, and when it was. I first put words to the page for this novel on February 11, 2022, a Friday eight months after Dad died unexpectedly and, it would turn out, just a month before Mom died. Leo is my father's middle name; my dad isn't Leo, but Dad's generous and loving soul is buried in this character I love as much as Gemma and Iz do. Leo's typewriter is my mom's (a 1946 Woodstock), as are Rebecca's legs. Rebecca's desire for Gemma to make friends was my mom's desire each time I started the six different grade schools I attended. Gemma comes from Meg run backward; like her, my writing began with journals and typewriters, and I don't know what it means to have a grandmother. There are shreds of my heart all over this one. Many weeks, the only time I wrote was the forty minutes I spent with Jenn, Ellie, and Sheryl—the JEMS, Ellie dubbed us, a name that I see only now is also echoed in Gemma's name. We began each Friday Zoom by saying what we were going to write. That morning, with my heart no longer in the novel I'd been working on when Dad died, I said I was just going to start something new, a novel about the Hollywood blacklist that had long fascinated me. What I wrote that morning was a scene with a writer like me facing the empty space where her grandfather, the only father she knew, used to be. Like Leo, I believe in beginning wherever I can.

A year later, Sheryl shared a question her mother-in-law, Helen

Solomon, had asked—"Who do I belong to now?"—which simply and movingly articulated what I was trying to dig out of my own heart. The question also inspired Ellie to write a poetic list of the people (and Tippy!) she belonged to, the last of which was "my Friday writing group that gives me love, encouragement, a quiet space, a respect for routine. Mostly that gives me myself." Me, I belong in that very same way to Sheryl and Jenn, and to Ellie, who passed away a few weeks ago.

I belong too to the Rough Drafts—Karen Joy Fowler, Elizabeth McKenzie, Susan Sherman, Peggy Townsend, Jill Wolfson, and Kathleen Founds—who gave me Part I encouragement and thoughtful rough-draft love. I belong to my brother, David Waite, with thanks for the bourbon toast and everything else, and to the rest of my family and so many friends, but especially Eric and Elaine Hahn, who provided a temporary Palo Alto home when we so needed it, and the experience of drinking great wine in a room of glass walls that slide away to make an open-air space.

I am so grateful to my editor, Sara Nelson, and to Katie O'Callaghan, Katherine Beitner, and everyone at Harper—Jonathan Burnham, Doug Jones, Leah Wasielewski, and Tina Andreadis, to name a few—whose extraordinary efforts to get *The Postmistress of Paris* published while Mom was alive brought her so many moments of joy and laughter, and to Edie Astley, Joanne O'Neill, Robin Bilardello, Nancy Singer, Lydia Weaver, Stephanie Mendoza, and everyone else at Harper who works on my books. Kristin Hannah's kindness and generosity started a flood of fellow-author kindness that I will never forget; thank you all. Christina Baker Kline allowed me much-needed quiet time in Maine to finish the first draft of this one. My agent, Margaret Riley King, deserves some kind of Oscar for all she has done for me, with Sophie Cudd and Meagan Irby deserving nominations, at least, as do the many booksellers all over the country whose efforts to put my books in readers' hands give me the miracle of a whole writing life. I learned so much about screenwriting (and how much I still have to learn) from my Writers Lab friends, especially Elizabeth Kaiden and Nitza Wilon, Robin Swicord and Mary Jane Skalski, and Karen McDermott and all the alums who keep me involved even as I am writing novels. I'm grateful to Meryl Streep, Nicole Kidman, Oprah Winfrey, and everyone else funding this amazing effort to bring more women's voices into film.

This novel is also an homage to Carmel-by-the-Sea and Carmel Point. I am grateful to the Robinson Jeffers Tor House Foundation, which keeps Jeffers's remarkable home and evocative poetry available to us all, and to the guides and staff who inspired me with their stories and answered my many questions. I hope my new Carmel neighbors will forgive me for taking some liberties in order to, for example, allow Gemma to sit out on Flat Rock some years before storms sheared the rock to create the ledge, and to put my fictional Fade Inn and Manderley across Ocean View from Hawk Tower and Tor House and, in the more contemporary chapters, build Sam's fictional house on a lot that doesn't exactly exist. I hope the owners of the real Carmel Dog Bar will accept my apologies for moving it up the road. Most of what I've included about Carmel is what I understand to be true: Memory Bench is real (thank you, Marcia!), as is the little cove where Leo wrote, where we have found many tree-stump offerings, including one beautiful poem written in French that we first read as "I follow you a poem." But while many Hollywood stars did come up to Carmel in the 1950s, whether they came to testify in secret executive sessions, or have abortions, or sleep their way into roles, I do not know. It happened. It may have happened here. No doubt the truth is buried in some file in some government basement, like so much of history we don't like to face.

The late Laird Koening gave me the title that started this book, and with our mutual friend the late Fred Klein, helped me understand what it was like to be gay before that was a choice the law allowed. Thanks too to all the Facebook friends and followers who answered my repeated calls for information and advice, including Susan Koeppe Archibald (for the name "Nyx") and my car-naming team of Joy Tyler Riley ("Buttercup") and Vivian Fotos Rose ("Tubby"). I'm grateful too to Jessika Auerbach for fixing my German. To André Jackson for allowing me to use his name for this character who inspires Sam just as the real André inspires me. And to the whole Maggiori clan for the inspiration for Isabella's name; I hope by the time Isabella is old enough to read this, we women who have come before her will have managed to clear a wider path.

Martha Lauzen and her Center for the Study of Women in Television and Film, and Stacy Smith and her Media, Diversity, & Social Change Initiative at USC's Annenberg School do incredible research on gender in media. The *Washington Post*, the *San Francisco Chronicle*, and Susan Brenneman at the *Los Angeles Times* all gave me space to proselytize about women directors and writers long before it was fashionable to care. Tarana Burke first coined the term "Me Too." Ashley Judd first spoke on record against Harvey Weinstein. The Pulitzer Prize–winning reporting of Jodi Cantor and Megan Twohey helped drag into the light the stories of all the brave woman who, in going public about their own experiences of sexual harassment, allow us to know we're not alone.

My apologies to the late Nedrick Young for giving my fictional Leo the very real Oscar awarded him for *The Defiant Ones* under the pseudonym "Nathan E. Douglas" (cowritten with Harold Jacob Smith); Young's credit was restored in 1993. Apologies also to Justine Triet and Arthur Harari for stealing their writing Oscar for *Anatomy of a Fall* and giving it to Gemma; she felt quite guilty about taking it.

The sources I turned to for this book include the documentaries *Hollywood on Trial* and *Alfred Hitchcock: Master of Suspense*; the books *Scoundrel Time* by Lillian Hellman, *Naming Names* by Victor Navasky, *Shedding Light on the Hollywood Blacklist* by Stanley Dyrector, *The Sun and her Stars* by Donna Rifkind, *Inside Out* by Walter Bernstein, *The Dark Side of Genius*, *The Art of Alfred Hitchcock*, and *High Society* by Donald Spoto, *Ideal Beauty* by Lois W. Banner, *Elizabeth Taylor* by Kate

Andersen Brower, *The Fixers* by E. J. Fleming, *Alfred Hitchcock* by Patrick McGilligan, *Hitchcock* by François Truffaut, *Hollywood: The Oral History* by Jeanine Basinger and Sam Wasson and *The Star Machine* by Basinger, *Women vs. Hollywood* by Helen O'Hara, *Tab Hunter* by Tab Hunter, *Hitchcock on Hitchcock* edited by Sidney Gottlieb, *Scandals of Classic Hollywood* by Anne Helen Petersen, *Hitchcock's Blondes* by Laurence Leamer, *The Twelve Lives of Alfred Hitchcock* by Edward White, *The Selected Poetry of Robinson Jeffers* by Robinson Jeffers, edited by Tim Hunt, *Robinson Jeffers: Poet and Prophet* by James Karman, and *The Stone Mason of Tor House* by Melba Berry Bennett; and the archives of the *New York Times* and the *Carmel Pine Cone*. The writing of this book was also a lovely excuse to again watch Hitchcock's films; my favorite remains *Rear Window*, which I so wish I could watch one last time with Mom.

Chris and Nick, along with the newest member of our family, Lizzy Mays, remind me through their love and laughter that, as the Hitchcocks said of movies, it's only a book. Mac, who understands that I don't exactly believe that any more than I expect the Hitchcocks did, helps me make my words the best I can write while, at the same time, keeping me in clean clothes, good humor (I'm a sucker for his puns), and great love. I am so glad to belong to all of you.

ABOUT THE AUTHOR

MEG WAITE CLAYTON is the *New York Times* bestselling author of eight previous novels, including the *Good Morning America* Buzz Pick and *New York Times Book Review* Editors' Choice *The Postmistress of Paris*, *The Last Train to London*, and *The Wednesday Sisters*. Her books have been published in twenty-four languages and have been finalists for the Bellwether Prize (now the PEN Bellwether), the National Jewish Book Award, and the Langum Prize. She also writes for major newspapers and magazines, mentors in the OpEd Project, and is a member of the National Book Critics Circle and the California bar. She lives in California and Connecticut.